Someday the future of civilization w
along Filipinos as part of the story

Kevin F Owens

Sep 2013

To Alissa

Here's a story I wrote about
our future Sci-Fi. Frontier's
you like the adventure

Kevin F Owens

Kevin

Martian Panahon Virus

An epidemic begins when a young
Filipino prospector escapes from Mars
infected with a Paleolithic virus.

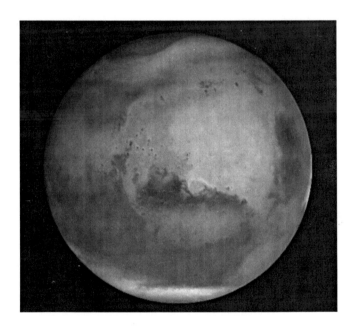

Kevin F. Owens

authorHOUSE®

AuthorHouse™
1663 Liberty Drive
Bloomington, IN 47403
www.authorhouse.com
Phone: 1-800-839-8640

First published by AuthorHouse 12/16/2009

ISBN: 978-1-4490-2736-0 (e)
ISBN: 978-1-4490-2734-6 (sc)
ISBN: 978-1-4490-2735-3 (hc)

Library of Congress Control Number: 2009910611

Printed in the United States of America
Bloomington, Indiana

This book is printed on acid-free paper.

Cover images are stock NASA artworks.
NASA takes no position concerning the book.

LIST OF CHAPTERS

Author's Prolog

The history of human enthusiasm for the Martian frontier began in the 1890's when American astronomer Percival Lowell published articles describing the red planet as an abode for life. Using his Arizona observatory, Lowell saw dark agricultural regions on the desert world that changed colors with the seasons. He mapped webs of canals designed to move water from the melting polar ice to thirsty vegetation nearer the equator. Other reputable astronomers, not all, supported Lowell's Martian life observations. Enthused fiction writers then transformed Lowell's Martian theories into stories about Martian civilizations with tales like H.G. Wells' 1898 "War of the Worlds" and Edgar Rice Burroughs' 1912 "Princess of Mars". These adventure stories motivated young engineers, like Robert Goddard and Werner von Braun to attempt to build spacecraft capable of going to Mars.

Early space probes were a disappointment. The canals mapped by Lowell proved to be illusions. There were no Martian crop fields or cities. Mars proved to be a small, cold, dry, nearly airless world too harsh for familiar life. However, more space probes revealed evidence of permafrost below ground; water that is essential to all life forms we know about. Even if the first astronauts find no life on Mars, the existence of water sources will make it possible for explorers to bring civilization to the red planet. Immigrants will breathe life into the Martian landscape creating the next frontier, similar to the European development of the Americas.

Beyond Mars, the frontiers suitable for human settlements that wait us are Earth-like planets orbiting nearby stars. Because distances are so great, missions to those stars will take years, even when technologies come that enables us to move at near light-speed velocities. Communication with those first interstellar explorers, even at the speed of light will be virtually impossible, that is unless there are forces in the universe that are not restricted by the limits of time and the speed of light.

DEDICATION

This story is dedicated to my Filipina wife, Maurese,
and to our daughters, Tanya and Michelle.
The future frontiers are waiting for them.

PART A

PROLOGUE

Chapter One

Martian Funeral

Brandy, Caesar Canyon, Mars

Earth Date:	Nov 8, 2215
Mars Date:	K-Mmon 7, 1173

Sonia felt herself shaking with the vision. It was as if she were looking through Jim's eyes. Carefully he approached the canyon wall. The last detonation had failed to go off. He could insert another explosive to detonate the last charge, but if that did not work, what would he do? He was halfway to the cliff face, up the bank of loose rocks, when he stopped and looked up. The face of the cliff exploded, throwing chunks of rocks in all directions. One hit his arm, spinning him off balance. A split second later, a sharp-edged rock smashed into his helmet faceplate, cracked the clear ceramic, and broke the sealing gasket. Jim fell backwards under the cascading rock ejecta. He felt his face puff up with the loss of pressure before he inadvertently exhaled what was in his lungs. There was enough time to feel the frigid cold, and he gasped for air that wasn't there. The pain of depressurization was intense. He watched as the avalanche of boulders came crashing down on him. Sonia opened her eyes. She did not want this vision to be her last memory of Jim.

Silently, Sonia Androff stared across the gravesite at Fisk Banzer, her stout, balding business partner. Fisk stood stone-faced beside Jim Everly's widow, giving her an arm to hold. Tears trickling down Hummy Everly's cheek were obscured by the black lace over her face. Her son, Little Willy, gripped Hummy's other hand. The five-year-old (nine Earth years) looked dazed. Like everyone else at the funeral service, the color setting on their environmental pressure suits had been set to black. All sported collapsible helmets hanging from the back of their necks. Sonia felt uncomfortable watching the family's anguish.

The ceramic casket was motionless over the burial pit. Sonia had not seen Jim's body since it was returned to Brandy, and she did not want to. Just the same, her mind filled with images of a broken, dehydrated, disfigured friend. 'Accidents' like these manifested grotesque effects with instant, Martian freeze-dry depressurization. Her thoughts drifted from the macabre to the gold-prospecting gamble that she, with Jim and Fisk, had been planning for the El Dorado Badlands.

Fisk and his wife, and Sonia and her husband, had been independent mining partners since the war. A year after they formed the partnership, Fisk's wife and Sonia's husband ran off together, abandoning their respective spouses and the business. Dejected, Fisk and Sonia thought they had lost everything. They got mad together, and then got drunk together. Then they decided to keep the business going, promised that they would treat each other as if they were cousins doing business together, avoiding romantic, sexual compromises that had already destroyed both of their marriages. For twenty Earth years they worked together as prospectors. Their relationship had grown very comfortable with time. Both pursued romances independent of their relationship.

For years they worked as independent subcontractors to the major mining companies, finding a number of ore deposits that made those corporations rich. Each time they got paid a finder's fee, they winced at having lost out on the real value of their find. However, when they tried to go on their own, searching for asteric crystal deposits in the

Grand Mariner Canyon, their claim was jumped. By the time they got back to the Bureau of Mines in Crater City to file a claim, they found that claim had been countered by the Polaris Metals Corporation. They learned to be careful who they trusted.

Fisk, Sonia, and Jim Everly spent a lot of time studying the old mining records, mineral satellite surveys, and prospecting reports to come up with a hunch on Princess Dejah Canyon. They had flown over the canyon with Fisk's multi-spectral cameras. They knew there was gold in the canyon.

Jim would have been their geochemist, but now he was dead. There was no proof of foul play, but Sonia sensed his death was more sinister than an inadvertent accident. She also found it troubling that the Redrock Mining representatives just happened to be visiting Jim when the accident occurred. It surprised her that Redrock vice-President George Pilsner had the gall to be at Jim's funeral.

Sonia listened to the priest. She was not Catholic. The priest eulogized about Jim having gone back to God. Sonia silently prayed for the soul of her friend, for the future of his family. Standing under the portable, pressurized, transparent dome covering the gravesite, a hundred mourners patiently listened. Sonia only knew a handful of the guests. Most were Jim's relatives or friends. She recognized the famous face of Brass Newton. A friend of Fisk's, Brass was a noted bio-engineer, married to a media star, and heir to the Newton Enterprises Corporation. Tall, blonde, and Nordic, he was in his mid-twenties (forties Earth age). She had never actually met him. Although he was chairman of the board of Newton Industries, Brass was noted more for his work as a top genetic engineer. He garnered fame at the Life Sciences Institute, designing new agricultural life forms adapted to the harsh Martian climate, but everyone recognized him more because his wife, Terra, was a popular Martian media journalist. That someone of his credentials would be at Jim Everly's funeral surprised Sonia. She also had never met George Pilsner. Thin and white-haired Pilsner was vice-president of Redrock Mines. She did not like Pilsner because neither Fisk nor Jim trusted him or his company.

Inside of the portable pressurized dome the air was comfortable. A pleasant sunlit landscape beyond looked deceptively warm and inviting, but the miniscule carbon-dioxide air pressure, freezing temperatures, and high solar ultra-violet radiation levels were all lethal. Like submariners working Earth's oceans, the new Martians knew they would die quickly if it were not for their mechanically engineered thermal and pressure protections.

Down the hill from the grass-covered cemetery, the dusty copper mining town of Brandy was laid out like a map. Typical of Martian towns, most of the homes, businesses, smelters, and warehouses were underground, linked together via pressurized tunnels. However, the town's surface had its own enticing beauty. Pressure-bubbles covered yards, gardens, and parks, all displaying rainbow colored gardens. Dark paved streets created a contrasting grid to highlight the strings of street lights and bright colors from those garden bubbles. Beyond the town the multi-hued, high, stratified cliffs of Caesar Canyon opened to the vastness of Grand Mariner Canyon beyond.

The words this priest spoke over Jim's body were familiar from any other eulogy. He reminded the mourners that Jim was an independent prospector, who spent his time searching the desolate Martian deserts for valuable ores, selling mineral rights to the major mining companies for a royalty. He was taking ore samples from the side of a cliff when that rockslide took him out. Sonia glanced again at young Willie. She empathized. Back when she was a child, her own father had kissed her forehead goodbye for the last time the morning of his accident. It took her a long time to overcome the gnawing in her stomach created by the emptiness of a daddy she loved who would never come home again. She wanted to take the little boy in her arms to cry with him, to let him know that the pain he was feeling would some day fade. She also knew he was not ready for someone to understand. Losing a father was like breaking a leg. She had done that, too. It hurt like hell. No matter how bad the stories were of someone else's pain, it did not lessen your own. No, she would be supportive, be a friend, but leave Willie and his mother alone to deal with their loss as best they could.

When the priest finished speaking, there was a momentary pause. Jim's uncles stepped forward to slowly sing "Danny Boy". At the end of the song, as if on queue, Fisk released the hand of Jim's widow. He moved one step closer to the casket. Fisk said, "Jim was my room mate in college… many, many years ago. We served in the militia together during the war. We prospected as a team for a long time. He was my best man when I married. He was my best friend when she left me. After he married, his wife made their home my home. Damn, Jim, we need you. We will miss you. I miss you." With that, Fisk leaned forward, and placed a gold pendant on the casket.

Jim had been a friend who often dropped by to drink or play poker. Sonia thought of the times he joined them for some crazy prospecting hunch, hunches that were mostly time consuming treks with no reward. She took a daisy from a large vase of flowers, stepped forward, and placed the flower on Jim's casket. Other guests did the same. She turned to face Hummy and Willie, breathed deeply, then reached to hold Hummy's arm.

"I know," Hummy responded, "I don't know what to say either."

When Sonia opened her mouth to speak, another voice jarred her senses. "Mrs. Everly, I'm so sorry about Jim." George Pilsner was abruptly next to Hummy. "If there is anything I can do, let us know." Pilsner was closely followed by an associate who looked more like a stone-faced athlete.

Although Pilsner was handsome and charming, Sonia found it upsetting that he would even be at Jim's funeral. Maybe Hummy did not know about Pilsner. Sonia remembered the last time she saw Jim. He complained then that Pilsner cheated him out of royalties for a titanium discovery. Jim had sold the mineral rights to Redrock in return for a discovery fee, plus a standard royalty percentage. According to Jim, Redrock altered the electronic contract documents in a way that deleted reference to royalties. Even the documents filed with the Bureau of Mines had been altered, leaving Jim no way to support his complaint.

"George," Fisk pursed his lips, and then exhaled; "Your audacity never ceases to amaze me. Why are you here?"

With a look of mild astonishment for such a query, he responded, "I'm here to pay my respects to Jim, to his family," Pilsner bowed slightly, reaching for Hummy's hand. "I want to apologize for previous misunderstandings."

Fisk smiled, "You going to give Hummy the royalties you owed Jim?"

Pilsner shook his head, "I wish I could. It is out of my hands. The board is unwilling to discuss the 'White Star' claim any further." He turned once more to Hummy. "I am here to say goodbye to a friend. Mrs. Everly... Hummy... I feel a great sadness for you. I wish this had never happened."

She smiled and accepted his hand clasp.

Before releasing her hand, Pilsner said, "I understand that Jim was planning an expedition to the El Dorado badlands. I'm willing to offer you a handsome reward if you allow us to continue his exploration."

She continued smiling, "I'm sorry. He did not discuss prospecting plans with me. I can't help you."

"If you allow us access to his logs, we will work with you."

"George," Fisk interrupted, "She doesn't have the records. I do. Jim was working with Sonia and me. I'll make certain Hummy is taken care of."

There was a moment of silence. "Fisk, you've worked with us before. I think we can work on this matter in a way that will benefit everyone."

"It wouldn't benefit Jim. He was my closest friend."

"I understand," Pilsner stared into Fisk's eyes. His gaze shifted to Sonia, then to Hummy. Returning to Fisk, he said, "I'll send you a proposal you may like." He turned once again to Hummy. "I know this is a poor time to talk business. I'll leave you now. I agree with the priest. I know your husband has gone to a better place."

Sonia quietly watched as Pilsner and his assistant backed away. The two of them secured their pressure helmets, and then left via the nearest airlock. Once they were gone, Fisk spoke before Sonia could, "I think we have a problem. I don't trust him."

"I don't trust him either," Sonia watched Pilsner getting into his private vehicle. "He should not be aware of El Dorado. Have you talked to anyone?"

"No," she elbowed him. "You know better. The best I figure, it was the sample Jim left with the Bureau of Mines. Redrock has agents in the Bureau."

An hour after the burial service, Sonia and Fisk were seated on cushioned chairs at Jim's modest home in Brandy, while other guests milled about the pressurized garden patio on the surface above. Willie was in the kitchen with his mother and aunt.

"What do you think of Pilsner?" Fisk swirled the liquid in his cocktail glass.

"Maybe he was there to mourn for Jim," Sonia took a bite of pastry. "But he seemed anxious about El Dorado. I wonder what he knows."

"You know Jim… He liked to talk about what he was doing... to anyone... at bars... at poker games."

Sonia put the remainder of her pastry back on a small plate on the end table. "I wonder how soon before 'the accident' that George asked Jim about El Dorado?"

Fisk pondered, and then said, "Redrock never crossed me, personally. But I've heard stories."

"What should we do about our plans?"

"I've been thinking about that for some time. We need a mining crew, but you don't know who might be working for Redrock on the side. However…"

"However? What?"

"The last time I went to Earth, I traveled with Brass Newton. We stopped in Manila." He pulled a Zerta notepad from his breast pocket.

"You didn't tell me you traveled with Mister Newton," Sonia was perplexed. She looked across the room at Newton. "I'm supposed to be your partner!"

"Relax," Fisk unfolded the small notepad to a flat clipboard sized computer screen. "We were on the same flight to Earth. He has business operations in Manila. He invited me to join him."

Sonia once again looked toward Brass Newton. He was busy trading jokes with other men.

Fisk handed the notepad to her. "Brass introduced me to some Filipino miners interested in visiting Mars. They want to come just for the adventure of going somewhere different. They live in a remote, primitive barrio in the Luzon Mountains. Their village is something out of antiquity, but they understand mining, and they work hard."

On the notepad screen was a series of photographs of dark, smiling Filipinos standing on the porch of a bamboo house. "Maybe we could bring in a team that no one on Mars knows."

"How do you propose to do that?" She studied the images of a dozen Filipino miners on the screen. She knew she had never met any of them, but for some reason they seemed familiar, particularly the youngest. Pointing to the image of the teenage Filipino, she asked, "Is his name Apollo?"

Fisk checked his notes, and then stared at her. "You've met him?"

"Has he been here? I know I've met him. I just don't remember where or when. I sense that he likes exploring caves… like me."

"I didn't know you'd been to the Philippines?"

"I haven't been. I must have met him here. I don't recall when, but I know I've met him"

"Terra Newton did a special on his village about five years (nine Earth years) ago. He would have been a child at the time. Maybe you saw that show."

"I don't remember a show like that." Sonia reached for her wine glass. "Maybe I'm confusing him with someone else."

Fisk said, "Next month you're going to Odessa to that family reunion. You could make a side trip to the Philippines… to see what you think of them."

"Me? You could do that." She handed the notepad back to Fisk.

"Redrock watches me like a hawk. If I went, Redrock would follow. However, you'll be at your reunion. An excursion to Manila would appear innocent. We'll give you a cover… taking a package of business papers for Brass."

Sonia stood. "I'll think about it." She walked to the staircase leading to the surface garden.

CHAPTER TWO

STARFLIGHT UPDATE

Martian Broadcast Agency
The Weekly Terra Antoni Newton Report
Crater City, Mars

Earth Date: Nov 11, 2215
Mars Date: K-Mmon 10, 1173

"**M**ission Control received the midpoint communiqué from the manned starship on its way to Tau Ceti Two, an earth-like planet circling the star Tau Ceti, roughly twelve light years away."

Sonia looked up from her computerized spread sheet to watch the commercial telecast. The printed words on the screen, over the talking image of Martian media commentator Terra Newton, read: 'Terra Newton Chronicles. Starship update.' Even after twenty-three years (twelve Martian years) as a star journalist, Terra maintained a popular following on Earth as well as Mars, and she sported an immaculate, attractive appearance to help sustain her appeal. Her short, black hair remained stylish, her on screen environmental suits were always the latest fashions, and her face was as wrinkle and blemish free as it had been during her teenage years.

The screen changed to split image, with Terra Newton on one side, video from the starship on the other. "This mid-course message was sent from the Starship six years ago, an automated data transmission from the manned spacecraft. All supervised systems on the space craft appear to be operating normally, with minor adjustments being made automatically. The one hundred and forty pioneers on board the spaceship remain in hibernation, not to be awakened until they decelerate into orbit around Tau Ceti Two, which will take place ten years after this message was sent, or four years from now." The message images showed the starship's instrument panel, hibernating crew, life support machinery, and the propulsion systems. Two external telescopic views showed looking forward looking toward Tau Ceti Two, still just a blue-white dot circling its star, even at high magnification, and a similar image looking back toward the familiar inner solar system planets of Earth and Mars. All of these planets were being seen from a midpoint distance of six light years.

Concluding the update, Terra Newton said, "Although the Starship will arrive at Tau Ceti in four years, images of those first steps on the shores of a world in a different star system will take twelve years more to reach us. Civilization has come a long way, now that we are able to migrate to other star systems; but it is regrettable that the creator has not granted human genius a way to communicate with those distant frontiers at speeds faster than light."

The newscast switched to a different journalist reporting on a political campaign. Sonia muted the telecast to return to her record keeping. She stared at the spread sheets, but could not focus on the data. She leaned back to think about Fisk's proposal for her to go to the Philippines in search of a prospecting team, Filipino miners who were friends of Terra and Brass Newton. She pushed a button to save her accounting spreadsheet for later. She then asked the computer for a media library index of Terra Newton's broadcasts about the Philippines. Her curiosity was peaked.

CHAPTER THREE

CHRISTMAS EVE

Baguio City, Philippines

Earth Date:	Dec 24, 2216
Mars Date:	K-Mmon 51, 1173

S onia wiped sweat from her forehead. Despite her fashionable dark-blue environ-suit, she was unprepared for Earth's humid, tropical air. Overhead, the huge, hot noon sun peeked through fluffy white clouds dotting a pastel blue sky. She had adjusted to the strange sight of blue sky during her family reunion in Odessa, but the thick, warm, humid air was something else. She envied Roberto DeNila, standing with her on a stony hill overlooking the mine entrance in the canyon below. The husky, middle-aged Filipino miner was cool and comfortable wearing a cotton shirt and trousers. Suddenly, something caused an irritation on her bare left hand. A mosquito. She swatted with her right.

Roberto was oblivious. He ignored the mosquitoes as he continued his Filipino accented English narrative about the Benget mining operation, pointing out the multiple entrances to the Santos copper mine at the head of the box canyon. With his hand in motion, he detailed how the various stretches of conveyors transported raw ore a hundred yards beyond the entrance to a processing building where a crusher pulverized the rocks. Automated spectrometers separated the crushed stones into ejected piles of greenish ore bearing gravel or gray waste. Waste rock was moved via another conveyor a mile down the valley, where it was poured into a planned foundation to create a dam. Although the open-pit mine area was void of vegetation, the crest of the canyon around the mine was green with pine trees, wild grasses, and bamboo accented with the vivid colors of tropical wild blossoms.

"I'm amazed," Sonia scratched the mosquito bite, "That copper ores are mined this way. Why don't you just scrape away the face of the cliff to bring out the ore? That's how we recover Martian copper." Briefly glancing down at the back of her hand, she inspected the bright red discoloration of the insect bite. "Why use so many people? Much of what your men do, we do with robots."

"You Martians no worry about disrupting nature." Roberto responded. "The laws here require we do not disrupt the wildlife." He pointed to the conveyor moving the waste rock down the canyon. "That junk rock is going to create a water dam. The company got the government to approve that." His attention then returned to the tunnels at the base of the canyon cliffs. "Your question about robots … Santos management likes to hire miners. It is work for the men of my barrio." The conveyors were no longer moving. Miners streamed from the tunnels. "What did you think of my men?"

She pondered. In the early twenty-third century, with so many variations of artificially intelligent machines to do physical labors, such as mining ores, she was amazed that any business would still have men doing that physically grueling work. "Impressed. Hard workers. Are they taking a lunch break now?"

"On most other days," Roberto answered, "Today, we quit at noon!"

"Noon?" Sonia was puzzled.

"This is Christmas Eve!"

It had slipped Sonia's mind. "I'm willing to hire six of you. That's all I can take, okay?"

"That's what Sonny says. You want to pick? Or, do you want me to pick?"

"You pick, Roberto. You know who can work in a pressure suit … who can be gone for a long time … Shall we get together in Baguio? I'll treat everyone to lunch."

"This is Christmas Eve," Roberto lifted his left wrist, glancing at the time before speaking to the built-in comm unit. "Six-Three-Bee!" While waiting for a response, he told Sonia, "On Christmas Eve Sonny invites everyone from the Barrio to his home in Baguio. Lots of food, people, singing … he has a beautiful view of the canyon below Baguio. We can talk to the men there."

"I wouldn't want to impose on a family affair." She scratched the mosquito bite again. She was curious. Before leaving Mars for her family reunion in Odessa, Brass Newton arranged with his Manila friend, Sonny Ortigas, for her to travel to the Philippines to meet with Sonny's brother-in-law, Roberto. At first she could not understand why Brass Newton, heir to a corporate fortune on Mars, would have close connections with such primitive people as Roberto and his family. The media archives from Terra Newton's shows clarified the matter. Sonny was a private detective in Manila. Terra hired him twenty years ago to research the Manila murder of a Martian Customs official, and they had been friends since. Ten years later Terra prepared a special report about Roberto's hometown, an isolated mountain barrio where the way of life had not advanced in centuries. Locals still lived in bamboo nipa huts, planted crops by hand, and centered their lives around their parish church.

"Not family… barrio. Sonny sent you here on Christmas Eve. He is my wife's brother. He would want to know who goes to Mars." Roberto finally noticed her scratching the back of her left hand. He said nothing about it. "This morning you watch everyone work, but we could not talk. They were busy. It would be funny in front of Company bosses. At Sonny's place, everyone will be clean. We can talk … meet their families …. You might have fun. Have you ever seen a Filipino Christmas before?" He stopped talking with Sonia to concentrate on a discussion with his comm unit to talk to his crew. He then turned to her to ask, "Miss Androff, you have a rental van.

Can we use that to get home?" After she agreed, he spoke again to the comm unit to tell Emilio Perez to proceed without him.

For the grand tour of the area, Roberto directed Sonia's rental van computer to drive along graded mining roads of the Mount Atop area. This was the first time anyone from beyond the Benget Mountains had shown interest in the work he did, and the interested party was a beautiful blond woman from Mars. He wanted to make a good impression. As a mine supervisor, he granted himself leeway, wearing a new outfit to work, rather than the stained outfits he donned most days. He even had a new haircut. He had walked her through the mines, explaining the operation of boring vehicles, shoring equipment, and the way miners determined where the rich ore deposits were. On the way back to his barrio, "Maliit na Ulap", he took her to the canyon where a levy was being built using the waste rocks for a dam destined to create a new water reservoir. He took her by several mines that had been tapped out, showing her one that had been a gold mine a hundred years earlier. He pointed to flakes of gold still spotting some of the rocks.

Eventually, they went up a winding mountain road, passing the ancient multi-layered rice terraces inter-spaced with pineapple farms, dense brush undergrowth, and scrub pines. Blooming morning glories and other wild flowers added colors to the greens and browns of the hillsides. The van rolled into town and quietly pulled up in front of Roberto's home, three buildings from the stone church. Roberto's own vehicle was parked beside his house. The other miners were already cleaned up and hanging around his front porch; drinking beer and swapping jokes.

'Maliit na Ulap', a barrio with little more than a few huts, was located on a flat rocky plateau extending from the flank of the mountain. Thirty primitive homes were strung along the side of the dirt road, with a general store and a small stone church in the center of town. Behind the town the sharply rising mountainside was thick with bamboo and pine trees. On the other side of the road, the hillside sloped down to a rice terrace, then to another terrace, and to a third below that. Hundreds of years old, Maliit na Ulap was a village frozen in a time long gone. Families choosing to remain were like primitive peoples anywhere, aware of the outside modern world, but preferring to live the way their ancestors had.

There was no hint of the typical factory fabrication in any of the buildings. The stone church and masonry general store had been there for centuries. The homes, made with bamboo walls, palm leaf-thatched roofs, and large covered front porches, were something out of story books.

Before getting out of the van, Roberto handed his electronic clip board to Sonia, with six portrait images displayed on the screen, "Here is my recommendation for a crew," Roberto pointed to several of the Filipinos in front of his house. Emilio Perez, Jun Ventuno, and Celso Cruz were laughing with each other over some joke. Each had a beer in his hand. He then pointed at Doug Manglapus, who was approaching from the general store. These men were Roberto's close friends who grew up with him. They worked the Benget mines together, and were part of each others barrio lives. They were life long friends.

"Then, I would include myself and my nephew, Apollo. I wouldn't want to take more, because the mine crew here would be too short handed. Most of the rest would not be able to leave anyway", Roberto said exiting the van.

"Roberto!" A heavy-set, fifty-year-old Filipina woman stepped out on the bamboo porch, "Where were you so long? You know Sonny wants me quick-quick!"

"Celia, my bulaklak (flower)! It is Christmas. We have a guest all the way from Mars."

Celia stopped, stared at Sonia. She said, "When you said a prospector was coming, you did not say it was pretty woman."

Sonia felt awkward. Standing on the bottom steps, she said, "Merry Christmas, Mrs. DeNila. I'm sorry to come when you have a family reunion."

Appearing in the doorway was the young Apollo Panahon, dressed in dark slacks with a white pineapple fiber barong tagalog (loose-fitting translucent dress shirt). Sonia stared at the thin, bronzed teenager. Again, she knew she had seen him, but did not know why or where. She had noticed him in the mine, where he piloted a boring machine with the ease of someone who had been doing it for twenty years. He was polite, intelligent, and enthusiastic for his work. When introduced he had the innocent shyness of his youth. He silently stared back, but said nothing. She returned her attention to Celia and Roberto.

Roberto had a friendly smile, "Your brother told you she was coming. You no need me to repeat."

"Sonny tells me what he tells you," Celia stared at her husband, then at Sonia. "He say his friend Mister Newton asked if Filipino miner would talk to a prospector from Mars. Sonny no say the prospector is pretty woman!"

Sonia again stared past Celia at Apollo. Roberto had explained that nephew Apollo and his younger sister were the children of Roberto's late sister, and that Apollo's parents died five years earlier in a crash. Roberto and Celia adopted their orphaned nephew and niece afterwards. Sonia could not shake the feeling that somehow she had known Apollo all her life. He sat himself on the veranda to make music with a small guitar. The traditional Christmas tunes he played were recognizable favorites from as far back as the early twentieth century, when the Philippines was an American colony. Ending the tunes, Apollo looked up at Sonia with a puzzled expression. He stood, smiled, and told Celia that he was going to get his girlfriend, Nina Perez. He descended the steps and walked away.

Sonia felt uncomfortable. Roberto was a knowledgeable miner, a natural supervisor for the other Filipinos, and likable. It was obvious his wife was the jealous type who did not trust her husband around other women. Her mind churned with thoughts of Roberto having had affairs in the past, or of Celia being self-conscious because she was aging with a weight problem. There was nothing Sonia could say to overcome the obvious problems. It was up to Roberto to deal with his own wife.

Once more, Sonia scratched the itching insect bite on her left hand. This time the scratching brought pain, similar to a burn. Looking at the back of her hand, the area around the bite was swollen and bright red.

"What happened?" Celia descended the steps from the porch. "Did spider bite you?" She pointed to the discolored circle on the Sonia's hand.

Sonia stared at Mrs. DeNila, then at her own hand. "I think it was a mosquito. We don't have any on Mars!"

Celia took hold of the hand to inspect the inflammation. "Is this your first time in the Philippines?"

"This is my first time on Earth," Sonia sighed, "I'm just getting used to the gravity... the air pressure..."

"Roberto," Celia glared briefly at her husband, "She has allergy to mosquito. Get alcohol and Thelax Cream." She took Sonia by the arm, leading her up on the porch. "Sonny's wife has a doctor brother. He will be at Christmas party in Baguio. He fix your kagat na lamok!"

Whereas the barrio homes of the Filipino miners were primitive nipa huts made of bamboo and nipa leaves, the Baguio vacation home of Sonny Ortigas, Roberto's brother-in-law, was a modern masterpiece of contemporary home construction combined with traditional Filipino designs. Jenny Ortigas, Sonny's picture-book-perfect beautiful wife, gave Sonia a tour of her home, elaborating that twenty-third century factory-built aristocrat's home had been airlifted in sections onto a concrete foundation. The home had all the sealed environmental controls, self-cleaning floors, computer-controlled cooking systems, and household robotics that most Martians were accustomed to. Assembled near the top of a canyon, with a terrific view, Jenny told of falling in love with the home when they first got it. However, Sonny missed the traditional barrio architecture he had been raised with. To satisfy him, they hired a contractor to modify the overlook, and build a wood and bamboo recreation room and deck overhang above the concrete back deck. The deck overlooked the canyon. As a native Martian, it was a building idea Sonia had never seen. Jenny made this vacation place sound like the greatest home in the world.

Everyone from the barrio, all sixty of them, were able to be comfortable in the two floors of recreation rooms. A section of one wall had opened to display an automated food layout, offering a feast of holiday foods that the Ortigas' computerized kitchen prepared automatically. Those dishes were inter-spaced with home-made dishes the women of the barrio brought. Guests at the half-dozen small tables entertained themselves with dinner groups, poker, or mahjong.

Many of the guests ate from dinner plates while standing, perfectly comfortable, balancing their plate in one hand while maneuvering their forks with the other. Roberto played a localized card game with a handful of other miners at one table. A cluster of women sat on a couch discussed fashions. Another group of the men watched a holographic broadcast of a basketball game. On the lower concrete deck, Apollo strummed more Christmas music on his guitar. Most of the barrio teenagers sang along. Nina Perez, a pretty, petite teenager, was obviously infatuated with Apollo, sitting close to him, singing along with his music. Sonia smiled, thinking back to her own youth when she used to get infatuated that way with a musician. On the wooden second-level sun deck, Sonny spent an hour with the barrio priest discussing philosophy.

Sonia liked the people, and they were all overly attentive to her, but she felt out of place. The warm, thick, moist air, spiced with the aroma of tropical bushes surrounding the house, air that everyone else found refreshing, made her feel uncomfortable. She wished she were back on Mars. She felt silly for feeling uncomfortable. Shrugging off the discomfort, she approached Sonny to ask how he knew Brass. The story he told was fascinating.

Sonny explained that he was a close friend of Blue Heidleburn, who flew transports between Manila and Crater City. He got to know Terra when she hired him, a Filipino detective, to help solve the Manila murder of a Martian custom's inspector. They have been friends since that case. By the time Sonny finished his stories, Sonia had completed her platter of Christmas dinner.

Sonia looked again at the Filipinos playing cards nearby, at the young boy leaning against the railing making Christmas music with this guitar. During a brief pause in the music, Nina leaned to kiss Apollo on the cheek, and then offered him a beverage glass.

"I'm curious," Sonny accepted a San Miguel Beer form the roving robotic server, "Why you think it's necessary to come here to hire a prospecting team? There are so many back on Mars, and they are adapted to the conditions?"

She accepted a white wine, "I thought Brass and Fisk explained that. There is a dominant mining consortium on Mars run by men we do not trust. They screwed Jim Everly out of the royalties on one mine he found. They were at his funeral asking directly about the effort we are trying now. They should not even know about that. We are worried that any Martian-based crew would include their agents."

The two of them watched as Sonny's stunningly beautiful wife approached. "Have you ever had Filipino cakes?

Part B

Martian Gold

CHAPTER FOUR

PRINCESS DEJAH CANYON

El Dorado Badlands, Sytris Major Region, Mars

Earth Date	July 1, 2216
Mars Date	C-Mmon 19, 1174

"Roberto!" Sonia repeated to the comm unit. "We're waiting."

"Teka, teka!" He replied, "We need to finish putting things away. We'll be down in a minute."

It took several months for the Filipinos to reach Mars. First they had to arrange a leave of absence from their jobs, from their families. To get certification to work on Mars, they had to take a two-month training course in Antarctica where they learned to work with simulated Martian gear. This was all done inconspicuously because Sonia wanted to make certain no Martian competitors knew they were coming. After the miners landed at Crater City, the Martian capitol city, in the shadow of huge Mount Olympus, Roberto rented an overland rover. The rover's computer drove them several hundred miles to Wells for a secret rendezvous with Fisk and Sonia. Leaving the rented rover parked in a garage, they boarded the prospecting crew's caravan for the long drive half way around the planet to the El Dorado Badlands.

Emerging from the cave into the bright morning sunshine, tightly gripping the handle of an ore sample case, young Apollo gingerly scampered down slope. He carefully picked the boulders he used for steps. Bouncing from stone to boulder in his full pressure suit, he eyed the array of prospecting vehicles two-hundred yards down the pediment slope, parked on the flat canyon floor. Half a mile away, across the flat canyon base, the high south-cliff wall remained in dark shadow; a high, shear cliff, rising two-thousand feet to the rim, just like the north face behind him. The noise of his own breath inside the pressure helmet no longer seemed unnatural, the way it had when he first arrived on Mars. After a month in the trackless Martian deserts, he was comfortable in the pressure suits, having adjusted to the discomfort of the breathing gear. In the one-third gravity of Mars, the air control packs on his back felt no heavier than a suit of clothes back in the Philippines.

Even with the difficult, uneven pace forced by having to choose each step carefully, Apollo needed only a minute to reach the caravan rovers and trailers. He circled around to the entrance of the control rover, a van a little bigger than an old-fashioned bus. Over his shoulder he glanced back up the face of the cliff he just left. His eyes squinted, pinpointing the small cave where the shear rock wall rises vertically from the apex with the sloped pediment. Above the pediment slope, the north face of the canyon wall rose a third of a mile toward the sky. He leaned his head back to get a clear view, noting that even at mid day, sunset colors dominated the air above. He was awed by the enormity of the cliff faces, higher than anything he remembered from the Philippines. The north wall of the Princess Dejah Canyon displayed multi-colored rock strata, horizontal bands of gray, orange, brown, ochre, and black.

He pushed the button to open the vehicle airlock, and then stepped up into the entrance. Within moments, the double chambers had pressurized his environment to normal levels. The airlock's automatic sliding interior doors opened, allowing him into the rover. He opened the visor to his pressure helmet and inhaled the fragrant, warm, pressurized air. "Maganda!" He removed the helmet, hanging it on a hook reserved for headgear. Slowly, he approached the backs of Sonia and Fisk. Both were preoccupied, preparing to launch a seismic survey of the canyon's north face.

Geochemist Dave Crane watched from a console at the back of the van. He got up to return to his seat at the geologic chemist's station. Dave Crane, a single, pale, curly haired chemical engineer, was intelligent, had a pleasant manner, and a good sense of humor. He had worked for the Bureau of Mines before approaching Fisk for a job. He left to get away from government work, to be part of prospecting paydays. Fisk liked him, and trusted his talents as a geochemist. "Have a seat, Apollo. Did you follow another maze of tunnels?"

"Not today." Apollo responded, "Did you want me to?"

"That was quite a trek yesterday," Sonia turned to him. "I checked the samples you brought back last night. Your data recorder showed you went about eleven miles to the surface. With all of the collateral tunnels, how were you able to find a route to the top?"

Apollo grinned. "Just like back home ... long ago those caves were made by underground water. I tried to figure out where the water came from, and kept following it up."

"You're an amazing kid", Fisk looked around. "I would have been lost fifteen minutes into the climb. How did you find your way back?"

"He left reflective markers," Sonia said, "Like you and I do." She smiled at Apollo. "What did you bring this time?"

Apollo lifted the ore sample case and placed it on the counter top between Sonia and Fisk. Both glanced at it. They then ignored it, as they returned their attention to the control instruments in front of them.

"Relax, Apollo," Sonia again looked briefly over her shoulder at him. She smiled. "We will see what you brought after this." She returned to the video screens. Her very short blond hair and hint of middle-age facial wrinkles did not detract from her natural feminine beauty. Apollo knew all his uncles whispered humorously among themselves, wishing for her to smile at them. They all knew that wish was futile. Her smiles toward him were warmer than those for the others. He convinced himself he was misinterpreting the attention she granted him. She probably thought of him as a kid. She was friendly the way she would be to a nephew. Apollo thought she was beautiful.

During the drive from Wells Sonia took a lot of time to explain to all the cave exploration differences between Earth and Mars. The frigid, nearly airless conditions on Mars meant that survival required prospectors to always wear full pressure suits. They could not feel or smell rock surfaces they were looking at. She made clear that if they were chipping out rock specimens, an inadvertent slip with a pick could tear their pressure suit and that would expose them to traumatic hypothermic depressurization. At a few rest stops during the drive, she led them into small canyons to show them how to search for trace samples of valuable ores. Apollo's uncles would tire of the field trips quickly, and return to the trailers to play cards. However, Apollo maintained an excitement about the Martian geology she was teaching. He listened, asked endless streams of questions, and adapted quickly to the quirks of Martian prospecting. Sonia enjoyed working with a young student, enthusiastic about the geology she loved. Apollo was excited to finally find an adult who loved rock exploration as much as he did. Fisk was aloof. Apollo's uncles were miners because it was what they did to earn a living. Sonia was different. She loved exploring the rocks.

"What I found may interest you," Apollo started to open the case. He stopped when he noticed Sonia raise her hand as a signal not to proceed.

Sonia said, "I'll look at your discovery in a moment. First, we set the probes." She spoke softly, "I thought your 'Filipino uncles' were coming with you. Are they coming out? We hope to launch in a few minutes."

"They know. Should I call them again? Apollo settled slowly into a chair behind Sonia. With his fingers, he brushed back the locks of his straight, black hair drooping over his forehead. He was fascinated with the exotic computerized geological survey equipment Sonia was controlling. He lacked the education to understand what most of it meant. A bank of fifteen small video screens in front of her, each monitor displayed a slightly different coloration of the same view of the two-thousand foot high face canyon wall they were surveying.

The different screens illuminated the signature of fifteen different single-frequency laser strobes used during the night to get these unique reflective images. Three larger screens displayed the computer-enhanced interpretation of those combined images superimposed under normal daytime lighting, giving a false color image of where concentrations of various metal ores could be found. Superimposed on that screen were eighty electronic crosshairs, showing the aiming point for the array of penetrator missiles about to be fired.

Apollo's desire to talk to Sonia about his discovery in the caves could wait. He quietly watched. On another set of video monitors, one screen was turned to a commercial television newscast. With the volume turned down, he had no idea what was being said, but he did recognize the newscaster, Terra Newton. Uncle Sonny had once brought her to the barrio so she could do a story about native Filipino life.

Fisk spoke to the comm unit in the control console in front of him. "Roberto. We fire the probes in a few minutes. If the blasts blow ejecta in front of your cave, you may want to be back here." Fisk's bald head was slightly sun-burned. His perpetual squint made it hard to read his eyes. "Besides, your scanners don't show anything of interest."

Sonia turned to Apollo, "You'd have a better view from the observation trailer," She smiled at her young friend. "When this is over, could you bring coffee? The galley in here is empty."

Roberto's voice responded from the control comm unit. "We're on our way. Did you see the sample with Apollo? You may want to hold off blasting. This is an interesting cave."

"The cave will still be there," Fisk responded. "Just get down here."

One surveillance monitor focused on the entrance to the cave Apollo had just left. Five figures in full pressure suits slowly emerged to begin the long descent down the pediment's jumble of boulders. Fisk turned to Apollo, "What's the big surprise?"

Apollo was leaving for the observation trailer. He stared briefly, paused. He turned back and opened the three-foot stainless steel case on the counter. Inside, a transparent container, sealed to maintain

Martian surface conditions, was an ore sample that looked like a mixture of granite and rock ice. It had been cut from something bigger with a laser knife.

"Gravel and ice?" Fisk read the data display on the container, then scratched his head, "What's so special about the ice? There's underground ice everywhere on Mars."

Sonia inspected it more closely. Before the usually tongue-tied Apollo could think of the right words to use, Sonia squealed, "Look! Plants! Fish!"

Dave rose from his chair and approached the sample. Fisk leaned to look more closely. Lifting the container, Sonia placed it in the recessed evaluation cubicle for analysis. "Computer, give a biologic readout for the plants and animals embedded in this enclosed ice sample. Screen four."

The image on screen four adjusted to a view of the sample, then to a spectral analysis. The message was short and startling. Aquatic grasses and fish. Genetic code not in data bank. Biologic and ice air pockets carbon dating estimate age at one hundred million years plus.

"This is a joke?" Fisk turned to Apollo. "Roberto is making another joke with us?"

Apollo shrugged, and then pointed, "I found an ice pool in the cave, under a layer of sandstone. It did not look like a joke."

"Someone was in this canyon before." Dave shook his head. "Set up an elaborate prank." He snickered. "Something I would have done in college!"

"But, how?" Sonia inquired. "The carbon…"

"This can't be right," Dave added, "Biologics that old should be fossilized."

Fisk added, "My guess is that this came from someone's aquarium. They aerated the aquarium with prepared carbon dioxide to simulate a decay age of a hundred million years. They then poured the aquarium in the cave and covered it with sandstone. A joke… waiting for the next stupid prospector checking out this canyon."

"Sounds like an elaborate façade," Sonia responded, "You're probably right." She winked at Apollo. "We'll check out the cave after the launch. Now, go to the observation trailer and watch the fireworks."

Fifteen minutes later, Apollo was in the observation trailer sitting with Uncle Roberto and the four other Filipinos, sipping coffee, waiting for the launch. Rugged facial features, barrel-chested, Roberto, along with Emilio, Jun, Celso, and Doug laughed in unison when they heard the reaction the ice sample had drawn from the control team. They agreed with Fisk's assessment, that it was probably an elaborate hoax. The only life forms on Mars were the genetically engineered biologics that human immigrants had created during the most recent centuries. Early pioneers discovered ample examples of aquatic fossils from long gone eras, but Mars, and especially that canyon in the Syrtis Major basalt regions, had not had running water for millions of years. The genetically engineered arctic grasses growing in isolated patches along the canyon floor had been designed by people to extract water from the frozen permafrost below ground. Apollo laughed with the men, thinking what fun it would have been for some earlier visitor to the Princess Dejah Canyon to set up such a prank.

Something did bother Apollo, however. If an earlier visitor had deliberately manipulated the carbon isotope mix to make the ice sample seem old, why couldn't the computer identify the biologics? Twenty-third century computer data banks were programmed to identify every life form man was familiar with, and any created or brought to Mars would be in the computer. He knew he lacked the education to understand it all. Apollo focused his attention on the unfolding events. He looked up at the cliff face, just as the control trailer dialog announced the decision to fire.

One at a time, a series of brilliant exhaust flames of eighty penetrator missiles followed the accelerating rockets as they lifted from the launch trailer. The fast, upward trajectories slammed the missiles into the cliff, burying each penetrator approximately six feet into the rock. With each silent impact, a small ball of flame highlighted the stone ejecta thrown from the contact point. Spaced a hundred meters apart, the penetrators formed a grid a thousand meters wide by eight-hundred meters tall, beginning at three-hundred meters above the canyon floor. Half of the embedded penetrators housed calibrated seismic sensors, the rest contained precise explosives awaiting the detonation signals from the control rover.

One of the two wide monitor screens below the window showed a view of the cliff face with eighty electronic target crosshairs identifying where each penetrator had impacted the rock wall. The second screen gave a technical readout of the embedments. Near the center of the grid a large silent explosion spit a cloud of dust and rocks from the face of the cliff. The readings for each of the seismic sensors displayed the technical readouts, which meant nothing to the six Filipino miners watching the show. A few minutes later, the second detonation did the same thing. Then the third.

By noon it was all over. The computer had combined those seismic readings with the strobe laser spectral survey of the canyon wall. That gave the independent prospectors in the control room what they wanted; a mineral image of the north face of Princess Dejah Canyon. Sonia, Fisk, Dave, and their mechanic, Japa Reese, joined the Filipino workers in the observation trailer for lunch, where they discussed the morning's events.

Roberto directed the kitchen computer to prepare for him some chicken adobo and rice. He followed Jun to the table. Apollo sat next to them, quietly eating as he listened to the conversations of his elders.

"Okay, boss," Roberto asked, "What do we have up there?"

Dave Crane finished a mouthful of scalloped potatoes. "There's a little ore. Looks like veins of copper … lead … zinc … at nine-hundred feet up. Behind that seventy-foot layer of granite, five-hundred feet up, is a network of caves … lots of quartz … looks like there once was underground water deposits … a huge buried cavern."

The monitor image used false colors to show what Dave was talking about; a cavern obscured by the thick layer of granite. The actual view of cliff did show hints of the ancient water deposits. Directly below, where the sensors implied caverns, were eroded rocks. It was obvious that a waterfall had been there once, eons ago, when water flowed on the surface.

Sonia interrupted Dave. "Nobody cares about the quartz or granite. Tell them what you found!"

The Filipino men stared; first at Sonia, then they focused on Dave. Her outburst surprised them.

Fisk quietly ate his lunch. Putting his fork down, he said, "If the computer reads those seismic patterns correctly, we have a vein of gold ... a large vein."

Roberto slowly smiled. So did his friends from Northern Luzon. He finished eating what he had in his mouth. "How big?"

Fisk stared at the miners, then smiled at his partner, "Sonia, you do the honors."

Everyone turned to the wide screen monitor below the window. The three dimensional display illustrated the cliff in blue, the gold vein in yellow. The data screen gave the figures. Average at thirty inches high, sixty feet wide, and two-hundred feet into the cliff. There were air pocket caves adjacent to the vein with sedimentary settlement pools. Preliminary estimates suggested at least eighty-thousand tons of gold.

"Maganda!" Jun stood up, "When do we go up?"

"Tomorrow," Japa responded. "This afternoon we'll put up the equipment platform. We will go up in the morning." He pointed to the image on the screen. "That empty chamber to the right of the main deposit looks big enough for an operations trailer. I'll set the platform there. Looks like we only have to go through ten or fifteen feet of granite to get to the chamber."

Jun returned to his meal. Roberto leaned back. "What do we do about the biologic? Other than the ice, I did not find any ores in the cave to get excited about. I guess those mineral grains we sampled in front of the cave yesterday came from further up the face of the cliff."

Fisk put his fork down, leaning forward with his arms on the table. "Roberto, I think it's a gag. If we announce it, you know what happens."

"I know," Roberto reached up to scratch his head. "The government will have the Lowell Institute send out a team for a full biological investigation. Our mining efforts in this canyon will stop until we are cleared to continue. Then, the fact that your miners are here on tourist visas will get everyone in trouble."

"I looked at your journal video," Dave commented, "It looks like you thawed some of the ice."

Roberto eyed Apollo. "The boy wasn't certain. Thought the specimens should be fossils. We took the sample in the tent and melted the ice. He removed two half-inch fishes and a water plant. Those looked like something that had been thawed from a storage freezer."

Sonia looked at Apollo. "You shouldn't do that. Any unfamiliar biologic should be thawed in quarantine."

Apollo grinned sheepishly, bowed his head, then nodded, "I'm sorry, Miss Sonia."

She reached over and patted his arm, "Don't do it again. After lunch, while the men are putting the platform up there to get the gold, let's you and me analyze these biologics the right way."

Apollo, still somewhat embarrassed, raised his head, smiled and nodded in agreement.

CHAPTER FIVE

UNDERGROUND CAVERN

El Dorado Badlands, Sytris Major Region, Mars

| Earth Date | July 1, 2216 |
| Mars Date | C-Mmon 19, 1174 |

"Japa!" Fisk was double-checking; "You clear?" His eyes focused on the visual countdown display.

Eleven. Ten. Nine. Eight.

"I'm clear! Roberto's with me. The crew's in the trailer."

Four. Three. Two. One. Zero.

A bright flash from the missile launch trailer precursored a fast penetrator rocket streaking up into the cliff face, sixty feet above the suspected gold vein. The "harpoon penetrator" towed a thin, sturdy twin set of wires behind it. Gray rock chunks and dust of the impact ejecta shot in a spray outward, and then slowly looped downward to settle on the canyon floor five hundred feet below. Roberto, obvious in his black and gold pressure suit, grabbed the twin lead wires where they attached to the launch trailer, and slowly walked up the pediment slope, lifting and then dropping the line to make certain it was clear of any snags. Meanwhile Japa attached one end of the split line to the wench reel, and the other end to the pulley. He activated the wrench motor, sending the pulley up the tow wire to the protruding shaft of the penetrator. Once the pulley reached the harpoon penetrator, the unit automatically clamped itself to the end of the penetrator's protruding shaft. By the time this was finished, the rest of the Filipino mining crew had joined Roberto and Japa to help guide the main lift cables being pulled up through the just installed pulley. Within thirty minutes of the missile firing, a cable loop was in place between the pulley on the harpoon shaft and the elevator wench motor mounted to one of the construction trailers. A butterfly support bracket trailing twin cables was lifted up the main hoist cable. The nose of the bracket connected itself to the pulley, and then the wings of the bracket opened like a huge letter "A" stretching ten-feet on either side of the penetrator shaft. Automatic anchor bolts at the ends of the brackets drilled themselves into the rock face. The platform hoist cables were in place.

"Who you calling?" Fisk looked over his shoulder at Dave's geochemist station. "I don't want anyone to know about this yet."

"Tapping into my library back in Crater City." Dave responded without looking around. "There's nothing for me to do 'til we get up there. Thought I'd cross check the mineral findings with my own computer."

"Shut it off," Fisk said, "No outside communications until I'm ready."

Dave did as ordered. "Yes, sir!" He turned to watch the operations outside. "I think you're being paranoid."

"Humor me." Fisk stood. "Let's go help Roberto set up the platform."

Per Roberto's instructions, Apollo sat in the control rover, watching out the window as the crew spread out the three hoist cables to lift the work platform to the five-hundred feet level. The men did not want an inexperienced teenager in their way during this risky operation, so Roberto asked him to remain inside with Sonia, where she managed communications and surveillance systems. Sitting at the console with little to do, she also watched the men preparing to raise the work platform. Glancing back, she asked, "Apollo, is this your birthday?"

He glanced at her, smiled, and then nodded agreement.

"Earth or Mars?"

"Earth," he continued smiling, "I'm eighteen. I don't know what that is on Mars."

"Happy birthday, Apollo. That would be nine and a half Martian years."

Apollo accepted a glass of mango juice from Tessie, the shapely robot. He sipped the drink. "Did you check my file?"

She used her thumb to point toward the mining crew working outside. "Roberto told me. They plan to set you up with Tessie."

Apollo stopped drinking. His tan face noticeably flushed. Wearing loose coveralls over her feminine shape, the beautiful oriental robot returned to her vertical closet, assuming the standby mode until called for. Tessie was a playmate robot Fisk had rented for this expedition to keep the Filipino mining crew entertained in the evenings. During the day Fisk changed her programming to an alternate domestic helper selection. Young Apollo had been too embarrassed to participate with the robot to this point. Apollo swallowed hard. The thought of Uncle Roberto and the rest of the Filipino crew watching and laughing as he made a fool of himself with a sexual robot terrified the teenager.

Sonia glanced at Tessie, smiled quietly, and then she turned to Apollo. She realized she had shaken him. "Sorry if I put you on the spot. Once again, I wish you a happy birthday!"

He paused to swallow, then muttered, "Thank you."

"Are we the first Martians you ever met?"

He looked at her, and then pointed to the commercial television beside the mining monitors. Another show was on the air with the newscaster who had been to his barrio. "I met her. She is a friend of Uncle Sonny!"

"I think maybe all Filipinos are relatives," She laughed, then glanced at the still silent commercial television image. "That's Terra Newton. She's the biggest video journalist on Mars. You know her?" She suddenly felt silly for raising the question. Sonia had not met her, but Terra's husband Brass had explained their connection to the Filipinos when he arranged for Sonia to hire the mining crew. Dumb.

"When I was little she made a show about my barrio."

Sonia thought about having reviewed that show. She tapped Apollo on the arm. "The men will take all afternoon to get up the cliff. This would be a good time for you to show me where you found the fish."

Apollo resumed sipping the mango juice. Turning from the window view of the work outside, he answered, "Yes, Miss Sonia." He stood up.

She smiled as she got up from her seat, reaching to retrieve her pressure helmet from the wall, "Could you leave out the 'Miss'? Just call me Sonia."

"Yes, Miss Sonia ..." Apollo blushed again, "Yes, Sonia!" He reached for his own helmet.

"Leave the receiver on for channel three, so we can hear what's going on out there," Sonia said, "But, we'll use channel eight for ourselves."

Apollo made the channel selections via his sleeve controller. He double checked his backpack readings. He pulled the gloves from the inside of his helmet, secured them over his hands, and then slipped the helmet over his head. Watching Sonia reach for the life sciences computer case, he followed her through the airlock to the dusty Martian surface. The sun-illuminated landscape looked as warm as a terrestrial desert, although the frigid, rarified air outside would kill unprotected humans within minutes. Despite the harsh conditions, small white and yellow flowers were blossoming within the scrub grass struggling to survive in the soil of the canyon floor. Immigrant genetic engineers had developed a lot of plants that could survive on the miniscule water available at the surface, plants that pushed roots deep into the soil below, searching for permafrost moisture.

The mining crew worked diligently with the hoist cables to hook up the first forty-foot long platform support beam. Apollo's expertise was as a boring machine operator. It would be at least two days before the work platform was in place and ready for boring efforts to begin. Following Sonia, Apollo climbed the two-hundred yards of jumbled rocks much more slowly than he would have had he been by himself.

She was more than twice his age. None of this prospecting outing was as much of an adventure for her as it was for him. At the mouth of the cave, he pushed a button on the box at the cave's entrance to activate the communications relays between the cave interior and the control rover. He led her along the twisting path a hundred more feet into a thirty-foot high cavern, still illuminated by the tripod mounted lights Roberto had installed the day before. The fifteen by fifteen pressurized tent was still inflated, positioned to one side of the cavern. A green light over the airlock entry to the translucent tent advertised that the air inside was safe. Scattered on the floor of the tent were several sleeping containers, a low coffee table, and a counter with drawers of cooking equipment, plus a few other miscellaneous items.

Sealed in his full pressure suit, Apollo approached the collapsible tables beyond the tent, where small sample collection pans of rocks were awaiting analysis. A mineral analysis chamber, and a data control computer sat quietly, unused, on the table beside the samples. Pointing to the rock samples, Apollo said, "Most of what we found in here are iron oxides ... quartz, sandstone, granite ... nothing valuable."

"I can see that," Sonia placed a hand on his shoulder, "Show me the ice."

Side stepping to another table, he lifted a pan with several chunks of ice and stone. "Right here, Miss Sonia." He put it down, and then reached for a second sample. "Here is one with some plants."

She took it, picked up a portable light to illuminate the sample. She peered through the flat surface where a laser had cut the ice. Stubby, brown grasses stood erect, an inch high, in the transparent ice. She looked to the control panel on the computer two tables away. Cave air temperature reading was a minus 120 degrees Fahrenheit. "Show me where you found it."

Pointing to the left, he said, "Down that auxiliary tunnel about fifty feet," He led the way through a narrow accessway, so constricted that both had to get on their hands and knees to squeeze through. After a rough, rock-strewn crawl through a twisting tunnel, they emerged in a vertical cavern, fifteen feet across, ten feet high. Using his helmet light, Apollo illuminated the ground underneath. A laser pick lay to one side of a pile of sandstone rocks. In the excavated pit was a layer of ice, about one foot deep.

There was a smirk to Sonia's tone. "Fisk thinks someone came down here to create a prank?" She raised her head, looked around the bay, then back down at the pit. "Please, get me another sample with some biologics!"

Apollo reached for the laser pick. He cut out a fresh section of covering sandstone to expose more of the ice deposit. Peering cautiously through the ice for several seconds, he began cutting. Putting the laser down, he lifted a twelve-inch cube of ice and handed it to Sonia.

With her focused spotlight, she studied the ice. There were two tiny fishes. No apparent eyes, but otherwise they were fishes. "This is good. Let's take it back to the main work bay for analysis."

Before starting toward the passage back to the tents, she asked, "Your adventure yesterday … going through dried aquifer tunnels to the top of the cliff … where are they?"

He pointed up to one corner of the cavern. Above was a dark, ragged, chimney-like opening going straight up. "I went through there. A few feet up, it angles to the left. There is a flat cavern thirty foot further."

"Would you show me, later?

"Of course; do you want to go now?"

"Later. You said the cave passages to the surfaces were over ten miles."

"Eleven," Apollo answered, "At least according to the instruments in this pressure suit."

"Lead me back to the tool bench."

A few minutes later at the work tables she did the mineral evaluation. However, through the ice she could not get a clear reading of the molecular make-up of the fish. "You say you thawed a sample? What did you use?"

He pointed through the transparent wall of the pressurized tent. Inside was a small counter with a microwave oven. "I used that."

Sonia stared in disbelief. "Do you understand that this is an unidentified life form? You were in direct contact?"

He nodded, embarrassed again. He was thankful that the gold sunscreen coating on his visor obscured his reddening face. "Back home, when I went fishing near the barrio … if I catch a fish I don't know, I tasted it to see if it is good."

"That's crazy. You should never eat unidentified substances. What if it were poison?"

He looked at her with an expression of worry. He had not expected her to be upset.

She patted him on the back, "That's okay. Be careful after this. Where's the fish you thawed?"

Again, he pointed in the tent, this time to a ceramic jar. Two fishes and a stock of seaweed were visible within. "I ate one. It tasted like raw fish."

She looked at the ice sample they had just retrieved, at Apollo, then at the jar inside the tent. "I'll analyze this in the trailer containment later. Let's take my life sciences computer in the tent. I can get a reading through the jar." She patted his shoulder again. "And I can give you a birthday present."

Approaching the tent airlock, she pushed a button to open the outer door. Both stepped into the compartment designed for two adults, then closed the door. Once the chamber was pressurized, the inside door opened, allowing them inside the tent. Sonia double checked environmental readings, then removed her helmet. "We'll be here for awhile," she put her headgear to one side, "May as well get comfortable!" She disconnected her backpack, and placed it in a corner.

Sonia removed her utility belt, unzipped the front of her pressure suit, and then removed the upper jacket.

Apollo smiled as he did the same. He watched her, but said nothing. He appreciated her full feminine form, now more visible with only the snuggly fitted thermal wear covering her chest. Her breasts were larger than what he was used to seeing on women back home. He flushed momentarily, embarrassed for having thought about Miss Sonia in that way. Uncle Roberto had joked with the other Filipino miners about her. They all assumed she was Fisk's fiancée. Nobody tried advances. The men had robot Tessie to resolve their amorous needs. Apollo often wondered why Fisk never seemed attentive to Sonia. He decided to change the subject. "Miss Sonia, Fisk and Uncle Roberto said this would be investigated by the Lowell Institute if they knew about it. What is that?"

"Please, don't call me Miss."

"But, you are the boss lady.

"I prefer if you just call me Sonia." She then responded to his comment, "The Lowell Institute? It's a government research organization that collects natural information about Mars … helps the politicians make environmental policy."

"Was Lowell the guy who started it?"

"You never heard of Percival Lowell?"

"Who?"

"In the nineteenth century … America … he was an astronomer, convinced that Mars was inhabited, that the citizens of Mars built a massive network of canals to transport water from the ice caps to equatorial farmlands. For nearly a hundred years he had dreamers convinced that they would find an advanced civilization here."

"But, there is an advanced civilization. You and Fisk and …"

"Until human pioneers came, this was virtually a sterile rock. Immigrants from Earth brought what life we have. Anyway, Percival Lowell created the dream of exotic, alien Martians … the Institute is named in his honor."

"Maybe when we get finished here, I'll read about him."

"You still have any of that mango juice here?" she asked. She opened the life science computer case, and removed a small bottle of liquid from the specimen compartment.

He opened the mini refrigerator, reaching inside for the mango juice. He located two glasses in another cabinet compartment. He filled each glass half full.

"My ancestors are from Odessa." Sonia opened the bottle. "Nothing makes a glass of fruit juice sparkle like a touch of vodka."

"You're from Earth?" He was not certain if he should be drinking alcohol.

"My grandparents immigrated. I've never been off Mars, except for small trips, like the one I took last Christmas." She added vodka to each glass. Putting the vodka down, she picked two hand-sized scanners from the case, and placed them on opposite sides of the ceramic jar with the fish specimens. Speaking to the computer, she said, "Full scan, wide range cross check."

She then picked up her glass, held it toward Apollo, and said, "To your eighteenth birthday."

He lifted his glass to click hers. The birthday present was his first taste of vodka. As they sipped, the computer said, "Genetic analysis: similar to arctic fresh water fishes, but no match. No known match on file. This is an unidentified species."

Sonia stared at the jar with the fish samples. "That's what I thought." She sipped her drink again. She then asked, "How did you get your family name?"

"Huh?" He also sipped again. "I was born with it."

"Ever since we decided to hire a Filipino mining crew, I've been researching your homeland. All of the men have common names, but your name ... Panahon ... there's only about a dozen listings in the interplanetary directory."

Apollo smiled as he removed his own pressure suit jacket. "Two hundred years ago my great, great ... whatever ... grandfather had no last name. He was an Igorot ... that's a tribe of remote mountain people. A mining company trained him to keep track of other workers ... when they work, when they go home."

"He was a timekeeper?"

"The barrio people started calling him "Panahon," which means "time". It has been the family name since." After finishing the cocktail, he poured more mango juice in the two glasses. "My first name is for a Filipino hero of long ago ... Apollino Mabini ... he wrote our first Constitution."

Sonia added more vodka to the two drinks. "Well, Apollo is also a Greek God. I thought you got the name from that first manned flight to Earth's Moon." She lifted her drink for another toast. "Here's to our God of Time!" She sipped, and then put the glass down.

Apollo followed her lead. The two cocktails were suddenly making him light headed. "Are you and boss Fisk ... a couple?"

Sonia laughed lightly. Running her fingers through her short, golden hair, she said, "No, Apollo. Fisk and I are business partners. That's all." She reached to take his hand in hers. "Tell me, do you have a girlfriend? I think I saw you with Emilio's daughter at Christmas."

Apollo watched silently as she gently massaged his hand with her fingertips. He thought of Nina, Emilio's sixteen-year-old daughter. He liked her. She liked him. But, they had never actually committed to each other. He slowly shook his head back and forth. "Nina is a close friend, but we aren't engaged. Why?"

She smiled devilishly. "Just curious. You're quite something. You're the first person I've met in a long time with a passion for crawling on the rocks the way I used to be."

Apollo studied Sonia's face. It was obvious that she had been a beauty when she was young. Apollo secretly wished their ages were closer. At twenty-two (forty-two Earth years), she still had a pixie quality to her, although a trace of wrinkles had become obvious from the corners of her eyes. Since he first saw her on Christmas Eve in Baguio he had fantasized about being with her, although he knew those thoughts were silly. He silently wished their ages were closer. He regretted being an inexperienced teenager that someone like her would never think about him in that way.

"Your Uncle Roberto wants to let you celebrate your birthday with Tessie. I know you've never been with a woman. Your first time should not be with a machine… it should be with a real woman. For your birthday, I'm going to give you a first time."

Apollo's mouth silently popped open. He blushed, looking down as her fingers gently rubbed his hand. He began to feel aroused. That embarrassed him even more. Following a few stutters, he mumbled, "Are you sure you want to do this? I don't really know…"

Sonia reached to his cheek. "I like you. Once upon a time I was young… and awkward… and afraid… just like you. I had a boyfriend, but was afraid to have sex. Then, my cousin flirted with my boyfriend and went to bed with him… in my own house," She leaned back propping herself with her arms. The posture pushed her ample breasts forward. "I was angry… at her, at him, at the world. I went looking for sympathy from Charley Yulanti, a restaurant owner… back then… he was a little older than I am now. I gave myself to him… that was my most memorable…"

Apollo watched her chest moving with each breath. "For your birthday," she leaned forward again. Took his hand, and placed it on her breast. "Your first time will be with a real woman who can share your excitement, the way Charley Yulanti shared mine. It will be better than making love to a machine that acts and speaks as it was programmed."

Apollo felt excited at the idea of trying something he had always wanted to do, but never had the opportunity. His face turned red, flushed with the embarrassment of what was happening. He felt guilty, thinking of Nina, that they were sort of special to each other. He thought of the few times he had subtly pleaded with Nina to sleep with him. She always rebuffed him, telling him they should both wait until they were married. Sonia's hand, holding his, drew his fingers to her breast. He briefly held his breath, and quietly smiled. He felt sexual excitement as he gently squeezed her large breast, which felt like a warm water balloon.

"That's fine," There was an impish smile on Sonia's lips. She uttered a nearly imperceptibly gasp. She lifted his hand to her lips, and kissed his fingers. "The secret to a good experience… one that many young men miss out on… is not to rush. Sex is like dinner. You can eat a sandwich quickly to end your hunger, or you can slowly eat a multi-course meal while chatting with someone who enjoys your company." She dropped his hand aside, and then placed her hands on his cheeks. She leaned forward to kiss his forehead, then his ear, and finally his lips. Apollo flushed a little. He was fully aroused.

Sonia grinned, leaned back, glancing down at his bulge. Her eyes returned to his expression. "Apollo, don't be embarrassed. I know you're getting excited. That's normal. Just don't rush. Let's help each other out of the thermal wear."

Still grinning, she reached to unzip his thermal vest. Slowly, she removed his vest, to expose a brown, freckled, hairless chest. He reciprocated by unzipping her vest. She opened it and pulled it back to drop off her shoulders, an action that caused him to gasp at the view of her ample cream-colored breasts. "Beautiful," he whispered. He stared at the protruding pink nipples. This was the first time a woman had ever undressed before him, creating an excitement that was nearly overwhelming. Her breasts were everything the other Filipino miners joked about over the months. His mouth opened in awe.

She rose to a standing position before him. "Apollo, I'd like you to take the time to enjoy this discovery." She snapped loose the waste removal belt so that it could be slipped down easily. "I want you to remove the bottom half of my outfit. Take your time. See if you can do it without touching my skin."

He pulled the elastic outfit from her hips, stretching the waist band far enough for his thumbs not to touch her. He couldn't help but admire her taut stomach muscles at the front of a very shapely body. The thermal slacks slid down her legs, exposing her shaved pubic area. Apollo quietly swallowed, continuing his wide-eyed stare.

Sonia stepped out of the outfit, one foot at a time. Giving him a moment to take in his first view of her nakedness, she then said, "Apollo, you'll stand now, and I'll undress you."

She dropped to her knees, leaned forward, and kissed his cheek. Squatting on her haunches, she motioned for him to stand up.

Trying to lower the waist band of his thermal wear past his erection was a little more difficult. "Oh, my... I'd say you are ready."

His face flushed a little. She winked up at him.

"Now, kneel before me, and take my hands in yours. We'll intertwine our fingers."

He did as instructed. He gulped, trying hard to contain the emotions.

"Take it easy, Apollo." She continued to talk in a cheerful whisper, watching his eyes closely. "We'll keep our fingers locked together. I'll lean forward and lightly blow air at your body. You will do the same for me."

"Okay, go ahead." He swallowed.

"By the end of this, we will both need a shower." Without touching more than his fingers, she began blowing light streams of air on his neck, then his chest. She continued down, she blew air at his belly button, bringing a tickled giggle from him. When her warm breath puffed against his genitals, he was unable to control his inexperienced arousal. He erupted in a way she had expected. He was embarrassed.

"You're doing fine," She smiled up at him. "Now, I want you to blow air on me."

An hour later, as Apollo lay naked across the blankets they had pulled from Roberto's bedding, The games enabled him to physically explore everything on her body, including bringing her to a sexual climax with his fingers. She had done the same for him. The novelty of sexual experiences for him kept him highly aroused throughout, even following multiple eruptions. Finally, she drew him into her, and guiding him into a prolonged, vigorous sexual intercourse that had both moaning in pleasure. Sonia lay beside him, propped on one elbow, running her fingers across his chest. Filled with a sense of adventurous accomplishment, his gaze moved from her pixie face to the nipples protruding from her breasts. "Thank you, Miss Sonia. I enjoyed this very much."

She ran her fingers through his hair. "You were great, Apollo. I haven't enjoyed sex this much in a long time. For someone doing this for a first time, you learn quickly, and you have the intensity I've watched you show for geology. You are really something special."

Taking a moment to quietly think, he finally looked up to her eyes, "Sonia, I didn't realize how great it could be. Will we be able to do this again?"

She smiled, and shook her head. "I don't think it so. That would complicate the business we have here. Treasure the memory. This was only a birthday treat. Okay?"

"I promise to be an attentive student."

She rubbed her fingers through his hair, "You'll just have to let Tessie work for you after this. For today... from me... Happy Birthday."

He felt disappointed that she was withdrawing any chance for more encounters. "I understand." He leaned his forward to once more kiss the nipple. "I will remember."

"If your Nina finally decides to sleep with you, just remember not to rush. Make it a slowly evolving game... the way I showed you."

He stared at her face again, "Have you ever experienced a robot?"

"Oh yes," She chuckled. "But, like most women ... I prefer the real thing. Robots are great for someone who only wants the mechanics of sexual arousal ... but I want to know my partner enjoys being with me ... is sharing something with me."

"Why did you choose to give me your love? Not Roberto or Fisk or the men who know what to do?"

"They know what to do, not how to make it a new adventure. You're a little awkward, but I enjoyed it." She did not explain that she was attracted to him for reasons she did not understand. She was thrilled to be with someone who enjoyed geologic exploration as much as he did. When she first saw his picture at Jim Everly's wake Sonia felt a sense of deja voux, that she knew him, and knew him well. That feeling surfaced every time she saw him. She did not know why, but there was something special about Apollo that she did not feel about anyone else she knew. She put her drink down, "These dark marks on your chest... are they freckles?"

"Freckles?" Apollo asked. "I have no freckles." He looked down at his chest. There were a dozen or more dark spots that had not been there the night before.

"Maybe it's your reaction to having a first time." She ran her fingers down his chest, across his abdomen, towards his manhood in an effort to see if he could be aroused again so quickly. He was.

CHAPTER SIX

GOLD STRIKE

El Dorado Badlands, Sytris Major Region, Mars

Earth Date	July 4, 2216
Mars Date	C-Mmon 22, 1174

It had been an exhausting three days, but a steel grating work platform was secured to the face of the cliff midway up, five-hundred feet above the canyon floor. In addition, a motorized equipment elevator had lifted a high-heat laser mole vehicle to that platform. With the dawn the crew was ready to go to work. Apollo's job was to bore an opening into the rock face to provide an access way to the hidden cavern, a cavern that would provide a stable work area to dig for the suspected gold vein. It was time to start digging.

Anxious to do more than watch the other men do the work, Apollo convinced Uncle Roberto to take him up, to let him bore the first entrance tunnel. Slowly, the wenches pulled their elevator over the two-hundred foot of sloped pediment up to that five-hundred foot elevation. Apollo, Roberto, and Jun stared at the grated work platform getting closer. The rising sun, barely above the eastern horizon made the landscape seem warm and bright. The data displays on the pressure suit sleeve reminded them that it was minus forty degrees, with the air pressure at seven millibars, less than a hundredth the pressure inside his suit.

Apollo silently endured pain in his back and legs, aches in his muscles that seemed more intense than the day before. The rash on his skin created itching irritations. Combined with a queasy stomach, he knew he had a touch of something. He kept quiet about it. He was tired of being treated like a child.

"Top floor," Jun opened the cage gate as soon as the elevator jolted to a stop, having automatically latched itself to the platform deck. The blinding sun reflecting from his gold-tinted visor hid his face from view. "Apollo, fire it up!"

Apollo slipped into the seat of the golf-cart-sized boring machine, and strapped himself in. The nuclear powered vehicle had an eight-foot diameter boring disc on its face. He connected a control cable from his belt computer to the appropriate jack on the cart's instrument panel. "On! Warm to two-point-three-kay (2300°F)!"

Slowly, the eight-foot crystalline laser disc at the front of the vehicle heated to over two-thousand degrees Fahrenheit. Apollo glanced over his shoulder at the small blinding sun, now well above the mouth of the canyon. The slopes of Burroughs Valley beyond, no longer in shadow, seemed green with the color of scrub grasses growing from the dry, cold soil. A near-surface permafrost layer provided the moisture needed for those plants to survive.

Roberto and Jun sidestepped around the machine to stand behind Apollo, positioning themselves to control the magma drain.

The color of the front face of the machine's laser disc changed from black to red, to glowing orange to yellow to bright white. When the temperatures on the disc's outer face reached the twenty-three hundred degree boring temperature, Apollo set in motion the six spinning concentric composite zirconium-tipped cutting rings. He checked the slag ejection tubes; they were properly set to expel molten waste to the canyon floor, while Roberto and Jun had it aimed away from the miner's caravan. According to the instrument readings, the cooling tubes behind the laser disc and wrapping the ejection tubes were operating properly. "I'm set, Uncle Roberto!"

"This is your buffalo, Apollo. Ride it in!"

Apollo talked to the computer, pushed a few buttons, and then steered the mole into the wall. Smoke began pouring from the contact point; vibration rattled the mole, the rock face, and the platform. Speckled gray granite changed to bright liquid lava, breaking into chunks with the pressure of the cutting blades. The magma flowed like liquid cement through the ejecta tubes under the vehicle, spewing a glowing mud-like stream of smoking lava in an arc down to the canyon floor. Slowly, Apollo pushed the boring machine into the rock face. A few inches. A few feet. Slowly, oh so slowly, the entire vehicle disappeared into a round, eight-foot diameter hole through solid rock. Advancing into the granite, Apollo had the boring machine release titanium-ceramic-steel rings from the back. These rings expanded in place, creating tunnel bracing. Water streaming from the perforated braces created clouds of steam to cool the man-made lava tube enough for the rock walls to harden. Roberto used a separate fire hose to spray water, pumped from a trailer below, over the hot tunnel walls.

It took Apollo a half-hour to bore ten feet. Seismic data imaging maps, created days earlier, showed that the tunnel had to be thirty feet to reach the underground cavern. It would take another hour. Inside the insulated, shock-protected cab for the boring machine, the environment duplicated an Earth-like atmosphere. Apollo didn't need his pressure suit, but he kept it sealed. He should have been advancing through the cliff in cool comfort, the way he had done so many times in the Benget Mountains of northern Luzon. This was different. Beads of sweat formed on his forehead. He heard faint whining sounds that he knew were not real. The dark freckles (rash) on his chest had multiplied since Sonia first noticed them. He thought he might be reacting to something he ate. Maybe it was caused by the fishes. He would continue to work, to say nothing.

He listened to the radio chatter of Uncle Roberto and Jun on the platform talking to Fisk and Sonia in the control rover below. Fisk directed Roberto to adjust the aim of the waste ejecta pattern. Occasionally, Roberto or Fisk gave Apollo verbal information, although most of what they said was displayed on his instrument panel. Shy Apollo preferred to listen, follow the instructions of his elders, and say very little that might make him seem foolish.

With time, the boring machine finally emerged through the rock wall, and on to the floor of a huge underground cavern bay. It was a cavern carved millions of years earlier when warm water flowed through underground aquifer streams, precisely where Fisk had predicted. Apollo turned off the laser disc, drove the vehicle sixty-feet across the dark cavern, and parked it. With a push of a button, an equipment access hatch opened in the vehicle roof. A rack of spotlights telescoped upward. The lamps flooded the huge cavern with light, while a video camera panned the surroundings. Pristine stalagmites proved that once upon a time these Martian crustal rocks had been warm and wet, but now scanned temperature readings of the far wall gave values well below freezing. Light from outside filtered through the steam still clouding the freshly bored tunnel.

"Uncle Roberto. The bore temperatures should be cool enough to walk on now. You want to come in?"

"Teka, teka (Wait a moment). See anything?"

The video image highlighted metallic sparkles from the walls, but that provided little real information. "Ewan ko (Don't know)! Bring the spectral strobe scanner."

With the boring machine silent and cool, Apollo sat quietly for a few moments. He did not feel well. He needed to lie down. He turned off the communicator to lean back and close his eyes. Something must be wrong with the equipment. He was still hearing faint voices, too faint to make out what was being said, but the muffled voices were definitely there. He sensed that he had a touch of flu. He tried taking his mind off the discomforts. Leaning back, his thoughts drifted once more to his birthday surprise. With his eyes closed, he visualized Miss Sonia in all her naked erotic beauty, taking the time to show him how to enjoy a sexual encounter. Was it possible that she may be interested in him for more than a moment of special fun? Logic immediately raised doubts. She was twice his age. It was just a birthday present, as she said it was. Would there be a second time?

His thoughts then went to that evening, and his birthday gift from the adult Filipinos. Roberto and the rest went to the observation trailer to play poker late into the night, after programming Tessie, the Asian featured robot playmate, to behave with Apollo as if he were a school boy anxious to share a first encounter. Apollo thought he would not like being entertained by a robot, but he enjoyed the evening despite the reservations. Tessie was designed to look, and feel, like a beautiful Oriental woman of his own age. She had soft, tan skin and delicate features. Fisk leased the robot programmed to speak two Filipino languages, and that included an intimate knowledge of Filipino culture. In addition, when Sonia was in Baguio to hire the mining team, she asked Apollo's Uncle Sonny to provide personal details about each of the six miners; data that was programmed into Tessie's computerized memory. Rather than rush into a sexual gift for Apollo, the way she was programmed for the older Filipinos, Tessie took her time. She had him stay at the table while she prepared arroz caldo (a rice and chicken soup with ginger and green onions). While cooking, she talked to Apollo about the older Filipinos, repeating jokes they had told her. She asked him about growing up in the Benguet Mountains. Programmed to duplicate human conversation patterns, she adapted to new information she heard. Her conversations reflected what she had learned. She was even programmed to eat and drink consumables that could be cleaned from her system later. For this occasion she wore an oriental dress that tended to accent her mammaries.

After feeding him and sharing a glass of wine, Tessie moved with him to the side of the bed. Standing in front of him, as he stared in wonderment, she slowly opened her dress, exposing her ample breasts to his view. She playfully grinned at him, letting the outfit drop to the floor. She had no underwear. With a smile and a whisper, she cooed for him to kiss her breasts, to do what he wanted. Programmed to behave much like Sonia had, Tessie seduced him one step at a time, like a teacher with a new student. Her programming was very good. After exhausting him in the bed, she brought him into the shower stall to clean up.. Slowly, they soaped each other everywhere. With shower water cascading over them, she proceded to seduce Apollo again, doing what she was programmed for to augment his arousal. Tessie's duplication of muscles were made of elastic fiber, and felt real. Her sexual arousal moisture and aroma seemed real. Still excited from the earlier birthday present, Apollo found that playing with Tessie was as entertaining as watching a rerun of an enjoyable movie.

When he finally went to sleep, tucked in a bunk with Tessie, he thought of Nina Perez, of how the year before they had talked about marriage. They agreed to wait until they both grew up. Now, he felt as if he had betrayed her. In addition, Emilio, Nina's father, arranged part of that betrayal. Emilio did not know about their relationship. The next morning Apollo woke without Tessie, hurting from muscle pains and sick to his stomach. He avoided talking to his Filipino 'uncles' about the sex or the symptoms, knowing they would just laugh at the confused little boy.

Roberto banged his pressure suited glove against the boring mole's cabin hatch window. Apollo opened his eyes, turned the communicator up again.

"Are you all right?"

"Yes, Uncle. Just tired."

"Open the door," Roberto signaled his nephew. "Let's talk with the steth-o-line."

The steth-o-line gave pressure-suited people a way to talk directly without radios. Apollo attached his steth-o-line to his helmet, opened the vehicle hatch, and then handed Roberto the connector for the other end of the line.

Making the connection to his own line, Roberto shook his head just slightly. "Don't let the bosses see you wasting time. If they think we are lazy, they might tell us to go away. On Mars, we have no place to go. We are not supposed to be working at all."

"I know, Uncle," Apollo spoke softly; "I'm just a little tired."

There was mirth in Roberto's next words, "Sonia told me about the birthday present. Thinking about it probably kept you awake at night. I'm not certain how things went with Tessie, but I assume you enjoyed it."

Apollo began blushing inside helmet. He was glad his uncle could not see. He felt betrayed that Sonia had told.

Roberto sensed the boy's unease. "She did not want to tell, but I was worried because you have acted strange the past three days. I was worried that you were getting sick. When she explained, I understood." He patted Apollo on the shoulder; "Miss Sonia gave you what she would not give to me, or the rest of the men. Be glad you had a good birthday. We have to make do with the robot playmate."

Apollo looked up at the glistening helmet of his uncle, "I thought you said that Tessie can do anything a real woman can do? She acted real when you left her with me."

"She is a great robot," there was a pause, "but, she is not a woman. She is a machine."

Apollo blushed once more, this time hoping to change the subject. "What do you want me to do now?"

"Move the mole machine to the right, out of the way of the tunnel. Boss Fisk is coming up now with a lot of equipment to sample the ores."

Apollo motioned for his uncle to step away from the hatch. "Okay, I move!"

Using the elevator lift Japa, Celso, and Doug brought up equipment carts with tables, tents, and instruments. Fisk, Sonia, and Dave came on the next elevator ride along with the rest of the equipment. Roberto and his crew worked quickly, inflating tents, erecting worktables, and hooking computers and ore testing carts to the power generator. Simultaneously, Fisk and Sonia used spectral strobe scanners to image the mineral information along various portions of the cavern bay. Using a pneumatic drill, Japa drove steel inserts into the rock walls at various locations; some were seismic sensors, others were explosive bolts designed to create shock waves through the rocks. Roberto and Apollo, using laser cutters and old fashioned shovels, dug several small pits into the loose sediment of the cavern floor.

The cave had been a natural underground cistern, where water flowing through cracks had settled temporarily before pouring outside through a small channel to cascade down the face of the cliff. The five-hundred foot waterfall would have been a beautiful sight. No water had flowed through this cavern for millions of years.

Roberto brought several pans of gravel from the cavern's sedimentary rocks to the Startech BR-16 Analyzer. "We have gold dust," he said excitedly. Watching the results on the instruments, he said, "Boss, you want to see this?" He looked over his shoulder.

Fisk and Sonia were preoccupied. They closely inspected a glittering gold ribbon stretching across the rock face to the left of the cave access tunnel. They both carried scanners, but neither paid attention to the instrument readings. Instruments were not needed to recognize a six-inch band of pure gold ore. "Amazing," Fisk ran his gloved fingers along the seam. "I've been prospecting all my life. I have never seen a strike like this one." He turned to Sonia, hugged her, and danced around a few steps. "We did it. We actually did it."

Sonia uttered a nearly unintelligible squeal of delight. "We're rich. We are really rich!"

Dave, always less excitable than the others, remarked, "It looks good, but it doesn't count until we record it. Should I call it in?"

"We need to finish the seismic test," Fisk was as giddy as a child at Christmas. "Dave, go ahead. Send it in. Send Tessie back up with lunch." He looked around. "We'll eat in the tent. Roberto, have your men put up a shield." He pointed to the boring machine, tents, and worktables to the right side of the cavern. He continued, "to protect the equipment."

Despite his flu-like symptoms, Apollo was as thrilled as the rest of the crew. Fisk had promised, in the event they found gold, a big bonus on top of what they were to be paid. Apollo worked with Emilio and Jun to stretch the telescoping cable mesh shield screen across the cave. He felt happy, but he was sweating. His stomach felt funny. He could hear unfamiliar voices talking, voices that lacked clarity. He could not make out what those voices were trying to say. He dared not tell anyone that he thought he was sick. It would jeopardize all the Filipino's chances to keep working, especially now that everything looked so promising.

The seismic tests were completed within an hour, with no ricocheting rock bullets to liven the day. Fisk mapped the buried gold vein to the limits of the seismic detector range. Greater than eighty-thousand tons was determined, with the vein extending beyond the limits of mapping. There was nothing more to do until Dave confirmed that their claim was registered with the Bureau of Mines.

Tessie, as sensuous as ever and not needing a pressure suit in the Martian environment, arrived in the cave with a galley cart. Wearing a loose fitting worker's uniform so as not to distract the crew while they were working. She could be programmed for most routine service functions. Emilio accepted the galley cart from her. He steered it through the airlock for the crew's tent.

Programmed for Martian and Filipino meals, the galley computer prepared the lunch menus everyone was yelling for. With the food dishes ready, they all entered the tent to settle at the table with helmets off.

Slowly sipping his soup, Apollo watched Roberto shuffle a deck of playing cards for the men's usual mealtime poker game. Soup was all he felt up to putting in his stomach. "Mister Fisk, I understand how you mapped out the gold up here. What I don't know is how you were able to determine this was the place to look?"

Fisk, watching the poker game with fascination, took another bite of his roast chicken sandwich. After chewing and swallowing, he said, "Research, Apollo. Lots and lots of research."

Roberto took a spoonful of his mixed vegetables with rice, put the bowl down, and then dealt the cards to the rest of the crew. "Red threes and black fours are wild. Double the usual stakes."

"Double?" Jun questioned.

"All this gold around us... You can afford it."

Sonia, watching the poker game, responded to Apollo's inquiry. "Fisk, that's a terrible answer." She turned to the boy. "Apollo, first we get a detailed geologic survey of the entire planet. We have the computer blank out any properties that been claimed. Then, we isolate trace concentrations of valuable ores we're interested in."

"You mean to say that you are the first to detect gold here?"

Fisk spoke, "No, not the first... the third."

"I still don't understand."

Sonia stared into his eyes. She reached across the table and patted his hand. "We looked at thousands of sites with geologic readings for enough trace ore readings to catch our attention. We cross checked those sites with the Bureau of Mines, with historical records. In the case of Princess Dejah Canyon, there are trace readings for gold and copper in the downstream sediment, along the entire canyon floor. Twice before prospectors came to this canyon to sample the sediment; they did not explore the mid levels of the cliff walls like we did. Directly below this cavern is where a waterfall once dropped a lot of gold dust."

Apollo nodded understanding. He felt a little uncomfortable that Sonia was staring at him. She had mentioned those freckles on his birthday. Many more had appeared, including on his face. He silently prayed that she would not make a public issue of it.

Reaching for a fresh hot roll, she ignored the blemishes. She watched as Fisk put money on the table to join the card game.

Roberto handed the deck to Emilio, as he raked his winnings to his corner of the table. He then reached for his fork. "You in, boss?"

"In," Fisk took another bite of his sandwich.

Emilio shuffled the cards, as he announced, "Face cards with mustaches are wild." He began dealing to the five players. Sonia, Japa, and Apollo watched from the sidelines.

Fisk shook his head, smiled, "You men are crazy with the wild cards. Tell me again what you call this game."

Jun answered, "Pusoy. Duce is higher than ace. Diamonds beat hearts beat spades beat clubs."

"Amazing!" Fisk picked up the ten cards he had been dealt.

"Computer," Japa turned to face the remote console cabinet, "Commercial television. Mars Broadcast Agency." A small monitor screen on the instrument panel illuminated with the ongoing news telecast from Crater City, half a planet away. The familiar face of media journalist Terra Newton appeared on screen. She was talking about an upcoming treaty between Earth and Mars concerning resource access for Venus.

"Venus?" Japa questioned no one in particular, "Why is there a need for a treaty about Venus?"

"Listen and find out," Fisk said. He concentrated more on the cards in his hand.

"Apollo met her," Sonia pointed to the newscast.

"Met who?" Japa asked.

"Terra Newton, the journalist. Apparently she is a friend of Apollo's uncle."

Fisk glanced at the newscast, at Apollo, then at Roberto. "This true?"

Roberto nodded agreement, as he played a card on the table. "Miguel Sonny Ortigas, my wife's brother, is a Manila detective. He did a homicide investigation for Terra Newton for a story about fifteen years ago. Sonny brought her up to the barrio when Apollo was small. She was doing another show."

"Well, Apollo," Fisk smiled at the boy, "Maybe you can get your Uncle Sonny to pull a few strings to get all of your Filipino uncles a work visa. Now that we have a big gold strike, it's going to be hard to go on with just your tourist visas."

Fisk's attempt at humor had the opposite effect. Everyone froze, stared at him. This was the unresolved issue central to everyone's concerns.

Fisk played a card, "Sorry, I shouldn't have said that. Jun, your play."

Sonia shook her head, "Fisk, you can't just fart in church and expect no one to notice. Tell them."

Jun won the hand. Fisk took the cards from the table to begin shuffling. "We like the way you work. That's why we brought you to Mars, even if it is as tourists. If things do not work out, what I promised you is guaranteed. Roberto, you know that. I put the money in your account before you came. Anyway, if things don't work out with the visas, Sonia and I promise a big bonus."

The silent Filipino crew continued staring at him. Finally, they looked at each other, and Roberto said, "Thanks, boss. Now, maybe I can win a few hands."

CHAPTER SEVEN

BETRAYAL

Princess Dejah Canyon
El Dorado Badlands, Sytris Major Region, Mars

Earth Date	July 6, 2216
Mars Date	C-Mmon 24, 1174

The bright morning sun, shining through the window, was higher in the sky than Apollo expected. He had overslept. He had to get moving, catch the elevator up the cliff to join the crew for breakfast. It was too late for breakfast. He would just go to work. He had to dig gold from the wall of the cave. Sitting up, his back and shoulders ached more than before. His muscles were too painful for him to move around, let alone work. He had no choice; he had to do his part. Stumbling into the trailer bathroom, he felt dizzy, nauseous, and weak. For two nights he had slept in the trailer, separate from the rest of the crew, fearful that they would know he was not well. Since the older Filipinos slept in the worksite tent in the cavern up the cliff, they had not watched him tossing and moaning in his sleep. Roberto, knowing Apollo was ill, suggested he sleep in the trailer.

Apollo promised he would do a medical computer evaluation, but had not gotten around to it. He did not want to find out. He was afraid that if Fisk and Sonia found out, they would send all the Filipinos home. Those crazy dreams had startled him awake several times during the night.

He needed a real shower, not just the ultra-sonic dry type. Removing his night clothes, he paused at the mirror on his way into the shower stall. His formerly featureless skin was a mass of small dots. Ignoring it, he stepped into the shower. The warm water felt good for awhile, washing away the sweat, smell, and irritations. He was frightened. He whimpered to himself while the water flowed over him. He wished he were home. He felt embarrassed, fearful that the crew would think he was such a baby if they saw him. He was sick, but he had been sick before. He would continue to act as if he were healthy.

Apollo slipped into his pressure suit, and then stepped through the hatchway of the crew's trailer into the connecting pressurized access tube to the observation trailer. He stopped at the galley for a bowl of chicken broth. His shaky stomach would not be able to handle solid food, and the last thing he wanted was to get sick inside a sealed pressure suit.

"Apollo?" Sonia's voice resonated from the communications console. "Could you come to the control rover for breakfast?"

"Of course, Miss Sonia."

He did not feel like eating. Leaving the nearly full soup bowl on the table, he put his helmet on, closed the visor, and stepped into the airlock. Walking across the dusty compound to the control rover, he noticed an unfamiliar rover among the vehicles. Glancing up the elevator guide cables to the work deck five-hundred feet up, he saw no activity on the outside. He kicked a little dust in the air before entering the airlock to the control rover.

Inside the pressurized rover, he left his faceplate down, hoping to obscure the new freckles. "Yes, Miss Sonia?"

"Just call me Sonia, please?" She was concentrating on the instrument panel in front of her. "Have a seat. We need to talk."

Apollo sat in a chair behind her, his helmet on, faceplate still down.

She looked over her shoulder, and exhaled. She twisted her swivel chair to face him. "Apollo, look at my face… my hands."

He was trying to avoid eye contract. He noticed that her hands were slightly wrinkled, light flesh colored, with small brown freckles, freckles he had not seen before. He looked up at her pixie-like face. More freckles.

"Whatever you have, I've got it now!" She patted his knee to comfort him. "Take off your helmet. Let me look at you."

Acid churned in his stomach. The birthday present. He gave her what he had. Slowly, he removed the helmet. Did he also give it to Uncle Roberto?

Sonia studied his face, carefully looking in his eyes, at his lips. "We need a medic evaluation on you."

Apollo waved her away. "No, I'll be fine in a day or two. It is not bad."

"Don't play this game with me," Sonia's tone hardened, "I have the same thing you do. I don't know how bad it is. I've already done my own medic review. This is an unknown."

"Unknown?" Apollo opened his pressure suit to comply with her commands.

"I have an unknown virus. It came from those fish you found, because I tested the samples for the same thing. There is no data bank record of a virus like it anywhere."

Apollo's hands began to quiver. "What does this mean?"

"It means that we may be in trouble." She pointed him to the medic evaluation unit to record his vital signs, including pulse, pressure, temperature, respiratory, neuron activity, blood analysis, urine sample, air sample, and perspiration analysis. While he dressed himself, the computer compared the new information to his previous readings, and to the computerized medical library.

"Same virus," Sonia said, "Same discomforts. You've been sweating too much, you're a little warmer than you should be. You've been dizzy, distracted, and nauseous. You've been hearing voices of people who are not there."

Apollo sheepishly nodded agreement.

She looked at the statistics on the monitor, "Just like me. You also have elevated secretions from the pituitary and unusual neural activity in the hypothalamus."

"What does that mean?"

"I wish I knew," Sonia returned her attention to the teenager. "I've been having wild dreams these past two nights... about you... about a lot of Filipinos."

"Me too," Apollo responded, "I had crazy dreams last night. You were in them."

They both went quiet for several seconds.

"Apollo, you and your uncles are the only Filipinos I know. I had dreams about your Uncle Sonny and his house... the one where we went for the Christmas party. In my dreams your Uncle Sonny was talking to his wife, Jenny. She is the prettiest oriental woman I've ever seen, but she does not look Filipino."

"Tita Jenny originally came from Laos." Apollo was curious, "What did you dream about them?"

"I dreamed they were visiting you at a hospital on the Moon. Sonny, separated from the rest of you, was at a communications monitor, talking with Jenny. She was with you, isolated from the outside, and you were asleep. They were worried. They were talking about the whole barrio being sick."

"The barrio?" Apollo breathed deeply. "I've never been to the Moon. This is the first time I've ever been away from Luzon."

There were several more seconds of silence. Sonia said, "Must have been just a wild dream." She reached for a cup of coffee still on the instrument panel ledge. "Tell me about your dreams."

"They were terrible. You and I were lost in the Martian desert, trying to get away from trouble. Uncle Roberto and boss Fisk and all of my Filipino uncles were dead. Boss Dave and a friend of his killed them. It was horrible. I was so glad when I woke up and realized it was only a bad dream."

Sonia's eyes tightened as she listened to his description. She continued to stare after he finished. "Is that all?"

"That's all I remember this morning. All the other dreams sort of disappeared from my mind the past few days."

She glanced at the bank of monitor screens showing the inside of the cavern. The Filipino crew was busily boring into the gold vein. Fisk was with Dave and Ghant Travis, a Bureau of Mines inspector who had arrived during the night.

She spoke to the communications console. "Show me the transmittals sent by Dave Crane to register this mining claim."

The monitor displayed the claim statement. She read it carefully. Nothing seemed out of the ordinary.

"Computer, double check the directory for the party receiving the claim."

The monitor displayed a listing for 'Redrock Mining Consortium, Crater City Headquarters."

"Redrock?" She muttered to herself. "Not Bureau of Mines?" Then she remembered. Ghant Travis was a vice president of Redrock. She had seen his name on a Redrock directory once a year earlier. She remembered it because of the unusual name. Ghant would not have been with the Bureau of Mines. Fisk had questioned it, but Ghant had legitimate credentials. She looked again at Apollo, and then turned and addressed the computer once more, "Give me a level six security check on Dave Crane and Ghant Travis. Look for intercepts with Redrock Mining."

"Ghant Travis is a continuing corporate vice-president of Redrock Mining. Dave Crane is listed as a consulting research director for Redrock Mining until last year, simultaneous with full time employment with the Bureau of Mines."

"Is there any record that Ghant Travis works for the Bureau of Mines?"

"Ghant Travis worked for the Bureau of Mines as claims director five years ago."

She had the computer connect to the traffic control satellite, and ask for the identity of any vehicles owned by Redrock Mining in the vicinity. One was parked next to her control rover. Four were in Burroughs Valley, twenty miles south of the entrance to the canyon. The last was on highway 'M-24' approaching from the west. Highway M-24 was the main Martian east-west highway, circling the globe near the equator

Sonia once more turned to Apollo, "You said you dreamed they were all dead?"

Apollo nodded, staring down. He was ashamed to be telling such a terrible dream.

"I hope our dreams were possibilities, not predictions. Your warning about Dave is right. He did not file our claim with the Bureau of Mines. They are about to jump this claim. We have to do something, fast."

"What can I do?"

"Quietly, connect a life support trailer to this rover. Bring Tessie in here. We may need her help."

"Are you going to warn them?" He pointed up.

"I'll try. Fisk is in the tent with Dave and Ghant right now. If I say they might be a threat, I may trigger your dream into reality. First, I'm going to undo what Dave did to our claim."

Walking around outside, Apollo realized that the nearest life support trailer was the observation trailer. Water, air, food, and supplies were stacked in storage tanks below the crew deck. Using a motorized tug, he pulled the trailer to the back of the control rover, and coupled it. His muscles ached, his head hurt, but he could not allow this virus to slow him. He forced himself to move quickly. Acid was eating his stomach worse than he could ever remember. He was now convinced that his dream of Uncle Roberto being killed was a premonition, a spiritual warning of what was about to actually happen. He found Tessie in standby mode, standing lightly dressed with a translucent nightgown in her closet in the crew's quarters. Apparently, the men had taken advantage of her entertainment mode the night before. Apollo ordered her to resume her domestic worker mode. She dressed herself in loose fitting coveralls, and then they proceeded to the observation trailer. Apollo was back in the control rover within twenty minutes.

Removing his helmet, he placed it on a wall shelf. He seated himself in a swivel chair next to Sonia. Sonia did not look at him, as she was too focused on watching the monitors. Apollo looked to the screens. Everything seemed normal. "Were you able to tell Mister Fisk?"

"I tried. I told him to go to the special channel. He asked me to hold for a half-hour. He said Ghant had a solution to the visa problem."

Apollo could see on the screens that the other Filipinos were putting down their tools, heading for the pressurized tent.

"I sent our claim to the real Bureau of Mines. Apparently, Redrock has already filed a claim through Dave."

"Buwsit (terrible)! Can you stop it?"

"I packaged our entire journal, from the initial research logs to the present, and transmitted it several places. If I don't countermand those instructions, those reports will go to the police, to the media, to my family."

"What about our virus?"

"If nothing happens, I can stop dissemination. If your dream is true, it won't make any difference." Sonia took a breath, "In your dream, did you know how they were killed?"

"Uncle Roberto was choking, gasping for breath!"

They both looked to the cave monitor image. Uncle Roberto and the Filipinos had entered the tent. Dave rose from a seat at the table. He exited the tent through the airlock to the depressurized cavern beyond.

Sonia pushed the emergency alarm. A flashing light on everyone's sleeve made clear that the alarm was working. All of them simultaneously reached to push the silence button. Fisk's voice came from the console. "What's so damned important that you have to push the panic button?"

"Channel, your sisters."

"Sisters?" He paused. He switched to channel three. Fisk had no sisters. Fisk and Sonia had agreed to this coded approach years earlier for just this type of situation.

"Okay, Sonia. What's wrong?"

"Ghant Travis is not with the Bureau of Mines, he's still executive vice-president of Redrock Mining. Dave worked for Redrock before he worked for the Bureau."

"What?"

"Our mining claim was filed with Redrock, not the Bureau. This is a claim jump."

66

"Are you positive?"

"Put your helmet on. I have reason to believe that Ghant intends to gas all of you."

Sonia and Apollo watched the multiple monitor screens. Fisk looked around the tent. Ghant had not opened his helmet. Fisk, Japa, and the Filipino crew had all removed their own headgear. Dave Crane was outside on the access platform. Ghant pulled a thermos from his case. Placing it on the table, he started to unscrew the lid. Fisk reached over, and with the back of his hand, knocked it out of Ghant's grip. The unscrewed cap came loose when the thermos bounced hard against the galley cabinet. The hissing of gas was unmistakable.

Fisk reached for his helmet just as Ghant slammed shut his own faceplate. Fisk started coughing. Moments later Roberto, Emilio, Jun, Celso, Doug and Japa began gagging. All reached for their helmets. It was too late. Fisk actually got his on. He tried to stand, but collapsed back down on the table. Roberto's coughing fit was accented with a spray of blood from his mouth. He fell out of his chair to the floor. In fifteen seconds all in the tent were motionless except Ghant. He was sealed in his ochre colored Bureau of Mines uniform pressure suit.

Sonia and Apollo, standing, silently watched in horror. She directed the computer to check the life signs from everyone's pressure suits. All in the cave were dead, except for Dave and Ghant. Ghant, exiting the tent, was obviously talking on another channel to Dave. The camera view from the access platform showed Dave boarding the elevator, waiting for Ghant.

"We have to leave," Sonia squealed, "Apollo, there's a laser drill in the corner. Go out … disable the other vehicles. Now. I'll get this ready to move."

Apollo donned his helmet, secured his faceplate, grabbed the laser drill and headed for the airlock. Rushing around the compound, he burned a slice through the wheel and the engine manifold on the four rovers. As he finished the last cut, he looked up the cliff at the elevator cage, already halfway down. As soon as he was inside the airlock, the control rover began moving.

CHAPTER EIGHT

EL DORADO BADLANDS

Sytris Major Lava Beds

Earth Date   July 6, 2216
Mars Date   C-Mmon 24, 1174

Apollo was shaking all over. Horrified at what just happened to Uncle Roberto and the rest of the mining crew, he was confused about what to do next. He was terrified for the uncertainty ahead. Gripping the armrests of his chair, he watched in silence as Sonia acted out with what appeared to be a determined plan. Was this another dream about everyone being killed? No, this time it was real. Sonia directed the computer to route the rover via the only exit from the dead end Princess Dejah Canyon; a tributary of the Burroughs rift valley. During the ten-mile run from the mining site to the canyon entrance, she diligently worked with the onboard computers to determine what they were facing, to plot an escape route.

A computer-generated map displayed roads, settlements, and remote man-made facilities of the region. Sonia had the computer use the navigation tracking satellite link to highlight all locally moving vehicles, and then to identify any local vehicles registered to Redrock Mining, the computer yellow color-coded six rovers. Ghant's vehicle was parked in the canyon, disabled. Another Redrock truck was on the main east-west highway M-24 a hundred and fifty miles away going the opposite direction. Four Redrock vehicles were in Burroughs Valley, twenty-five miles beyond the canyon entrance, but moving closer. Sonia asked the computer to highlight Redrock properties and parked vehicles in the Syrtis Major region. Five mining sites and one ore processing plant were concentrated in another canyon two hundred miles to the north. Over a hundred parked ore trucks and a half dozen rovers were at those sites. When she asked for a highlight of government vehicles and facilities, the computer highlighted a dozen vehicles, mostly on the main road, that were widely dispersed over the three-hundred mile stretch of the map.

"There!" she pointed to the map, speaking to herself as much as to Apollo. "We'll head north… use the John Carter trail out of the canyon. That will put us in the El Dorado Badlands above the canyon."

"Badlands?" Apollo questioned.

"Early prospectors searched for uranium in those hard, jumbled, black basalt hills. It is a hard land. There is erosion from ancient water flows, but no shallow permafrost underground to provide moisture to nurture vegetation. Very little uranium. No crystals. Not much precious metals. Just black basalts."

"Why is that a good way to go?" He was still trembling. He studied the map. The John Carter trail led up out of the valley, passing within a few miles of the top of the Canyon they were leaving.

"It gets us out of the Valley. If Redrock is determined to come after us, there are a lot of crevices and caves to hide our vehicle in. Also, it's only ten miles to the main highway from where the trail clears the Valley."

"I don't understand why this is happening? It was only a dream."

With the vehicle computer driving a programmed course, Sonia directed the communications console to report any non-ciphered transmissions concerning events in the Canyon. "I don't understand it, either," Sonia watched the communications panel display, "You had a dream last night that foresaw precisely what happened a few minutes ago. I had a dream visualizing your relatives... the people I met last Christmas... with you at a hospital on the Moon. I had no reason to think about those people or the Moon. Apparently, besides making both of us sick, this virus generates strange dreams."

"But, Uncle Roberto is dead," Apollo started shaking harder, "Really dead!"

She looked over her shoulder at him. "I know. So is Fisk. Fisk has been my best friend, my prospecting partner... for ten years (eighteen Earth years). He is dead. So is Japa. Japa has been fixing our vehicles since..." she stopped, paused, then said, "Can you talk to computers?"

"If they accept my voiceprint. I learned in school."

"While I get us out of here, get the medic computer to recommend remedies for our symptoms."

Apollo coughed before saying, "I thought this virus was unknown?"

"This virus is, but the ailments are flu-like. We have to find a way to control our discomforts until we get to safety."

Apollo stood, turned, and walked to the medic computer.

"Plug Tessie into the unit, too. Have the computer program her to the nursing mode."

"Tessie can do that?"

"She's a machine built to look like a sexy woman. She is hard wired to act like any woman we have a program for. We leased her to keep the Filipino miners entertained. Now, we need a nurse."

The control rover crested the rim of the valley half an hour later, heading north into the El Dorado Badlands. During that time robot Tessie quietly administered antibiotics and pain reliever to the two travelers, and then returned to her standby station. Sonia updated the claim report for the gold find to include the videos of the killings in the cavern. She continued monitoring the display screens while pondering where to transmit the report. Two Redrock rovers had turned from Burroughs Valley toward the mining site at Dejah Canyon, but the other two were now following Sonia's course out of the valley. There was considerable radio traffic to and from those rovers.

A light on the communications panel indicated an official bulletin about Princess Dejah Canyon. "Audio the report."

"Police alert, Syrtis Major Region. Redrock Mining Consortium officials report finding the murdered bodies of two independent prospectors on contract with Redrock. The dead are identified as Fisk Banzer and Japa Reese. Report claims there is evidence that their female partner, Sonia Androff killed the men, with the assistance of an unknown conspirator. Androff is missing. Report also notes that Androff filed a falsified counter claim to a Redrock Mining operation in Princess Dejah Canyon. Martian Global Police detective Ken Sylvester has been assigned to investigate. Any available data on the principals is to be forwarded to his office."

Apollo and Sonia both stared at the written screen display of the report, which listed the number to reach Detective Sylvester.

"Computer," Sonia coughed before continuing, "Cross check any files on Martian Global Police Detective Ken Sylvester with Redrock Mining Consortium."

"Detective Ken Sylvester is a first cousin to Redrock Mining Operations Vice President Ghant Travis. There are no other known connections."

Sonia stared at the display, and then studied the area map. The two Redrock rovers were definitely following her out of the valley. "Computer. Deactivate vehicle traffic transponder."

"That would be a violation of Martian statute MD-1678.9A2. Transponders can not be tampered with."

She rubbed her left hand across her face. "Pull to the side of the trail, and stop the vehicle."

The rover and trailer moved off the gravel trail to the jumbled rocks of the terrain then came to a full stop.

"This is a campsite. Shut down all operations for a mechanical overhaul."

The sounds of the motors, generators, and computers went quiet. Sonia stood, opened a cabinet beyond the computers, and pulled out a case. She grabbed her helmet and checked her backpack settings.

Looking at Apollo on her way to the airlock, she said, "Wait here. I'll be right back." She then exited through the airlock.

Three minutes later she was once again inside. She told the computer to begin moving the rover again. As expected, the computer warned her that there was a malfunction in the transponder traffic signal, asking if it should diagnose and repair. She responded that the damage was an exterior electrical short. She would assume responsibility for transponder down time.

Apollo, not used to computer operated survival vehicles, was amazed at what these rovers could do, and how someone who understood them could outsmart their systems.

"Display close up map on a scale that shows ten miles from rim of valley to Highway M-24. Highlight any abandoned mines suitable for storage of control rover and observation trailer."

Four sites appeared in beige. The nearest was to the right, off-road a mile, on the far side of a series of rock outcrops.

"Run on silent mode. Follow this course." She moved her finger over the monitor map display to plot a course, while instructing the drive computer what care to take for dealing with uncharted obstructions. She then turned to her "conspirator." She was perspiring, her fingers twitching a little. She coughed some more. "We'll be in a cave in a few minutes. Did you understand the police bulletin?"

Apollo shifted in his chair as the rover rocked going over rough terrain. "I come from an untechnical people, but I understand scams. The report on the crime scene listed Fisk and Japa as Redrock employees, and it did not mention Uncle Roberto, or the rest of our Filipino crew. They are hiding the Filipino bodies."

She forced a smile. "You're smarter than we give you credit for!" She reached over and patted his knee. "They had their own detective in the police ready to do the official investigation as soon as they called it in. They do not want an honest investigation of the murders, because the evidence will expose what really happened. That means they need to find us, kill us, and file an 'official' investigation report with no living witnesses."

The rover circled around a jumbled area of jutting blocks, then crossed the John Carter Trail on its circuitous route to the abandoned cave.

"Is that why you disabled the traffic transponder?"

She nodded agreement. "They will be trying to follow us with the transponder signals. They have not had time to get access to scanning satellite cameras to follow us visually, and will not want legitimate police to watch what they do too closely. If we get undercover, they may go right by us."

Still trembling, Apollo did not respond. It seemed logical. He wanted to scream, wanted to run, wanted to cry. He controlled his emotions. He coughed. He watched Sonia address the computer for an inventory of food, air, water, weapons, mining tools, and survival gear in the rover and the observation trailer. There was enough life support for the two of them for sixty days. There were no weapons. Three survival tents, complete with collapsable airlocks and life support cabinets, were on hand with their manual pull carts. By the time she finished the inventory; the rover had reached the entrance to the abandoned mine. Following a computer generated series of multi-spectral scans through the cave mouth. Sonia was able to determine the limitations they were facing. She instructed the computer to back the rover into the cave, trailer first; far enough to have the front of the rover recessed at least thirty feet.

"Apollo," she pointed to a cabinet at the back of the rover. "In there... get a shielded mini-camera and a communications antenna. Take two rolls of signal cable, and set them at the mouth of the cave. There's a box of ceramic 'boulder' covers that should fool any scan equipment. Put the covers over the camera and antenna."

"Why do you need wires?" He stood. At least there was something to do.

"Signal transmissions can be picked up by Redrock. The wire is shielded."

He collected the materials he need. Watching Sonia while putting on his helmet, he wondered what she was looking for in the tool cabinet. She pulled out a laser rock blaster and a collapsible flexible shield.

"Apollo, no channel communications." She pointed to the comm controls on the sleeve of her pressure suit. "Come back as soon as you're finished."

With the mini camera securely mounted on a flat rock, Apollo connected the signal cable from one of the rolls, and then placed a ceramic cover over it. He set a few real stones next to the cover to help obscure it. He did the same for the antenna. Unrolling the two spools of cable back into the cave toward the rover, he nearly tripped over Sonia. She had unfolded the flexible protective shield ten-feet in front of the rover, telescoping the tarp to a large enough expanse to obscure the entire vehicle from any scanner looking in. Using the rock blaster to knock dust and rocks loose overhead, she coated the surface of the shield with debris indistinguishable from the surrounding soil. Once the dust had settled, the shield would look like an uninteresting cave wall.

Back in the control rover, Sonia set the antenna for passive pick up of the traffic control satellite signal. She would use the rover computer to highlight any local Redrock Mining vehicles. The Redrock rovers that had been following them were topping the ridge where the John Carter Trail left Burroughs Valley. The data indicated that rovers were operating spectral scanners as they sped on, faster than it should for a careful surveillance. It slowed briefly where Sonia had stopped to disable the transponder, then moving on quickly. It rolled past the point where Sonia had pulled off the trail without slowing. Continuing along the trail, it passed the point where Sonia had brought the rover back across the trail. The Redrock vehicles increased speed, following the trail to an intersection with Highway M-24.

"They lost us," Sonia smiled, "They think we headed for the main highway. They should have called in the satellite cameras, but they outsmarted themselves."

"Does that mean we're safe?"

She exhaled, "For the moment. When they don't find us the easy way, they will go to Plan B."

"Plan B?"

"A cliché. That detective, Ghant Travis' cousin… he will issue a police bulletin confirming that I am a deranged maniac… sometimes coherent, but paranoid and delusional… there will be orders to stop us at all costs. If they catch us alive, we are to be turned over to them. If we have to be killed, that is regrettable, but we are dangerous."

"You seem so clear about all this."

"My uncle was a pathologist in Wells. I'm used to police procedures."

"Your uncle? Is he still around?"

She shook her head. "Killed in the war. I really miss him."

Apollo understood about the war. It was the only war on Mars, a few years before he was born. When Mars seceded from the United Nations, they fought their rebellion against a U.N. Space Force attempt to re-establish authority. After losing half of their invasion fleet, the United Nations gave up, and granted the planet its independence. This was history he had learned in school. He returned his attention to matters at hand. "Apparently we evaded their chase," he pointed to the surveillance map. The Redrock vehicles were approaching the main highway. "What do we do now?"

"Wait. Watch. Three... four days..." She coughed, and then stood up. Pausing momentarily, she swayed on her feet, and then sat down again. "Dizzy. I'll do that slowly."

She rose carefully to approach the galley cabinet. "Chicken soup. Traxel sandwich." She looked back at Apollo. "You need something to eat, too. What can you hold down?"

He sat quietly settled down. The adrenaline that had forced him into action since the killings began to subside. A wave of exhaustion swept over him. "I can't eat. I think I need to lie down."

Waiting for her food, she said, "It's too bad we didn't bring any of the sleeping trailers. Neither of us has a change of clothes, any personal effects. We have rover bunks. You want to sleep here? Or in the observation trailer?"

"It doesn't make a difference."

"Computer," Sonia pulled her food from the galley hatch. "Open two bunks, opposite the control desk." Two sections of wall, thirty by eighty inches, slowly descended over a counter. Each had thin, spongy mats covered with blankets. Not as comfortable as the beds of the crew trailers, but they were adequate for emergency situations. All Martian rovers are designed to support a crew of four for fifteen days in the open desert in the event of mechanical breakdown.

"Apollo, go ahead, get some sleep." Sonia said as she approached the galley for something to drink. "I'll watch the monitors awhile. This rover has a shower with a toilet facility behind the driver's station."

Apollo looked to the bathroom cubicle. He scanned the surroundings. He had nothing to change into. Everything was back in the Canyon. He looked at Sonia, and began to blush at the thought that he could not change from his outfit, that he had no privacy from her.

Returning to her seat at the computer, she smiled at his reddened face, "Are you embarrassed?"

He looked down to his feet.

"Oh, to be young and awkward again. We were naked together a few days ago, and you still blush at the thought. What is there to be bashful about that I did not see the other day?" She seated herself. "Go ahead. I won't look."

Apollo suddenly felt stupid. He slowly started removing his pressure suit. The aches in his limb muscles were painful again. He felt dizzy and sick to his stomach. He had to take a shower, and then get some rest. He quietly removed his thermal wear, dropping it in a pile with his pressure suit. Finally, he removed his underwear, and walked toward the shower stall.

CHAPTER NINE

EVENING STAR

Sytris Major Lava Beds

Earth Date	July 8, 2216
Mars Date	C-Mmon 26, 1174

Apollo was dreaming. The image he saw was of a little blond girl in a wheelchair at a Martian hospital observation deck. Beyond the pressurized dome was a magnificent panorama of the grand dry volcanic Mount Olympus rising eight miles into a sunset colored sky. A few wisps of ice crystal clouds reflected a brilliant white at the peak, accenting the dark basaltic rocks of the slopes. With a cast on her left leg; the child laughed with another small girl patient, whose right arm was in a sling. A throbbing headache once again disrupted Apollo's dream. The throbbing at his temples alerted him to again be aware of nausea in his stomach, harsh dryness of his throat, and burning of his eyes. He opened his eyes, glancing up at the lovely, attentive face of robot Tessie.

"Mister Apollo," her designed sensuality had been muted for the nursing mode. Apollo was too shy and too sick to be interested in her primary program. "We lack medicines necessary to control the effects of this virus." She gently washed his face and chest with a damp cloth. "Do you feel up to taking nourishment?"

The thought of food was revolting. "No food. Only water."

She handed him a plastic tube to suck whatever water he felt he could handle. He swallowed one mouthful. That triggered a coughing fit, followed by an acidic bile stirring up his esophagus.

Sonia abruptly appeared beside Tessie. She told the robot to withdraw to a standby position. Sonia looked down at Apollo. "Terrible. I hope you don't feel as bad as you look."

He noticed that her rash had intensified to a mass of small, dark freckles over her entire face and neck. Her eyes were bloodshot.

He could feel the heat in his dry eyes and perspiration building on his forehead. He tried to speak, but began coughing again.

"You've been asleep for thirty-six hours. I hope this breaks soon. I'm terrified for you."

He tried to sit up. His arms and back signaled, with aching pains, that he should not attempt it. He inhaled deeply, and then sat up anyway. Covers for all windows were closed to prevent light escape. "Anything new?"

Sonia helped him to a sitting position. "The sun is going down. There are a half dozen Redrock vehicles on the main highway… A few more at the canyon… Butterflies flew by twice, but did not detect us."

Apollo reached for the damp cloth Tessie had left on a nightstand. He wiped his forehead. "Butterflies?"

"I keep forgetting you are not of Mars. A butterfly is an insect sized flying surveillance drone. It looks for man-made heat sources and metals."

"I've seen them. Uncle Sonny uses those."

"Sonny?"

"He hosted the Christmas party. You dreamed about him and his pretty wife."

"Yes," she smiled, "I remember. Did you have more dreams?"

He reached for the plastic water tube. He swallowed a small amount of the water. This time it went down without trouble. "The only dream I remember was a few minutes ago. It was about a little Martian girl."

"Little girl?"

He dipped the damp cloth in the water dish on the stand, rang it out, and then pressed it to his eyes. "A strange dream. Two small children... six year old girls... Earth years... I guess they would be three on the Martian calendar. They were wearing aqua and silver pressure suits. Climbing a cliff in the Mount Olympus caldera, they ignored warnings from their father. The girl highest up the cliff stepped on a rock ledge that gave way, dropping one girl on top of the other, starting a small landslide. The girls tumbled ten-feet to the base. There they were hit with a shower of falling rocks. One of the girls got a broken arm, the other a broken leg. They were flown to Crater City Hospital for treatment. I woke when they were at the observation deck of the hospital. It was late afternoon. The sun was reflecting off ice crystals at the peak of the mountain in the distance."

Sonia's interest peaked. "Tell me about the girls?"

"The girl with the broken leg had medium cut blond hair, blue eyes. The other girl had curly red hair and a pug nose."

"My God," Sonia found a chair and sat down. "You've just described an incident from my own childhood. I broke my leg at Mount Olympus when I was little... climbing the cliffs of the caldera with my cousin, Ratina!"

Apollo removed the cloth from his eyes. He stared at her. "I do not know about your life before this year. How is that possible?" He tried to stand. It hurt to move. He sat again.

She patted his arm. "I have no explanation. I would not believe stories like this if someone else told me about it. I always thought these things were made up by people who wanted too hard to believe in something."

"Did you have more dreams, yourself?"

Sonia sighed before answering; "You were in it again. Now, I can't remember the details. I usually can't remember dreams an hour after I wake up."

He coughed again, and then reached for the water tube. Once more, the drink forced another cough. "Sonia, I'm scared. What are we going to do?"

She stared at him. Her eyes began to moisten. She shifted from the chair to sit on the bunk beside him, putting an arm around his shoulders. With her free hand, she wiped her eyes. "I'm frightened, too. For years I could always count on Fisk when I needed help. Fisk is dead. The people who did it want to kill me... to have a clear title to our gold strike. Right now," she squeezed his shoulders; "You and I have only each other. We're both sick with some unknown ailment, and can't get to a doctor. Redrock agents will kill us as soon as we try to leave here. If we don't try, this sickness may kill us anyway."

She hugged him the way his mother used to hug him. She was not his mother. She had given him a birthday present no other woman had ever given him... an experience she had not shared with the older, experienced Filipino men. She was just as frightened as he was. She had saved their lives so far, but was out of answers. Just like the little girl with a broken leg, she needed someone special to help her survive then, and now. He reached his arm around her waist, sniffled, and just quietly held her.

He started thinking about the problem. "Do you think those messages you sent out will work?"

She coughed, and then released him. "The police have raided all the friends I sent messages to, seized their computers. Detective Ken Sylvester has all of those messages."

Apollo felt coldness sinking in his stomach. What he thought was the solution was no longer an option. "What about sending it to someone like that Terra Newton, the journalist?"

"I thought about that. Terra's husband is the person who suggested the Filipino mining crew in the first place. However, the Redrock people apparently have phone tracers for my messages, because they located all the messages I sent out so far. I have that from their internal police bulletins. If I tried to contact Terra Newton, the police would convince her that it is a false claim, and I am deranged. She doesn't know me. Her husband barely met me. Dave knows everyone I would know. I can't contact anyone by signal. It has to be in person. As soon as we start to move, they have us."

Apollo released her. He looked at the console across from the bunk, at a monitor image from the cave entrance. The sun had just dropped below the horizon, and it was rapidly getting dark. Near the horizon was a familiar twin star, the brilliant blue-white earth with the dimmer, yellowish moon. He coughed, and then said, "They don't know who I know."

She had reached for a glass of fruit juice to quench a sudden thirst. She looked over at the screen image of the evening star, and then turned back to him. "Your detective uncle. Do you know how to reach him?"

"Can we send a signal directly to Earth?"

She sipped her drink, taking a moment to think. "I think... a ciphered message would be delivered without question. Redrock might detect the transmission, but would be unable to know where it went... unless they bring in the police of Earth." She stood and approached the galley cabinet. After she got herself a muffin, she returned to her chair. "Can you think of a series of names only your uncle could determine?"

"Code names to break a cipher. They work like a combination lock. Send a sequence of questions, where each answer opens one cipher lock. Four or five ciphers would unscramble a coded message. Ask his mother's maiden name, his hometown... things like that."

Apollo forced himself to stand. It was painful, but once he was on his feet, the pain subsided. Sonia stood, turned to the control console to arrange a collection of the evidence in the support of their story. "Apollo, before we cipher the message, I want you to record a personal message to your uncle. Tell him what happened, and why. I'll give him the details about where to find us."

"But, he's on Earth. How can he get here in time?"

"You said he knows Terra Newton personally, and as a friend. He probably has other friends on Mars he can contact discreetly. We have enough food, water, and air to last sixty days."

"And, if Redrock detects our transmission?"

"I see what you mean. Maybe, I'll take a remote transmitter out in the desert. Nah. We'll figure something. Let's just put a message together."

Apollo tried to think of questions only Uncle Sonny would understand. His mother's birthday? She was Uncle Sonny's sister. Historical questions about the Philippines? That wouldn't work. Anyone with a computer could find solutions. Filipino words? A computer translator would solve that. Nicknames of family members. That would work. He looked again at the video image of the darkening western horizon, of the double evening star. Home. It was so visible, yet so far away. Would he ever see it again? "My little sister, Madeline… her nickname is 'Baby'. Uncle Jun's son is Carlos. His nickname is 'Coconut'. Uncle Sonny calls his wife 'Christmas Rose'. I think I remember all of their birthdays."

"That will do. Type their full names and birthdays into the computer. That will be the code keys."

Apollo slowly stepped over to the computer and took a seat. He was in extreme discomfort. The dizziness made it very difficult to operate the keyboard. He forced himself to focus on the task he had to do.

Chapter Ten

Coma

Sytris Major Lava Beds

Earth Date	July 11, 2216
Mars Date	C-Mmon 29, 1174

H e drifted in and out of fitful sleep. Muscle aches made him too uncomfortable to fall fully asleep. His throat was dry and swollen, all his glands throbbed, and his head hurt, no matter how much pain relief Tessie gave him. When he started to drift into sleep the murmur of voices got louder, some words clear, but for the most part, indistinct. When he closed his eyes he saw people. People talking, people he did not know, saying things he did not comprehend. He continued sweating profusely, although he felt alternately hot then chilled. Tessie maintained her relentless surveillance of his condition, looking for medicines not available to treat symptoms that did not all seem to belong to one illness. When he would not eat, she fed him intravenous nourishment. When he messed himself during a rushed attempt to the toilet because of diarrhea, Tessie quietly undressed him, cleaned him, put him in another bunk, then cleaned his clothes and bedding. She redressed him when the clothes were dry. He remained too incoherent to be aware of what would have been the ultimate embarrassment in front of Sonia.

Sonia was not much better. The muscle aches, headaches, and loss of appetite had taken control of her. She kept her wits, forcing herself to eat, to move about, and to sleep regular night hours. Her survival, and that of her young friend, depended on her being ready to adapt to any new threat.

"How long have I been laying here?" Apollo forced himself to sit up.

She rose from her chair at the instrument console. Approaching him, she said, "It's been three days since you prepared the message for your uncle. You were up for a few hours yesterday. Don't you remember?"

He thought, then said, "Oh yes. I thought I dreamed about getting up, going to the trailer. That makes it five days since the killings. How do I look on the med computer?"

Sonia took the damp cloth from Tessie. She continued wiping perspiration beading on Apollo's bare chest. "Temperature of one-hundred and two, erratic pulse and breathing. The rash remains unchanged on either of us."

"What about neural readings?" He grunted as he forced himself to stand.

"Still elevated in the hypothalamus," She helped him up. "Do you feel you can handle food?" She studied his eyes. "Or do we continue intravenous?"

"Maybe some soup," He headed for a chair. Standing was too unsteady. "Anymore butterflies?"

"Tessie, get Apollo soup and plain bread." Sonia pointed to the console displays. "Nothing. I think they gave up on us. Redrock has moved a lot of equipment into the canyon. They are moving fast to take our gold." She stared at the traffic locator map, shaking her head. "Those dirty..."

"Did you transmit to Uncle Sonny?"

Turning back to him, Sonia said, "I didn't want to risk exposing myself with all that Redrock traffic." She sat down beside him. "I'll have to try something soon. We need to get you to a hospital."

Tessie quietly returned, carrying a bowl of soup with a plate of bread. She handed it to Apollo.

"I don't remember..." the bread looked unappealing. "Do we have rice?"

Sonia laughed, "Roberto insisted on rice when we hired him. Tessie, get Apollo a cup of rice. I'll eat the bread."

Apollo sat at the bank of monitors. The commercial channel again showed the media journalist his Uncle Sonny knew. The sound was off. What was her name? Yes, Terra Newton. Tessie brought his cup of rice. He had not yet attempted to eat anything. "Maybe she is our solution. I dreamed about her last night."

"She?" Sonia glanced first at Tessie, then around at the monitor screen. "Oh, yes, Terra Newton. Maybe your uncle can contact her. If we tried, I'm certain her staff would give our call to Detective Sylvester."

"Did we suggest that in the message for Sonny?"

She shook her head. "He'll know who to contact based on the story."

"Did you know her?"

"We're the same age. We were in the war at the same time. She was an officer at Mount Olympus. I was an enlisted soldier in Lowell Canyon. I never saw any action." Sonia studied the silent, talking image on the screen, "She was a public relations spokesperson. I remember her appeal to fight made me want to volunteer a second time."

"So, she was just a media personality..."

Sonia paused, and then said, "Apollo, you should try to eat." She picked up a piece of bread. "Terra was a lot more. She commanded an all-female artillery post. They were involved with shooting down U.N. troopship Landers. When one of those troopship Landers was forced down at her family's farm, she led the assault to rescue her own family. She was seriously wounded, and her best friend was killed."

"Is that where Uncle Sonny met her?" Apollo sipped the soup. He paused, waiting to see how his stomach would react. He swallowed another spoonful.

"I don't think so. She hired your uncle several years later to investigate the murder of a Martian customs inspector in Manila. By the way, what was your dream?"

Apollo sipped a glass of water. "I dreamed she was on the Moon... Earth's Moon... doing a show about a first ever manned landing on Venus. Only, everything was going wrong. A spacecraft landing on Venus had a mechanical failure... something clogged the coolant circulation system. There was an explosion. Terra Newton was reporting that the crew of six were all killed."

"Did you know when this was supposed to happen? According to recent newscasts, she is supposed to leave soon for Earth's Moon to cover a Venus Resource Recovery Treaty."

"I don't remember that. It just seemed that one of the crew was a personal friend of hers."

"I'll add that to this transmission. Just in case it means something."

Apollo took a bite of the rice. It tasted good. "Maybe we can hear what Miss Terra is talking about?" He took another bite.

Sonia told the computer to increase the commercial broadcast volume.

"... So I will be leaving for Tyco Lunar Station next week to cover the signing of the Venus Resource Recovery Treaty. As you are all aware, the resources of Venus have never been tapped because the climate on the planet makes access prohibitive. The high-pressure atmosphere, the nine-hundred degree temperatures, and sulfuric acid clouds made exploration of the surface difficult for ordinary unmanned spacecraft. However, the recently developed anti-gravity drive makes it possible to lift resources off the surface without exposed moving parts, without exposed engines. Since the United Nations signed the treaty recognizing Martian rights to control use of the anti-gravity drive, this treaty is necessary for any U.N. recognized business to..."

Apollo waved for Sonia to turn the volume down again. He ate some more soup. "Why does Mars control the anti-gravity drive?" He finished his cup of rice.

"That was another special event Terra Newton had a lot to do with. That customs murder your uncle was involved with... it related to an attempt by the U.N. Space Force to hijack the Martian-built prototype anti-gravity vehicle. Terra exposed the story, but they kidnapped her. The Martian government took the affair to the brink of war. The United Nations agreed to Martian control of the technology to defuse that crisis."

Apollo was feeling a little better with food in his stomach. He smiled. "She sounds exciting," He stood to walk to the toilet. Halfway to the bathroom a wave of nausea swept over him. He rushed to the bathroom, but did not make it. He began vomiting all over the bathroom door.

He tried to step in, to vomit again, but collapsed, hitting his head on the doorframe.

"Apollo?" Sonia dropped her bread as she sprung to her feet. She rushed to her falling companion.

He was unconscious.

"Tessie, bring the medic probes!"

Sonia's worst fears were realized. The food in Apollo's stomach had triggered a neural shock wave. The elevated brainwave activity in his hypothalamus stopped. Most mental functions had gone flatline. Only the involuntary neural activity seemed to be functioning, and those signals were erratic. His temperature, pulse, and respiration were fluctuating and abnormal. She carried him back to a bunk. He was motionless.

For a half-hour she stared at Apollo. He did not move, did not twitch, and did not blink. His pulse slowed and his breathing became minimal. His temperature dropped to one-hundred. His brainwave patterns remained unchanged. She had enough medical training to know what this meant. Apollo had lapsed into a coma.

Suddenly, Sonia felt alone. Even if he had been sick, Apollo would wake occasionally and talk to her. Why had she insisted that he eat? If only the rover had medicines. There was so little for this type of situation. She was convinced that if he did not get to a doctor, a real doctor, Apollo would probably die there in that isolated Martian desert cave.

Sonia began crying. She thought of her best friend, Fisk, dead in the gold mine. She thought of her mother, dead during the war. She thought of Apollo, her one remaining link to humanity in this most desperate situation. He was dying. She bawled uncontrollably for a half hour, unable to think clearly.

Finally, she looked up at robot Tessie, who was trying to treat Apollo. The vital signs remained unchanged. Sonia wiped her eyes, and then stood up. "Apollo, I am not going to let you die on me. At least not here." She went to her seat at the control console, and looked up at the traffic control map. "Where can I go? Where do I have friends?"

There was nothing familiar on the ten-mile map. She expanded it to a one-hundred mile scale. She muttered to herself, "A half dozen mining camps. A trucking station. Epsen Hauling Company, outside Sagan City. Eighty miles. Not much of a city. Population of ninety-six. A hotel, an airport, a uranium processing plant, and a trucking company. I know Flex Epsen. He used to haul ore for us."

She paused, and then asked the computer for traffic control information. "Highlight any Epsen Hauling vehicles on the map!"

Other than trucks parked at their facility in Sagan, there were three Epsen trucks on Highway M-24. If they maintained speed and course, one would be passing the intersection of the John Carter Trail in five hours. Checking the traffic control manifest, she noticed that Flex Epsen, himself was in that truck. There was a second Epsen truck thirty minutes behind the first. Both were heading for Sagan City. She called for highlights of all Redrock and government vehicles. Two eastbound Redrock trucks would pass the trail intersection within the hour. Everything else was in Princess Dejah Canyon, or parked at Redrock facilities a long distance off. The only government vehicles were in Sagan or the Canyon. They were all parked.

Sonia knew she could not drive her rover out in the open for that period. Even without a transponder, Redrock surveillance cameras would pick her up once she started to move. She zoomed the map back to the local area. She was four miles from the intersection with the main highway. A mile east of the intersection was a bridge over an ancient dried riverbed. That would work.

With a plan in mind, Sonia could once again act with determination. She looked over her shoulder at the sleeping young Filipino. "God, I hope this works. If it doesn't we'll both be dead by tomorrow morning."

CHAPTER ELEVEN

SAGAN CITY

Sytris Major Region, Mars

Earth Date	July 12, 2216
Mars Date	C-Mmon 30, 1174

MARTIAN VIRUS, DAY 12

Dressed in her full pressure suit, Sonia stood at the mouth of the abandoned El Dorado mine watching the orange sun drop below the western horizon. The Earth-Moon double evening star brightened in the rapidly darkening sky. "I hope this works!" She squatted, pushed a button on the pocketbook-sized transmitter, targeting its narrow beam antenna tracking focus on the Earth-Moon. With the antenna aimed, she set the transmission to begin in ten minutes. The encoded broadcast would repeat every ten minutes until the Earth dropped below the horizon. Once tracking had been lost, the transmitter would self-destruct.

Sonia pivoted, striding back into the cave. She double-checked the observation trailer. She had moved Apollo, Tessie, survival gear, most the control computers, equipment and ore samples to the trailer. Luckily, two emergency medical transport chambers were available in storage with the observation trailer. Designed to immobilize patients with life threatening injuries, such as a broken back, the med chambers were ideal for use in the hostile Martian environment; they could maintain life support and medical surveillance for long periods until the patient was delivered to a hospital. Apollo's med readings had not changed. Sonia stepped out through the trailer airlock into the darkening cave, walked forward, and entered the control rover airlock. She slid into the driver's seat. "Computer. Set. Let's go!"

In spite of the fact that both Martian moons were high in the sky, not enough illumination existed to give more than a visual outline to the rugged boulders along the route back to the John Carter trail. The rover's computer-operated infrared cameras brightened those images of the path ahead sufficiently for the automatic driver to steer the vehicle around obstructions. Sonia had instructed the computer not to use light beams, radar, or active illumination for navigating because she hoped for as much stealth as possible.

Ten minutes of backcountry bouncing and sharp turns brought the rover and trailer to the John Carter trail. The rover turned north on the trail, and accelerated. The traffic control map showed no change in Redrock or Police vehicle movement, no increase in communications. Traveling at thirty miles per hour, she made it to Highway M-24 in fifteen minutes. Still there was no change in signal threats. Sonia inhaled deeply, and then slowly exhaled. The Epsen trucks were still moving the same course and speed. They had not stopped or slowed. They were heading for Sagan City. The rover-trailer turned east on the highway, following a preset course to the bridge.

Shaking with chills, Sonia raised the temperature setting for her pressure suit, even though she was simultaneously sweating. Her head ached, her throat felt parched, but she could not allow herself to relax, to be sick. Thirty minutes had passed since leaving the cave, and there was still no activity from the Redrock vehicles. The monitor displaying a view of the western sky made obvious that the evening star was about to drop below the horizon. "Uncle Sonny, I hope you do something with this." She laughed to herself. The transmission suggested that there would be a follow-up message within a few days, once safe haven had been found. If the effect of the virus on her was the same as for Apollo, she would soon be in a coma. There would be no follow-up message. Right on schedule, the rover slowed, pulled off the highway, and routed down a gentle embankment to the bed of an ancient dried river gully. It followed the gully back toward the highway, and under the highway bridge. The rover and the trailer stopped and parked.

Fresh signals from Redrock vehicles were coming from the canyon; ciphered messages. Sonia was uncertain if they posed a threat. The Epsen truck would arrive in fifteen minutes. Donning her helmet, Sonia grabbed a remote computer case and two emergency light beacons and left through the vehicle airlock. Climbing the gully embankment at the bridge abutment, within moments she was on the sixty-foot wide concrete roadway surface over the dried riverbed. Moons Demos and Phobos cast a faint glow on the concrete deck, so much lighter than the surrounding igneous rocks. Earth was below the horizon. The automatic radio transmissions were finished. Opening her remote computer case, she studied the screen-generated map. The Epsen truck was three miles away, still coming at a speed of forty. Two Redrock rovers were moving from the canyon, rovers that had been parked minutes earlier. She mumbled to herself that this was it. She placed the two emergency beacons on the roadway, pushed the appropriate buttons, and then stepped aside to watch their red, white and blue flashings signal oncoming traffic.

At this moment, Sonia felt overcome with the effects of the sickness. She was terrified that the Epsen truck might just pass her by. If it did not stop, Redrock agents would kill her. She had thrown the dice in a desperate gamble for her life, and the odds were not with her. Sonia had never been religious, but she began praying as if she had been in church on a regular basis. "Oh, God. We need your help at this moment. Please, do not let me and the boy die here in this desolate wasteland. Give me a chance to make things right." The headlights of the oncoming truck got brighter and brighter. Would it stop?

As the truck approached the dual flashing beacons on the bridge, it slowed, and then stopped a few feet from Sonia. She glanced at the computer display. The two Redrock rovers had turned into Burroughs

Valley on a course that would take them to the John Carter trail. Sonia swallowed, approached the airlock of the truck, and plugged the communications cord from her pressure suit into the appropriate jack beside the door. "Is Flex Epsen driving?"

"This is Flex. What's your emergency? Did you crash off the bridge?"

"This is Sonia Androff. I need your help, desperately."

"Androff?" There was a pause. "Yes, I know you, Sonia. Did you murder Fisk?"

"No, I did not. He was my partner, you know that. Redrock Mining jumped our claim, killed everyone in our crew except for a boy and me. They are looking for us."

"The police say you went berserk. You're supposed to be a threat to the public."

"You've known me since the war. You've hauled our shipments countless times. I am not crazy, but I will be dead if you don't help. The police detective in charge of the murder investigation is a cousin to a Redrock vice-president."

A green light came on beside the airlock. "I believe you. I've dealt with Redrock before. Not anymore. Come on in."

"You don't want me to come in. The boy and I have some unfamiliar virus. He's in a coma at the moment. We need medical help."

"Coma? Virus?"

"My rover is under the bridge with an observation trailer. If you hook the trailer to the back of your truck, I have the rover programmed to continue north on the trail."

"North?" There was a momentary silence. "That trail goes nowhere for hundreds of miles. Bring your vehicle up. I'll come out and help you hook up. You can explain the rest via internal communications."

Sonia glanced down at the luminous instruments on her left sleeve and pushed a button. The control rover under the bridge automatically moved out, coursing its way along the gully to another gentle slope that it could follow out of the streambed. Within two minutes it had circled around to the roadway, and maneuvered to a stop alongside the truck. Following a conversation on the logistics of the arrangement, Sonia had her rover back the observation trailer to the back of the Epsen ore trailers. She uncoupled her rover from the observation trailer, and then coupled her trailer to the back of the Epsen assembly. She signaled her vacated rover to initiate its automated journey. Gathering the signal lights and the remote computer case, she looked up at the star-studded night sky, glanced at the tail lights of her rover dimming in the distance, and then climbed through the observation trailer airlock. "I'm in, Flex. Let's go."

Sonia fell against the airlock inside doorframe as the vehicle accelerated to normal highway speed. Tessie was still quietly monitoring Apollo's life signs. His condition had not changed. She settled in at the control console. The traffic control display showed the two Redrock rovers still in Burroughs Valley, approaching the trail. Her now automated rover slowed at the intersection of the trail and the highway, then turned north on the trail. Sonia had opened the engine heat vents on the rover to make it easier for Redrock to track it by infrared, although she left the transducer disabled so as not to draw suspicions. No other Redrock or police vehicles were moving in the area. "Please, follow the yellow brick road."

"Sonia," Flex interrupted her concentration on traffic. "Tell me what happened. If I'm going to help you escape, I need to know what we're up against."

Sonia's aching muscles, throbbing head, churning stomach, and burning eyes made her wish for sleep. She dared not until she knew those Redrock vehicles were going to follow her rover north, rather than east after the Epsen truck. The second Epsen truck was now fifteen minutes behind them, the distance closed by the delay on the bridge.

Sonia asked for a cup of plain tea, the only thing she felt she could keep down. She did not want to trigger what had happened to Apollo. She began relaying her story, with occasional questions from Flex, about the prospecting mission, the decision to hire a Filipino mining crew, about hiring Dave. Retelling the story absorbed her enough to lessen the pains of the worsening illness. She explained about the fish Apollo found, that the two of them were sick from a one-hundred-million-year-old Martian virus, a sickness that generated crazy dreams about the past and the future. She told that she had foreseen Apollo in a coma, and he had foreseen the Redrock murders.

By the time she finished, they were halfway to Sagan City. The Redrock vehicles on the John Carter Trail had both crossed the main highway in pursuit of the automated rover.

"I can hide you," Flex finally responded, "Indefinitely ... if you want."

"I need help to stop Redrock."

"Worry about justice later. First, you have to stay alive. If your story is true, that decoy moving north through the desert will not fool them for long. When they check the traffic records, they will come looking for me."

Sagan City was a small town built over a permafrost oasis. Most of the Syrtis Major basaltic plains were old, dry, dark bedrocks. In the twentieth century, before spacecraft visited Mars, astronomers observing the bright orange Martian disk thought that the dark regions on that globe, like the Syrtis Major triangle, got their darkness from local vegetation. Astronomer Carl Sagan, with a flare for publicity, argued that the dark areas were more likely just darker basaltic bedrock. Immigrant pioneers to the Syrtis Major badlands chose to remember the astronomer who guessed correctly what the area was by naming their first outpost after him.

A billion years earlier, when Mars was wet and warmer, the Sagan area had been a lake over an underground aquifer. When the heat underground dissipated, the aquifer froze solid, just like the underground ice at Princess Dejah Canyon. Around Sagan City the permafrost was close enough to the surface for genetically engineered plants to reach it. The barren desert of that former lakebed gave way to grasses, bushes, and trees planted by human immigrants trying to breathe life into the harsh cold world. Around Sagan were a multitude of farms, some with open grain fields, and all with pressurized dome crop fields. The pressurized domes were needed for most edible agricultural produce, except for the engineered grains. In the center of the former lakebed was a rocky outcrop, a former island used as a town center. Here, the founders of Sagan City had build another underground township with heated, pressurized tunnels connecting all homes and businesses with each other. The city also had a smelter to process locally any ores brought in from the Major

Syrtis region. The mining and agricultural businesses made the city ideal for trucking companies like Epsen's.

When Flex pulled into the smelter compound, company employees were waiting to move Sonia's trailer. Once uncoupled from the ore shipments, a golf-cart sized tug towed the trailer through a back gate into an abandoned tunnel once used for mining the permafrost for water.

Parked in a relatively secure hiding place, Sonia had nothing to do but wait. She wanted to avoid exposing anyone to the virus, meaning that she had to keep the trailer sealed. No excursions out of the trailer, no casual visitors inside. She warned Flex to only let visitors come in with quarantine rated pressure suits, and to have those outfits sterilized with decontamination hoses attached to the trailer airlock.

Flex agreed, promising to keep the trailer's existence a secret from everyone but the doctor, the trucking manager, and his co-driver. A half hour after Flex pulled into the compound, near midnight, six other Epsen trucks left Sagan City, each pulling shipments not actually scheduled to leave for a few days. Flex figured this would confuse Redrock observers suspicious of his stop on the bridge.

After reviewing the computer medical records for Sonia and Apollo, and studying the course of the viral infection, Doctor Wayne Follett returned to his office to do what research he could. The prescribed injection for Apollo made no change to his coma. The prescriptions Sonia took herself immediately deadened the pain in her muscles, head, and eyes. They also made her drowsy. Fifteen minutes later she was asleep, the first sound sleep she had in several days.

CHAPTER TWELVE

MOORELAND

Isidis Plains

Earth Date	July 13, 2216
Mars Date	C-Mmon 30, 1174

S onia abruptly sat up from bed, startled awake by an overwhelming sense of panic. The sudden motion forced shooting pains through her back muscles. She braced herself. Her head swirled with dizziness. Something was wrong. She had dreamed that she had seen Dave with Ghant Travis and Detective Sylvester meeting with several Redrock security guards in an observation trailer at the base of the canyon cliff. Through the trailer window was a conveyor system that moved rocks from a pile of raw ore being ejected from the high cliff gold mine to a processing trailer, which crushed the stones and separated the gold from the granite. The gold was transported on another conveyor that moved it into empty trucks. Detective Sylvester had explained that Sonia was in an abandoned tunnel in the Epsen compound in Sagan City. Sonia remembered looking at the trailer clock. Mars time showed a little after noon, on C-Mmon 32, 1174, or

July 14, 2216. It was a day in the future, and they would know where to find her if she remained in Sagan City. The dream-like visions faded. Why did she see this happening? Was this the "real" near future? She knew she had to leave Sagan quickly.

The dizziness settled. Slowly, she shifted on the bed, turning to put her feet down. She looked across the trailer at the life signs displayed over the med chamber holding Apollo. Dr. Follett provided two advanced med chambers, each with better stocked automated dispensaries. Apollo's condition was stable and unchanged; he was still in a coma.

"Good morning, Sonia!" The old doctor's face appeared on the control room video screen. "Do you feel better?"

Sonia looked up at the computer screens to check her own life signs. Temperature, respiration, pulse, and blood pressure were slightly abnormal. White blood cell count was high. Neural activity was abnormal, especially in the hypothalamus. Pituitary secretions were unusual. The viral concentration seemed less severe that it had been two days earlier. She studied her bare arms. The rash of dark spots remained unchanged. "I don't know. You have a recommendation? You see the same information."

Although the kindly faced doctor lacked humor in his expression, his eyes showed compassion. "You know what I recommend. You need to go to a hospital. You need isolation in intensive care."

"I wish I could, Doctor Follett. Any officials notified of my coming would tell the police. Detective Sylvester would make certain I was dead before I could tell any authorities my story."

"You may die anyway, if you do not get help. The boy especially; he is borderline between life and death. If that virus does any more damage, you will lose him. You have to get him to a hospital immediately."

"Redrock murdered his uncle and four other Filipino miners. The police are covering up that the Filipinos were ever here. What do you think will happen to him?" Tears were streaming from Sonia's eyes. Her crying even surprised herself. She stood and walked to the chamber encasing her young friend. His rash and vital statistics had not changed. Tessie remained in standby mode at the back of the trailer, with nothing to do as long as Apollo's medical needs were maintained by the chamber. "I don't want him to die here. I don't want official records to show that he never existed on Mars. She looked again at the video screens. "There has to be another solution."

"I have a way," Flex's face appeared on a separate monitor. "I've been talking to a space freight pilot in Wells. She says she met you … Octan Palmer … flies between Wells and Boston."

Sonia wrinkled her mouth, "I know her. She's a partner in a space transport business. Each of the four partners operate between different cities on Earth and Mars."

"You've met," Flex smiled. "Did you know she is a friend of Sonny Ortigas?"

Sonia was quiet for several seconds. "Apollo's Uncle Sonny?" She smiled. "I remember now. Sonny told me about it."

"Anyway, I told Octan I had a sick Filipino runaway who needs to get home. She was reluctant until I told her the boy is a nephew of Sonny. Apparently she owes Sonny some favors. She agreed to take Apollo back to Manila, no questions asked."

"That's perfect. If we can get Apollo back to his family, away from Mars… they can get him to a hospital." Her eyes began to well with moisture. "Great." Her face then contorted. "How much did you tell her… about this situation?"

"Just that we had a sick, dying boy in a coma with an unknown contagious disease… a nephew to Sonny." Flex remained stone faced as he talked. "This could work for you, too. Go to Earth and recover, then come back and make your case with the right authorities."

Dr. Follett made a suggestion. "I have a friend at the Hong Kong University Medical Center. I'll contact him to forward an order through channels to ship a coma case to them. We will give Apollo a Chinese name; say that he was part of the diplomatic corps. That will get the boy through customs. We could do that with both."

It sounded tempting. However, after a moment of consideration she said, "No, not me. We send Apollo home. If he dies, let him be with his family. I'm a Martian. Earth is too hot and too wet and the gravity is uncomfortable. If Redrock found out where I was, they'd put a bounty on my head. Even in an isolated hospital, they would take me out just to make certain that I never threatened to expose them." She approached the galley; asked for cup of tea. She pointed to it, looking to the screen with Follett's face for approval. The doctor smiling slightly, nodded. Sonia slowly sipped the tea. It tasted good, and it felt good going down. There was no reaction at the end. "What I need is a medical facility here on Mars, one that Redrock will not be able to find."

"I grew up in Lowell Canyon, in the Mariner Grand Valley," Flex said. "There are some old mines there that were transformed into quarantine compounds during the war… in the event that the U.N. tried to hit us with biologic weapons."

"I know that place," Dr. Follett added, "I was stationed there during the war. We ended up dealing primarily with normal war trauma victims. They still have a staff of research specialists. They do animal research on genetic mutations from the life forms engineered to survive on this planet. It's perfect for looking after you, Sonia. This new virus you have would be their specialty."

"What about the police?"

"I'll talk to them … I'll tell the staff to expect you … that you're a diplomat, that this must be kept quiet."

"I'll think about it. If they turn me into a lab experiment, I may never see the light of day again."

Flex interrupted, "Sonia, you don't know what you have. You may be a threat to everyone on Mars. Have you thought about that?"

Unfortunately, she had. She knew the options. That was why she had isolated herself and Apollo in the trailer. If she was a threat to life on Mars, she would be quarantined, studied, kept away from human contact. Once again, tears rolled down her cheeks. "Flex, wherever we go, we have to leave right away."

"You don't think we should lay low for a few days?"

"Remember what I told you about Apollo… knowing that Dave was about to betray us? Well, I woke from a dream… I saw things taking place two days from now. Detective Sylvester is going to deputize Redrock security guards, and come to this abandoned tunnel with a warrant. I have to be gone."

"It's too bad you're too sick to walk around," Flex laughed, "With this new talent, I'd like to go with you to a casino." He glanced from the screen to an information panel. "I figured on taking you both to Wells, leaving tomorrow afternoon. I'll speed that up, and leave after breakfast. I have six trailers of processed uranium oxide to deliver to Wells. We'll work out how to get you to Lowell along the way."

"Wells is six-thousand miles," Follett said slowly. "Even non-stop, sleeping on the run, that will take a week. Miss Androff and her young friend need to find medical attention before that. Apollo may be dead before you get him there."

"Could you come with us?" Sonia asked. "It might make the difference."

"I wish I could, but I have a clinic full of patients. I can't be gone for a week without finding a temporary to fill in. Besides, I am not an expert on infectious diseases. You need a specialist."

Flex smiled at the camera, giving a slight wink. "We'll handle the matter. Sonia, will you be ready to move in an hour?"

"I have a choice? I assume we are putting this trailer in your caravan."

Flex nodded, "It was dumb to ask. We leave in an hour." He turned his attention to the doctor. "When you arrange with Hong Kong to file for delivering Apollo to Earth, have the invoice specify the shipment via Sonny Ortigas in the Philippines."

"Sonny Ortigas? Who is that?"

"The boy's uncle."

The late afternoon sun on Highway M-24 eastbound created mirage-like atmospheric waves shimmering above the flat, featureless plain ahead. The road ahead was straight as an arrow, with no curves or hills for as far as the eye could see as they trekked across the brilliant ochre-colored sandy flatlands, deserts similar to pictures of the Sahara back on Earth. The air outside the vehicle, with miniscule surface pressure, was a balmy thirty degrees Fahrenheit. After sundown the thermometer would drop to a hundred below zero. The vegetation growing on the once shallow sea of the Isidis Plains east of Major Syrtis highlands seemed like a garden compared to the lifeless terrain of the basaltic highlands. Sparse outgrowth of wild grasses, bushes, and scrub conifers, genetically engineered to survive the Martian climate conditions, added patches of green similar to the deserts of Nevada.

Sonia's head throbbed, back muscles ached and stomach churned. She continued sipping the soup mix Dr. Follett gave her, something her stomach could handle with only minor queasy reactions. The doctor's medications had her symptoms under control, although they did not seem to be working for Apollo. At least his med-chamber had a wider range of medications and a computer program update to deal with a wider range of ailments.

"Sonia, you play poker?" Flex was on one of the console monitors.

"Who doesn't in the desert?" Sonia glanced to the adjacent screen where displayed a computer generated card deck was being shuffled. "Your deal."

"What game? Stud? Draw? Blackjack?"

Sonia glanced at Apollo, then at the console, "You ever hear of Pusoy?"

"What is that?"

"The Filipinos like to play that in the evenings. It's a variation of poker. Duce is the highest card. They use lots of wilds."

"Maybe another time." He looked away from the camera. "Lets just do normal seven card stud; no wild."

Sonia agreed. The computer started dealing. She got an eight of hearts; Flex a jack of clubs.

"Okay, no one is listening." Flex whispered. He bet two chips. The two men in his crew were absorbed in their own conversation at the driver's seat while Flex did bookkeeping and talked and played cards with Sonia. "We are not driving all the way to Wells. I'm separating your trailer from this truck at Mooreland Airport. A friend agreed to fly a special cargo to the Wells spaceport for an extra bonus.

"Extra bonus?" Sonia called the bet. Her next card was a six of hearts.

Flex got the ten of diamonds. "If your dream is accurate, that detective will have deputies swarming all over Sagan tomorrow afternoon. With a little SWK truth serum they will know what Dr. Follett knows before sunset. If we are to get that kid off Mars, we have to do it by tomorrow morning."

"I thought the same thing. I figured I had no options, since I have to remain isolated, and take any route I can to evade the police."

"The guys don't know about Mooreland, yet. The pilot, Jake Andrews, thinks I'm trying to avoid customs duty on something being shipped to Earth. I'll let him think that."

The hand of seven card stud on the screen continued. Sonia got two more hearts. Speeding up the trip to Wells improved her hopes of saving Apollo from the Redrock killers. "Are we still going to Lowell?"

"It would be ideal," Flex won the first hand with a pair of jacks. "The quarantine facilities, the medical specialists are there. However, I'll know that by tomorrow night, Redrock will know, and they will have agents waiting to intercept us."

"So, where can I go?"

"I haven't figured that out. You have any ideas?"

After sundown, the desert landscape turned black. The temperatures dropped. A sparkling array of small lights ahead, to the right of the main highway, highlighted the desert town of Mooreland. Located in a gentle depression at the eastern edge of the Isidis Plain, the town was surrounded by open wheat fields; that wheat taking advantage of the frozen aquifer a few inches underground. There were dome-covered cattle ranches, chicken farms, and huge hydro phonic warehouses. Homes, built into rock islands rising above the former seabed, were mostly underground. The lighted garden domes and parking facilities at every home and business, however, made Mooreland sparkle with lights. At night those lights could be seen from a hundred miles away. A permafrost water processing factory was at the outskirts of town. Ice-laden permafrost was trucked into the factory where it was heated, changing the mud embedded ice into steam; that steam was then condensed back into pure water for use at the local farms.

Just past that factory, Flex's truck turned off the main highway, routed down a side street through the city's light industrial section, to a local Epsen Hauling Company compound. Once inside the compound, Flex had his crew park the trailer to one side, and couple two more freight trailers to the back of their load. Without letting them know what they had been hauling, he sent them on their long journey to Wells, a city on the other side of the planet.

After checking with his field office, he personally drove a yard tug, a golf-cart-sized towing vehicle, to Sonia's trailer. Once the trailer was connected to the yard tug, he non-chalantly drove out of the compound, down a side road behind the permafrost plant, then to the freight entrance of Mooreland's airport. There, a dragonfly transport was parked to one end of the tarmac, near the perimeter fence. Ignoring the pressurized hangers for the terminal, Flex drove directly into the plane's open cargo hold.

Sonia watched what was transpiring using external monitor cameras. In accordance with plan, she remained quiet, so that Flex could convince the pilot that the trailer held a delicate, expensive mystery cargo. The plane ride would cut the travel time to Wells from a week on the road to ten hours in the air.

Sonia's head was hurting. She checked Apollo's statistics, and then returned to her bunk. She lifted the blankets, kicked off her footwear, slipped into bed, and snuggled to a pillow. Moments later she was sound asleep.

CHAPTER THIRTEEN

WELLS SPACEPORT

Western Flank of Arsia Mountain, Mars

| Earth Date | July 14, 2216 |
| Mars Date | C-Mmon 32, 1174 |

MARTIAN VIRUS, DAY 14

The black dragonfly cargo plane, with a yellow stripe down the center of either side of the fuselage, circled at three-thousand feet above the topside streetlights of Wells, waiting clearance to land. Named for the nineteenth century novelist who wrote "War of the Worlds", about a fictional Martian invasion of Earth, Wells was the metropolitan area that suffered the most damage when Earth invaded Mars during the Martian war for independence from the United Nations. Five thousand space force troops, who survived the descent from orbit to Wells, were angry that half of their comrades were shot out of the air in the attempted landing. Once in the underground tunnels, they wrought vengeance on the citizens of Wells with a killing spree that left thousands dead and destroyed an entire section of the business district near the spaceport. The twenty-three years since the war had eased painful memories Wells had to live with. It had been rebuilt and recovered from the devastation. From the air, the lights of the surface roads, the domed parks and gardens, and the transparent private observation deck bubbles created an illuminated cityscape, like a street map of sparkling diamonds on a black velvet cloth. Up the flanks of the pitch-black Arsia volcano, there were long twisting lines of roadway lights and a few clusters of mining camps.

Flex always enjoyed the stark image of cities from the air at night, when cities seemed more pristine. The instrument panel clock displays read: "Wells: 9-83-22 MT", nearly midnight local time; the reading for Sagan City local time was "5-32-22 MT", slightly past noon. If Sonia's vision about a Redrock raid on Epsen Company was a prophecy, it would be happening as they landed. The plane banked to line up with Runway 25-165, and began descending. Jake Andrews, the young, thin pilot let his computer finish the landing. He had given up trying to get Flex to tell him what the cargo was, or why he was so nervous about the flight. He had known this hard-driven friend since he began flying, and had never seen him as high-strung as he was during this flight. He quietly watched Flex monitor information from the secret cargo trailer. The computer displays of medical statistics let him know that the cargo was human and in bad shape.

As the dragonfly glided to a touchdown, Flex called up traffic control maps for Sagan. A convoy of police and Redrock rovers were on Highway M-24 approaching the city. Sonia was right. Once more he called up medical surveillance data to the monitor screens in front of him. Apollo was still in coma, no change in condition. Sonia was sleeping, with erratic life signs. Flex signaled the computer to wake Sonia. This display indicated that the trailer alarms were working. There was no indication that Sonia was coming out of her sleep. Flex looked more closely at the brainwave patterns. Sonia's sleep was like that of Apollo. Except for normal, involuntary functions, the neural consciousness patterns had gone flatline. She was in a coma.

Flex grimaced, reached up, and brushed the lock of hair that had dropped across his forehead.

The runway lights rapidly got closer. Jake Andrews ignored the view out the window. Turning to Flex, "You are pale as a ghost. Is something wrong with your passenger?"

For a moment Flex continued looking at the video display of Sonia's brainwave patterns. He turned his head to stare at the pilot, not speaking.

Jake motioned toward the display in front of Flex. "It's obvious your secret cargo is a sick someone. Care to tell me a little more than you have?"

Flex smiled. The plane jarred as the wheels came in contact with the concrete runway. "You are better off not knowing!"

"Want me to guess?"

He shrugged. "Give it your best shot."

"You arranged for me to park this plane in the interplanetary custom's area. Whatever you have in that trailer is going off-planet. You've been monitoring abnormal life signs for two individuals. You have two sick passengers. You've been monitoring global police reports. Your passengers must be wanted. You've been monitoring traffic patterns near Sagan, and the police are presently moving that direction from Burroughs Valley. The only police news from that area in the past week has been the killing of those prospectors in Princess Dejah Canyon, and the manhunt for the killer and an unknown accomplice. I think the chief suspect..." He pushed a button on his own computer display. An image of Sonia appeared on screen.

Flex felt a churning in his stomach. "Did you plan to do anything about your guess?"

"Flex, Flex, Flex..." Jake put his hands behind his head, lacing his fingers together. "I've known you for what? Eleven Earth years?" The plane had slowed to a stop. Automatically, it began moving again, routing off the landing strip to a taxiway. "I've never known you to do anything illegal, unless the law was obviously wrong. If you're convinced that it is important to evade the police, to send these people off planet... I flew you here, didn't I?"

Flex relaxed slightly, although he was much on edge. "Thanks for that."

"I don't mind helping, but if you have me mixed up with a fugitive escape, I wish you could give me the score."

Flex briefly looked out the window. They were rolling toward the parked spacecraft at the eastern quadrant of the spaceport. "You're right. I should tell you." He pointed to the traffic control display for Sagan. "I picked up Sonia and her accomplice three nights ago. She showed me control rover videos of the killings in the canyon. Dave Crane, a geochemist working for her, was with Redrock Operations Vice President Ghant Travis. They killed Sonia's partner, Fisk Banzar, Japa Reese, their mechanic, and five Filipino mine workers."

"Filipino mine workers? The police reports only identified two victims."

"Sonia and a Filipino kid escaped. They are both sick with some unidentified virus. The police detective in charge of the case is a cousin to Travis."

"Virus?" Jake's eyes were focused out the window. The plane rolled to a stop at an inspection tarmac. He glanced at the medical statistics in front of Flex. "Now, I see the problem."

"They both need advanced medical attention."

"And they are both in coma," He pointed to the display, "You sending both to Earth?"

"The boy. Sonia wants to stay… to fight if she can."

A tarmac tug, pulling three spacecraft cargo containers, approached from the nearest hanger airlock. "Is that for us?"

Flex nodded. "They're picking up a package of 'agricultural experiments' for Hong Kong University. Sonia was supposed to have it ready for off loading." He frantically pushed buttons on the instrument panel. "There's a robot in standby mode in the trailer. I don't have the access code to Sonia's computer, so I can't call for the robot to prepare the cargo."

Jake shook his head, "And the sealed trailer is carrying some unknown contagious disease." He half whistled, blowing air through his lips. "Problem."

"Do you have a decon hose?"

He was adjusting controls on the plane's console, "Yeah, I forgot about that. Never needed it before." He got up. "I'll hook it up."

"I'll go in for Apollo. Don't want to risk both of us."

Jake looked out the window at the cargo tug parked beside his plane. "You going to send both to Earth?"

"I can't do that to her." He put his helmet on, then adjusted the exterior settings on his sleeve from Martian night surface (-100°F, 8 mb) to include exposure to hazardous biologic contaminants, an adjustment that would set the air regulator to internal recycle only, sealing out all external atmospheres. "If the story she told me is right, then Redrock jumped her prospecting claim. She claims they discovered a minimum of eighty-thousand tons of gold. If she gets back, she could offer a big reward for helping her."

"If she dies, we get nothing. If Redrock catches us, we die with her."

Flex waited for Jake to decide.

"Someday, I may need help. I'll gamble a few days with the plane. Let's move the cargo, and then get the hell out of here."

Flex snapped the faceplate down, and headed back into the cargo bay to the observation trailer airlock. He waited long enough for Jack to pull the decon hose from the plane's equipment hold and connect it to the trailer airlock. Once the airlock sealed him in the outer compartment, the hose issued a caustic gas spray designed to chemically breakdown any unprotected organic molecules. After the fifteen second pressurized decontamination, the decon hose sucked out the gas, then pumped in fresh air, and initiated normal airlock operations. Flex passed through the inner airlock door to the observation trailer.

Speaking as he moved via channel five to Octan, who was outside on the tarmac, Flex explained that he was running a little late because the package had a leaking pressure valve. Pulling back the bedding from Sonia's bunk, he stripped Sonia of all her clothing, dressed her in a medical control pressure suit, and then placed her in the second med chamber. Carefully, he attached the waste removal connections, the intravenous feeding tubes, the air regulator mask, and the life support surveillance devices. He sealed her chamber and pushed it aside. Next, he double-checked the external shipping label on Apollo's med-chamber: "John Doe. Coma victim. Diplomatic sensitive. Route to Miguel Sonny Ortigas, Makati, Philippines for eventual shipment to Hong Kong University. Medical authorization signature, Doctor Wayne Follett, Sagan City, G.P." The lid setting was for transparent, quarantine mode. The rash colored face of the young Filipino looked as if he were sleeping peacefully. Flex disconnected the chamber from the trailer computer jacks, telescoped the rack wheels under the chamber, and then rolled Apollo's med-chamber towards the equipment airlock at the back end of the trailer. "Jake? Is the decon attached?"

"Send it through!"

Flex opened the airlock door and pushed the med chamber in. The sliding door closed behind him. As soon as the lights indicated that the door was sealed, a fog of decontamination spray filled the chamber. After the fifteen second wait, the air cleared. The outer airlock door opened, allowing Flex and the med chamber to enter the plane's cargo bay. Jake depressurized the bay, and opened the plane's cargo doors. He then helped Flex wheel the med-chamber down the loading ramp to the tarmac, where spacecraft pilot Octan Palmer was waiting with spaceport cargo handler, Bryce Vern.

"This the package?" Octan, in her pressure suit, approached the med chamber. Using a glove embedded spotlight, she peered through her darkened visor into the transparent lid of the chamber. If it weren't for the life signs on the chamber display instruments showing he was a very sick patient, she would have concluded he was dead. She carefully read the routing instructions, and then looked up. "This matches the shipping orders from Sagan and Hong Kong. Bryce, show this to customs, and then load it in cargo hold three."

"Yes!" Bryce Vern grabbed the med-chamber handles and loaded the unit on his own motorized cargo cart. "Are you coming with me?"

"I'll be there in a minute. I have to talk to Jake."

Bryce got back on his cargo tug and pulled the loaded carts toward the customs hanger. A bright exhaust flame from a commercial spacecraft lifting off from the other side of the spaceport briefly illuminated the tarmac. The darkness once more enveloped the background. Nearby were a line of parked, colorfully marked anti-grav shuttles, Octan's shuttle among them. Standing like an old-fashioned rocket, her winged shuttle had the dual fusion engines protruding under its anti-grav deck.

The trio walked back into Jack's cargo hold. Another anti-grav shuttle lifted off the tarmac. There was no flame or noise on take off.

That shuttle quickly rose into the air, attitude controlled by nitrogen jets. At a thousand feet above the tarmac, the flames from the fusion thrust engines cut in to propel the shuttle to an orbital velocity. The view of the anonymous launch disappeared when Jake closed the cargo doors. Repressurizing the hold, Jake led Flex and Octan around the observation trailer toward the cockpit.

They all seated themselves and removed their helmets.

Octan then asked, "Tell me about Sonny's nephew. What am I dealing with?"

Flex said, "Picked up an unknown virus in Burroughs Valley. He's in a coma. I don't know if he will survive the trip. He should still be with his family."

"I know." Octan said, "We talked about that. Where's Sonia? She was going to give me instructions… to pass on when he gets to Manila…"

Jake pointed back toward the observation trailer in the cargo hold. "Sonia is in a coma. It's contagious. I don't know what her instructions were, except to get the boy to Sonny Ortigas, and to do your best to keep him alive. The people tracking her will kill him if they can. We have to figure a way to get Sonia medical help to keep her alive."

"No instructions?" Octan accepted coffee from Jake. She looked back through the cockpit window at the cargo bay.

"I don't know her computer access codes. Everything is in the computers. If she revives, or if I figure it out, I'll transmit what you need. The med-chamber should maintain the boy as long as he's in a coma. If he wakes enroute, keep him isolated."

Octan patted Flex on the shoulder. She looked out through the cockpit window at the activity on the tarmac. "This whole thing scares the hell out of me." She pulled a computer plug out of a pressure suit. "This is my personal cipher this month." She glanced at Jake, smiled, then said, "Transmit as much of the story as you can tomorrow. I don't know what I'm dealing with; that makes me nervous."

"When do you lift off?" Jake asked.

"Half an hour. I delayed for your package. As soon as Bryce loads it, I leave."

"Good," Flex said. "The sooner you get that kid off Mars, the better."

Octan sipped her coffee, leaned back and said, "Before I go, tell me what you know about this. I'm doing this for Sonny, because I owe him, but I have no idea what you've gotten me into."

Jake shook his head. "Flex?"

Flex said, "I wish I knew the whole story. All I have are pieces from Sonia. I'm convinced that if she… or that boy… are to survive, we have to move fast. I'll tell you what Sonia told me."

Three hours later it was after midnight. Wells Interplanetary Spaceport was behind them. Octan had taken Apollo into orbit, and docked to Octan's main transport ship. Customs agents from the orbiting "Olympus Snow" space station were onboard the transport double-checking the cargo manifests to release the freight shipment from Martian space. Jack's dragonfly plane, with Sonia's observation trailer in the cargo hold, was airborne and eastbound towards the Grand Mariner Canyon.

PART C

QUARANTINE

CHAPTER FOURTEEN

HILTON HOTEL

Pompeii, Italy

Earth Date	July 20, 2216
Mars Date	C-Mmon 38, 1174

A slight yellow haze colored the air over Pompeii, intensifying the stifling summer heat of southern Italy. The brown, towering slopes of Mount Vesuvius seemed indistinct beyond the reclaimed ruins of the ancient Roman city of Pompeii, shimmering through the thick humidity. Seen from the rooftop of the local Hilton Hotel, those reclaimed ruins spread out like a relief map. The cobblestone streets, the plaza pillars, the formerly ash buried homes of ancient Pompeii had become an interplanetary tourist attraction for people from everywhere searching for a bridge to history. Tourists could stroll ancient walkways and listen for the sounds of a long dead civilization whispering in the wind. A breeze slightly cooled the late afternoon heat, bringing momentary relief from the humidity, but not much. Under the shade covering the hotel's rooftop terrace, Sonny Ortigas did not mind. The weather reminded him of Manila.

The view of the buildings of the ancient Roman city fascinated him as much as it did other tourists.

Sonny Ortigas, a Manila-based private detective, specialized in recovering stolen properties for the insurance commission. He did not have to. He had partial partnership in a space freight business that paid him well, but he did not like flying cargo and did not like leaving Earth. His passion was unraveling mysteries. A Space Patrol investigator in his youth, and a U.N. police detective after leaving the military, he quit the U.N. Police because his superiors did not like his creative ways of solving crimes. Starting his own detective business, he found that insurance commissions were lucrative.

Heinrich von Dietrich, world famous art dealer from Bremen, Germany, sat across the table from Sonny. He did mind the heat. He was wearing a temperature controlled thermal outfit to keep his body cool, but his exposed head continued to perspire heavily. He lifted his beer stein for a long, cool drink, and then returned it to a coaster on the table. "Sonny, where are they? If they don't arrive soon, I'll leave... Come back after sundown."

"Heinrich," Sonny smiled, and then drank from his own beer. "You must learn not to mind a little discomfort. They make the pleasures of life much more enjoyable."

Heinrich grimaced. "You have such a relaxed approach to life. Are you sure you are not part Italian?"

"Born and bred Filipino. We are just as laid back as any southern European", Sonny sipped the beer again, "Looks like we don't have to wait any longer," He glanced toward the terrace restaurant's glass doors. She was in her late twenties, an attractive Italian woman in a casual dress, accompanied by a fifty-ish man with graying, bushy hair. They were speaking to a waiter at the door, who pointed to Sonny's table. Slipping around other tables to approach, the young woman spoke first, "Mister Dietrich?"

Heinrich put his beer mug down. "I'm Heinrich Dietrich. May I help you?"

"I'm Ucello. We talked in Bremen … at Herr Vogel's reception last month."

"Ya vol, meinen Fraulien," He motioned for her to take a seat. "Ich Weirstahe. Haben ein sitz, bitte!"

"Danke." Motioning for her companion to take a chair, she seated herself beside Heinrich. "If you don't mind, my German is, shall we say, limited..."

"Ya. Und meinen Italiano is nicht ser gut. Shall we speak English?" As the waiter approached, Heinrich motioned with his hand toward Sonny. "My friend from Manila doesn't speak German or Italian. I believe you know Sonny Villamore." (Sonny had established the Villamore alias for this investigation).

Ucello's eyes twinkled at Sonny. "Oh yes. Sonny brought me to the Vogel reception." She looked up at the waiter to order a glass of rose wine. Her companion, Charn Bendino asked for red. Sipping the beverages on the terrace in Mount Vesuvius' shadow provided a moment to relax on the hot, humid afternoon. All four offered a few minutes of small talk and attempts at humor before broaching the matter that brought them together.

Lloyds of London had contacted Sonny in April about three missing paintings from the National Museum of Art in Rome; art treasures that included two DaVinci's and a Rafael.

For two months he had studied and restudied the police reports, repeating their investigation interviews. He revisited the crime scene many times, and researched the intricacies of the underground fine arts world.

During his tour of duty with Space Force Intelligence, Sonny mastered the manipulation of sensitive computer systems. For his own benefit, he programmed his own secret code entries into the military intelligence computer network. This allowed him to learn any diplomatic and military access codes. With those codes, he could access any computer in the world, a resource that served him well as a detective. He discovered clandestine inquiries made within the underground arts community searching for the highest bidder for the three paintings.

Working with Lloyds of London, he created a computer record for himself under the name "Villamore", and arranged a partnership with Heinrich Dietrich. It was an elaborate ruse, but Lloyds was paying a ten-percent finders fee for the art, plus expenses.

Sonny's investigation focused early on Ucello Scapallini because of clues the police had missed from the original evidence. Ucello had a record of dating recognized art thieves, of living far beyond her means. Early in their investigation, the police found that for two months before the theft she was in the United States. At the precise time of the theft in Rome, Ucello was at the Corcoran Art Museum in Washington, D.C., accompanied by three United States Senators. Those facts convinced the police that she was not involved with the crime. When Sonny studied security video records of the Rome Museum, he found that Ucello had been a regular visitor during the year before the theft. She knew the curators. Although they told Sonny that Ucello's special interest was twentieth century art, she often brought friends to see the displays of DaVinci and Rafael. Sonny's suspicions were confirmed as he restudied the security videos, where he recognized a gold lapel pin she wore. He had several versions of that lapel pin himself, a disguised mini video camera. A year before the theft, Ucello was making videos of all aspects of the museum. Sonny surmised that Ucello may not have been in Rome at the time of the crime, but she was most likely the mastermind.

After the men listened to Ucello finish telling of a recent humorous skiing incident, they were ready to get down to business. "I enjoy listening to your stories, Miss Scapallini," Heinrich finally remarked, "You are a most remarkable, entertaining woman. However, I assume that is not the reason we have been here in the heat so long."

Sonny smiled. Poor Heinrich just could not deal with the heat and humidity.

Ucello sipped her wine, looked at Charn, and nodded almost imperceptibly. Looking to Heinrich, she asked, "Do we have an offer?"

Heinrich waited for Sonny to speak for both of them.

Sonny reached for his beer, took a sip, and then put it back on the table. "First, we need confirmation."

Charn motioned for everyone to pick up their drink. He placed a computer case on the table. He looked over his shoulder at the bar inside, at the commercial video screen embedded in the wall. It was tuned to a local news program. He opened the case, allowing the tri-screen display to telescope out of the case like a pyramid on its side. The image on the screens was the same as the commercial show in the bar. "This is the real time confirmation." Charn said, "A television in the midst of the merchandise display."

Sonny motioned for them to continue. Ucello leaned back to not interfere with Charn's demonstration. "Zoom back to full scope," The image of a television monitor shrank on the screens. The three missing paintings appeared on the screen, behind the news program television monitor.

"You now have an image of the merchandise." Charn said, "The camera transmitting this image is actually a ZRT-60 scanner. I assume you are familiar with the unit."

Both Sonny and Heinrich had used the scanner. It operated with frequencies from far infrared through visible light and ultraviolet to x-ray. It was able to illuminate and receive in narrow or wide band of select frequencies.

"You want to let me do my own tests?" Heinrich asked. He motioned with one finger to the image on screen.

Charn stared before speaking to the computer. "Create labeled grid. Approve voice access for Heinrich Dietrich in German, Italian, and English." Charn pushed the unit across the table to Heinrich, "Your I.D. card?"

Heinrich found his standard identification card in a chest pocket of his environmental suit. He handed it to Charn, who ran it through the computer, and then returned the card.

Sonny lifted his own computer case from beside his seat, and sat it on the table beside Charn's unit. Opening the case, he pulled a cable from the side, handing the end to Charn to plug into the jack. He handed a microphone to Heinrich.

The German drank from his beer once more, and then spoke. "Picture one, Grid coordinate M dash 12. Multi-step scan, pigment dating."

The screens on Charn's computer zoomed to a six inch square section of the Rafael painting. Slowly the image coloration changed in flashes of x-ray, ultraviolet, infrared. During the sixty seconds it took the ZRT-60 to scan that portion of the painting, the four "tourists" leaned back quietly with their drinks. Ucello nervously eyed other tables to make certain no one was paying undo attention.

Outwardly, Sonny maintained his air of nonchalance. His appearance as a hustler had to remain unquestioned. "I assume this is stored nearby," Sonny asked.

Ucello winked. "Never assume anything." She lifted her wine glass. "But if all goes well, you should have the merchandise within a few days."

A flashing yellow light on his environmental sleeve caught Sonny's attention. It was a communications emergency. He pushed a button to turn off the warning. It had already attracted Ucello's watchful eye.

"That was an emergency signal," she smiled. "You should take it. Heinrich will need at least an hour."

Sonny was in a quandary. If he postponed answering the call, Ucello would get suspicious. Every police report he had ever seen on her showed she would cancel any deal where she felt something was not right, and then just disappear. If he tried to leave the table, and take the call privately, she would be suspicious. Ucello, the Italian word for bird, was appropriate. Beautiful, she seemed so innocent, and at the slightest concern, she would fly away. The only one who had his present emergency number was Zhenny with Lloyds. She would not have put through this signal if it was not critical. Hopefully, she will be careful.

Sonny had to avoid creating suspicion with a secret communication. He needed to avoid secret calls, or Ucello would get nervous. He put down his beer to speak to his sleeve attached button phone. "What is it, Zhenny?"

"I know this is a bad time. You have a special problem back in Manila."

"Special problem?" Sonny gritted his teeth. Ucello was acting coy, but watching with intensity. If Zhenny said the wrong thing, it was all over.

"A medical chamber arrived from Mars unannounced at the Manila Spaceport. It's addressed to the Hong Kong University Medical Center, but the instructions are for you to take possession. Inside is a young man in a coma."

Sonny could not understand why Zhenny would call with this. Ucello was especially interested. Heinrich was engrossed in testing the paintings, while Charn quietly followed his actions. "Have Lydia sign for it, and route it to Hong Kong." His stomach was getting acidic. Zhenny should never have been his contact person.

"The young man inside is your nephew, Apollo. According to the pilot, he's been in coma for two weeks, and apparently someone put a death mark out for him."

The report of the death mark sounded good. He knew Ucello would check that out as soon as she was away from the table. Hopefully, Zhenny knew enough to create a background for this story. Apollo is in a coma? He was supposed to be looking for gold on Mars. Where was his brother-in-law, Roberto?

"Have Lydia sign for it. Tell her to get Jenny to take Apollo home. They'll know what to do." With a few more pleasantries, Sonny ended the call. He wondered if that radio message that came in ten days ago had anything to do with this. On the road for two months, he was unable to deal with it. Apollo had coded the message, and he was not there to decipher the encryption codes. Sonny had assumed the message was a normal report about the Filipino crew on Mars. Now he was not so certain. He had no choice. It would have to wait. Jenny would have to take care of Apollo.

"Family troubles?" Ucello put her wine glass back on the table.

He had been staring into space. He turned to her. "You overheard the conversation?"

"Hard not to."

"My nephew. He just returned from Mars in a coma. No details with the med-chamber, except that someone is after him."

"Do you need to go home?"

"He has a lot of family up in the Benget Province. I told Zhenny to have his Aunt Jenny take charge. She'll know what to do."

"I'm sorry to hear this. I hope he gets better soon."

CHAPTER FIFTEEN

JENNY

Manila, Philippines

Earth Date	July 21, 2216
Mars Date	C-Mmon 39, 1174

MARTIAN VIRUS, DAY 21.

"Good morning, Bibi," Jenny Ortigas pushed a button on the comm console in front of her. "We know our shipment landed last night. Matt is coming to the Spaceport this morning to take delivery."

Bibi Sandoval, an attractive sixty-year-old Filipina with gently wavy hair, smiled back from the phone monitor. "Kumusta, Jenny. One of these days I have to get you to tell me how you never seem to age." She paused, but not long enough for the Jenny to react. "I know you don't need to be reminded to pick up Lee's cargo. It's at the hanger." Bibi's smile evaporated. "This call is a personal matter."

"Personal?" Jenny tried to think of what would be personal from Bibi, from E.M. Transport. She waited clarification.

"Octan Palmer brought a special shipment from Wells, specifically consigned to Sonny. I called Lydia. She tried to contact Sonny, but he's out of town. Apparently, he needs for you to pick up the package."

"Package? For Sonny?" Jenny was puzzled. "He never mentioned a special order from Mars. Sonny is in Italy for a month… under cover. What package?"

Bibi exhaled sharply, trying to phrase the matter properly. "It's your nephew, Apollo. He is…"

"Apollo? He's with Roberto on Mars. They're on a prospecting expedition." Jenny held her breath, thinking the worst. "He is a package?"

"No, he's not dead, if that's what you're thinking." Bibi understood Jenny's reaction. "He's in a coma. Apparently he's been in a coma for two weeks. Octan said she had to take him off Mars secretly and in a hurry. Someone powerful is stalking him, but Octan does not know details because the woman who saved him is also in a coma."

"Woman who saved him?"

"Do you know Sonia Androff?"

Jenny nodded. "She was at my house in Baguio last Christmas. She's a partner of Fisk Banzer. They hired Apollo … Roberto … six miners in all … to search for a goldmine. What happened? Where is Roberto?"

"Octan doesn't know. All we know is that Apollo is in a coma… sealed in a med-chamber … suffering from an unidentified disease … and someone is after him. He needs medical attention immediately. A private security agent from Martian Metals stopped by three days ago asking about the sick diplomat Sonny is supposed to escort to Hong Kong. This was before the package arrived. I called Lydia. She knew nothing about it, but told the agent that type of information would be privileged. Last night Apollo arrived with a John Doe diplomatic identification. The instructions are for Miguel Sonny Ortigas to deliver the patient to Hong Kong Medical University. A coded message from Mars arrived a week ago, but Sonny has not been in his office for a month. I have no idea what it says. Can you pick up Apollo?"

Jenny agreed, ending the call.

She called her husband's Manila office. Lydia, Sonny's office manager, explained in more detail what Bibi said, but could offer no additional insight.

"Apollo is in a medic chamber with instructions to deliver him to Hong Kong University Hospital via Sonny. The routing clearance is to a doctor in Hong Kong, signed by a doctor in Sagan City. It's sealed with an infectious disease classification. I didn't want to accept it. I tried to call Sagan City, but the doctor is missing. Same with the doctor in Hong Kong. It scared me. I'll go with you if you want to claim it."

"I'll be by your office in an hour." Jenny shook her head. "I really need Sonny for this."

Jenny called Octan in Boston at her home. On the comm monitor behind Octan was a younger, athletic male with his shirt off. "Good evening, Jenny. It's been a long time. How's the baby?"

"It's morning in Manila. Baby Teddy is now four years old," Jenny smiled. "You haven't been to Manila for awhile."

"I guess not. I really plan to come again."

"We have a second house... up in Baguio. You're welcome to stay anytime you want." Jenny continued to smile, "Bring your friend."

"I'll keep that in mind," Octan slapped away the young man's hand rustling through her hair. "I assume you called about Apollo?"

Jenny's smile disappeared. "Yes."

"I don't know where Roberto is," Octan was straight faced, "or any of the Filipino crew. I don't know why Apollo is sick, but he is sick... and someone wants to kill him. Private agents were waiting with customs when he was off-loaded at the Spaceport. Once the customs inspector realized that Apollo was being transported as a secret diplomat in medical quarantine isolation, he refused to grant access without a court order. Apollo needs hospital attention immediately, quietly. The trucker who brought Apollo to me said someone wants to kill him to keep him from revealing secrets. That's all I know. He's been in a medic chamber for ten days coming here. He never woke up. There were fluctuations in life signs, but the chamber kept him stabilized."

"What can I do with him?"

"Take him home, hide him, and find a doctor to check him out." Octan accepted a glass of wine from her off-screen friend. "Don't you have a doctor in the family? If I remember …"

"My brother, Kai. He's a doctor at the Tycho Lunar Medical Center. He specializes in infectious diseases."

"Call him."

With the end of the call, Jenny looked at the wall in front of her desk. She reached to the console at her desk, and then the wall once more became a transparent partition. Lee Chang, her sixty-year-old boss, was busy with two customers in the office lobby; pointing out the window of the elevated second floor office to something on the warehouse floor below. She recognized one of the customers, Yugo Danford, a food products expediter, who she knew well. Years earlier, when Jenny was a child prostitute, Danford was a client. He had treated her right, and paid well. Then Lee rescued her from the streets, taking her in as an adopted niece.

Jenny, not her birth name, was originally La Trang, the eight-year-old daughter of a remote Laotian mountain farmer when bandits attacked her family. Her parents were murdered during the intrusion. She and her younger brother Kai were abducted and sold to flesh peddlers in Hanoi. Separated from her brother, La was sent to Manila where her name was changed to Jenny Ho, and she was turned into a child prostitute. A year later a police raid rescued her, and placed her in a Catholic orphanage. The little Laotian girl ran away from the orphanage within six months. With no family to go to, she continued to sell sex on the streets. That is where she first knew Yugo Danford. He introduced her to Lee Chang, an import-export businessman. Lee liked the charming little girl, but was not interested in the sex she was selling. He offered her a job as an office girl. Over a period of time, she charmed Lee into claiming her as a niece, and she helped his business by becoming a business expediter with men who found her exceptional beauty irresistible.

Jenny got to know Sonny Ortigas when he was hired by Martian Media star Terra Antoni to investigate the Manila murder of a Martian Customs agent. Sonny looked into Lee Chang's connection to the murder victim, and reciprocating, Lee sent Jenny to seduce Sonny in an effort find out what he knew. A talented detective, Sonny was prepared for Jenny. He had tracked down what happened to Kai Trang, her long missing brother. In exchange for information about Lee Chang's connection to the murder victim, Sonny told Jenny about her brother. The Hanoi flesh peddlers, who sent Jenny to Manila when she was eight, sent Kai to Manchuria. Kai was rescued there by a Methodist Minister. Sonny set up a meeting between Jenny and Kai, by then a young doctor. The collateral circumstances of all this was that Jenny and Sonny fell in love with each other. He maintained his detective agency, and she continued to work for Lee Chang.

Jenny pushed another button on the console. Lee asked, "Jenny, are you coming in?"

"Lee, I have a problem. I can't tell you now, but I have to pick up a package at the spaceport for Sonny, and take it to Baguio."

Lee stared, saying nothing. He glanced toward the two customers with him. The customers could not hear what she was saying to him. Lee's expression of disappointment was obvious. He was expecting Jenny to take the customers to lunch. She had a way with businessmen. "An old friend of yours is here. He asked if you could join them for lunch."

"I know," Jenny said. She felt guilty asking to leave at the moment, "Tell Yugo I'm still married. Get Letty to go with him. I have to go. I have no choice."

"I'll take care of this. He wanted to talk to you about a shipment to Sonny from Mars." Lee responded, "How long do you need to be out?"

"A few days. I'll call from Baguio." With that, Jenny stared at the screen. Why was Danford asking about a Martian shipment for Sonny at this moment? Something was not right. She called the Saint Anne Children's center in Marvelles to arrange to pick up Teddy from day care. She zipped up her white environmental suit, adjusted the settings to deal with the warm weather, and then headed for the exit.

The Manila Spaceport, on the Bataan Peninsula across the Bay from Manila, is located at the outskirts of Marivelles. Jenny was in no mood to admire the tropical beauty of the rugged, jungle-clad mountains, the deep blue of the South China Sea beyond the rocky cliffs to the west, or the quiet waters of the Manila Bay to the east. After picking up four-year-old Teddy, she went to the Manila Bay beachfront offices of E.M. Transport Company just long enough to pick up Bibi. Together, they headed directly to the E.M. hanger at the Bataan-based spaceport.

Inside the hanger, two blue-tinted eighty-foot anti-grav shuttles were parked, silently waiting for the next mission. The cargo door to one of the spacecraft was open. Near the cargo ramp a half-dozen containers were being unloaded by a swarm of workers, robots, and tugs. Quan Pena, Bibi's transport pilot, was in negotiation with a customs inspector and three Mindoro Fabricators representatives who were there to pick up deliveries.

Quan turned when Inspector Pryne Callahan pointed out Bibi approaching with Jenny and the small boy. "Morning, Bibi!" He greeted her with his usual grin. "Looks like we have everything cleared. All our customers were here on schedule." His eyes shifted from the matronly Bibi to the stunning, sensuous Jenny. "Jenny," He reached around her arm and hugged her with the usual familiarity. "It's been a long time."

Pushing away from his embrace, she patted his cheek. "Behave yourself, Quan." She glanced down at Teddy, then stepped back another pace. "This is my son. I'm here for a package for Sonny."

Quan winked at Teddy, who tightly held to Jenny's hand. Quan then said, "I figured as much. While you're here, I have two containers for Lee... Newton Industries asteric crystals and Rama environmental suits."

"Matt will be by in an hour."

"I'd rather help you with it." He winked. Quan handed his clipboard computer back to the customs inspector, asking him to finish the cargo clearance for Mindoro Fabricators. Jenny, still holding Teddy's hand, followed Bibi and Quan to an eight-foot long medic chamber sitting by itself against a back wall of the hanger. Customs had already signed the release for the chamber.

Jenny lifted her curious son to her hip so that they could both look at the chamber. Through the transparent, sealed cover lay Apollo, who appeared to be sleeping peacefully. Remembering the boy's almost flawless complexion, Jenny was taken aback by the mass of small, dark discolored dots on his face. She sighed, not knowing what to say, where to direct questions. A quick glance at the computer display of life signs were inconsequential to Jenny. She knew nothing of technical displays.

"Mommy, why is Apollo sleeping in that box?"

"I don't know, Teddy." She continued staring into the canopy cover, "He is very sick."

"Poor child," Bibi did understand the display. "Low pulse, low respiration, low temperature. Allergic shock. Intravenous feeding and bladder drainage seems to be working properly. White blood cell count is high. Those brainwave patterns are somewhat erratic."

"You understand all this?" Jenny asked.

"My parents sent me to nursing school. But, I preferred a business office to bedpans."

"I didn't know that," Jenny turned to face Bibi. "Can you come with me to Baguio? I don't know what I'm looking at here."

Bibi took Jenny's arm. "I can't. She waved her arm toward the activity on the hanger floor. I have to settle these accounts, and then get the ship ready for the outbound return to Mars." She looked again at the sleeping Apollo. "Have you decided where you will take him?"

"His family is in a barrio outside Baguio. Sonny and I have another home in Baguio. I'll take him there. I already called my brother. He'll be here in three days."

"You should get him to a hospital," Bibi pointed to the text display on the chamber control panel. "Did you see that message?"

Jenny leaned forward to read: "Patient contaminated with unidentified infection. Maintain sealed isolation. Check chamber for microbe analysis." She straightened up. "What does that mean?"

Bibi pointed directly at the message. "It means that whatever is making Apollo sick is contagious and can't be identified by normal medical computers. He should be in a hospital."

"Until I know who is after him, I can't risk that."

"At least send a copy of the medical record in the chamber's computer to your brother. He will better know what to do when he gets here."

Jenny was frustrated. Medicine was not her area of expertise. "Bibi, I don't know about this stuff. Can you send it for me? You understand."

"Of course," Bibi was sympathetic to Jenny's plight. "I'll do what I can. Quan," Bibi spoke to her pilot, "Fly them to Baguio. Call it a practice flight to Vigan. Do not log who you have onboard."

"No log?" Quan was puzzled. "Why? Who is this patient?"

"Sonny's nephew. Other than that, don't ask. We'll let you know what it was all about when it is over."

Quan stared at his boss for several seconds, turned to look at Jenny with her son, and then down at the medic chamber. He lifted his left arm, spoke into the button phone on his sleeve, "Computer, send a tug to put this medic chamber on the Pelican. Warm the engines. We'll be leaving in…" he looked at Bibi, at the activity around the cargo containers, then back at Bibi.

"I have all the invoice logs," Bibi said, "I'll take care of clearing out the hanger. Go on, now."

"We'll be leaving in twenty minutes."

Teddy, still held by Jenny against her hip, was attentive to the activity around him. "Mommy, are we going on an airplane?"

Jenny carefully looked around, suspicious of everyone else in the hanger. "Yes, Teddy," she whispered.

CHAPTER SIXTEEN

TYCHO CONTACTS

Martian Broadcast Agency
The Weekly Terra Antoni Newton Report
Tycho, Moon

Earth Date	July 21, 2216
Mars Date	C-Mmon 39, 1174

"Do you understand the information from the med-chamber?" Jenny asked. She was irritated with the delay for each portion of her phone call to her brother's office on the Moon. Those delays were unavoidable; communications at the speed of light had a three second round-trip delay between the Earth and Moon. Jenny's brother, Dr. Kai Patterson was a staff doctor with the Tycho Quarantine Center on the Moon.

Kai responded, "According to the diagnostic data from the med-chamber, the patient was placed in the med-chamber on July 11th already in a coma. Notes were added the next day by a Dr. Wayne Follett in Sagan City, Mars; but they are encrypted. I need for Follett to decipher his notes. The diagnostics shows unusual blood chemistry and a virus our computers can't identify. Tell me about the patient?"

"The patient is Sonny's nephew. The chamber arrived from Mars addressed to Sonny, but Sonny is unreachable. The transport pilot warned me that someone with official Martian credentials is stalking the patient. I'm moving him to Baguio. Call me there in an hour."

After another three second delay, he said, "I'll talk to the Director. I'll call you back. By the way, your friend from Mars is here, in Tycho."

"My friend?"

"Terra Newton. She's on the Moon … to report on a Venus Resource Treaty. She's broadcasting at this moment. If the patient has problems with Martian officials, you may want to contact her."

"I'll check the show." Jenny thought about Terra. If there was Mars troubles behind Apollo's coma, Terra would be the best contact. She waved at Bibi. Bibi, holding Teddy's hand, signaled Jenny to move towards the plane. She adjusted her computer to the Martian network. Terra Newton was on the air from the Moon. She adjusted the computer to copy the program for playback later, and then walked back toward Bibi to get her son.

Once Jenny and Teddy were strapped into their seats for liftoff, and Teddy was occupied with his own small computer, she returned her attention to the Martian broadcast.

"Reporting from Tycho Media Conference Center, this is Terra Newton." Terra's image filled the left side of the screen; on the right were video transmissions from a remote robotic probe sitting on the hot, dry surface of Venus, looking across the scorched landscape at the golden flanks of the Mount Rhea volcano. The bright, yellowish haze of the overhead smog diffused the sunlight so there were few sharp shadows. Venus' bleak broiling landscape was hard and lifeless.

"Unmanned probes are in place ready to video the planned first manned Venus landing next week. The pioneers, expected to be the first to walk the surface of Venus, will arrive in local orbit within a few days. Their anti-grav shuttles to Venus will be Martian built by Aster Corporation, specifically designed to operate in the broiling, high pressure atmosphere of Venus."

The images from the fire-view cameras faded, replaced by a picture of the empty conference room at the Tycho Media Center. "And here is where the historic Venus Resources Treaty will be signed next week by the governments of Mars and Earth for a joint exploration of that planet. Government and business leaders invited to this event are not yet on the Moon, but they will be arriving within a few days."

Jenny closed her computer, folded it, put it back in her handbag, and then turned to look out the window at the green hills below. She thought about the first time Sonny introduced them when they attended Terra and Brass Newton's wedding on Mars. That was Jenny's first time to leave Earth. Sonny maintained an informal connection to them over the years. If the problems with Apollo were complicated, and Sonny remained unreachable, Terra would be someone to ask for help.

CHAPTER SEVENTEEN

BAGUIO CITY

Benget Province, Philippines

Earth Date	July 21, 2216
Mars Date	C-Mmon 39, 1174

"Thank you, Bing!" Jenny gave the airport cargo handler a hundred peso bill. Bing Mendoza thanked her for the tip, and then started walking toward the door.

"Teka, teka!" Quan stood at the picture window. He looked out at the canyon below, and the lush green of Camp John Hay Regional Park across the chasm. He turned to Jenny. "This is the first time I've been here. Terrific view." he glanced at Bing, and said, "You want me to stay, or should I head back to Manila?"

She glanced at the medic chamber, positioned on a rolling cart in the middle of the lounge room. "I'll take it from here. Go on home. If anyone asks, you never saw me or Apollo." Her eyes turned toward the stairway leading downstairs. Teddy had disappeared to his own room to look for toys.

"How could I say I never saw you," Quan winked, "Every time I see a pretty flower, I see you in my mind." He nodded as Jenny grimaced at the unsolicited compliment. "Bibi made that clear. We have to cover your movements." He approached the heavy-set Filipino cargo handler on his way to the door. "Bing, if you're in no hurry, I know a great bar down on Session Road … called the Silver Challis. The owner's a friend!"

"Silver Challis?" Bing smiled. "The hospitality girls are expensive, but it's worth it." He smiled at Jenny, "Unless Jenny would like me to stay." His silly grin said that he already knew the answer.

She smiled in return, "Try the Silver Challis!"

"Oh, my darling Jenny," Bing lifted her hand to kiss her fingers, "You're breaking my heart. Alas … I must go." He turned and followed Quan out the door.

Jenny grinned to herself. As a former child prostitute, she wanted to forget about that life. However, the appeal she had for men was still there, even when she did not want it. "I'll see you in Manila."

Once alone in the house with Apollo, she told the house computer to serve a light lunch on the observation deck. Out there she could sit in the open air overlooking the canyon below. She needed to think. How could she explain this to Celia, Roberto's wife? Apollo was supposed to be on Mars with Roberto earning money on a mining expedition. No one knew where he was … or Emilio, Jun, Celso, and Doug. Celia would not understand. She would be angry and frightened. Jenny was frightened, too, but she had years of practice covering her true feelings.

The cusinart robot rolled from the kitchen to the deck, the sliding glass doors opening automatically to allow for the delivery. Jenny followed the squat robot to the deck, accepting a platter with a sandwich, a salad, and a cup of coffee. She felt a breeze fluttering the cut ends of her shoulder length, black hair. Lowering herself into a chair, she stared out at the rugged cliffs of the other side of the canyon. The sky above was covered with light layers of white clouds. The colors of the trees and rocks on the other side of the canyon were muted pastels, lacking brilliance, lacking shadows. "Computer," She said, "Call Celia DeNila in Barrio Maliit na Ulap. I'll talk to her as soon as you have her."

Jenny loved her Baguio vacation home. For their fifth wedding anniversary Sonny bought the house from Ferdinand Cruz, a Philippine Senator. The Senator's teenage daughter had been raped, beaten to death, and thrown in the ocean near a beach resort. The lack of substantial evidence stymied the police investigation, who had other cases to worry about. Senator Cruz hired Sonny. He used his access to government intelligence computer systems to track the killer... a visiting South African businessman. Besides paying Sonny handsomely for his work, the grateful senator sold him the Baguio vacation home for a fraction of its value. It was an immaculate house, of the latest design. The house computer maintained temperate, fragrant, clean air through the entire building. The building had maintenance robots to do cooking, cleaning, and repairs on voice command.

Jenny loved the house. It gave her the sense of value that she had never had before. It was worth far more than any home they could afford at the time. Sonny was not so certain. He did not care for all the technical advances. He came from a poor barrio where the people still built homes from wood and bamboo, much as their ancestors had for centuries. Sonny granted Jenny the ultra-modern house, but contracted a local builder to add an old fashioned wood and bamboo observation lounge over the immense backyard patio deck. It had capiz shell windows with screens that defeated the environmental controls, although those windows could be sealed if climate control was necessary. It had a chandelier of dangling capiz shell disks refracting the illumination from a light source within. At first Jenny feared that mixing the old and new would be an aesthetic disaster, but the Ilocano contractor knew what he was doing. They blended. The observation lounge extension added a feeling of antiquity that had been missing. When they were in Baguio, Sonny loved to sit in the lounge to work with his computers, read mystery stories, play poker with his friends, or sit and stare across the canyon at the thick brush and rugged cliffs. When Jenny wanted to be amorous, Sonny's lounge was the place to snuggle while watching a sunset. This lounge was where Teddy was conceived.

Sitting quietly on the observation deck eating her sandwich, the house was far from her thoughts. Apollo had her concerned, confused, and terrified. She could not even guess why he was in a coma, why someone was after him, where Roberto was, or if Apollo's sickness was a threat to her and Teddy. These were questions Sonny would find answers to quickly if he were with her, but she had no idea when he would be back from Europe. All her questions were questions Celia would ask, questions that Jenny could not answer. Unable to get answers, Celia would be angry.

Celia had not liked Jenny from their first meeting, when Sonny brought her home to Barrio Maliit na Ulap. A Laotian by birth, Jenny was not a natural Filipina. That bothered Celia. Jenny's natural sensuous beauty drew the attention of all the barrio men. That upset Celia, even when Jenny remained unresponsive to all of them. That Jenny had been a child prostitute created a questionable history. Lee Chang, who had rescued Jenny from the streets, and raised her like a niece, was of questionable character. His import business was frequently associated with smuggling operations. In addition, that Sonny did not come much to the home barrio bothered Celia. She blamed Jenny for keeping him away.

Jenny continually tried everything she could to make friends with her sister-in-law. The fact that Sonny and Jenny had two homes, worth more than the entire barrio of Maliit na Ulap created animosity. When Roberto or Apollo spoke glowingly of Jenny's charms, Celia was troubled. Jenny got along fine with Lolo (Grandfather) Raul, with everyone else in the barrio, but there was always something just a little amiss between her and Celia. They talked, they cooperated, but Jenny knew that Celia considered her an outsider.

The thought of having to bring Apollo home to Celia had Jenny tied in knots. There was no telling how Celia would react. If only Sonny were home. He should be the one to deal with this matter.

"Mommy," Teddy came running out on the deck. "Kuma kain ka na? (Are you eating now?)" He was carrying the stuffed puppy she bought for him in Baguio months earlier. It was a toy, hand made by natives of the hills.

He stood on the deck, closely inspecting her salad and sandwich. He squinted, shook his head, and then said, "Hindi, salad." Looking around, his attention focused on the gate to the concrete steps leading down to the lower patio deck. Just beyond the steps was a banana tree growing in the steep hillside. He pointed to a huge bunch of six-inch bananas. "That!"

Jenny grinned. "Sure, Teddy, help yourself. Be careful not to fall down the hill."

"Yes, Mommy." He scampered through the deck gate to the bananas. In a moment, he was walking back with several of the small bananas in one hand, the stuffed puppy under his other arm. He sat at the table, and began eating one of the bananas, offering another to his stuffed puppy.

"Jenny," the computer's soft feminine voice drifted with the wind from obscured, embedded wall sound units. "Celia DeNila is ready to talk to you."

Jenny pushed a button on the side of the deck table. A video screen rose from the center of the table. Celia was smiling. From the familiar pictures on the rataan wall behind her, it was obvious she was sitting in her own living room. Celia said, "Good afternoon, Jenny. I'm surprised that you're in Baguio. I thought you had to work this week?"

"Hello, Celia. Are you busy?"

"Not really. Is Sonny with you?"

Jenny shook her head gently. "He's on a job. Can you come here? It's important."

"I wish I could. My van is in the shop for repairs. What's so important?"

Jenny's stomach was churning. She had to think clearly. "Celia, could you plug in the cipher Sonny gave you? Set it for channel ... four."

Celia stared momentarily. She reached to adjust the communications controls. The image in front of Jenny went to static, and then cleared when she adjusted the cipher setting to channel four. "I'd like to chat, Jenny, but I have a million things to do. What is so important?"

Jenny concluded the only approach was the direct one. "I got called at work this morning. Apollo was brought back from Mars ... in a coma ... sealed in a medic chamber. He was landed secretly. Apparently someone is trying to kill him. I have him with me now."

Celia's expression changed from a polite smile to angry disbelief. For several seconds she did not react at all. Finally she asked, "Is Roberto with him?"

"No one was with him. I sent a message to him, but there was no response. Has he said anything to you?"

"I haven't heard from Roberto for more than two weeks. Where is Sonny?"

"He's in Europe. He does not know yet."

"Has a doctor seen Apollo?"

"The pilot who brought him from Mars told me to keep him hidden. He needs to see a doctor, but whomever is after him would find him if I took him to a regular doctor. I called my brother, Kai. He's a doctor at Tycho. He'll be here the day after tomorrow."

"Can I see him?"

Jenny instructed the comm computer to get an image of the medic chamber. The image on screen showed the chamber in the middle of the lounge floor, as seen from a wall mounted camera. Slowly it zoomed to the sleeping face inside the chamber.

"My god," Celia's voice raised an octave. "What are those dots on his face? What happened to him?"

"I don't know," Jenny responded. "I wish I did. You are his ... stepmother. What should I do? You want me to take him to the Baguio hospital?"

"Not if someone is after him. Can you bring him here?"

"Don't you think my house is better?" Jenny knew she should not have said that as soon as the words were uttered.

"No." The screen image returned to that of Celia. She paused. "Maliit na Ulap is a little more isolated than Baguio. It would be easier to hide him from whoever is after him."

Jenny did not want to risk antagonizing Celia. "I'll bring him as soon as I can."

Barrio Maliit na Ulap (Village of the Little Cloud) was a fifteen mile drive outside of Baguio, on a gravel road off the main highway near Mount Atop. Primarily a village of Ilocano terrace farmers and copper mine workers, the barrio had thirty houses, a general store, and a church. A walk down the unpaved main street of Ulap was like stepping several hundred years back in time. The residents were simple hill people, building homes and lives from local raw materials, as their forefathers always had. Most who had left for the modern cities had found the dirty, meager struggle to survive in a modern city dehumanizing. Some made it, the way Sonny had, but most languished in abject poverty surrounded by poor, embittered neighbors, they were looked down on by the rest of the Filipino society. In the barrio nearly everyone was poor, but they looked out for each other. They shared with their neighbors, and all found a sense of community, of family, of belonging even without the material trappings of the big cities.

By the time that Jenny's van arrived from Baguio, Celia had alerted the rest of the barrio. The families of the men who had gone to Mars with Apollo and Roberto were waiting in the yard of Celia's nipa hut home. A very pregnant Angela Reyes, wife of miner Celso Reyes, was standing on Celia's porch with two of her other children, anxious to hear any news from Mars about her husband. A misty shower was falling through the thin foggy haze, adding a muted dreariness to the homecoming. Some miners who had not gone to work congregated under the front patio overhang of the concrete block general store. All were friends, all were curious about why there had been no messages from Mars, about why Apollo was returning sick and alone. After the van's robot unloaded the medic chamber to the roadway in front of the house, four of the men took charge of Apollo's container, lifting it from the dusty roadway up the steps to the wooden front porch. They then wheeled the chamber into the house.

Nina Perez, and Apollo's fifteen-year-old younger sister Madeline 'Baby', gasped when they saw the rash covered face in the chamber. As Jenny followed, holding Teddy's hand, Nina grabbed her arm. "What happened? Where is Tatay? (father)."

"Tatay?" Jenny puzzled, and then remembered, "Yes, you're Emilio's girl. You were Apollo's girlfriend." Jenny grasped her arm in return, shaking her head. "I wish I knew. All I have is Apollo. I don't know why he is sick … I don't know where Roberto or your father are… I don't know who is after them…" She looked beyond Nina and Baby to Sol, Nina's mother. Sol squinted with serious concern for her missing husband, Emilio Perez. Sol accepted Jenny's response to Nina quietly.

"Teddy! And my lovely Jenny!" Lolo (grandfather) Raul sat forward in his easy chair to hug the little boy. He then got up to hug Jenny. "I'm happy to see you. Is Sonny with you?"

Jenny smiled at her aging father-in-law. "I'm happy to see you, too, Lolo." She shook her head, "No, Sonny is working. He wasn't able to make it this time."

After a few minutes of polite chatter, the old man, with his age induced incomprehension, returned to his easy chair and the video show he had been watching. Everyone else ignored him.

Celia and Ruby Cruz approached the medic chamber to stare through the transparent lid. Celia glanced at Ruby, her closest friend, "I have to believe Roberto sent him home because he is sick. We have not heard from them because they are working on Mars with tourist visas. They are not supposed to be working there. "

To Jenny, that perspective sounded logical. It sounded far more optimistic than she felt. Silently, she prayed that was the situation.

"This fancy box is probably keeping Apollo asleep," Celia began looking for the latching controls. "If we open it, it might wake him up. He can tell us what happened."

"I don't think that is a good idea," Jenny released Teddy, putting a hand on Celia's shoulder. "We don't know why Apollo is sick. The medical report says that it is contagious."

Celia straightened up, turning to her sister-in-law. "You tell me Apollo has been like this for two weeks, in this box; that you can't take him to the hospital. Maybe he needs the air from home. I take care of him when he has flu. I take care of him when he has measles. I take care of him whenever he is not feeling well because he sick with something contagious. I made him better before and no one died." She looked past Jenny at the other barrio people in the room. She turned her focus to the crowded porch beyond the doorway.

"Please, Celia … I'm afraid …"

Celia stared at Jenny, then down at Apollo. She looked up at the ceiling, silently praying to the Virgin Mother. With a hand in motion, she gave the sign of the cross in front of her chest. Then she said, "I open. I take care of Apollo." She twisted the latch controls. There was an audible click, followed by a whirring sound. The transparent cover automatically receded into the side of the chamber.

"Martian air!" Jenny muttered. "That smells like the air from spacesuits of the transport pilots, like the disinfectant the Martians use." She bent forward, "Also the smell of sickness and bad breath."

"If you were in a box that long," Feni Ventuno (the wife of Martian miner Jun Ventuno) said, "Your breath would smell just as bad. We will fix that."

"Aster," Celia spoke to another woman, "Make some broth. We will feed Apollo a little, even if he is not awake."

Nina pushed her way past Apollo's kid sister, through the people crowding around the medic chamber, to get close to Apollo. "Apollo, my poor Apollo," Tears rolled down the girl's cheeks. She reached down to brush away a mosquito from Apollo's arm. She leaned over the chamber, kissed Apollo on his cheek. "Maybe his is like the story of Sleeping Beauty. He needs a kiss from the girl who loves him to wake up."

Apollo did not wake up. He continued to look like a pale, rash-covered, sleeping teenager. More mosquitoes landed on his exposed flesh.

Celia faced Jenny, "When can Sonny come? He is detective. He should find out who wants to hurt Apollo, why he is this way..."

"According to Lydia," Jenny stooped a little to brush a mosquito from her son's neck. "Sonny can not talk to us for a few days. She promises to get him home."

CHAPTER EIGHTEEN

MALIIT NA ULAP

Benget Province, Philippines

Earth Date	July 24, 2216
Mars Date	C-Mmon 42, 1174

MARTIAN VIRUS, DAY 24

"Mommy, my head hurts." Teddy fidgeted in his bed.

Jenny was worried and anxious. She continued to sponge the perspiration from the brow of her young son. The small dark blemishes all over Apollo's skin now appeared on Teddy. She wished she had been more forceful with Celia, had stopped her from opening the lid to the medic chamber. Half the barrio was now infected with whatever it was that put Apollo in a coma. Teddy had it. He was complaining of flu-like symptoms. Looking up to the wall mounted security surveillance monitor, she stared at the pine tree lined residential road winding up near the crest of the hill. The sky overhead was blue, with scattered small puffy clouds. An ambulance abruptly appeared at the crest, and then quietly approached along the road. Pulling to a stop in her driveway, the vehicle door opened automatically. Jenny's brother, Kai Patterson, got out at the entrance to the house. "Computer. Open the front door. Greet Dr .Patterson, and direct him to this room."

"Mommy, will Uncle Kai make me better?"

"I hope so," She continued watching the monitor.

The computer automatically slid the door into the wall for Kai, where he found Jenny seated in front of Teddy's bed. He said, "I'm confused. You told me Sonny's nephew is sick, not his son. What are we dealing with?"

Jenny looked up at her brother. "I did not know what I could tell you. According to the pilot who brought him back from Mars, Apollo is in a coma from an unknown sickness. Someone in position of influence is stalking him, and Apollo needs medical attention, immediately. I do not know who is after him. That is why I contacted you through unorthodox channels. Did Bibi send you the medic chamber report?"

"Unorthodox is right. That report is why Tycho sent me here. What is wrong with Teddy?"

"I think it's the same sickness. Apollo is covered with a lot of these same little dark spots." She pointed to Teddy's face.

"I thought you said Apollo was isolated in a medic chamber? I thought we had it contained."

"He was. Sonny's sister felt the enclosure may have been responsible for keeping him in coma, so she opened it. Now, Teddy is sick. So are a dozen people in the barrio."

Kai shook his head in disbelief. "You should have followed Bibi's suggestion, and moved him to a hospital. Even the Tycho Medical Center computers have no record of a virus like the one Apollo is suffering with." Kai lifted his arm, speaking via his sleeve communicator to a robot medic. "Ula, bring a medical diagnostics unit. The house computer will guide you." Looking to his sister, he asked, "You have Teddy's med stats card updated?"

"You told me to have it ready for Apollo." She pulled a plastic card from the night stand at the head of Teddy's bed. "I figured the same for Teddy. What do you think this is?"

"Give me a chance!" Kai pulled surgical gloves from his pocket. As he put them on, he asked, "You say Apollo has this same rash?"

"According to the pilot, a Sagan City doctor looked at him, who consulted with a friend in Hong Kong. They were unable to figure it out." Jenny used the damp cloth to wipe Teddy's face.

"Uncharted virus…" Kai put his arm on Jenny's shoulder. "If this is contagious … and dangerous … you may want to limit your direct exposure to Teddy."

"Too late, I've been carrying him around the past two days. Since he started feeling ill, I've been hand feeding him." She continued to wipe the perspiration from Teddy's face.

Robot Nurse Ula, manufactured to resemble an attractive female nurse, entered the room carrying a large case. Stopping in front of the doctor, the robot asked, "Which patient am I to test?"

"Both ," Kai responded. "The child first. Here is his medical file." Kai handed the med stat card to Ula. "Teddy contacted an unknown viral infection. Give us the best diagnostic you can get."

As Ula opened the stainless steel case, Kai turned to the young patient, squatting to his level, "Teddy, Nurse Ula needs to know what's wrong with you. Have you done this before?"

He nodded, "Oh-oh (Yes)!"

"I have to ask you to take off all your clothes, and let nurse Ula dress you in a special suit, including a special hat. Is that okay?"

Again, Teddy nodded. He slowly sat up. Jenny began unbuttoning the child's sleep shirt.

"To test what's in your blood, there will be a small sting on your finger. Are you tough enough to take a small sting?"

Once again Teddy answered, "Oh-oh!"

Nurse Ula will need for you to … wee wee into a tube in the outfit she puts on you. Can you do that?"

"I try," Teddy forced a smile.

Ula approached with a medic diagnostic outfit sized for the four year old. Jenny and her brother stepped back to allow the robot enough space to work. Giving a cursory glance to the robot dressing the boy, Kai turned to the open case, reaching down for a diagnostics suit sized for his sister. "Go to your room to change! I should remain with the boy at the moment."

She smiled, accepted the outfit, and then exited into the hallway.

Fifteen minutes later the diagnostic evaluations were complete. Kai had plugged his med computer into the house system so that information could appear on a large wall screen, "Do you understand what we're looking at?" He asked.

"No," she lightly swatted Kai's arm, "And don't make me feel like an idiot because I don't understand."

"Sis, you're being too vain. Let me do what I know," He pointed to the magnified image of an isolated virus on the wall screen. "There's the bug in Teddy's system. Apparently it attaches itself to red blood cells, somewhat like malaria, but it is vastly different. There are no known relatives, so we doubt that it is a transformed virus, or genetically engineered one. The bug is totally new. You did say first contact was on Mars?"

"I don't know anything more. Apollo sent an urgent message to Sonny just before he went in coma. Lydia has it at her office, but it arrived ciphered and coded. I don't know Sonny's coding systems. Lydia did not know this one, either. Sonny's in Europe doing an undercover job for Lloyds of London. He left instructions for no one to contact him until he calls in."

"Well, I doubt that Apollo will know more about this than what I see right here. I'll look at the medic chamber file when we get there. You do not have any hint of the virus. How did Teddy get this? Did he touch Apollo? Get close to his breath? Pick up something of Apollo's?"

Jenny shook her head. "When Celia decided to open the medic chamber, I kept Teddy back. The pilot warned me it might be contagious. I should have insisted. Celia is a barrio woman. She doesn't understand most technical advances."

"We probably would have been the same way if our parents had lived, and we grew up in the Laotian mountains. Don't be too hard on her, "He stood up, "I think we should go to the Barrio and check Apollo."

Jenny slowly rose from her chair, "What about Teddy? He isn't feeling well."

"Bring him. He already has the virus. You do not. I'd like to find out why." Kai looked her sister in the eye. "My director is worried about this virus. I have an emergency quarantine team on call at the Baguio airport. If this is as bad as it seems, I may have to call them in. Do you understand what that means?"

Jenny was not clear, but she caught the drift. "You may have to isolate the barrio ... Apollo ... Teddy ... me! I talked to Bibi yesterday. She told me the same thing. I understand. I don't think the barrio will."

"We may not have a choice." He rubbed a hand across the back of this neck. "Will you help me talk to them?"

She felt acid churning in her stomach. Once more she was going to be the harbinger of very bad news, "On the way out of town," Even though it was seventy-eight degrees outside, Jenny put a sweater on her son. "Let's go to Session Road. I have to bring something to eat."

"Eat?" Kai asked. He then instructed Ula to close up the case and take it to the ambulance.

"Celia blames me for what happened to Apollo ... blames me for Sonny not being here when the family needs him ..."

"Sounds like she is angry because of these troubles ... she doesn't know what to do. You brought Apollo home in a coma, and others are now getting sick. You told them someone is stalking the boy, and you don't know who."

"I understand why she said what she said," Jenny responded. "If I am going to bring in my 'rich, foreign, doctor brother,' I better combine it with a little standard Filipino hospitality." She paused, and then spoke to the wall, "Computer. Call Rollo's Restaurant. Order enough lechon, pancit, adobo, kae-kare, and ... mango ice cream ... to feed fifty people. We need it in twenty minutes. Include picnic plates and utensils."

"Twenty minutes?" Kai's eyes popped wide, and then returned to normal. "You can call a surprise order like that for twenty minutes?"

She laughed, "Probably not. Rollo knows me. He'll call back and let me know what he can provide. I have customers for Chang's come up here once in awhile, and I hire Rollo to cater for me. He'll think of something!"

Ninety minutes later the ambulance rolled to a stop on the dusty driveway in front of Celia's house in Barrio Maliit na Ulap. Rather than the lechon (roast pig), which was not ready, Rollo had just finished baking enough bangus (milkfish) to cater the expected crowd. Otherwise, he furnished Jenny had asked for. She then called ahead to Celia that she was coming with a doctor to check Apollo and everyone in the village, detailing how much food she was bringing. She was thankful that it was a dry, sunny day. It was possible to get the whole barrio over to Celia's yard to eat, to meet with the doctor, to get diagnosed by robot Ula. At the urging of her brother, Jenny wore a full body environmental suit, including domed head covering. He wore the same type of unit as protection. Getting out of the ambulance, Jenny carried Teddy in her arms.

Celia directed the other barrio families to bring tables and chairs, setting them under the scrubby trees in her yard. She directed the men to help unload the food from the back of the ambulance, and then she stepped up on her porch to join Jenny, Teddy, Kai, and robot Ula. Celia was obviously exhausted. She took Jenny by the hand, and said, "I'm sorry for what I said to you yesterday. I no mean to say that. It just that so many are sick from Apollo … I don't know how to help … I know you tell me not to open the chamber … I was foolish!"

Jenny smiled. After letting Teddy down to walk on his own, she patted Celia's hand. "You did what you thought was right, what you've always done when someone was sick. You are tired and frightened. We all are. I'm so scared because Teddy is sick, too."

"I know …"

"How many," Kai asked, "Have the rash?"

Celia and Jenny turned to the doctor. Celia answered, "Twenty … maybe twenty-five!"

"You do not have the rash?"

Celia shook her head. "I do not have it. I don't know why. I clean Apollo, I feed him. Lolo not touch him, but he is sick. Angela Reyes is six months pregnant. She has the rash. We are so worried that it will hurt her baby."

"Show me Apollo, please."

"Of course," Celia led the two of them through the door. She guided them around Lolo (Grandpa) Raul, who was lying on the couch. He was covered with the rash. Baby Madeline, Apollo's fifteen year old sister, with a less intense rash, was on a mattress on the floor. She was moaning lightly. Kai signaled for Ula to test the two. Nina, who seemed healthy, was helping those who were sick. Within moments Ula reported, "Madeline Panahon is suffering the same ailments as Teddy Ortigas. Raul Ortigas is no longer alive."

Everyone came to a stop. All eyes turned to focus on the body of Lolo Raul, lying quiet, cold, and pale. He looked normal, except for the rash.

"No ... no ... no ..." Celia screamed. She stepped to the couch, taking Lolo Raul's wrist to check his pulse. Tears began pouring down her cheeks at the realization that her father was dead. "That can't be. He was talking to me thirty minutes ago."

Robot Ula responded as she had been programmed for this situation. "I'm sorry, Mrs. DeNila ... Raul died of heart failure eighteen minutes ago. It is too early to know if it was caused by the virus."

"Lolo," Jenny squatted to take tighter hold of her son, "This can't be ... Lolo ..."

"What's wrong with Lolo, Mommy?" Teddy stared at tears welling on Jenny's cheeks. He looked at the very still Lolo Raul, who had greeted him so warmly a few days earlier.

Jenny ran a hand through Teddy's hair. She swallowed uncomfortably, and then said, "Teddy, I think Lolo has gone to be with God. We will say a prayer for him."

"But, he is still here. We can just wake him up!" Teddy had a very sad face, amplified by the rash, sweating, and drooping eyelids.

"I wish we could," Jenny picked up her son, standing to face her brother with a look of desperation, a silent plea to keep the virus from killing more, from killing Teddy.

Kai felt helpless. Everyone in the barrio was looking to him for professional help, and he had no idea yet of what he was dealing with. Now that Jenny's father-in-law was dead, three days after exposure to the virus, the urgency had just become acute. He crossed the room to the medic chamber under the open window. Apollo was still unconscious in the chamber with the lid open. A mosquito net was draped over it. A small table had been placed in front of the chamber, to display a Catholic religious statue of "Santo Nino", decked in an ornate, intricately gold embroidered robe and red cap. Father Salvador Roxas was rising from his kneeling prayer before the table, still chanting Latin prayers to Saint Jude. He excused himself. Giving last rites to Lolo Raul was the urgent task for him to attend to at the moment.

Kai ignored the priest. "Celia, why the mosquito net? You should have closed the chamber lid."

"I think the boy needs real air. Mosquitoes were all over him. They like him. I don't understand. They don't bother him before. They don't bother me."

"Kai looked around at Lolo and Baby, at Celia and Jenny. "The mosquitoes are transmitting the virus."

"Mosquitoes?" Jenny asked. She thought back three days to when Celia opened the chamber lid. She remembered brushing a mosquito from Teddy's neck.

Kai lifted the netting to get closer to the chamber. He studied the shipping instructions, sent by Dr. Wayne Follett of Sagan City, Mars to Dr. Lin Chow of Hong Kong University Medical Center, care of Miguel Ortigas via Manila Spaceport., the same coded notes Jenny sent days ago. The medical statistics update showed the same virus identified on the file transmitted to him on the Moon, the same virus he found in Teddy's blood. Blood sugar, glandular secretions, neural activity were still off. Unusual strains of Feldermite hormones were coming from the pituitary gland, chemical anomalies that concentrated in the hypothalamus. From the medic chamber computer files, he noticed that thinking skills had been flatline for two weeks, except for several episodes of dream enhancements. He connected his sleeve's computer link to the chamber's jack to download what information there was.

Kai stepped back from the netting. The priest began chanting prayers for the soul of Raul. Father Roxas had a few rash spots appearing on his own face. Kai directed Ula to diagnose everyone in the barrio. He had Jenny follow him to the front porch. Celia was close behind.

"Can you help Apollo?" Celia pleaded.

"I think I understand what's happening. The virus has closed certain neural pathways in the brain. That's probably what triggered your father's heart failure. I think I might be able to revive Apollo at Tycho. As to this virus, this is new. We need lab experimentation to break it down."

Jenny breathed a sigh of relief. "He'll be all right, then?"

Kai shook his head. "I can't say that." He keyed on Celia. "Mrs. DeNila, do you understand what we are dealing with? These are your relatives ... your friends ... your town."

Celia's weathered cheeks were still damp from tears. She swallowed before responding. "My father is dead. Apollo is sick ... like malaria or typhoid ... everyone else is getting the same sickness ... the men Apollo went to Mars with are missing," She looked over her shoulder through the window into the house, then back to the doctor. "Mosquitoes have spread it?"

"That's right." He picked his words carefully. "But, Apollo got this virus on Mars. Mars has no mosquitoes ... he caught it in some other way. You have been treating Apollo, and Jenny has been treating Teddy, and neither of you have it. ... this brings up questions I have no answers to. However, we do have the makings of a dangerous epidemic." Kai looked at the street beyond the porch. Ula had collected medical stats from everyone in the yard. "This is a brand new disease. I have no idea how bad it will get. It has similarities ... to a dozen types of sickness, but is like none of them. How many are sick in their homes, not able to come?"

Celia looked across her front yard, quietly checking the people eating against her mental roster of who lives in town. "There are eight not here. Four are small children."

"Could you take Robot Ula to them? I need to get med stats from everyone."

"Yes, doctor." Celia was very respectful, more so than Jenny expected. As soon as Celia went down the steps to lead the robot to the correct homes, Jenny asked her brother. "What do you plan to do?"

"The shipping documents give the names of a Martian doctor who shipped Apollo as a diplomatic John Doe, and a Hong Kong doctor who agreed to receive him. I plan to contact those two first."

"I tried yesterday. Lydia called from Manila. Dr. Follett in Sagan City is missing. Doctor Chow in Hong Kong knows nothing, except that Dr. Follett asked him to requisition Apollo as a sensitive diplomatic coma case. He told Lydia that Dr. Follett promised a transmission with greater detail, but that transmission never arrived. Apparently, a security agent from Interplanetary Metals Corporation visited Lydia after I brought Apollo to Baguio. They are looking for Apollo and a woman who was with him ... Sonia Androff. Supposedly, both are wanted by the police on a classified warrant."

"Classified?" Kai looked up, watching Celia lead Ula into the white painted concrete general store half a block away. He looked back through the window at the chamber where Apollo remained in coma, at the priest who was still begging the Lord for guidance. "Why would corporate security guards ask about a classified warrant suspect, rather than the police?" He noticed that Celia was returning without Ula.

Jenny shook her head. "I don't know. Until Sonny is available to look into it, I don't think we will know. All I know is Octan Palmer warned that someone is stalking Apollo, and that we have to keep him hidden." Jenny took Kai by the arm. "What are we going to do?"

Celia walked up the stairs, "Doctor, little Dolphi is getting sick all over the floor."

He nodded acknowledgement to Celia, then answered his sister, "I have no choice. I have to quarantine this barrio."

"Quarantine?" Celia was surprised. "We can't be closed off. If the men no work at the mine, they all get fired. If others don't go to the rice field, we have no food."

"Kai," Jenny added her own concern, "If someone is after Apollo, this will make it easy for them to find him."

Kai accepted a cup of fruit juice from a young boy coming up the stairs with a tray of drinks. "Even if the only danger of transmission is via mosquitoes, this could spread world-wide in a short time. Apollo is in a coma. Raul is dead. This may happen to all of you if we don't deal with it quickly. Please help me before it gets beyond Ulap."

Neither woman liked hearing what he had to say, but both knew he was right. "What do you want us to do?" Jenny asked.

"Celia, this is your town. Will they all stay if you ask them to? If you tell them it is important not to let this sickness go any further than Ulap?"

"Everyone has a family member who is sick. They suspect that is like typhoid, and that they can't go to see others. I'll tell them. They will stay." She paused to breath softly, and then asked, "Will you help feed us until this is over? We no have enough food for very long."

Kai was surprised by the question. He laughed lightly. "You'll be taken care of, I promise. If I have to do it myself, you won't go hungry." He patted Celia's shoulder. "Has anyone left town since this started? Did anyone go to work, or to Baguio?"

Celia thought a moment, "You know about Jenny. Art Cordero and Boni Sunga went to work in the mines. Lotty Hernandez sells at the Baguio market. She went there. Everyone else stayed to work in the rice fields." Celia pointed to the stepped rice terraces down the hill. "There were no visitors. Everyone else stayed home because they are sick."

"I have to call this in. I'll try to keep it as quiet as I can. We don't want any news media involved until we can contain the spread of the virus." He walked down the steps with Jenny to his ambulance.

Jenny watched over his shoulder as he seated himself at the comm unit behind the driver's seat. "Control, this is Dr. Kai Patterson, Tycho Medical Center. Direct this message to Director Rochelle Bond … Rochelle; I have a code six-six virus alert at the Philippine Barrio Maliit na Ulap, in the Benget Mountains. Isolation of the victim has been compromised. There are now over two dozen patients. Early symptoms compare to combination dermatology allergic reaction, influenza ailments to respiratory, digestive, and cardiovascular systems. Unusual glandular inflammation, particularly the pituitary. Neural system becomes erratic. Initial patient has been in coma for more than two weeks, enclosed in a Mars originated medic chamber. Doctor on Mars who shipped John Doe to Philippines is missing. No data file available on the source of the virus. Apparently comes from Mars via John Doe in coma. Observable transmission appears to be via mosquito. John Doe needs protective security … is being stalked by unidentified trackers. We need to quarantine this barrio immediately. Three residents are in public. We need isolation for fifty residents for a code six-six. We need to avoid public attention. Attached are files for entire village."

CHAPTER NINETEEN

QUARANTINE

Tycho Medical Center, Moon

Earth Date	July 25, 2216
Mars Date	C-Mmon 43, 1174

MARTIAN VIRUS, DAY 25

The first of the United Nations health emergency hovercraft appeared on the main street of Maliit na Ulap following sunrise. Six officials disembarked from the twenty-third century version of a limousine helicopter. All were sealed in hazardous duty environmental suits, complete with backpack air purifiers and gold-tinted faceplates. All six gathered in the middle of the road for consultation with Doctor Patterson. Their anonymous, uniform, non-human appearance made their presence all the more ominous to the town's people. Some of the Filipinos whispered of efforts to leave for the hills before it was too late. Five minutes after the V.I.P. landing a squadron of thirty white hovercrafts quietly drifted into position just above the tree line in a half-mile radius, circling Ulap. A dozen pressure suited agents, all sealed in the same frightening outfits that obscured their features, disembarked from each hovercraft, forming a closed human barrier around the entire barrio. Some of the women began to cry. Men were cursing in their native Ilocano tongue.

"What are you doing?" Celia approached Doctor Patterson. "Everyone is frightened."

"This is normal quarantine procedure for a deadly contaminant … we have to isolate Apollo's virus." His full white environmental suit still covered his whole being. He reached to take her hand for comforting. "Tell everyone to gather their personal effects … clothing, photo albums, and family heirlooms. Do not bring plants or food or …"

"Why?" Jenny asked, "What are you about to do?" Jenny, unlike the barrio natives, was sealed inside an environmental suit similar to what her brother was wearing.

"If mosquitoes are spreading the virus," Kai responded, it could be in any water source … on any pig or chicken…"

"What?" Celia looked horrified. The rest of the barrio was beyond earshot, but all watched her discussion intensely, "You're going to burn our barrio? We have been here for two hundred years."

"Homes and gardens can be rebuilt. Take a look at Apollo. He is barely alive. Your father is dead. The rest of you will probably be like Apollo within a few days, maybe worse. We have to prevent this from going further."

Celia looked around. Sitting on the porch of the next house, Bobbit and Faye Quintos were oblivious. They were too old to understand the problem. The others, not yet sick, were congregated in her yard, or at the entrance to the General Store. They waited for information from her. All appeared terrified.

"Are you going to destroy Jenny's house in Baguio, too? She took Teddy home after they got sick."

Jenny was thunderstruck. That special house, the home that she and Sonny hoped to retire to… was she going to lose it?

"I know," Kai looked down at the ground rather than into his sister's eyes. "Right now it is beyond my control. I can petition to have it sprayed, sealed, and observed … I can't promise."

"Can't promise?" Jenny pushed at his shoulder, "That's my home. This is Celia's home. That means everything to them. Have them spray here first. What about Rollo's restaurant? We stopped there yesterday to buy food. Are you going to…"

Doctor Patterson lifted his sleeve. "Captain, there will be no burning. Use the spray, the defoliant, and the x-ray burst … do not damage the facilities. I assume responsibility." He looked up at one of the anonymous white environmental suits.

The outfitted health official gave thumbs up. "On your authority, we will do decontamination only."

Celia and Jenny both smiled, having won a small concession in the face of eminent disaster.

"The medical space transport will arrive in fifteen minutes," Doctor Patterson said, "Gather what you can. There are only fifty of you. The shuttle can carry two-hundred, so you can bring extra suitcases."

"Where are you taking us?" Celia asked.

"Tycho Medical Center. We have the best isolation facilities anywhere."

"The Moon?" Jenny questioned. "I have not talked to Sonny. He is still on a case in Europe."

"I know," Kai responded. "I need to talk to Sonny, too. He has to decode that message from Mars … that would give us a hint where this virus came from."

"I've never even been in an airplane," Celia said as she walked with Jenny up the gangplank into the United Nations Medical Emergency anti-grav shuttle parked in front of her house. "I really do not want to do this now." She looked back at the stack of her suitcases filled with clothes and heirlooms from her house. These travel bags were among the many deposited by the rest of the barrio.

Sometimes, governments are capable of moving efficiently during times of crisis. Jenny Ortigas observed in amazement that her brother accomplished just such an action. She had nothing to pack, as she had come to Maliit na Ulap with her brother, bringing only the sealed environmental suit she was wearing, and her son. While the rest of the barrio's citizens were being fitted with medical environmental suits, she called her house computer to seal up, and to set internal environmental controls to sterilize all air. She called Lydia, Sonny's office manager, to explain the situation, pleading for her to get hold of him as soon as possible. Finally, she called Lee Chang, her boss, with the disquieting news. He was disturbed, but was in no position to do anything at all.

The one-hundred foot tall anti-grav shuttle, encased with a ceramic coating, had no windows beyond the cockpit. However, the quarantined Ulap citizens had good external video views on screens around the passenger compartment. A prerecorded message explained the strange sensations created with an anti-grav liftoff, but it still came as a surprise to most passengers. Once the anti-grav drive was powered, the passengers felt the abrupt reversal of the gravitational field, from being pulled toward the Earth to being repelled towards the sky. The individual passenger seats rotated to create the proper body alignments simultaneous with the craft lifting from the streets of Ulap. The images of the town, the rugged hills, the terraced rice fields, and the green carpet of vegetation as individual objects shrank with increasing altitude. Within moments the craft was above the scattered white clouds, heading for space.

The majority of the people of Maliit na Ulap had never been airborne in their lives, only having made rare road trips to Baguio or Manila or the beach. For Celia, the experience of leaving the earth was an exhilarating, but frightening adventure. The uniqueness was exciting, even if it was for tragic reasons and taking them into an uncertain future. Some of the passengers were excited, watching all the beauty displayed on the video screens as they soared so high that the Earth below became but a big blue and white ball. Others curled up with inward terror at having lost control of everything, at being thrust into these alien space environs. The remainder were too sick to be much aware of what they were going through, drifting in and out of sleep, feeling flu-like discomforts.

The shuttle flew past the orbiting Pacific Blue Space Station, a space base positioned in a synchronized stationary orbit twenty-two thousand miles above the International Dateline. All other vehicles leaving the Earth were required to get inspections before proceeding, but the U.N. Medical Shuttle had authorization to bypass exit inspections. Using the mix of anti-grav and fusion drives, the spacecraft accelerated on out-of-orbit for its six-hour flight to the moon. Behind were the swirling white clouds accenting the receding deep blue globe of home, ahead was the golden cratered terrain of the waterless, airless moon.

Jenny, still in her full environmental suit with face plate, remained close to Teddy. He slept through the entire launch. His medical stats seemed stable, although his temperature was high, blood pressure low, and neural activity chaotic. She prayed for Sonny to hurry with whatever it was he was doing in Europe. She hoped that by praying intently, he would sense they needed him. Kai and robot Ula were slowly making the rounds to everyone, double checking medical stats for each passenger, too busy to pay attention to family matters. Fifteen-year-old Baby Madeline was alert, but obviously uncomfortable. Even with the medical suit giving her prescribed medications, she was shaking, sweating, and pale. Celia watched both Madeline and the barrio priest, Father Salvador Roxas. The priest slept most of the way, waking occasionally for a sprint to the bathroom to throw up. Celia's aging neighbors, Bobbit and Fay Quintos showing symptoms of the virus, were quietly watching video images from the exterior cameras. In the cubicle beside Jenny, three of the village miners had switched their video screen from the view outside to a commercial news broadcast. Jenny paid little attention until a familiar face appeared, Martian media journalist Terra Newton. The screen image showed Terra at a discussion table with two unfamiliar men. A map of the surface of Venus was electronically displayed behind them. Checking the channel on the image, she switched her own monitor to the same show.

One of the men, Professor Rhet McIntosh, a seventy-year old astro-climatologist from Oxford, talked about Venus, "... the conditions on the surface have been just too extreme for man and his machines. At nine-hundred degrees Fahrenheit, with a carbon-dioxide atmosphere a hundred times denser than Earth's air and with corrosive sulfuric acid clouds at altitudes where the temperatures and pressures were more tolerable, Venus has always been too inhospitable for man to survive, for man-made machines to operate. For two hundred years we have been developing colonies on the Moon, Mars, Mercury, and the satellites of the gas giants. We presently have a manned expedition on its way to a planet circling a star twelve light years away. But,

Kevin F. Owens

Venus, the planet closest to Earth... just slightly smaller than Earth ... man has never set foot on the surface... because the temperatures, pressures, and acids made it impractical... until now."

"Professor McIntosh, could you tell us," Terra was obviously directing a previously rehearsed line of questioning, "How the Venus Resource Treaty will change that?"

"The anti-grav technology makes access possible. The anti-gravity phenomenon is created by passing electrical current through asteric crystals at cryogenic temperatures ... near absolute zero. This allows the spacecraft to land and takeoff, carrying massive loads, without rockets, without jets, without external moving parts. Until now, shuttling between the planet's surface and orbital space needed rocket fuels that are uncontrollable in the Venus atmosphere. Anti-gravity does not expose fuels to those conditions, does not depend on exhaust thrust, but on magnet-like gravitational repulsion. We can land and takeoff. Using habitats and vehicles air conditioned to operate on the surface of Venus, we can be there."

"Have you tried it?"

"The cooling systems have been tested in blast furnaces. They work for extreme temperatures far higher than those on Venus." The video display behind the panel of speakers showed a moving image from a robotic surface explorer. It was following an identical automated vehicle driving along the base of a Venus volcano. "These images are live from Venus. The two robot vehicles have been exploring the surface for forty days now, with no ill affects. In a few days, a manned anti-grav shuttle will land and retrieve the vehicles, including ore samples these vehicles have collected."

Kai Patterson seated himself next to his sister. After a quick glance at the Teddy's medical stats, he looked up at the screen. "I didn't realize your were interested in Venus. You surprise me."

Turning her attention from the screen, she gently rolled her head left and right, "Generally, I'm not, but Terra Newton interests me." Jenny turned the volume down.

"Her?" Kai looked up at the woman on screen. Martian commentator Terra Newton, at forty years old, looked ten years younger.

158

"Sonny worked for her several years ago," Jenny explained, "Terra might be the person to ask to help locate the Filipino miners who disappeared."

"Sonny knows Terra?" Kai rubbed his chin. "Does she know you?"

"I went to her wedding, because Sonny was invited. "

Kai ordered robot Ula to bring coffee. With a continuing half-gee anti-grav field, the passengers avoided the disorienting discomfort of extended zero gravity common to other forms of space travel. It also meant that his liquid coffee stayed at the bottom of his cup. "If we remain viral free at the Moon, maybe you can contact her for help."

"I'm not leaving Teddy, virus or no."

"I understand," Kai sipped his coffee once more. "But, this virus comes from Mars. We don't know its origin, how Apollo got infected, or who else is contaminated. If security agents from Interplanetary Metals Corporation are stalking Apollo, then we don't know who to trust on Mars. I'm willing to bet that Terra Newton is not involved. She lives for exciting stories, and what is more exciting than this? If Sonny helped her once, maybe she could be persuaded to help him… to help save his son."

"Good argument," Jenny accepted the coffee. "If I can be free of the quarantine … if I can come back in to care for Teddy… if Lydia is unable to get Sonny's attention. I'll try to talk to her."

"Please. It may save Teddy's life. He's not getting better."

Pondering briefly, she asked, "What about Apollo? Any change?"

"As a matter of fact, mental activities have picked up, especially in the dream centers and the hypothalamus."

"Dream centers? I wonder what someone in coma for several weeks dreams about?"

"I've arranged to find out," He put his coffee down. "We have C.N.A. Units at Tycho. The team is bringing the equipment tomorrow morning."

"Tomorrow? How do you know what day it is on the Moon?"

"We synchronize Lunar activities to New York … area lighting, work hours …"

After a pause, Jenny asked, "What is C.N.A.?"

"Cerebral Neural Activity, a brainwave analysis machine. Once calibrated to an individual's mental functions, it can create a video image of what the brain is visualizing.

"Really?"

"If Apollo is dreaming, we'll be able to see what he is dreaming about. We might get a clue where this virus came from."

"Can we watch?" Jenny motioned with her hand to others in the room, "Celia has been foster mother to Apollo since his parents died. Roberto, her husband was on Mars with Apollo. So was Emilio Perez, Nina's father. They are missing. Maybe this C.N.A. Unit can let us know what happened to them."

Kai pondered the matter before answering, "The neural activity in Apollo's brain comes from the hypothalamus and the dream center. Dreams are not conscious thoughts. They may be nightmares. They may be sexual fantasies. Do you want Celia and Nina to see that unedited?"

"I see your point," Jenny continued relaxing in her seat. She glanced at her son, then returned her attention to her brother. "I'd like to be there. I can deal with teenage fantasies. I'd like to see how it works."

A flashing signal on Kai's sleeve attracted his attention. It was a communication from his robotic nurse. "Doctor Patterson," Ula said, "Patient Angela Reyes needs attention."

Doctor Patterson was moving when he asked, "What's the problem?"

"Angela Reyes is going into premature labor. According to the med stats, the fetus has lost life signs."

"Oh, my God," Jenny got up.

Angela Reyes was screaming in pain, with Celia DeNila trying to open the crotch to Angela's medical control outfit. Nina Perez was on the other side holding Angela's hand.

"Let me through," Doctor Patterson pushed past three on-looking passengers. "She needs my help."

The Tycho Medical Center Quarantine Facility had a spacecraft landing area separate from the rest of the Tycho Metropolitan area. Passengers and cargo could be transported in total isolation. After the shuttle landed at the special pad, a spaceport tug was brought out on the tarmac to tow the spacecraft through the multiple airlock doors to a huge bay pressurized hanger. A telescoping access tube reached out from a second floor lobby to the spacecraft's passenger door, allowing the citizens from Maliit na Ulap to disembark. Pressure suited agents directed the patients through the isolation lobby, along another access tube, into a waiting lunar bus.

The Facility, constructed back in 2075, only a few years after a permanent manned presence had been established on the Moon, was one of the longest lasting profitable facilities on the Moon. Built as a combination government base and private enterprise settlement; the designers saw great potential for a lunar medical facility. The one-sixth gravity of the Moon automatically reduced the gravitational pull on two hundred pound adults to thirty three pounds, making it perfect for patients with bone, obesity, paralysis, or elderly ailments. The lack of an outside atmosphere made it possible to isolate patients with contagious diseases. Infectious bacteria could not inadvertently escape into the atmosphere, as there was no atmosphere, and the intense, unfiltered solar radiation was useful in sterilizing circulating air within the compounds.

Jenny was once again feeling the strange sensation of weight at one-sixth what she was used to. Instead of her one-hundred and ten Earth pounds, on the Moon she weighed eighteen. There was considerable bounce to each step, but not as much as the children, who were experiencing Lunar gravity for the first time. Just walking through the corridors was as much fun for them as being on an endless trampoline. At least some were finding a lighter side to the viral infection.

The ride in the lunar bus took ten minutes to reach the rim of the Tycho crater. Uninfected and only mildly suffering Filipinos enjoyed the view out the window of golden rocks, the view of a big blue and white half globe hanging in the black star studded northern sky. Family members embraced each other, not certain whether to enjoy the excitement of a new adventure, or dread the unknown terrors that may be waiting them. Father Salvador Roxas, who had been quiet for the trip, began reciting a prayer; his rash had gotten much worse. Half of the alert passengers picked up on the religious chants. Taking out their rosary beads, they began praying along with their priest.

Except for a recreation observation dome and the air purification arrays, the quarantine facility was built entirely underground. This was typical of off-Earth metropolitan planning to maintain even temperatures, pressures, and protection within the facility. Moved into isolation compound 'Delta', all families were assigned quarters sized for the number of guests. They were treated to a community first 'Chinese' meal in the dining room, where a staff dietician asked those who understood their culinary needs to help program the galley computers to prepare foods they normally ate. Other staff workers helped the guests sort through the luggage they brought so that they could cart them to their individual quarters.

The only luggage Jenny brought was the stuffed puppy Teddy took everywhere. She regretted that she had not been allowed to go home for her own clothes and cosmetics. A staff worker brought her to a computer tailor, suggesting that she fit herself with whatever outfits she needed to feel at home. Stripping to her underwear, she stepped inside for the machine to create a laser grid pattern of her body. A few hours later she had dresses, environmental suits, and casual outfits custom-made for her. Finally, she returned to Teddy, finding him sitting up with his stuffed puppy, watching a video show. She picked him up. His forty-two Earth pounds had been cut to seven pounds on the Moon. She carried him through the halls, and up the stairs to the observation deck. There, among the planters filled with blooming marigolds, she settled on to a park bench. Pointing to the brilliant half-Earth in the northern sky, she explained that was where they came from, where home was.

"Is that where daddy is?" He asked.

"Yes, Teddy," She carefully studied the rash on his face. There was little change, although he did seem to be feeling better. "Daddy's still on Earth. I hope he comes soon."

CHAPTER TWENTY

DREAMWORLD

Tycho Medical Center, Moon

Earth Date	July 28, 2216
Mars Date	C-Mmon 46, 1174

MARTIAN VIRUS, DAY 28.

Still asleep, Apollo lay in a large containment bed, sealed in an intensive care isolation room. A massive number of the sensor attachments covered his new medical control suit. His football-helmet-like ceramic C.N.A. (Cerebral Neural Activity) Unit scanned his brain's neural signals. Kai, Jenny, and Teddy (Teddy now in a sealed medic chamber) watched from a quarantine isolation observation booth. Beside that was an outside visitor's booth, where Director Rochelle Bond watched the C.N.A. Unit Control Room. A bank of monitor screens under the windows of each of the four rooms displayed images the C.N.A. was getting from the helmet.

Rochelle turned from the control staff, to stare at Apollo, peacefully sleeping. Returning to her seat, she adjusted her comm controls. Then she spoke to Jenny. "Mrs. Ortigas, I'm so sorry for you and your people. I sincerely hope we find a way to check this virus quickly."

"Thank you. Please, call me Jenny."

"Jenny. Kai told me about you, about your husband. I hope he can help us soon."

"So do I." Jenny accepted some colorful low-gee lunar pastries from a robotic domestic.

"Doctor Patterson," Rochelle said, "Have you seen our preliminary results yet?"

"Two hundred Petri dishes and a hundred lab animals have shown that this virus does not react to most antibiotics, or to most human temperatures. It is unstable in dry, open air, but as long as it is attached to moisture it survives. It can be transmitted by sweaty contact, but not through the air. I hope we don't have to destroy the barrio. You have me isolated with the rest of the quarantine. Is there something I should know?"

"This is different from any virus we've ever seen. This is a new one. Let's name it after the first victim… Panahon."

"What else can you tell me?"

"Apollo had a full spread of inoculations before he left for Mars, and those did not protect him. We've infected a test segment of lab animals with the virus, but those tests will take time. I don't think we have a lot of time. Every lab rat we infected with the virus is dead within an hour. Same with white rabbits. We have brown rabbits from Australia that seem to be immune."

"Australian rabbits? What's the difference?"

"We don't know. It may be glandular differences."

"Glandular?"

"Everyone from Ulap is under close medical surveillance. A major difference between those infected and those free of the virus are the glandular secretions, especially from the pituitary."

Kai accepted a cup of coffee from the robotic galley unit. "The Feldermite hormone … I saw that in Apollo's readings … levels do seem extreme."

"Extreme?" Rochelle laughed, "That's such a rare hormone that we've never been able to get a large enough sample to run tests with it."

Kai spoke to his sister to clarify what was being discussed. "Jenny, this particular Feldermite hormone is a secretion from the pituitary during times of extreme stress, usually brought on by an adrenaline rush combined with mental anguish … someone dying from trauma. But, the levels of this hormone even then are miniscule. It wasn't even discovered until the year 2112."

"This 'hormone' is in Apollo?"

"Apollo. Teddy. Angela. Lolo Raul … everyone infected. And in large quantities."

"What does it do? Is it the body's defense against the virus?"

Rochelle responded, "It seems more likely that the virus altered the chemistry of the pituitary, and triggered the pituitary into producing the hormone in volume. The Feldermite is affecting neural activity."

"Is that the reason Apollo is in a coma?" Kai asked.

"We think so." Rochelle answered, "The autopsy of the old man gives some clues. I think we may be able to come up with a vaccine to help. I have all the Medical Center research computers working only on this virus. We'll know in a few days."

"A few days?" Jenny looked through the transparent cover over her young son, then up at Rochelle. "I may not have a few days."

"Jenny, consider yourself lucky that you called your brother," Rochelle responded, "that he brought you here. We have the authority to do experimental testing that no other medical facility can do … since this is a special treatment."

"What does that mean?"

"It means we will be looking for volunteers for anything that looks promising with lab animals."

"Lab animals? This is my son … everyone else is from Sonny's barrio!"

A voice from the intercom interrupted the discussion. "Director, we're ready to start."

She held up a thumb for those in the control room to see.

The images on the screens below the windows began changing to different forms of static.

Jenny studied the images, and then asked, "What can you tell me about these images? Most the monitors have nothing on them."

"The monitor with the clear image of the room ceiling is obvious," Rochelle remarked. "The nameplate reads 'helmet camera view." The next two blank screens 'optic nerve view' and 'visual cortex' have been calibrated to what Apollo's eyes see at the moment, which is actually nothing. His eyes are closed, and the neural activity is negligible. Those screens filled with static are what we are trying to calibrate now, the dream center and the subconscious memories. That is where he has considerable advanced neural activity. The hypothalamus is not known for sensory imaging, but it also shows intense neural activity."

"If we can calibrate," Kai continued his explanations, "we will be able recreate the visual images of his dreams. We could then use that center to reach into subconscious memories. That is how we will be able get Apollo's memories of what happened on Mars."

The dream center monitors suddenly switched from static to a clear, unfamiliar image.

"We're in." Rochelle sat up straight in her chair. "What are those extracts about?"

The image was a visual recreation from a man standing in a doorway, looking out across a manicured yard at a street scene under a darkened sky. Fire flickered from a metal bowl on a post near the front of the walk. Two wheeled carts, drawn by oriental men dressed in robes, with broad, straw hats, were rushing down the street, hurrying to unknown locations. A cherry tree in the front yard displayed a full spread of green leaves. The view changed like a video image, as if Apollo were walking out along the stepping stones of the lawn's walkway. The scene turned, as if Apollo were bidding farewell to several silk-robe dressed Orientals coming out the door. The four Asian men and two women each bowed in a rehearsed politeness. The monitor zoomed slowly to the face of the prettiest of the young women, then back to her slender, silk robed figure. They were obviously talking, but there was no sound.

"Beautiful view," Rochelle said. "Too bad they haven't calibrated the audio yet." She paused before continuing to talk, "Is this what Apollo's barrio is like? Nothing on Mars looks like that!"

"That is not the barrio," Jenny commented. "There is nothing in the Philippines like that, with human drawn carts."

"Rickshaws!" Kai said. "Those are Chinese or Japanese rickshaws. They haven't been used since… the early twentieth century. The bowing, the robes… they're nineteenth century Japan."

"Are you certain?" Rochelle asked.

"I minored in Asian history in college. I'm certain."

"Why would he be dreaming about ancient Japan?" Rochelle asked.

"Who knows?" Kai answered, "Maybe he saw a video about shoguns. Maybe he studied it in school. Try to understand your own dreams."

"Will we be able to get to the memories?" Jenny asked.

"Hopefully," Kai said, "That takes longer, especially if they are not active. Right now, control is trying to bring in the audio."

The image shifted, as if from the camera held by someone walking through an ancient Japanese house. Walls were made of rice paper. Servants walked barefoot on floors covered with straw mats. The view proceeded through the house, through another sliding door to a walled-in rear garden. A plum tree was growing in one corner of the garden, beside a rock encrusted pond. At the other side of the garden was a wooden gazebo deck, where a bearded European was peering through a brass refracting telescope. The man, wearing a black jacket with long tails, stepped back from the telescope, put his silk top hat on, and began talking to Apollo. Apollo's view moved forward, past the bearded guest, up to the telescope. Looking through the lens, the circular dark sky suddenly focused on a small bright orange ball with a white cap.

Everyone in the booth recognized the image – Mars, as seen from Earth's surface through a small telescope. The image seemed to enlarge, showing the contrast between the rust-colored deserts contrasting the darker triangular region of Syrtis Major. Then lines started appearing on the Martian world; faint, barely visible thread-like lines. Then the lines disappeared. The image through the lens disappeared, changing once again to the bearded European. The dream view showed Apollo's hand pointing to the sky, to the reddish star above the horizon. It was not Apollo's hand, but that of an older Caucasian wearing a ruffled silk cuff.

"...look closely," the unfamiliar, antiquated English audio began blaring from the C.N.A. speakers, "There are lines, just as the Italian observed..."

"Your eyes are better than mine," the bearded European responded. "I see nothing. Only the reddish deserts, the darker patches, and the white polar caps."

Suddenly Apollo's young, Filipino-accented voice added to the audio mix. "There is ice on the Martian polar caps. Engineers build canals so that when it melts it flows toward the equator for the cities, the crops..."

The voices disappeared again. The images continued as the European guest in the view moved to a garden table, pulling out a chair to seat himself. He motioned to a servant to bring his tea. He then picked up a folded newspaper. He glanced at it, said something that was not being made audible by the C.N.A. controls, then handed the paper to Apollo. A headline for an article in the Boston Globe read: "First Official Korean Delegation Meets With President Hayes in New York."

Abruptly, the image disappeared, turned to static.

Kai and Jenny looked to each other, then again at the screens. Finally they turned to Rochelle. She spoke to the controllers. "What happened?"

"Don't know. Neural shift. End of dream. Electronic adjustment on the machine. Give us a few minutes."

Jenny stood to look in at the peacefully sleeping Apollo. This was fascinating. She then looked down at Teddy. He was sleeping. His neural sensors were much closer to normal, but he was also very sick. Would he be like this for another month, just like Apollo?

"The dream ended," a voice announced from the control room. "Look at Apollo's neural readings. The dream center just went quiet. We'll continue to monitor."

There were several minutes of silence as they waited for new material from Apollo. Nothing more happened.

"Rochelle," Kai leaned back, "Are your going to the Mars Broadcast Conference at the Media Center?"

"Mars Broadcasting?" She stared at him, "Sometimes I don't know about you. Here we are getting a most fantastic dream ... this kid visualizing something straight out of a historical movie, and you ask about a totally unrelated conference."

"Sorry." He reached for his coffee, "Jenny was at the wedding of Terra Newton fifteen years ago. Apollo got his virus on Mars. We have no idea how. It just …"

"I read you, doctor. I can't let you or Jenny out of quarantine. Give me a message for Terra Newton. I'll make certain that she gets it." Rochelle lifted her sleeve to speak, "Computer.; access historical libraries. Cross check the information derived from Apollo Panahon's dream. Caucasian in Japan at the time of American President Hayes meeting Korean diplomatic delegation, and has connection to Boston. Interest in amateur astronomy."

Kai asked his own questions, "Computer, cross check entertainment industry for material on these issues that may have been shown in the Philippines or on Mars during the past several years."

A few minutes later they had their answer. Percival Lowell, from Boston, was in Tokyo to study in the Orient during the early 1880s, and at the request of the American delegation to Japan, he escorted the first Korean delegation to New York in 1883. He also took a temporary fascination, at that time, with an attractive female Japanese dancer. All his life, he had interest in Mars. He was convinced that Italian astronomer Giovanni Schaperilli had observed water canals on the surface of Mars. This was ten years before he left the Orient to build his own observatory to search for Martian life. Although there were several video stories about Lowell's quest for canals on Mars, none telecast in the last fifty years made mention of his years in Japan. Apollo would not have been casually aware of these events.

Jenny called Celia. Once the images had been replayed to a very astonished Celia, she confirmed that Apollo had never exhibited a fascination with abstract history, nor had he ever mentioned Lowell. Apollo may have read about Lowell while on Mars, but Celia doubted that he would have explored Lowell's life deeply enough to know what Lowell was doing in Japan.

Kai listened to the discussions as he studied those around him. Finally, he said, "If Apollo revives, we'll ask him. In the meantime," he pointed to the medic chamber with the sleeping Teddy inside,

"Teddy's hypothalamus and cerebral dream centers are active, just like Apollo was a few minutes ago. Maybe…"

Rochelle rose to her feet, looking through the window at Teddy's medic chamber. She glanced briefly at Jenny before speaking, "Do a C. N. A. on the child!"

Staff workers rolled Teddy's medic chamber into the isolation booth with Apollo. They made the appropriate adjustments to a C.N.A. helmet in order to fit the child's head without disturbing his sleep.

The optic nerve and visual cortex images were blank. The view from the cerebral dream center displayed an image of a white wall above a plush, beige floor carpet. Three easel tripods in front of the wall displayed three beautiful, antique Italian paintings.

"Those are the paintings stolen from the Rome Museum," Rochelle said. She briefly glanced at Jenny, "I assume you took Teddy to Rome recently?"

"He's too young to appreciate art. I've never shown him these artworks… not even magazine pictures of them."

The image shifted to an elderly man, obviously German, dressed in a conservative business environmental suit. Perspiration was beading on his forehead. A voice blared from the audio speakers. "Heinrich, are you convinced? Shall we accept?"

"That's Sonny's voice!" Jenny gasped.

"Daddy!" Teddy's voice came next. Everyone looked through the window at the medic chamber. Teddy was still in peaceful sleep. Once more, Teddy's unspoken voice called out, "Daddy, I'm sick. I need you."

The German in the image responded, "I'm satisfied. "Let's settle."

The image panned back to the paintings, again to Heinrich, and finally to another man. This younger man was obviously of Mediterranean descent. Once again, Sonny's voice came from the speaker. "Mister Bendino, I wish Ucello could be here. This is her deal."

"Sorry," the man just identified as Bendino responded, "She is cautious. Now, as soon as we confirm payment, the contents of the room are yours."

The image panned the room, focusing on a door where two very tough looking Italians stood. The view shifted to the paintings, then to Heinrich, and finally to Mr. Bendino.

"Let's do it." On a table where two open computer cases were waiting. One of the computers zoomed in, as if a video was being walked towards it. The computer displayed "August 2, 2216, 10:32 a.m., Hotel Aqua Mediterranean, Naples, Italy." Below that was listed a Zurich, Switzerland Bank account number with instructions to transfer funds to an account in another bank. Sonny's voice became audible. "Charn! Which bank?"

Again, Teddy's small voice came from the speaker, "Daddy, daddy, I need you."

"Bern, Oberstein Bank. Account number 66004-BTG-32891-AAZ-0000977." The account number appeared on the display as Charn Bendino spoke it.

"Heinrich?"

The old German stepped up to the computer, put his hand on a ceramic plate designed for hand print and DNA identification, then said, "Heinrich Dietrich, 54550-778-91124, of Bremen, Deutschland."

A written text read. "Transfer complete."

Bendino was watching his own computer, through a separate network. He smiled, closed the case, and then reached over to shake hands with Heinrich and with the source of the imaging. "Thank you. Enjoy your purchase." Bendino left with his two bodyguards, closing the door as they left.

An environmental suit sleeve appeared on the dreamscape monitor, with another hand pushing a button on the sleeve's communications controls. "We have possession. Secure this room."

A female voice asked, "And the money? Do we still have control?"

Once again the computer screen appeared. Unfamiliar numbers were legible on the display. Sonny's voice said, "We have it. The payment went to Oberstein Bank, then immediately to an account in Geneva at Bergenmeister Bank. The tracer attached to the account is doing its job. The computer is double checking the account transfer as a routine. The money should be returning to Zurich in thirty minutes."

Teddy's dream center image changed to static. Suddenly the optic nerve and visual cortex shifted from the deep blue, to red, to white, to images identical to the helmet camera. Teddy was awake. "Daddy? Daddy?"

Jenny standing beside the med chamber was anxious to calm her young son. "Teddy," she reached to the comm controls on her sleeve, "Teddy, this is Mommy."

"Mommy? Mommy! … Where am I? … Where are you?"

Jenny turned to her brother for help.

Kai turned to Rochelle.

Rochelle said, "Go in!" She addressed her sleeve, "Teddy is awake. Take Mrs. Ortigas to see her son."

Once she had left the booth, Celia DeNila asked, "Was that a dream, or was it something more?"

"Did you see that clock?" Rochelle said, "I double checked. If that is Italian time, then what we saw won't happen until tomorrow."

"…no!" Celia said, "Teddy is a little boy. That was just a dream. He wants his daddy."

"Well, if it is more than a dream," Kai said, "We should know tomorrow. If Sonny finished … is about to finish his job … finding his family will be the first thing he does next."

"I'm glad we have this recorded," Rochelle said. "No one will believe it." She spoke to her sleeve. "Do we have a detailed account of what was happening inside Teddy's brain?"

"As detailed as the C.N.A. will do," The male control room voice sounded elated. "The levels of the Feldermite hormone were up, and the neural activities in the hypothalamus were peaking. That seemed to be regulating the messages to the dream center."

CHAPTER TWENTY-ONE

FATHER ROXAS

Tycho Medical Center, Moon

Earth Date   July 30, 2216
Mars Date   C-Mmon 48, 1174

MARTIAN VIRUS, DAY 30

"Can we go home, Mommy?" Teddy sat in Jenny's lap, leaning against her. He held tightly to his stuffed, cloth puppy. "I want to go home. I miss Daddy!"

Jenny ran her fingers through the child's matted, sweaty hair, "I miss Daddy, too, Teddy. But, we can not go until you and Apollo are better."

He huffed a breath of exasperation, but said nothing. The red blemishes still covered his face. He seemed a little more energetic, but not much.

Jenny, sitting in her private cubicle, waited as her brother took another blood sample from Teddy. "Kai, did the Director get my message to Terra Newton?"

"Sure did," He handed the blood sample to Ula, who stood by, waiting for Kai to move to the next room. Kai continued speaking, "She promised to come after this morning's show. That should be over in twenty minutes. I'm sorry about Mrs. Quintos."

"Show?" Jenny looked out the open door of her cubicle at the gathering of the women of the community. Four of the barrio women Jenny barely knew were at a table playing mahjong. It took a moment for the expressed regret about elderly Mrs. Faye Quintos to register. She had died during the night, the fourth barrio fatality from the virus.

"Another special on Venus. Want to watch it?"

Jenny was not particularly interested in Venus at the moment. However, she felt she should be up on what Terra Newton was excited about. "Twenty minutes? I'll turn it on … see what's happening with the treaty." Her brother disappeared beyond the door.

Jenny had joined the mahjong game the night before, thinking she should make friends with the barrio women while they were all isolated on the Moon. These barrio lives were right out of antiquity. They cooked over open fires, washed clothes in the stream, planted and harvested food by hand. Jenny understood none of that way of life. During the mahjong game the women talked about people who had moved from their village, people Jenny did not know. Occasionally, they would ask Jenny questions about cooking or cosmetics or the way she raised Teddy. From the emotionless way they dealt with her, Jenny sensed that the innocent questions were more inquiries for future gossip than compassionate concern about a new friend. After playing a few rounds of mahjong, she feigned drowsiness to get away. She went to bed convinced that her standing with the barrio women was probably related to how Celia felt about her. Lulu Alsona ran the Sari-Sari store. Ruby Perez, Nina's mother, was a seamstress. Feli Hernandez worked in the rice terraces. Marcia Paz was also a seamstress, making stuffed dolls similar to the one that Teddy carried around.

The next day, Jenny noticed that the four were once again totally focused on their mahjong game. There was nothing else to do during the lunar quarantine.

Four teenagers were absorbed with a comedy television show. A group of men, clustered around another screen, were cheering a soccer match. Celia, seated on a sofa, was in deep consultation with Bobbitt Quintos about the death of his wife, Faye. Bobbitt was ill himself.

Madeline had slipped into coma during the night. Nine other adults from the barrio were also in comas. Thirty were sick with nausea, headaches, sweating, diarrhea, chills, and high temperatures, as well as the ever present rash.

Nina appeared in the doorway, holding her artist's comp-pad in one hand. That computer sketch pad was a two-foot long tube when not in use. The artist could pull a sketch pad up to three foot long from the tube. Using the attached electronic sketch pens and unit controls, artists could free-hand sketch on the pad, electronically modify or color the drawing, and save to the computer to print out later. Nina opened her comp-pad to show Jenny a drawing she had sketched of Teddy with his stuffed puppy.

"Nina, that is very good. Do I get a copy?"

"If you want, I'll send it to you comm unit." Nina stepped over to the console included with Jenny's cubicle; there she transferred the sketch file. She said, "Tita Jenny. Would you like me to watch Teddy? You haven't been out of your room all morning."

Jenny stared without speaking.

"I don't have anything else to do." The peppy, petite teenager had no signs of the rash. "I know Teddy is sick. You should walk around a little. You'll go crazy."

Jenny looked down at her son, "You want to be with Nina awhile? Hear her stories?"

Teddy smiled, "Nina tell funny stories."

Jenny thanked Nina, got up and walked across the lounge to the open airlock leading to the observation deck. The path took her along a long corridor to another airlock, up some stairs to a third open airlock, which opened to the observation deck. All of the internal airlocks, positioned at critical points to automatically close in event of contamination or pressure leak, were open and inactive. At the deck area several men congregated watching the televised soccer game. Not far from the soccer fans, sitting at a table among the flower planters was sickly Father Roxas, laughing at the jokes of two of the barrio miners. Jenny ambled to an isolated bench near the edge of the transparent bubble dome. The view looked across the crater at the lengthening shadows from the rim. Lights sparkled from the multiple observation decks of the Tycho metropolitan center, several miles away, near the crater center. She sighed. The view of the nearly full Earth offered her solace, an opportunity to think quietly for a few moments. She missed her job at Chang Exports. She imagined Lee Chang's reaction to the quarantine, and then her mind wandered to thoughts of Sonny and the revelation from Teddy's dream about his father's work.

A cough from behind her distracted her solitude. She turned her head. "Father Roxas. I thought you were…"

"Miss Jenny," He came around the end of the bench. "I was with Bato and Andy. They wish they could be back at the mines. Up here, with everyone so sick, there is nothing for them to do."

Jenny looked closely at his face. "I understand. I wish I were back in Manila." She had not talked to Father Roxas since Christmas. The elderly, but once robust barrio priest now looked so sickly. He was pale with dried lips, bloodshot eyes, perspiration beads on his forehead, and a face covered with the rash.

Father Roxas sat beside her, "The Earth is lovely tonight, my child; and a long way away. It seems almost as beautiful and alone as the wife of Sonny Ortigas."

She smiled, wrinkled her eyebrows, then said, "Father Roxas, you are being … silly."

"That may be. Someone has to be. This place is depressing. It needs a touch of levity. I've been bouncing around as if I weighed only forty pounds. It is like having springs in my shoes."

She pondered the profound nature of what he said. She nodded, "On the Moon you weigh only forty pounds."

"Bato was at the Christmas party at your Baguio house. He said that you and Sonny played poker with Roberto and him that afternoon. We have cards."

Jenny looked over her shoulder at the table Father Roxas had come from. Bato and Andy were looking back at them. Bato lifted a hand to show the deck of cards. She focused again on Father Roxas. With a smile, she said, "Why not?" She followed him to the table.

Within a few hands of the poker game Jenny understood everyone's style. Twenty-year-old Bato Tolentino was cautious; he bet high with a good hand, dropped out with bad cards. Andy Lechica, a father of four, was a reckless gambler. Father Roxas was good at the bluff, telling jokes as he played. Jenny had learned poker as a child, something she used to entertain men as part of her role as a hospitality girl. Later, when Lee Chang took her off the streets, he taught her that games of chance were a good way to develop business skills, to understand the minds of customers and competitors. Consequently, while raising her to be a talented business lady, he trained her to be sharp with card games.

"… and with that," Father Roxas coughed, then finished his joke, "Saint Peter told the priest that the shuttle pilot got ahead of everyone because that pilot had scared the hell out of more people in a week than the priest had in thirty years." With the end of the joke, Father Roxas laughed at his own humor. He raised the most recent bet.

Jenny watched Bato groan at such an old joke. Andy smiled, but said nothing. Jenny, figuring that Father Roxas was bluffing again, matched his raise, she then raised again. She chuckled at the joke she had heard a hundred times since childhood. "Cute story, Father. Did Sonny tell you the one about the priest, the aqua farmer, and the politician being stranded in an undersea habitat?"

Andy spoke up, "Is that the one with a robot playmate programmed as a cargo handler?" He matches the two raises, calling the bet.

"Yeh," Bato grimaced at the betting, dropping his cards face down to the table. "The joke Sonny never told us last Christmas. Fold."

"I wasn't there last Christmas," Father Roxas matched Jenny's bet, then raised again. "If you had all been to mass like you were supposed to, I probably would have heard it, too." He coughed again. Reaching for a cloth, he wiped the perspiration from his forehead. "Child, tell me this joke that everyone else has heard."

Jenny matched his bet. She winked at him. Want to show me those two pair?"

Andy also matched the bet. "I have to see it."

"My, my, my child," Father Roxas placed his five card hand face up for everyone to see. "A pair of fours and a pair of eights, with no wild. Did you perchance see my hand?"

Andy laid down his three kings with two nothing cards, glancing up to Jenny.

Jenny peeled the cards out one at a time. Four successive hearts plus a wild card. Flush. "Thank you, gentlemen. Father, I believe you have the deal."

Father Roxas took the cards to shuffle. His effort at shuffling was unsteady, "Do I get to hear the story?" Suddenly he turned pale. "You have to excuse me." He stood, put a hand to his mouth, and then headed for the men's room.

The other card players, none yet displaying symptoms of the virus, watched him disappear into a descending staircase. For a moment no one said a word, and then Bato spoke to his sleeve, "Father Roxas seems to be getting worse. Have a medic check him at the deck men's room."

Jenny thought of continuing the card game with Bato and Andy, but with Father Roxas too ill to continue, she lost interest. Telling the two that she would continue the game later, she excused herself. She needed someone she could talk to. She went inside in search of her brother. He was in a staff lounge watching the Venus show he had mentioned earlier was on.

He motioned for her to join him, "This is a prelude show to the treaty."

She settled in beside him. "Is the treaty signed?" She signaled the galley computer to bring her mango juice.

"Not treaty. That's tomorrow." Kai said. He asked the computer to turn on Terra Newton's program.

"Professor Rhoc Stenner." On screen the seated familiar, immaculate, dark haired Terra Newton was talking to a thin red-haired man of thirty-five. "You believe the unusual rotation of Venus was caused by Earth's Moon. Please, tell us what this is all about?"

The large video screen split its image into two elements, the right side continued the view of the two people, while the left side displayed graphics display to illustrate the issue. A chart of the inner solar system inside Earth's orbit, showed the planets following their normal courses around the sun.

"Except for Venus, all of the planets in the solar system, and all of their moons, rotate on their axis as if they were rolling around their orbits. Some, like the Moon, have a tidal lock, with one bulging face always pointing towards the center of the orbit. Mercury has a slow roll, completing three rotations for every two orbits. Earth and Mars have twenty-four hour rotations. All of these worlds roll around their orbits. Venus, on the other hand, rotates in the opposite direction. Why?"

The images illustrated these planetary spins. Terra asked, "We have been taught to believe that the rotation of Venus was a quirk of nature. Do you have reason to believe otherwise?"

"The mechanics of the Venus rotation are such that it has exactly five solar days... that is, a point on Venus will pass through noon exactly five times, between successive conjunctions with Earth." The graphics highlighted this effect.

"We all know this from school," Terra said. "So that the same point always faces Earth when they come into conjunction."

The professor continued. "Between those successive conjunctions, there are exactly twenty lunar solar orbits of the Earth. To within a few degrees, the Moon is in the same position between successive conjunctions."

"Isn't this just a celestial oddity? Of no particular significance?"

"It has been for three-hundred years. I disagree."

"Tita Jenny," Nina was at the entrance to the lounge. "Can I talk to you?"

"Teka, teka!" Jenny responded, pointing to the screen. "Let me see this first. Is someone with Teddy?"

Nina found a chair to seat herself. "Tita Celia is watching him. Teddy's asleep."

Terra's show continued with the professor clarifying his theory. "I theorize that a billion years ago the solar system passed through a galactic dust cloud of ionized gasses. If solar storms created massive electrical currents through these gasses, the motions of the planets would have influenced the directions of those currents. The Moon circling the Earth created a disturbance in those currents that affected the metallic core of Venus, an influence that changed the rotation of the entire planet to be in alignment with the motions of our Moon."

"That's an interesting theory," Terra said, "I have a feeling that we just left a lot of people confused. Do you have evidence that a cloud of this nature ever passed through the solar system?"

"We have not found the cloud, if that is what you're asking. There are indirect indicators, such as magnetic field reversals on Earth, layers of unique dust layers in Martian polar ices..."

Jenny turned her attention from the interesting, but technically confusing show. "Nina, how can I help?" Father Roxas entered at that moment.

"Tita Celia told me about the dream machine hooked up to Teddy and Apollo." Nina said, "... about the visions of Percival Lowell ... of Tito Sonny!"

"Did you want to see those images?" Jenny glanced at Kai. "I think we could let you see them."

Nina stood, taking hold of Jenny's arm. "Apollo was my... we were special friends. We talked about the future, our future." She looked around at the priest. "Hello, Father Roxas."

Jenny glanced up at Father Roxas, "Are you feeling better?"

He seated himself, raising his hand silently to signal he was all right.

Jenny turned again to Nina. "I didn't know. I'm sorry. He may still come out of it." Jenny returned to her seat.

Nina sat with her, "I understand that. I know we all have to deal with this sickness. I pray all the time for him to wake up."

Jenny was uncertain what Nina wanted.

"Did he have any dreams about us? About me?"

"All I saw was the one from him," Jenny looked to her brother. "Kai, have you gotten anything else?"

"Another dream about Percival Lowell. It was as if he were walking up a Japanese mountain with friends, to an elevation above the clouds ... like a religious retreat. Lowell was in the presence of Shinto priests. Once again, Apollo was talking to him about life on Mars, about there not being enough air or water, so that people have to find ways to process what they need. It seems as if Lowell thought he was hearing voices inspired by those Shinto priests. Do you want to see that?"

"I want to be near him," Nina said, "I want to talk to him. Maybe my voice will bring a dream of our barrio. Maybe it will be like the fairy tales … when the one who loves him is there … if I touch him it will help him wake up."

"Is that a good idea?" Kai asked. "No one can control their dreams. What if he has a nightmare … or dreams a sexual fantasy? Could you deal with that?"

Nina was silent briefly. "I can deal with it. What I can't deal with is being locked in here, not able to go home … seeing my friends sick and dying … caring about Apollo, wanting to talk to him, to hold him, to feel… and not even being allowed to be in the same room."

"Okay," Jenny nodded her head, "If it were Sonny in there, I would feel the same way."

Kai looked at the screen. The abstract show about Venus was still running. "I'll talk to the director. Terra Newton is not scheduled to be here until tomorrow evening."

Nina looked up at the show where Terra was interviewing Professor Rhoc Stenner. "She's coming here? Even if we are all sick?"

"She'll keep separate from us," Kai smiled, "I don't think anyone in this center wants to be held responsible if we infect her." He addressed his sleeve. "Rochelle, I'm bringing Jenny, Father Roxas, and Nina Perez to see Apollo."

Father Roxas patted Nina on the shoulder. "Nina, Apollo will wake up tomorrow."

"Tomorrow?" She swallowed, looking to the aging sickly priest with doubt.

"Everyone with this disease is having dreams … about other people … about the past, like Apollo … about the future, like Teddy. I dreamed that Apollo will wake tomorrow … and he will be talking to," He pointed to Terra on screen, "that Martian newscaster about this virus."

Jenny looked up at Father Roxas. He looked ghastly. The rash covered his face and hands. He was perspiring. "Are you well enough to be walking around?"

"Jenny," he forced a smile as he stood to join them. Carefully studying Kai and Nina, he said, "I'll come with you. I have to hear what the priest and the aqua farmer did with a badly programmed playmate robot."

She smiled, "Of course."

Father Roxas took her pressure suited arm with one hand, patting it with the other. "You know, I've been jealous of Sonny for years."

"Father Roxas! You're a priest!"

"I know, I know," He winked at her, "at least you could come to mass once in awhile… when you're in Baguio."

"When this is all over, I promise I will."

Father Roxas's expression turned more serious. "Jenny, I've been having those dreams, too. If they are accurate … Teddy will be better tomorrow. Baby Madeline will take another week. You won't get sick yourself."

"You saw that in your dreams?" Jenny asked. "I hope it's true. Then, we can go home and rebuild Ulap. I know I haven't been to church very often, but I promise… when this is over, I will come to your services anytime we are in Baguio."

He laughed, "Child, I wish I could hold you to it."

"What do you mean by that?"

"I won't be going back to Ulap. God will take me home from here."

"Father," Nina gasped, "Are you dying? No…"

Father Roxas reached to grasp the hand of the young girl, "I also saw that in my dreams. I do not have long. This virus is very hard on those my age. I wanted to say goodbye to you, to all of you. Do not feel bad for me… or about Lolo Raul… or Faye Quintos… we will all be with God."

"Father Roxas," Jenny was standing. "How can you be so certain? You are still walking around… there is no coma."

"I feel the sickness in my stomach, in my head, in my lungs… and I saw it, the way Teddy saw Sonny. Please don't feel bad for me. I have had a full life."

Kai stood up to examine him, "As a physician, I do not know how to… to deal with all the strange anomalies associated with the virus. Father Roxas, I do not know you. My stepparents raised me as a Methodist… if what you are saying is true…" he stopped himself before he got too emotional. "Come with us. Say a blessing over Apollo. Maybe it will help him... Help us all to understand."

In the laboratory observation booth, Jenny settled into a chair with Teddy on her lap. Nina and Father Roxas took stools. In the booth for the first time, they both stared through the window at Apollo enclosed in his chamber. The monitors displaying Apollo's neural dream center activity showed static. There was something different about his med stats display. The flatline neural patterns of the cognizant areas of the cerebral cortex had changed. There were wave-like synaptic patterns on the charts.

"Father Roxas," Kai pointed to the brainwave patterns, "You may be right. Apollo's mental functions are fluctuating again."

Father Roxas turned from his view of Apollo to look to the face of the doctor, then glanced down at the diagnostic displays. His ability to deal with technical information was almost as limited as Celia. The information meant little to him. He spoke to Kai. "I know not about this, only what God told me through my dreams. "

Kai pondered, then addressed his sleeve. "This is Patterson. Who's at control?"

"Jackson. No dream activity at the moment."

"Get the Director. I want to put a C.N.A. unit on everyone with the virus. Seems like everyone is having visionary dreams."

"You didn't see her in the dorm? She's already doing that. I'll get the units for the patients you have in the booth."

"Father Roxas has the virus. Jenny, Nina, and I are unaffected."

"Director Bond ordered everyone, just in case there are new cases."

"Doctor Patterson?" Nina questioned, "Can I go in with Apollo? Can I talk to him? Can I touch him?"

"You should not touch him. You are clear of the virus right now."

"Father Roxas has it, and I've been in contact with him … same for Baby Madeline … and Tita Faye … and…"

"You've made your point." He spoke again to his microphone. "Jackson, Nina Perez will enter the room with Apollo. Let her make physical contact."

"You're the doctor."

183

Father Roxas settled into a chair beside Jenny. Kai led Nina to her sleeping boyfriend. With the lid to the medic chamber open, she reached down to brush a lock of hair from his face. She whispered softly to him that she wanted him back. She pleaded with him to tell her where to find her dad, Emilio Perez. She whispered that she wanted him to be well again.

"Showtime, doctor." Jackson's voice was audible through the speakers. "Dream images coming on line."

The C.N.A. monitors showing images from optic nerve and visual cortex remained blank, as before. The memory center electrical graph, along with the hypothalamus, showed neural activity. The cerebral dream center screen offered a view from inside the Martian prospecting trailer parked in Princess Dejah Canyon. Through the windows the landscape was very dark. It was obviously a night setting. The screen displayed a view of a dining table where five Filipino miners were playing a game of cards. Beverages were resting on the table next to each player's poker chips. Roberto DeNila dealt cards to each player. Doug and Celso quietly picked up each card dealt them, sliding them into their hands. June Ventuno chuckled, sipping his drink. Emilio Perez was conferring with a most attractive, Asian-featured woman.

"Tessie, today is Apollo's eighteenth birthday," Emilio smiled as he talked, glancing at the woman, then at the screen image source, "Take Apollo to the crew's quarters... give him a full treatment as best you can."

"But, Tito Emilio," Apollo's voice came from the speaker, "I really don't want to do this." A separate sound from a different memory circuit gave audio to Apollo's thoughts. "If Nina finds out, we'll both be in trouble." The image followed the approach of the dark haired robotic playmate, Tessie, who began removing a loosely fitted jacket. Underneath was a fitted satin blouse that emphasized her ample curves.

"Apollo, please come with me." A soft, whispery female voice was audible. Tessie reached to rub the side of Apollo's neck. There was a C.N.A. Unit indicator identifying the scent of perfume. "We have our own party to celebrate. I will show you how my programs can make your birthday the most memorable celebration you've ever had."

"Tessie is just a machine!" At the table Emilio Perez was picking up his cards. "This night will be between me … you … the crew … and Tessie. I won't tell Nina if you don't."

"Daddy!" Nina had focused on the monitor images in front of her. "Apollo, this is terrible."

The dream images showed Apollo shutting himself in a pressure suit to follow Tessie, who did not need pressure gear, through the observation trailer airlock to the Martian surface for the walk to the crew's quarters.

"No!" Nina put her hands to her cheeks. She screeched. She turned away from the screens, from Apollo. She left the laboratory room.

Jenny rose to her feet in the observation booth. She knew she needed to comfort Nina, to talk to her. She glanced down at Teddy, then up at her brother.

"Go ahead," Kai pattered her arm, "Talk to Nina. I'll stay with Teddy."

Jenny glanced at the dream monitor as she left. Tessie was helping Apollo remove his clothes. Her blouse was unfastened to the waist. Apollo's attention focused on Tessie's large breasts pushing at the satin materials; her obvious little nipples making the blouse even more suggestive. Jenny knew the medical staff needed to continue recording whatever it was that Apollo was dreaming, as there may be clues to what had caused the virus. She glanced at Father Roxas to see if he was following the show. He looked like he had fallen asleep.

"Asleep?" Jenny asked her brother.

Kai looked at the priest. He checked Father Roxas' med stats, and then spoke to his sleeve. "Emergency! Father Roxas is in full cardiac arrest."

Kai reached for the priest, pulling him from the chair to lay him flat on the floor. Using the devices built into the medical control suit the priest was wearing, he administered electro shock to the chest. Father Roxas jerked in reaction. The electro-cardiogram showed a blip, and then went flatline. Kai ordered the control in the outfit to inject a stimulant, and then administered another shock. Once again there was nothing more on the EKG than a mild blip. Father Roxas was dead.

"My God!" Jenny squealed. "He told us he dreamed he was about to die, and ..."

Kai was squatting over the priest. Looking up, he said, "I'll take care of Teddy, of Father Roxas. Go talk to Nina." He glanced at the monitors. Tessie was guiding Apollo's hands in removal of her blouse. Her perfectly shaped breasts were very sensual. "Jackson, cut the dream images from the room and from the test room. Keep recording."

The screens went blank.

Kai spoke to his sleeve communicator. "Contact Celia DeNila. Have her come here. He looked once more at his sister. "Go, Jenny. Nina needs you to talk to her."

CHAPTER TWENTY-TWO

MARTIAN JOURNALIST

Tycho Medical Center, Moon

Earth Date	August 1, 2216
Mars Date	C-Mmon 50, 1174

"Director Bond." The tallest of the three men addressed her through the isolation window. "I am Doctor Cal Reston, with the Martian Global Police. Officer Danford and Officer Quinn are my assistants. We need to talk to two of your patients."

"I'm surprised you came all this way without an appointment." Rochelle said. "Do you realize that this is a quarantine facility?"

Kai and Jenny were seated in an isolation booth, adjacent to the director's lounge, quietly observing. They had been expecting advance agents for Terra Newton. Once they realized that this was something else, they chose to let Rochelle do the talking. Jenny did not know Reston or Quinn, but Danford she knew. He had high thin cheeks, gray bushy eyebrows, and thin lips; he was dressed in a blue-gray business pressure suit, matching the outfits worn by the other two. On his shoulder, near the helmet flange, was a slightly off colored repair patch. It looked like a hurried repair over a tear.

"Of course," Reston had no emotion to his tone, nor in his expression. He repeatedly tapped his fingers on the table. "That's why I was sent here… for a visit. We are prepared to follow prescribed quarantine contact procedures."

"Which patients did you want to visit?"

"They may have come as unidentified admissions with the recent epidemic arrivals from the Philippines. One is a blond forty-year-old woman… Sonia Androff. The other is a teenage male Filipino, name of Apollo Panahon." Reston signaled one of his assistants to insert a computer plug into the wall control junction. "Here are our credentials, the warrant for the two suspects, and a search authorization approved by the United Nations Patrol. Do you have the suspects?"

Jenny watched as Rochelle reviewed the documentation on a monitor. Jenny only knew Danford. He was looking back at her and smiling. He winked. Danford had been with Lee Chang the morning she left work hurriedly to pick up Apollo at the Bataan Spaceport. In Manila he was a purchasing agent looking for a shipment; here on the Moon he was a police officer.

The computer confirmed that Cal Reston was a doctor. Yugo Danford and Scranton Quinn were listed as Martian detectives. The warrant, issued by Police Chief Ken Sylvester and signed by a Martian justice, authorized an interplanetary search for suspects Sonia Androff and Apollo Panahon. The U.N. Patrol in New York had also signed the search authorization. "Suspects? For what?"

"They are wanted as material witnesses related to a murder investigation on Mars. It is important that we talk to them."

Jenny remembered that Yugo Danford. Twenty years earlier, when she was working the streets of Manila as a child hospitality girl, Danford had been a customer. He was a purchasing agent for a food distributor in Manila. He paid ten-year-old Jenny well to show him a fun weekend at a Mindoro beach resort. She met him again when she was eighteen, after Lee Chang had adopted her off the streets. She entertained him for business purposes, as she often did for Chang's customers back then. Yugo Danford was no detective.

Rochelle eyed Kai and Jenny sternly. Surprised by the charges, she would not break proper procedures, nor would she attempt to run afoul of an official investigation. Returning her attention to the men, she said, "I'm afraid you've wasted your time. No one in this facility resembles the suspect you identify as Sonia Androff. Apollo Panahon is with us, but he is in quarantine and in a coma. He is in no position to see anyone."

"Can we confirm this patient?"

Rochelle asked the facility computers to show a surveillance view of Apollo Panahon. The view displayed the medic chamber he was in along with a reading of his vital statistics. He was still covered with the rash, still unconscious. "There will be no direct contact."

Following an exchange of pleasantries, the three visitors excused themselves. On his way out, Danford glanced back, smiled once more at Jenny, and then disappeared through the door.

Rochelle spoke to her companions. "There's something you're not telling me."

"I told you that someone is stalking Apollo," Kai responded. "We don't know why, only that it involved officials from Mars. Everyone who went to Mars with Apollo is missing. The Martian doctor who sent Apollo to us is missing, as well as the woman they just mentioned."

Jenny asked, "Have you had inquiries like that before?"

The question took Rochelle by surprise. "Many times. It is not unusual for the police to make inquires concerning patients ... or suspects."

"Have you ever been approached, here at this facility," Jenny rephrased her thinking, "in an official inquiry with no police along?"

Kai looked at Jenny with astonishment. "Is there something you want to share with us?"

"That one detective, Yugo Danford... I know him. If he's a detective, it's a new line of work. These 'officers' found what they wanted. Apollo is here. Sonia Androff is not. If someone is stalking Apollo, we just told them where to find him."

After a moment of silence, Rochelle spoke to her sleeve. "Security, this is Director Bond. Seal off Ward forty-three. Class five control.

No visitors, no outsiders of any kind except those that I personally authorize. Confirm the identities of the three detectives who were just here."

"Does that 'no visitors' order include the Martian journalists? Three of them are in a taxi heading this way now."

"Is Terra Newton one of them?"

"Newton, plus two of her staff."

"Send her to the lobby. I'll deal directly with her."

Terra's oval face looked as young, delicate, and fair as in pictures from her very public wedding fifteen years earlier. Her short, dark hair was stylish, without a hair out of place. The popular media star from Mars went to great lengths to maintain her appearance. However, when she looked through the lobby's isolation window at Jenny she felt absolutely plain. She almost envied the woman who never had to try to look better. Despite looking depressed and exhausted, Jenny had the aura of a fashion model. Terra glanced over her shoulder. Chet, her cameraman robot, was positioned to record everything. Terra then spoke to Jenny. "We are alone now. My staff is busy with the Director. Jenny, it's been a long time. Too long. I'm really happy to see you."

"Thank you. I'm sorry we've not been to Mars more often. I know how you feel about Earth." Jenny envied Terra's ease before the cameras, although she would never admit it. The monitors on her side of the cubicle showed Nina beside Teddy's bed, reading to him from a book. Teddy listened, quietly hugging his stuffed puppy. His medical stats showed improvement, but it was obvious that he was not one-hundred percent. He was still covered with the rash, even though it had diminished. For Teddy to lie quietly in bed when he was awake was not normal for him.

"What is this all about?" Terra asked, "Your message was short and disturbing. Director Bond told me about the virus … a new one from Mars. Where is Sonny?"

Jenny said, "He's in Italy tracking stolen art. I hope he calls soon."

"Stolen Art? Italy?" Terra's voice rose with excitement. "Rome Art Museum. Two DeVinici paintings … and a Rafael?"

"I think so," Jenny stared intensely. "I hope he calls. We have a lot of disasters waiting for him."

"Disasters?" Terra muttered, and then said, "Let's get to the point. What happened? I have an overview from Director Bond, but I want your story."

Jenny pointed to Chet. "It may be too early for public release."

"I understand. I need to keep a record. I won't release anything until its ready. I'll keep what you tell me exclusive until you agree to make it public. That is a promise."

Jenny had no choice. She had to trust someone, and Terra had never given reason for doubts. "One week ago Bibi Sanchez called from the Manila Spaceport. You remember Bibi, she runs the E.M. Transport business. Bibi had a John Doe coma patient from Sagan City, Mars routed to Hong Kong Medical University through Sonny. The John Doe was Sonny's nephew, Apollo Panahon."

"Apollo?" Terra asked. "The little boy from the barrio in the Philippine mountains?"

"You did that barrio report ten years ago. Apollo is now eighteen."

"You said he is in a coma?"

"He still is. He is infected with an unfamiliar virus. Sonny was in Italy, so I took Apollo home to the barrio. His Aunt Celia opened his medic isolation chamber. According to my brother, the virus spread by direct contact, or through mosquitoes, all over the village. My son is sick with the virus. Sonny's father died from it. So did Salvador Roxas, the barrio priest."

"Does everyone have the disease?"

"No. I don't have it. Sonny's sister, Celia DeNila doesn't have it. We test positive for the virus, but there is no sickness. Just over half of the village is sick with the virus. The others have no symptoms."

"On the news there were reports of a new strain of malaria in the Philippines. I understand another four-hundred patients have been quarantined in Baguio. You say this is a deadly epidemic?"

"Four hundred more in Baguio?" Jenny's mouth dropped open. She quickly recovered. "No one mentioned anything here. My God, that means it is spreading." She wiped her lips with the back of her hand, and then cleared her throat. "There is more. We know the virus came from Mars. Apollo sent a coded transmission to Sonny from Mars before he left the planet, but Sonny has not been back to Manila to decode it. The doctor who shipped Apollo home is missing. Five Filipino miners who went to Mars with Apollo are missing. According to the news, Fisk Banzer... he's the Martian independent prospector who hired the Filipino crew... was murdered by Sonia Androff, his partner. She is also missing. Three men, claiming to be Martian investigators were here just before you arrived, looking for Apollo and the Androff woman. Director Bond sent them away."

Terra accepted a cup of coffee from the rolling galley unit. After sipping, she asked, "Have you talked to the police?"

"Do you remember Octan Palmer?"

Terra thought for a moment. "She was one of Blue Heidelburn's partners in the space transport business. If I remember..." Terra turned to Chet, asked for a check on Palmer, and then returned her attention to Jenny. "Her operating bases were between Boston and Wells."

"She brought Apollo from Mars. She said that this Sonia Androff is also in a coma, that someone high up on Mars is after both of them. A trucker, name of Flex Epsen, brought Apollo in the med chamber to Wells Spaceport."

"Flex Epsen? Of Epsen Trucking?" Terra asked. "His sister was in my unit during the war."

"That was the name Octan gave me in confidence."

Terra asked Chet to check the name Sonia Androff. He looked down at the screen on her unfolded computer case. "She is charged with murdering Fisk Banzer and Japa Reese, prospecting agents for Redrock Mining Company. The killings were at a gold discovery in a remote canyon in the Syrtis Major highlands. She apparently disappeared with an unidentified male accomplice."

Jenny replied, "Fisk Banzer and Sonia Androff hired Apollo, his uncle Roberto, and four other Filipino miners to join a prospecting venture. Banzer was not certain he could trust local Martian miners."

Terra sipped her coffee once more. "There is no mention of Filipinos in this report. A new, deadly Martian virus has forced the quarantine of an entire province. Half a dozen Filipinos are missing on Mars, miners hired by a murdered prospector, and someone with authority is chasing after Apollo." She shook her head. "What a story."

"There is more." Jenny had a sheepish grin, quietly pondering the Apollo's recorded sexual dreamscapes.

"More?"

Jenny's expression turned more serious. "This virus creates strange side effects. Are you familiar with C.N.A. units?"

"Cerebral Neural Analysis. I did a story about them years ago."

"Apollo was showing unusual brainwave activity, so the medical staff put one of the units on him. They recorded him dreaming about Percival Lowell in the nineteenth century ... the world through Lowell's eyes."

"The astronomer who mapped non-existent Martian canals. That's not unusual. He probably saw a show about Lowell."

"According to Celia, Apollo had never mentioned the name before, and she was unaware of him showing any interest in history before. The computer checked the library listing. There have been no video portrayals of the period in Lowell's life we saw through the C.N.A. Apollo's dream was like a real time image of a house in Japan in 1883. The images match the written historical records for Lowell from that time."

"Interesting. Maybe I can give this data to Professor Chester."

"Two days ago, Father Roxas told me he dreamed he was going to die of the virus, but that my son would soon feel better, that Apollo would be waking up very soon. Father Roxas died yesterday. My son is improving. The neural readings from Apollo have been improving. We put the C.N.A. on Teddy while he was in deep sleep. We got an image through his father's eyes of a resolution of his investigation. I've been waiting for Sonny to call to confirm if what we imaged was an actual forecast."

"Amazing. I need to look into this. I almost wish I didn't have the Venus story to do. When Sonny finally calls, have him contact me."

Jenny checked the monitors in front of her. Teddy was sleeping peacefully with Nina still beside him. Apollo was in the med-chamber, still not moving. "I haven't been watching the news that closely. What exactly is this treaty you're reporting?"

"You understand that Venus is too hot, with too much sulfuric acid in the clouds, for a normal spacecraft to land and takeoff?"

"Yes. I know that much."

"A prototype anti-grav spacecraft has been built that should be able to land on Venus and bring mineral resources back to orbit. The United Nations treaty signed fifteen years ago grants Mars control of the anti-grav technologies, so a treaty has to be signed by the Martian government to permit using the anti-grav for this purpose."

"My boss, Lee Chang Exports, has a few agreements like that. Who all is involved?"

"Government officials from the United Nations and from Mars, Newton Enterprises, that's my husband's family business with the patents to the anti-grav, and some mining corporations."

"I forgot about Newton Enterprises. Is Brass here?"

"My husband?" Terra laughed lightly. "It may be a family business, but he's too busy with the Life Sciences Facility. His uncle is here to represent the company."

Jenny then asked, "Is Redrock Mining represented?"

Terra responded, "Their C.E.O. is here with the Martian President. I've already interviewed them. I think it may be premature to talk to Redrock about this. Please, have Sonny call me as soon as he can… especially if that transmission from Mars has anything relevant. I'd like to help resolve this case."

CHAPTER TWENTY-THREE

ART THEFT RECOVERY

Naples, Italy

Earth Date	August 2, 2216
Mars Date	C-Mmon 51, 1174

MARTIAN VIRUS, DAY 29

The sealed, insulated automated van had no windows, no external sounds, and an excellent suspension that masked rough roads. Sonny glanced at the indicator on his sleeve. There was no signal from the traffic control satellite. The van was shielded. Even the magnetic compass was not working. He smiled. Sonny had anticipated these precautions, hoping the efforts would put the art thieves at ease. The mini-gyro built into his briefcase could not be shielded; it tracked all motions of the van regardless of the course adjustments the van took to create confusion. Programmed for transmissions to remain inactive until a clear link to the traffic control satellite had been re-established, the computer would transmit a micro-burst of information once a connection was established. That micro-burst would appear as nothing more ominous than a spark plug misfiring. Channeled to Lloyds, the transmission would include all data gathered during the wait, including location. Sonny waited. He noticed the jeweled watch Ucello wore on her wrist. It was ten in the morning, local time. The deal should be complete within the hour. He thought of his wife and son. It had been a long, difficult effort to close this deal, necessary because Ucello was nervous about everything. Sipping from the wine glass she handed him, he pondered asking Lee Chang to give Jenny a few days off so that she and Teddy could go with him to Baguio for a holiday.

Heinrich von Deitrich, the sweating German art buyer did not want wine. He preferred a chilled stein of beer. For this ride, however, he accepted the wine. He sipped. Across the table Ucello continued telling Heinrich about her skiing and camping trip to the Bavarian Alps when she was a teenager. Sonny knew the story was a fabrication. She had been many places, but the Alps was not part of that history. As a teenager she had actually worked in a fish processing plant in Salerno. Her story was intended to relax the nervous Heinrich. Sonny said nothing.

Ucello's assistant, Charn, had the flare of a talented waiter. Charn stood, spun around the travel lounge at the back of the van, as if doing a dance, to reach for the 'Asti' sparkling wine, and then returned to his seat. He added a little more wine to Sonny's glass. "Amore vita!" He moved the bottle toward Heinrich's glass.

"Nein, danke," Heinrich put a hand over his glass. "Das ist wiel vino. Haben sie kalt beer?" He paused, and then repeated in English. "I would prefer a cold beer, please."

Charn winked, formed an okay symbol with his fingers, and then danced back to the galley for a beer. He opened the bottle, handing it to his guest.

Ucello sipped her wine, then placed the glass on a table. "We're here."

While watching Heinrich accept the beer from Charn, Sonny sensed that the van had stopped moving. He continued to sit with a nonchalant expression, waiting to follow Ucello's lead. The data on his sleeve confirmed that they were at the Naples Hotel Aqua Mediterranean. Sonny had stayed at the hotel in the past.

"Heinrich," Ucello stood, lifting her glass in toast. "Charn will bring you in a few minutes. I'll go ahead to make certain there are no surprises."

Again, this was expected. Ucello was always cautious. Inwardly, Sonny was very nervous. If Ucello suspected what he was doing, and she had doubts, this exchange could be a trap. Lloyds could lose the money and the masterpieces. She smiled, winked at Sonny, patted Heinrich on the shoulder, and then turned to leave. When the van door opened to the underground garage, Sonny glanced at his sleeve. There was still no satellite link. The section of the hotel garage was also shielded.

The van door slid closed behind her. Charn returned to his seat. "Well, gentlemen, you will earn a nice commission on this deal. You drive a hard bargain."

Sonny sipped his drink. "You've had me anxious all week. It seemed you would never get down to what our people were willing to offer." Sonny knew that was not the reason it took so long. Ucello was careful. Heinrich had offered enough; she just liked to watch buyers before an exchange, to give them time to make mistakes if they were not who they seemed. Heinrich had played his roll perfectly. The only potential problem was the message from Manila that Apollo had arrived in a coma from Mars. Hopefully, Jenny had solved the problems.

Drinking his beer, Heinrich continued chatting quietly with Charn, leaving Sonny to be alone with his thoughts. Ten minutes later Charn got his signal to bring the guests to the exchange. When the van door opened, he directed Sonny and Heinrich through the garage toward the elevator.

Ten flights up, they stepped out into a corridor. Sonny's computer established a satellite uplink, and transmitted the microburst. Within a few steps he had confirmation from Lloyds Insurance that they were reading him. Thirty feet from the elevator, Charn opened the door to a suite, directing Sonny and Heinrich inside. Two big, muscled guards stepped to one side to open a path into the room. Window drapes were tightly drawn. The normal hotel furniture had been moved from the living room to an adjoining bedroom. A long cherry wood conference table had been placed in the center of the room. Three padded chairs were waiting at one side of the table. Beyond the table, standing against the blank, white wall were three easels displaying the renaissance masterpieces. Near the easels were depressions in the beige carpet where the feet of a sofa had left their signature.

"Gentlemen," Charn motioned to the table. "Please put your cases here. Go ahead, do your confirmation tests."

"Danke," Heinrich seated himself first, opening his computer case. A video screen rose from the unit.

Sonny remained standing while he put his computer on the table. Pulling a wire from the case, he connected the unit to the hard-wired phone line waiting on the table for his use. "Where is Ucello?" Sonny had expected her to be gone. He did hope she would be there for this end game.

"Nearby," Charn put his own computer case on the table. He connected his unit to a waiting telephone jack. Both settled back to wait as Heinrich did his confirmation tests. Once more he initiated the infrared, ultraviolet, and x-ray analysis techniques. His computer verified that the brush stroke patterns matched existing files. The tests lasted approximately twenty minutes.

Sonny's concentration on the exchange was interrupted by thoughts of Teddy. It felt as if he were hearing his son's voice calling him. Looking around, there was nothing but the two expressionless guards. Convincing himself to ignore the thoughts, he sat, studied each of the three paintings, and then turned to stare at Heinrich.

Heinrich smiled, and then leaned back. He was sweating despite the air conditioning.

Sonny asked, "Heinrich, are you convinced? Shall we accept?" Before Heinrich could respond, Sonny once more sensed Teddy's presence in his mind. He heard, "Daddy. Daddy. I'm sick. I need you." Sonny did not know what to think this. Nothing similar had ever happened before.

Heinrich said, "I'm satisfied. Let's settle."

Sonny studied each of the paintings. He shifted his gaze to Heinrich, then to Charn. "Mister Bendino, I wish Ucello could be here. This was her deal."

"Sorry," Charn responded. "I'll let her know that you miss her. Now, as soon as we confirm payment, the contents of this room are yours."

Sonny looked back at the doorway where the guards were watching him. He again looked at the paintings, then Heinrich and Charn. "Let's do it." He sat down and activated his computer. July 28, 2215, 10:32 p.m. Hotel Aqua Mediterranean, Naples, Italy. The link was to a bank in Zurich, Switzerland. The connection numbers and account identifications began filling the monitor screen. "Charn. Which bank?"

Charn worked his own computer. "Bern, Oberstein Bank. Account number 66004-BTG-32891-AAZ-00977." The data began appearing on both computers.

Once more Sonny heard Teddy calling, a voice coming from everywhere, from nowhere. He tensed. He could not allow himself to think about something so abstract. That would spook Ucello and Charn. There would be no second opportunity. Sonny maintained his non-reactive little smile, looked to his partner, and said, "Heinrich?"

The old German stepped up to Sonny's computer, put his hand on a ceramic plate designed for hand print and DNA identifications, then muttered, "Heinrich Dietrich, 54550-778-91124, of Bremen, Deutschland." Following computer confirmation of his identity, he said, "Transfer payment by authorization." A message confirmed the transaction.

Charn, watching his own computer through a separate network, smiled. He closed the computer case, and then reached to shake hands with Sonny and Heinrich. "Thank you. Enjoy your purchase."

Charn waltzed through the door, followed closely by the two guards. The door closed automatically behind them. Sonny lifted his sleeve to speak. "We have possession. Secure this room."

The voice of Zhenny, Sonny's contact with Lloyds of London, was finally audible. "And the money? Do we still have control?"

Sonny looked at his computer monitor. "We have it. The payment went to Oberstein Bank. It was immediately transferred to an account in Geneva at Bergenmeister Bank. The tracer I attached is doing its job. The computer is double checking the account transfer as routine. Your money should return to Zurich in thirty minutes."

"Good," Zhenny responded. "We are tracking those Que dots you gave Ucello and Charn. They both left the hotel, and are heading in separate directions." Sonny had slipped the taste-free miniscule-sized 'Que Dots' into the wine Ucello and Charn were drinking in the van. Reacting to a very specific low-frequency radio wave, the "Que Dots" retransmitted signals every few minutes. Using the traffic navigation satellites, the Que Dots located whomever had swallowed the dots. It was an inexpensive, yet effective tracking tool. Ucello was heading for the Naples airport. Charn was in the van going in the opposite direction.

"Zhenny," Sonny seated himself in front of his computer. He glanced at Heinrich, who had moved closer to the paintings. Heinrich was an art connoisseur. Sonny knew the old German would kill to have these paintings in his personal collection. He also knew that Heinrich's moral code would stop such thoughts before they got out of control. Zhenny's image appeared on Sonny's screen. "We have a half hour before we confirm return of the payment. Have you been in touch with my wife?"

"Not directly. I talked to your secretary. Lydia is dealing with Jenny."

Sonny tensed, not certain he wanted to know what was actually happening. "Is everything okay? Did Jenny take care of my nephew?"

"You have been out of touch, haven't you?"

Sonny frowned. "Zhenny, I had to remain out of touch to avoid scaring off Ucello. What happened?"

"There is a health advisory to avoid the Philippines. A new virus is loose in the mountains of Northern Luzon. It's a disease your nephew brought back from Mars."

"What?" Sonny felt a sinking in his stomach." Where is Jenny? Where is my son?"

"Tycho Medical Center, in quarantine. They were sent there along with the entire village of Maliit na Ulap." Zhenny paused, watching Sonny's contorted expressions. "Lydia said that Martian security agents have a warrant for your nephew, Apollo. The U.N. Patrol has authorized them to pursue him. Lydia still has the coded message from Apollo that he sent from Mars. She has not decoded it. You should call Lydia when you get the chance."

Sonny wanted to call Jenny, but stopped himself. If the authorities from both Mars and Earth were stalking Apollo, he had to proceed with caution. First, he needed to complete the art deal. One more hour would not make a difference in the Philippines, but it would make a difference in Naples. "Zhenny, send a coded message to Lydia. I'll be in Manila this afternoon. Tell her that I said five of diamonds." That was his detective's code to not say anything over the electronic communications lines. They would talk in person at the office.

A knock on the door disrupted the communication. Sonny asked the room computer to identify the visitors. A video image on his monitor showed that four Lloyds security agents were outside the door. Sonny instructed the computer to open the door. The security agents, all wearing uniform gray-green environmental suits, moved swiftly into the room, maneuvering between the old German art connoisseur and the masterpieces. A computer driven storage cart followed them to the paintings. Heinrich stared with disgust at such a rude interruption.

"Time to wake up, Heinrich," Sonny smiled, accepting a cup of coffee from an approaching automated galley unit. "Let's give it back to the museum."

Heinrich grimaced at the security men, and then smiled. "But, my Filipino friend, to be in possession for such a brief moment was worth the long wait." He accepted a cup of coffee from the galley unit, and then sat down. "I think I actually enjoyed this caper. I'm tired. I don't think I want to do it again, but it was an adventure."

PART D

TIMESCAPE

CHAPTER TWENTY-FOUR

PHILIPPINE EPIDEMIC

Manila, Philippines

Earth Date   August 3, 2216
Mars Date   C-Mmon 53, 1174

MARTIAN VIRUS, DAY 34

Everything about the Manila Spaceport passenger terminal had changed. Spaceport workers on the tarmac wore sealed environmental suits, complete with pressure helmets and air sterilization filters. All windows were sealed. Gardens were empty of flowers and living plants, their bushes now leafless bundles of twigs. The usual flower-scented air had been replaced with the faint odors of disinfectant. Armed guards were faceless behind their tinted faceplates. At the arrival terminal Sonny rode a robotic passenger cart through the airport. He had no direct human contact at the baggage claim cubicle. Agents at customs check points were also sealed in full pressure suits. The passage to the terminal beyond customs no longer led directly to the spaceport lobby. A series of computerized medical booths blocked the corridor, where incoming visitors were first screened with a robotic medical examination, while at the second booth the Health Department furnished environmental suits to anyone without them. Sonny wore his own. A third unmanned, computerized booth warned visitors that anyone infected with the new strain of "malaria" would be quarantined.

Warned before leaving Italy, Sonny was prepared for the situation in the Philippines. Change to the usual bustle outside was just as dramatic. All pedestrians were sealed in environmental suits, breathing sterilized air. Open air vehicles, popular in tropical Manila, were no more. All windows were sealed, each with air purifiers humming. In front of a medical tent at the terminal's entry were uniformed medics, robots, and security guards watching everyone passing through medical scanners. Sonny's automated airport passenger cart took him to a rental vehicle parking lot. It stopped behind a small van, and then transferred his luggage into the rental van. Once inside the van, Sonny spoke to the vehicle computer. "Before we leave, are any tracking beacons locked on?"

"That is not a proper inquiry."

"Excuse me," Sonny pulled a small cylinder from his pocket, and plugged it into one of the computer jacks on the dashboard. The cylinder established a comm link between his portable personal computer and the van's control system. His own computer responded. "The global traffic locator has a tracking instruction to follow you, U.N. Patrol authorized. All information is relayed to the office of Interplanetary Metals on Roxas Boulevard."

Sonny sighed. He looked around. Another van beside his was about to pull out. He asked his computer. "Get me a readout on rental unit PBS-4457."

The computer responded. "Felix Boutista, of Olongapo, returning from Sydney, Australia.

"Good. Code UNSP XXR6. Traffic locator control, mix signal from passenger this vehicle with that of PBS-4457." Sonny called up the appropriate locator indicator for his computer. The display implied that he was in the other vehicle.

"Van, code UNSP-TQQ. Mask passenger manifest of this vehicle from traffic control. Take us to E. M. Space Transport Office."

"As directed, sir." With that, the van began moving.

Two miles from the Spaceport, the van pulled into a sandy, palm-tree shaded parking area in front of the E.M. Space Transport business office, a complex of bamboo-covered prefab buildings. Just beyond the buildings was a stretch of Manila Bay beach. The office entrance had changed; an airlock had been installed at the door. Sonny watch the automated van drive away to return to the Spaceport. He then glanced at local pedestrians walking by sealed inside environmental suits. When he left for Italy those same Filipinos would have dressed in short pants, loose shirts, and straw hats. He placed his luggage on the outer porch near the airlock, and then went through the quarantine airlock. No one was in the lobby. One wall displayed space freight rates for delivery to several popular destinations on Mars, along with timetables for the departures and arrivals.

"Bibi," Sonny said. "Sonny Ortigas. Open up."

The display of timetables and shipping rates abruptly faded to a transparent wall. Beyond the partition was a business office with wood panel over prefab office walls. There were five desks, but only two people in the office; Reni Treilio, a young expediter, and Bibi, owner-manager. Bibi told the computer to open the wall. The transparent partition slid into an adjacent wall. She stood to greet him, "Sonny! Why are you here?"

"I love you, too, Bibi," He said as he walked in, "I called Lydia... my office is under surveillance. They probably are wired into my comm system. I figure I should approach Manila unannounced."

"Did you lead them here?" Bibi gently slapped Sonny's arm. "They've been watching me, too. Your nephew was returned to Earth on one of our transports."

"They didn't follow me."

Bibi studied her old friend. "Don't tell me how. I don't want to know." She motioned toward the galley, "Something to drink?"

"San Miguel Beer," Sonny patted Bibi's shoulder. "Actually, if you have pancit and bangus... real food. I'm sick of pasta."

Bibi asked the galley computer to prepare what Sonny requested. Returning her attention to Sonny, she asked. "Are you up to date on the situation?"

"I called Lydia as soon as I finished in Italy. She explained about Apollo and the epidemic and said she was being watched. I told her to say nothing more until I got home. Here I am." He settled into a padded rattan chair. "I watched the news about the epidemic. Five hundred have been moved to Tycho. Twenty are dead, mostly elderly. The U.N. Health Service established an infectious threat warning for Luzon, with the Benget Province sealed off. The news claims the epidemic is from a new strain of malaria."

Bibi eased into her own chair. She briefly eyed Rene, and then once more spoke to Sonny. "Jenny said this 'malaria strain' is what your nephew brought back from Mars. It spread from Apollo to others in Maliit na Ulap by mosquitoes. Malaria is a convenient health threat that offers a believable excuse for spraying agricultural areas, and testing inhabitants."

"I just came from the spaceport. Unbelievable. It doesn't look like the Philippines."

"Neither Lydia nor I have told anyone about the transmission from Mars. We were tempted because of the precautions the Health Service imposed, but with someone stalking your nephew..."

The computerized mobile galley rolled up to Sonny's chair, extending a food tray for him to take. "Call Lydia. Tell her the shipment she was expecting from Naples has arrived. Suggest the 'red sun' approach."

"Red sun?" Bibi squinted. She took a mango juice, and then leaned back. It dawned on her this was Sonny's typical use of codes. She said, "Computer, call Lydia. Tell her the package is here from Naples. Use the red sun approach."

"Before we continue," Sonny placed his food tray on an empty desk. He placed his computer case beside the tray, "Do you have any security systems in place?"

She laughed. "You were Blue's friend. He designed this office."

"You have security. Have you checked it?"

She took the queue. Moments later the office computer identified an unfamiliar microphone at Bibi's desk, a tiny video camera attached to a wall, and a tracking transmitter embedded in her hair. Sonny methodically destroyed the three units, and then said, "The stalkers know I'm here. In an hour Lydia will meet me on the Rock with what she has. I need to see that message from Mars, see what Lydia has from other sources on these stalkers."

"The Rock?"

"Corrigedor... Malinta Tunnels. If there are any micro bugs on either me or Lydia, the signals will be useless from deep underground. If we are followed, I can neutralize them down there." He put his fork down, and then picked up the beer, waving his other hand in the direction of the spaceport. "This Health Service isolation of Luzon is terrible. Everyone is afraid to breathe air. If that message can solve the nature of this epidemic, I have to get it to the authorities. First, I have to find out who is threatening Apollo, and why."

Bibi sat her glass on the desk. "Lydia told me the transmission is coded. If you're isolated in the tunnels, will you be able to decipher the message?"

"Lloyds of London told me that the key to the cipher is the nicknames and birthdates of three people he and I both know. Apollo used a code I would know, that no one else could figure out. My computer has vital statistics for everyone from Maliit na Ulap. I'll figure it out."

Bibi asked, "So, is there anything you need me to do?"

"That's why I'm here. I need a plane and a pilot. After I meet with Lydia, I'm going to Baguio. When I get back, I'll visit Interplanetary Metals. I'll need a van."

"Baguio is quarantined. Is that a good idea?"

"It's a good idea." Sonny replied. "Relax. I know what I'm doing."

Company buildings along the beach at the back of the Transport office were used as guest quarters and entertainment facilities for customers. Beyond the buildings was a dock leading across the pebble beach to the gray waters of Manila Bay. These buildings had been the home of space freight pilot Blue Heidelburn before he accepted the Martian offer to fly the first manned interstellar mission to a planet circling Tau Ceti, a star twelve light years away. When he left, he transferred his third of the space freight business to Bibi.

After cleaning up in guest quarters, Sonny took a company owned hover craft, from a garage beside the dock, out over Manila Bay to the island of Corrigedor. A gentle breeze from the ocean eased the humid warmth of the morning. Sonny was sealed in an environmental suit fitted with a medical air purifier. Sonny wished the quarantine rules were not so rigid; he wanted to feel the breeze in his hair.

Out on the Bay, his computer's surveillance program did not notice any water vehicles following, and that there were no aircraft, drone or manned. However, during the five minute ride to Corregidor, the computer did report that Interplanetary Metals Corporation had locked on to his vehicle traffic transponder. He expected that. The same traffic control satellite gave him Lydia's coded transducer signal. She was waiting for him at the entrance to the Malinta Tunnel.

Corregidor was a rocky island jutting from the middle of the water passage between Manila Bay and the South China Sea. The view from the docks of the palm trees and rugged mountains of the Bataan was beautiful. For three centuries, Corregidor had been a historic attraction where tourists could recall the war of 1942. Abruptly, Corregidor had changed from a popular historic sight to a symbol of the fight against a new plague that threatened civilization. Now, tourist shops were covered with inflatable domes, and the tunnel entrances were covered with disinfection airlocks. Illuminated signs at the landing docks made clear the situation: "Tourist facility closed"; "Quarantine Isolation Facility"; "Restricted Access, Medical Emergency". Robot soldiers, armed with an array of weapons, were positioned every ten feet. Nobody could enter or leave Corregidor without security approval.

Sonny docked the hover van up on a concrete ramp. A robotic hovercraft approached to warn him not to disembark until given permission. Slowly circling Sonny's van, the robot scanned everything for hint of the virus. The craft then offered Sonny access to a Health Department communications console. Filipino officials on screen asked for identification, status, and purpose of visit. Sonny then said, "I am here on personal business."

"What business?"

"I am a private detective investigating this health threat."

There was a long pause. The doctor on the screen disappeared from view. When he reappeared, he said, "You can enter. If you become infected, you will be quarantined."

"Understood."

Sonny drove up the hill, passing a multitude of domed isolation facilities, into the entrance to the Malinta Tunnels. The entrance was covered with a transparent tarp, protecting the vehicle entrance and dual personnel airlocks. Inside the tunnel Lydia was waiting.

"Sonny!" She glanced down at the two cases he had asked her to bring, she then reached to hug him. "Finally."

"I don't know what to say," He eyed health service workers wandering by. "Do you have a room to use?"

She released him, "Follow." She reached for the two bags, but he motioned he would take them. "I arranged to meet the Health Service Chief. Since this epidemic started with your relatives, he wants to talk to you."

Carrying his own bags, Sonny followed. "Can he tell what this virus is? What is actually happening? I assume he understands I've been out of touch, that I know less than anyone."

Lydia said, "This infection started with your nephew. The chief, here, has the report from Tycho. He hopes you can find answers. He will brief us on the epidemic, and give you time to get involved." They strolled down the main tunnel causeway. She explained, "Five hundred are in isolation here. Baguio has several thousand testing positive for the virus. Burnham Park and Camp John Hay are now quarantine facilities. This epidemic began spreading only four days ago."

"This can't be. Apollo arrived only a week ago. How could a bug one kid picked up be moving this quickly?" He followed her around a tunnel lateral to temporary trailers that had been set up as offices. Many workers, obscured in medical environmental suits, scurried in various directions, paying no attention to the two of them.

"Jenny's brother, Dr. Kia Patterson, stalled telling the Health Service about this message from Mars. You were in Italy, and someone is after Apollo. He asked me to get it decoded, get anything relevant fast."

"I'll see what I can do. Tell me about the virus."

"Apparently it does not survive in open air. It lives in liquids, and can be transmitted by shared food, by sex, by mosquito. That's why Health Service control is so stringent." Lydia led him to one of three field office trailers parked in tandem. An illuminated sign mounted beside the main door read: "Administration Chief, Corrigedor Medical Isolation Center, United Nations Health Service."

The receptionist led the visitors past a maze of staff workers to a private office. The automatic door slid closed after she left, leaving Sonny and Lydia facing the facility administrator. Belisario was leaning back in his chair studying a wall screen displaying a spread sheet detailing routing of food supplies destined for the island patients. The man was sixty, short and chubby. Belisario leaned forward, supporting himself with his arms on the ceramic-resin desk. "Miguel Ortigas," he glanced briefly at the monitor on his desk where a U.N. file on Sonny was openly displayed. Belisario stood, smiled, reached for a quick handshake. "You've had an interesting life. I was just reviewing your report about the Rome art case. I'd love to hear the details."

Sonny grabbed the extended hand. "I'd love to tell you sometime, Mr. Belisario … over a beer. However, at the moment…"

Charles Belisario concluded the handshake. "Agreed." He motioned toward the chairs in front of his desk. "Please." Sonny and Lydia accepted the hospitality. Belisario sat back down. "Lydia told me you just returned from Rome, that you have been isolated from… this situation."

Sonny maintained his pleasant, disarming smile. "Can you bring me up to speed?"

Belisario quietly studied Sonny before responding. "A week ago Tycho Medical Center got a call from your wife that your nephew had been returned from Mars in a coma, sealed in a medic chamber, under very strange circumstances." He paused, took a breath, and then continued. "She sent a copy of your nephew's biostats from the chamber to Tycho, along with a plea for caution about an unidentified stalker. The boy's stats showed that he had been in coma three weeks with a new viral infection. The sealed medic chamber was opened in the barrio of Maliit na Ulap before health care professionals could evaluate the situation. Mosquitoes spread the infection."

Sonny stared, and then interrupted. "My nephew caused this quarantine?

Belisario leaned back. "The virus caused it. Your nephew is the first victim. Now, a great many people are infected. I need your help to track it back to its source."

"I'm not certain I follow…"

Charles addressed the computer. "Wall screen … display Ward Six. Hand held remote zoom control." The earlier spreadsheet display faded from the wall, replaced by a panoramic view of a sixty-bed sick ward. "This virus survives in most fresh water and biologic liquid sources. Frozen, or absent nutrients, it is dormant. In a blood stream it becomes active, and it can be transmitted by insect, by fish, by contaminated food, or by sexual intimacy. It can survive in plants, although there is no noticeable affect on those plants."

He zoomed the image to the bed of a young woman. Attractive, except for the dark spots covering her exposed flesh, matted hair, and glistening sweat. She had dark circles under her eyes. She grimaced in discomfort. "The symptoms, other than what you see on the outside, include fever, nausea, diarrhea, headaches, chills, hallucination, and coma." Belisario explained. The video image moved from one patient to the next, slowing at each. "These are the young adults. The older patients go into cardiac arrest with the coma."

"Interesting," Sonny responded. "This helps me understand what the virus does, but, still…"

"Relax, Mister Ortigas," The image switched to a file record from Baguio. It began with aerial footage of the town. The golf course and ballfields at the Regional Park Camp John Hay were packed with inflatable isolation tents. It looked like a military bivouac area among the landscaped pine trees. "There are several thousand patients in Baguio. Everyone from Maliit na Ulap is in isolation on the Moon. The town, along with nearby vegetation, has been sprayed to destroy this virus. The virus escaped. It is ravaging Baguio. It just started in Manila. We can't take all of them to the Moon."

"Have you found any antibiotics that work with it?"

"None. Some animals are immune. About half the people are immune. We do not understand the mechanics of this virus, why it does what it does."

"Informative," Sonny said, "However, I am not a doctor."

Belisario looked at him. "You're a detective. According to your file, you are good at it. We have a virus never seen before, and it spreading like crazy. The doctor on Mars who sent your nephew back to Earth is missing. The doctor in Hong Kong he was sending the boy to was surprised. He claims no contact with Mars. The men who were with your nephew on Mars are missing. An unknown stalker is following him. The man your brother-in-law was seeing on Mars was murdered. According to the Martian police, he was killed by his partner in a fight over a mining operation."

"Are you trying to hire me?"

"I assume you will be doing that anyway. My concern is where did this virus come from? Did someone create a doomsday bug, give it to your nephew, and ship him back to Earth? If this bug came from Mars, why is no one on Mars sick?"

"You think it may be a weapon?"

"Possibly, but I doubt the Martian Militia would deliberately start this. However, if they developed the virus, and some crazy worker took it to friends with a political agenda…"

"I see your point. Give me a day to think about it."

"I can grant you special U.N. investigative authority."

"I need to talk to my wife, to check a few things… here … and in Baguio."

"Understood. Keep in mind, this virus is deadly and not controlled. Your family is in quarantine. Your father is dead. If it is a weapon, whoever created this may have an antidote. Time is not on our side."

"I have to talk to my family first, and they are quarantined on the Moon." Sonny stood, signaling Lydia to follow. "I'll be in touch. I'm inclined to take your offer. I need to check a few things. I don't want to start blind."

Lydia led Sonny to another lateral tunnel, into a prefab building marked "Power Generator". She said, "I figured this would mask computer signals. Is anyone following?"

"They're tracking us into the tunnels, but down here those signals are lost."

Just beyond the power generator shop was a maintenance office. Lydia had paid the maintenance supervisor to make the room available. She handed Sonny the computer plug with Apollo's message from Mars. Placing his computer on the cleared table, he pulled up a chair to view the message.

The monitor display of the July tenth message showed a sickly Apollo looking back at the camera. His face was covered with a rash, his hair matted, forehead sweaty, and eyes bloodshot. "Tito Sonny, this is Apollo with a coded message from Mars. The keys to decode are the full names and birthdates of Baby, Coconut, and Christmas Rose. The remainder of this message is restricted and private." The screen image changed to freeze frame.

"Jenny should know these," Sonny grimaced slightly. "Did you ask her to decipher?"

"I told her the codes were nicknames of your friends and family. She didn't think she could help."

He thought about the three nicknames. "Baby is Apollo's sister, Madeline. What's her birth date?"

"I don't remember." Lydia manipulated the controls on her computer. "That's why we have calendars." A moment later, Madeline's birthday was on screen.

"Christmas Rose is Jenny." Sonny recalled. "The first time I dated Jenny she delivered that single yellow rose to my office."

"I was there." Lydia swatted Sonny's arm. "You were out when Jenny brought that rose in. What's her birthday?" Seconds later the computer displayed the date.

"Coconut? That's Emilio's son. What's his name? Carlos Perez?"

"Not Emilio Perez, Jun Ventuno!" Lydia smirked. "Jun. His son's name is Carlos."

Lydia had the computer display the information requested for the three nicknames. Apollo's commentary then continued. "Tito Sonny, I am not feeling so well. Last week we were exploring a subterranean cave in the Princess Dejah Canyon. I found a deposit of ice under a layer of sandstone deep underground with small fish embedded in that ice. I thawed and tasted one of those fish. That made me very sick. The rash on my face came from the fish. Miss Sonia Androff got the sickness from me, and she also has the rash." His eyes were moistening. "We are getting worse. Sonia will tell you the whole story."

The screen image switched to Sonia, also with a face filled with the rash. "Miguel Ortigas," a tired Sonia smiled from the monitor. "Tito Sonny, as Apollo calls you. We met at your Christmas party in Baguio. Fisk Banzer and I and Apollo and his Filipino uncles discovered a major gold deposit in the Princess Dejah Canyon. Our mission was sabotaged by a predatory corporate mining company. They killed Fisk, killed our mechanic Japa Reese, and killed the Filipino miners with us … Roberto DeNila, Emilio Perez, Jun Ventuno, Doug Manlapus, and Celso Cruz. The killings were done by Ghant Travis, Redrock Mining Operations vice president; Dave Crane, who was working for us as a geochemist; and Police Captain Ken Sylvester of the Martian Global Police. Our records and government files have been altered to imply that we were Redrock employees, prospecting under a company contract. Following this introduction, you will find the files of our business, a recording of the murders, and the statistics on the frozen fish Apollo found."

"Apollo and I are recording this message while hiding in a cave in the El Dorado badlands, not far from the John Carter trail leading out of the Burroughs Valley. The virus we are infected with has multiple symptoms that worsen with each passing hour, a sickness that may kill us before we find help. We will try to get to a hospital, but with Redrock stalking us, the odds are not favorable. If we disappear into the vast desert wastelands of Mars, this recording may be the only testimony left about what really happened in the Canyon."

"There is one more matter. The virus has an unusual side effect. It generates vivid mental images that accurately glimpse unfamiliar past and future events. In the attached recordings, Apollo had a prophetic dream of the murders in the Canyon before they happened. That revelation gave us advanced warning, or we would also have been killed."

"Apollo tells me that you are a friend and confident to broadcaster Terra Newton. If you get this to her soon enough, I trust that she may be able to save our lives. I am sorry about your Filipino friends. I hope this transmission will get justice for them."

That introduction was followed by a series of files, including the discovery of the fish and the bio-scans of the specimens; and the medical diagnostics reports for both Apollo and Sonia. Business records showed all aspects of the prospecting mission. The message finished with a video of the murders and details on how the official records were altered.

Sonny sighed, and then said, "This was transmitted three weeks ago. Do you have anything else?"

"Boss," Lydia sat up. "This is the first time I saw this."

"I'm not trying to blame anyone. It was coded for me to decipher. If I had been here, this epidemic would not be ... my wife and son would not be on the Moon."

"You did not know, Sonny," Lydia took his arm. "You had no way to know. What do we do now?"

"What do you have that can help me?"

"Octan Palmer brought Apollo from Mars. She told me that someone high in government was stalking him. I contacted the Ekakaidis Detective Agency on Mars to check on Fisk Banzer, Sonia Androff, Redrock Mining, and Interplanetary Metals. Interplanetary Metals sent agents to Bibi and to me to look for Apollo. You did a file search on the credentials for Fisk Banzer and Sonia Androff last Christmas before Apollo and Roberto went to Mars. Those credentials don't match what Ekakaidis got back. Sonia was right. The records were altered."

"You have the records with you?"

"Oh, yes," she handed the computer plugs to him.

"Go back to the office. If anyone asks, you have not seen Apollo's message."

"Are you going to show this to Charles Belisario? This confirms where the virus came from, and that it is not a weapon."

"Roberto was killed by an executive of Redrock Mining with the help of a Martian Police. They have people tracking Apollo. If I give this transmission to Belisario, he would be compelled to contact Martian authorities. They would rush to that Canyon to locate the virus, which would give the killers time to go underground. I can't share this yet."

"What are you going to do?"

"Offer to work with him. I'll ask for Health Service support, but explain that I have to work on my own. He'll understand."

"Where will you start?"

"Baguio. I need time to study what we have. Then, I visit Interplanetary Metals."

"Baguio is quarantined. Your house is sealed."

"As long as I stay sealed in this suit and go through all the sterilization checkpoints, I should have no problem. Belisario will give me the authority to get through."

CHAPTER TWENTY-FIVE

RECOVERY

Tycho Medical Center

Earth Date	August 5, 2216
Mars Date	C-Mmon 54, 1174

MARTIAN VIRUS, DAY 36

"Amazing," Kai put a hand on his sister's shoulder. "Teddy is free of the virus. Like you. It's as if he never had it." Kai watched the precocious Teddy chasing Nina around the observation deck, which provided a magnificent unimpeded view of the Tycho Crater from its southern rim. Hanging in star-studded sky above was the ever present blue-white Earth.

"He's completely recovered?" Jenny's gaze followed Teddy running back past the bench, a moment before he dashed out of sight, with Nina in hot pursuit. "Can we go home now?" The brilliant sun near the western horizon along with the huge Earth in the dark north sky seemed surreal compared to the familiar evening sky she was used to seeing in the Philippines.

"Not that simple. Teddy's stats are back to normal, except for a residual trace of the pituitary enzymes. In fact, all of the children under ten are in full recovery. However, we do not know how much of a threat they would be to someone who has not yet been exposed."

Jenny pleaded, "If I am not infected, and Teddy is better…" she looked at the crowd of alert patients on the far side of the deck. One of the miners was obviously telling jokes to the laughing crowd of nine. Even Celia seemed to be enjoying what she was hearing.

"I did not say you are not infected. You are not affected. It seems you are immune to the virus in your blood. We don't understand why you are unaffected, or how Teddy's system overcame the virus. If we can isolate why, we may be able to come up with a cure. Until then, you have to remain in quarantine."

"But, if we are improving? This place is so depressing."

"The U.N. Health Service brought six-hundred more patients from the Baguio area while you were sleeping. We did not eliminate the threat by sterilizing Maliit na Ulap." Kai looked up from his computerized clipboard. "They're in an isolation ward a mile from here."

"Six hundred? From Baguio?" Jenny remembered stopping by the restaurant to get food for the barrio. "Did I do that?"

Kai's gloved hand patted the arm on Jenny's pressure suit. "I don't think it was you. We found bats with the virus. They were eating infected insects. Apparently it makes bats more aggressive. They're attacking people in broad daylight."

"Sounds like rabies," Jenny sighed, "Then it wasn't me." She looked out through the transparent dome at the ochre-gray floor of the Tycho crater. The sun glistened from the hundreds of metal towers and transparent domes of the city twelve miles away. A tongue of flame followed an accelerating cargo ship lifting from the spaceport. "Why am I immune?" A light was flashing on Jenny's sleeve.

"You… Celia… Nina have type 'O' Negative blood. Everyone who is sick with the virus has either type 'A' or 'B' positive blood. It seems that 'O' Negative has properties that inhibit the virus, enables the body's defenses to fight it off. There are no clear solutions, yet."

Jenny did not understand a word he was saying, other than something about blood types making a difference. She lifted her sleeve. "This is Jenny Ortigas."

"We have a call from Manila." The computer generated voice responded "Sonny Ortigas. Do you want it there with the audio only?"

Jenny looked around to see who was nearby. Nina and Teddy were returning to her bench again. The rest of the barrio patients, not bedridden, were still together listening to funny stories on the far side of the observation deck.

Nina stopped her tag game with Teddy to come up to Jenny. "Is that Tito Sonny? Did he find out what happened to Apollo? Does he know where my dad is?"

"I haven't answered the call yet," Jenny patted Nina's shoulder. "Let me talk to him, privately. Please." She glanced down at Teddy, then once more at Nina.

"I understand," Nina took Teddy's hand to lead him out. "We'll be here."

"I'll look in on Apollo," Kai said. "You need to talk privately." He stood simultaneously with his sister. They walked down the stairs and through the corridors to the communications center. He left her to continue his rounds to visit patients. Jenny focused on the monitor screens. One message read: "Jenny Ortigas. Return call to Sonny at Manila office. Blue cipher."

She removed a case of six small computer inserts from her pocket. Plugging the blue one into the computer, she then set the console to record. "Sonny, we are in trouble. I'm sure Lydia already told you. I keep her updated. I miss you terribly."

Following the three-second delay for transmission travel time to the Earth and back, his image appeared on screen. His welcoming voice reached her ears. "I miss you. Very much. I'm sorry I was away. Yes, I know about the quarantine. Our Baguio house was sterilized." Sonny had a grim expression, blood shot eyes. "Teddy is going to be upset that the banana trees are gone, but there was no choice. I'm glad he is feeling better. I want to say a lot about my dad, about Father Roxas. I feel terrible. I did not have a chance to say goodbye … This will wait. I'll talk to Celia in a few minutes."

"Our house? What did they do to our house?" Jenny was frantic. She imagined the worst.

Seconds later he responded. "All plants, food… curtains… linen… the fish tank… have been removed by the Health Service. Everything was sprayed. Four times. The house is still intact. Our insurance will restore the garden and the clothing. It's not too bad. How is Teddy now?"

Jenny felt sick to her stomach. All those beautiful flowers were gone… her flowers… the rose bushes, the banana trees that Teddy loved. She visualized the house being empty of cloth and plants. She wanted to be angry, but knew that would only make matters more difficult for Sonny. "Teddy is better today. He's up on the observation deck playing with Nina. If Lydia told you everything, did you decipher that message Apollo sent from Mars?"

"Yes." Sonny paused before continuing. "The virus came from a fish Apollo found on Mars."

"Fish? Mars has no fish."

"The fish was frozen in buried ice for millions of years. Apollo thawed it, tasted it."

Jenny looked away from the telecommunications screen to the surveillance monitors. Apollo was still in his deep sleep. Kai was watching one of his dream sequence interpretation. "This strange disease came from an old, dead fish? That is hard to believe."

"Anyone with you from Ulap?"

"No. You want me to get your sister?"

"Not yet. Roberto is dead!"

"Dead? Apollo said that?"

"They're all dead. Emilio, Jun, Doug, Celso. So is Fisk Banzer, the man who hired them."

"Dead?" Jenny thought about the reports of Sonia killing Fisk Banzer. "Why? How?"

"Murdered. Fisk's partner, Sonia Androff saved Apollo's life. She sent the message. She has the same sickness as Apollo. She got it from him."

Jenny was shaking. She did not want to deal with these revelations. On a monitor view of the observation deck Nina still played with Teddy. Nina had been upset over Apollo's fantasy arousal dream with a playmate robot. A second sexual revelation would be more than the girl could handle. That news would be coupled with a report that her father had been murdered. On another screen Celia had left the crowd exchanging funny stories, looking tired. She approached the stairway leading from the deck down to the subterranean facilities.

"Don't talk about this to anyone else, yet," Jenny said. "Nina is already upset. Did you get the imaging videos of Teddy's dream?"

"I got it. I don't understand how, but Teddy saw the actual art deal transaction through my eyes before the transaction took place. Even the bank account numbers he dreamed were accurate. It was unreal. Does the medical staff has an explanation?"

"They do not understand. Terra wants to send the material to some professor she knows on Mars. I asked her to wait until you agreed."

"You met with Terra?"

"She's here to cover the ratification of the Venus Resources Treaty. She's interested in Apollo's story."

"Tell her to expect me at Tycho tomorrow. I have more from the transmission on Apollo's dreams, and about where the virus came from. Give her the green cipher. Have her track me through my office."

"If you know where the virus came from, my brother needs to know. Six-hundred more victims just arrived from Baguio."

"I know. There are several thousand positive cases in Baguio. Another five-hundred are isolated at Corregidor. I'll talk to him tomorrow. I need to control how this news gets out. The people who killed… killed Roberto … will probably try to make certain that no one survives to tell the story."

"Sonny," Jenny felt acid in her stomach. She was convinced this warning was the cause. She chose her words carefully. "I miss you terribly. I want to cry on your shoulder. But don't come here. If you do, you will be in quarantine, too. I need for you to find out who is stalking Apollo, find out why we can't talk to the police."

"I came to the same conclusion. I'm checking a few leads here before I head for the Moon. I'll talk to you again before I leave. I love you." He paused, and then said, "Is Celia close enough for you to speak?"

"Teka, teka," Jenny answered. The locator map of the compound showed Celia heading to her own cubicle. Jenny signaled her. Moments later Celia was in the communications room talking to Sonny. Jenny excused herself to allow them privacy.

In the hallways Jenny sighed at Nina approaching with Teddy. Nina asked, "Did Tito Sonny find anything about my tito (father)?"

Jenny said, "Can you watch Teddy for a little while? I need to talk to Doctor Patterson."

"Of course, Tita Jenny."

"I'll tell you after I talk to Kai." Jenny walked through the doors to the corridor. Along the way to Apollo's room, she paused at the observation windows to the room where most of the coma patients' med chambers were isolated. Carlos Bentua, Teresa Reyes, Madeline Panahon, and twelve others were in coma, enclosed in individual chambers. C.N.A. helmets were on all of their heads. Two medical technicians at Madeline's enclosure were making adjustments to the settings. Both were sealed in isolation pressure suits with Tycho Medical Center Quarantine Facility staff patches on their arms. An off-color gray patch was visible near the collar on one of the technicians.

She lifted her sleeve to call her brother. "Kai, who are the technicians in the central intensive care isolation ward?"

"Now?" He responded, "I don't know. I'm busy with Apollo. He is dreaming. I think he is waking."

"There are two staff medics at Apollo's sister's chamber. Can you verify who they are?"

During the pause Jenny alertly observed as the two technicians abruptly straightened from their hunched positions at Madeline's chamber. Looking around, they glanced at Jenny. The tinted faceplates obscured their faces. One picked up a small case from beside the chamber, then followed the other to the staff door.

"Jenny," Kai's voice was again audible through the suit communicator, "The two technicians were visiting from the geriatric treatment center three miles away. They should not be in the isolation ward. They have been told to leave."

"They left. One of them has a repair patch on his sleeve identical to one Yugo Danford was wearing. Danford is one of those detectives looking for Apollo."

Kai responded. "There are no changes to Madeline's stats, and no signs of adjustments to the I.V. medications. A doctor is on the way to double check."

Jenny remained at the window watching Madeline's chamber until a doctor she recognized entered the ward. She then continued on to join her brother. Because Apollo was the first recorded victim, under mysterious circumstances, and exhibited the most pronounced hypothalamus side effects, Rochelle had elected to keep him isolated under a John Doe listing.

"Sharp eyes," Kai said. Jenny entered the observation booth. He continued, "Security is trying to stop those two before they get away."

"I just talked to Sonny. He says that message from Mars warns that the people who killed Fisk Banzer may want to make certain there are no witnesses." She looked through the window at Apollo's chamber. There was no activity inside. She glanced at the technicians in the control room, and then looked at her brother. "You said he was waking up?"

Kai pointed to the monitors below the window. "His stats are normal. His brain activity, other than the readings from the hypothalamus, is comparable to light sleep."

"Are you trying to wake him?" Jenny studied the monitors. She did not understand the technical displays. The dream monitors showed a view of Terra talking to Sonia. The dream image showed them in a wood paneled dining room with a number of unoccupied tables beyond them. Embedded in one of the walls was a huge, internally illuminated room-sized terrarium enclosing small conifer trees, ferns, and flowering rhododendron bushes.

"We don't want to force it," Kai responded, "We've been piping audio broadcasts into his earphones. Hopefully, the soft conversations will stir him awake."

"You're playing Terra Newton broadcasts," Jenny pointed to the visualization of Apollo's dream. "Is that why he is dreaming of her?...

and Sonia? That dining room looks familiar. I've seen it before. Is it in Baguio?"

"I don't know," Kai said. "Watch if the view shifts to the entrance. Look at the time display."

The image shifted to an approaching waitress, a pretty woman, with wavy red hair. She looked to be about fifty, familiar.

"Starr. Starr Swenson." Jenny pointed to the screen. "She's a recording singer. She owns a night club in Crater City, called the Club Fir Tree. That image is one of the dining rooms in her club."

"We figured that out," Kai said. "The computer identified Starr, and the club. They've been talking about the virus and frozen fish in the Princess Dejah Canyon."

Jenny turned her attention to her brother. "Sonny is arriving tomorrow. He told me that message from Mars… Sonia Androff sent it. The virus came from a fish Apollo found frozen in a cave in the Princess Dejah Canyon. He thawed and tasted it. That's how he got sick. Sonia got the virus from him."

Kai pondered what she said, then pointed to the monitor. The view looked over Sonia's shoulder at the entrance to the dining room. Above the doorway was an electronic time display giving time and date for Seattle and Crater City. Appropriate for a place called "Club Fir Tree." The Earth date read: "August 26, 2216," three weeks into the future.

"This dream of Terra Newton talking to Sonia is about the near future? It's like the dream Teddy had about Sonny."

Kai paused before asking. "Did Sonny confirm Teddy's dream?"

Jenny nodded. "He did. Even the bank account numbers were accurate. How does this happen?"

"How?" Kai spread his arms in mock surrender. "I don't understand. Rochelle does not understand. We've never seen anything like this before. It has to be related to those new hormones causing unfamiliar neural activity in the hypothalamus. The dreams appear to be accurate images of the future… like this one… like Teddy's… and of the past, like Apollo's dreams of Percival Lowell."

The image had disappeared into a pattern of red and pink, and then changed to a faint, ghost-like portrait of Apollo's face overlaying ceiling lights.

"He's awake," Kai sprang to his feet. "Control, open the lid. Apollo is looking at his own reflection from the cover of the chamber."

"Miss Sonia?" Apollo spoke his first words in several weeks.

Kai told Jenny, "Apollo knows you. Turn to channel seventeen."

Jenny adjusted the settings on her sleeve. "Apollo, this is Tita Jenny."

"Tita Jenny? Are you on Mars? Is Sonia with you?" He tried to force himself to sit up. Technicians were already at his chamber, helping him to sit erect. "I thought I was in Crater City with Sonia and Terra Newton. Are we still there?"

"You were dreaming. Sonia sent you home several weeks ago. We are on the Moon."

"The Moon?"

"The sickness put you in a coma. You've been asleep for a long time."

"Where is Sonia?"

Jenny paused before responding. "We'll discuss that. First, try to wake up. The medics will help you."

The technicians adjusted the chamber for the side to drop down, and then cautiously aided Apollo in his efforts to sit up.

Kai said, "Don't attempt to walk yet. Your weight is one-sixth normal, and after a month in a coma, you need to approach it slowly."

Apollo lifted his arm, staring at his hand and wrist. "It's gone. The rash is gone."

Kai answered. "Your virus seems to be receding on its own."

Apollo looked up. "The dreams. I remember a lot of dreams…"

"We'll talk about that soon. Are you hungry?"

CHAPTER TWENTY-SIX

VENUS RESOURCE TREATY

Tycho Convention Center

Earth Date	August 6, 2216
Mars Date	C-Mmon 55, 1174

Spectators packed the auditorium at the Tycho Convention Center, anxious to be on hand for history in the making. VIP's seated at the tables nearest the stage included foreign secretaries for the thirty-two space faring nations of Earth. On stage, tables on either side of the podium were reserved for the Governor General of the Moon, the Martian Ambassador to Earth, the President of the U. N. General Assembly, and the corporate executives ready to participate in the new interplanetary venture. U. N. President Charles Petrivich spoke from the podium about the importance of the Venus Resources Treaty, illustrating how this agreement would make the hot, corrosive surface of Venus accessible for enterprises, exploration, and human expansion. President Petrivich mentioned his campaigned to open the surface of Venus to mankind. This treaty would make his promises a reality.

Behind the podium was a huge monitor with a four-way split screen. The four views included a live action image of the President speaking, then a robot camera view from the surface of Venus near the Rhea Mountain; the third view was a zoom from a communications satellite orbiting Venus that focused on the spacecraft designed to land a crew on that hostile surface; and last was a camera pan of the crowd in the auditorium.

Sitting in the press booth above the convention floor, Terra knew the President's speech would take thirty minutes, leaving her nothing to do until it was over. She leaned back, accepting a cup of coffee from Ness Trenton. "Thanks, boss." She sipped, watching as he settled into a seat. "Why are you here? You want to do a commentary?" She pointed through the window toward the stage. "After he finishes?"

"That's what I pay you to do. I'll be out before the President finishes. Is the follow-up ready?"

"All these years, and you still have to ask." Terra put her drink on a side table. "I've edited the major players and added their artwork. We have six hours to fill after the signing before the landing. I can fill the entire slot if you need it."

Ness rolled his head back and laughed. "You'd do it, too. No, your competitors would," he reached in a vest pocket, pulled out a small cylinder, and handed it to her. "You have a message from the Medical Center, marked urgent. You went there a couple of days ago. This may be relevant...What was that visit all about, anyway?"

She took the cylinder, rolled it in her hand, and then pulled an electronic clipboard from her pocket. The size of a pack of cigarettes, the touch of a button automatically unfolded and expanded it to a flat video screen. Plugging the cylinder into the top, she then asked for a display. The screen read: "To Terra Newton from Jenny Ortigas. Apollo awake. New dreamscapes. Sonny arrives today from Manila, Asean Spaceflight 568. I can't leave quarantine. Please meet him. He needs to talk to you. In the transmission from Mars, Apollo foresaw the failure of the Venus landing. Stop it if you can." After reading the message, Terra looked out at the U. N. President, who was still talking. Above the podium were the live action images of Venus.

Terra handed the clipboard to Ness.

Puzzled by her expression, he read the text. He looked up at her, "Who is Jenny Ortigas? What is this?"

"I've been holding back the quarantine story. A barrio from the Philippines has been quarantined on the Moon. Do you remember Sonny Ortigas?"

Ness nodded. "I've seen the news on the new malaria epidemic. Is that what this is about? Sonny Ortigas? The Manila detective? Fifteen years ago..."

"Sixteen years. Jenny is his wife. You met her at my wedding. And other times when they came to Mars."

"Oh, yes, her. I could never forget."

"Boss, she's not your type."

"Envy?" Ness smiled. "Terra, I'm surprised."

Terra grinned in return. "Silly. She's the most... sensuous... woman I've ever seen. She doesn't flaunt it. Her concern is her family, her town... male staff were going crazy trying to do favors for her."

Ness shook his head. "Yeh, she... never mind. Tell me about her situation."

"Jenny... Sonny's hometown is quarantined here at Tycho. The U.N. Health Service announced a health emergency for the Philippines. The reality is that it is strange disease, picked up by Sonny's nephew on Mars, and it is now loose on Earth. One side effect of the sickness is vivid dreams, more like prophetic visions that cut through time."

"Cut through time?"

"I watched a replay of a C.N.A. recording of a dream by Jenny's four-year-old son. His dream visualized his dad solving an Italian art theft. The C.N.A. showed details that include bank account numbers. The transactions took place several days later, just as the child dreamed it."

Ness glanced at the clipboard, and then handed it to Terra. "I think someone is playing a game with you."

"I hope you're right. I'm tempted to do something about this warning."

"Do what?" Ness took a moment to sip his coffee. "This sounds like occult hocus-pocus. If you stop it, then the prediction never happens. You look foolish for interrupting a historical climax to the treaty signing."

"If I say nothing, and it happens as predicted, I will always ask myself if I could have saved some lives." She looked very concerned. "We have nineteen minutes left of the President's speech. I'll call Jenny and ask for details."

"I'll call. You don't have time. If there is a warning about something specific, I'll call mission control with the advisory."

Terra smiled, and then nodded agreement.

At the end of President Petrivich's speech, Terra went on the air to summarize his thirty minute speech in thirty seconds. "The United Nations President just told us that the Venus Resources Treaty will be a milestone that opens the surface of a deadly planet to human development. It will make the resources of the planet Venus available to all of us. Mineral deposits on the surface have never been altered by water. The secret to access to Venus is the anti-gravity spacecraft that can land, that can lift huge loads without rocket engines, without jet or piston engines."

"The United Nations is required by an interplanetary agreement to allow the Martian patent holder, Newton Enterprises, control of the anti-gravity drive. This treaty reaffirms that agreement, and establishes an initial joint venture exploration of Venus by a consortium of two Martian mining companies, Redrock Mining and the Lyndon Corporation, and two Earth based companies, Reynolds Corporation and Mitsunomi Limited."

"Martian President Bollen H. Knotts will be speaking next about what the Martian contribution means to this venture. Following that speech, the two Presidents will both sign the treaty, making the Venus Resources Treaty official. President Knotts is stepping to the podium now."

As expected, the Knotts commentary was shorter than that given by the U. N. President. "For two-hundred-and-fifty years human spaceflight has been pushing the frontiers further into the depths of the Universe. We have reached out and civilized the Moon and Mars. We established viable mining colonies on the moons orbiting Jupiter and Saturn. Mars, now a world independent of Earth, remains part of the combined human civilization, much as a grown child remains part of the family he came from, even after he has set out on his own. Sixteen years ago, Mars launched the first manned interstellar pioneering mission to the second planet circling Tau Ceti, twelve light years away. The Martian spacecraft will not even arrive at its destination for five more years, and we will not receive radio signal confirmation of its arrival for twelve years after that. They are gone from our solar system, probably forever. Like those human explorers to Mars, they take their heritage with them. They will transmit reports back. If they are successful, others will follow to Tau Ceti. Someday their grandchildren may come back to enrich us with what they created on that distant world."

"We, of the ever advancing family of man, are once again about to reach out to another world that had been written off as inaccessible. Since the dawn of civilization Venus has beckoned like a goddess. However, since the early days of spaceflight we have known that the beauty of Venus is a deception. High pressures, hot temperatures, and corrosive clouds create a lethal trap at the surface, a climate that makes the planet inaccessible. This knowledge convinced us to give up on Venus... until today. The same Martian-based technology, the anti-gravity propulsion system, that permitted a pioneering star-flight mission to Tau Ceti, has made access to the surface of Venus a reality."

"No longer do we have to be concerned with trying to operate with temperature sensitive fuel propulsion systems in the nine-hundred degree surface temperatures of Venus. The anti-grav does not use fuel propulsion; it uses a magnetic-like anti-gravity field created by passing an electric current through super-cold asteric crystals. No longer do we have to worry about the ability of human explorers to operate on the surface of Venus, because for this cryogenic anti-gravity drive we have created new insulations and cooling technologies."

"Mars and the Earth's United Nations went separate ways following the Martian War of Independence twenty-three years ago, but we all contribute to the same future. Today, we sign an agreement that will have us working together for the common good of all mankind."

"With us at this table, to sign for the four companies dedicating their investor's monies towards making this enterprise profitable, are the C.E.O.'s of Redrock Mining, Lyndon Corporation, the Reynolds

Corporation, Mitsunomi Limited, and Newton Enterprises," President Knotts glanced towards the overhead press booths, focusing on the Martian Broadcast section. "Newton Enterprises designs and develops every anti-gravity drive system now in existence. Thank you." He returned to his seat. The master of ceremonies stepped to the podium to introduce the next speaker, Wes Chandler, C.E.O. of Redrock Mining Corporation.

The speeches finally wrapped up, and the treaty was signed, which started the countdown for the first planned manned landing on Venus. Following the treaty signing, Terra welcomed UN Space Agency Administrator Dax Umali to her press booth for an interview. She asked him to elaborate about upcoming landing.

Twenty minutes into the interview Ness returned to the press booth, just as Dax Umali finished his explanation of mineral resources on the flanks of Rhea Mountain on Venus. Terra decided to alter the script somewhat.

"Dr. Umali, our visitor is Ness Trenton, managing director for the Martian Broadcast Agency. Ness, are you here to add something to this discussion?"

"Yes, Terra," He was alert, though relaxed. "I'd like to ask Dr. Umali how confident he is with the spacecraft about to be landed at the base of Mount Rhea."

Umali responded, "You catch me unprepared, Mr. Trenton. We have shown the press the precautions we are following. Everything on this anti-grav Lander is new, tested, and certified. This is a dangerous landing. Over the past week, while in orbit over Venus, we retested every system. Is there a reason for this question?"

"Just a cautionary note," Ness was uneasy, despite his best efforts to conceal it. "An hour ago Terra told me that an individual, with unusual powers of perception, predicted a month ago that the Venus landing would run into trouble. I reviewed the recording of that prediction. There is a suggestion that there will be a problem with the cooling system's circulation during landing."

"Mister Trenton," Doctor Umali figideted in his seat, "I do not get excited by a fortune teller's stories of imminent disaster. However, I will order a flush check of the cooling system before the landing."

"Thank you."

"Who is this fortune teller? We may already have dealt with her."

"Him." Ness said. "But I am not prepared to give a name. However, I can almost guarantee that you have not dealt with him in the past." Ness stood. "I'm sorry to interrupt the interview. I was persuaded that there is more to this story than a phony fortune teller. You may return to your interview."

Ness's unusual interruption of a live interview had disrupted the thinking of both Dr. Umali and Terra. They continued to discuss how explorers would survive on the surface, but both wanted to cut the interview short. Dr. Umali left. Terra instructed Chet to run prerecorded stories in the arranged sequence until she was ready to come back on camera.

Once out of the press booth, she confronted Ness. "What was that? You told me not to bring this up. Then, you interrupt a live interview…"

He put a hand on her shoulder. "Terra, I know. I called the Tycho Medical Center. I talked to Jenny Ortigas. I talked to Isolation Unit Director Rochelle Bond. They told me about the C.N.A. Unit recordings of the dreams of all the patients with the virus. I then called the flight that Sonny Ortigas is coming in on. He will be arriving in four hours. He has a recorded transmission from before Apollo left Mars. He copied me a portion of Apollo talking specifically about a catastrophic failure of the cooling circulation system on the Venus Lander. I felt a warning may prevent a disaster. If it is a false warning, we get embarrassed. If it is accurate, maybe we can prevent it. If we don't prevent it, then you have and even bigger story than the Venus landing."

"Did they tell you that someone is stalking Apollo?"

"They told me. I felt this was vital."

"If this prediction is accurate, the interplanetary press will begin probing who Apollo is. Who ever is after him may use that attention as a way to come after him."

CHAPTER TWENTY-SEVEN

MESSAGE

Tycho Convention Center

Earth Date	August 7, 2216
Mars Date	C-Mmon 56, 1174

MARTIAN VIRUS, DAY 38

"Ness Trenton!" Sonny was surprised to find Terra's boss waiting to escort him. "Why are you here?" Sonny left the spacecraft docking tube, stepping into the Tycho Spaceport arrival lobby. Wearing a standard tourist pressure suit, he carried a small case in his left hand.

Ness shook hands with the arriving detective. "Long story." He pointed to a huge commercial video wall screen. The display image was of Terra interviewing a geologist about ores they expected to find on Venus at Mount Rhea. "That story is one she prepared two weeks ago. At this moment she's investigating the Venus Lander's cooling system."

Lightly springing up and down as he walked, Sonny smiled; he had forgotten about the Moon's gravity. The lunar spaceport looked like any spaceport on Earth, but the low gravity gave his 150-pound mass a lunar weight of twenty-five pounds. Walking through the lobby was like trying to stroll along a giant trampoline. "I watched you interrupt Terra's show. You shouldn't go public so soon." They approached the baggage claim area. "At least not until we talk to Apollo. Isn't this risky for you?"

"You're right. It is risky. If it all turns out to be nothing, then I look foolish. I've done that before. If it is a foresight into mechanical problems, maybe my going public can prevent a disaster. If it does happen anyway, as Apollo predicted, that's ... a very big story. It was worth the risk."

"What else do you know about Apollo's virus? I mean, other than that he is quarantined with an unknown sickness with unusual side effects? I withheld most of his message from Mars for a reason."

"Jenny told me the virus came from Mars, that someone from Mars is stalking Apollo."

At the baggage claim area, they entered a small stall. Sonny removed the glove from his hand, and then placed his palm on the handprint decoder plate. He announced his name and identification number. A video image confirming his name showed that he would receive four units of luggage. "Can you and Terra come to the Quarantine Center?" Sonny seated himself on one side of the stall. "There is more to this situation that you should know. Apollo is awake. I don't want to reveal much until we include him in the discussion."

Ness remained standing. "If I created a problem for you... for Apollo..."

Sonny waved half-heartedly. "You did not know. You did what you thought was right. Never apologize for trying to do the right thing. We have to proceed carefully; I'll let you know more at the right moment." Sonny then asked the baggage computer to provide an automated luggage mover.

The suitcases appeared one at a time through an opening hatchway in the wall, branching off from the distribution conveyor tunnel on the other side of the wall. A self-propelled computerized luggage mover arrived simultaneously. Stopping in front of the shelf with the arriving luggage, the unit's arms reached out to pull the suitcases onboard. "Mister Ortigas," the mover's computerized female voice said, "Will you ride or walk to customs?"

"Ride. There are two of us." Sonny looked around for the agent who had followed him from Earth. Sonny had spotted him and had his office identify him as George Fuller, an independent investigator. Fuller was at a luggage arrival stall on the opposite wall. He had only his hand luggage. Glancing down at his sleeve, Sonny got a reading on the tracking device he had discreetly attached to Fuller's communicator. It was active.

A bench telescoped from the back of the luggage mover, wide enough for two passengers. Sonny and Ness seated themselves, and then the luggage mover rolled away from baggage claim, routing towards the garage.

The Tycho Convention Center was packed with visitors attending the Venus landing events. Ness led Sonny past the crowds to the Martian Media Press offices, ushering him into a guest suite so that he could clean up from the flight. Before stepping into the shower, Sonny had his computer scan his baggage, clothes, and body for any unregistered electronics devices. The scan found a micro transmitter attached to his computer case. He moved the tiny unit to a pack of travel brochures, put them in a box, and addressed the box to himself care of the main desk at the Tycho Agri Center. The Center, where lunar greenhouses maintained locally grown foodstuffs, was on the far side of the Tycho Crater. He then called for a delivery service to hand deliver the box.

An hour later Ness returned with Terra and her security robot to accompany Sonny to the medical center. Greeting Terra with a smile, Sonny said. "My lovely Terra, I've missed you." He took her hand, "Like a Manila sunset, so lovely, so exotic... an artwork." He gently kissed the back of her fingers.

Smiling, she took her hand back. "Sonny, I forgot about your style." She patted his cheek, "You should come to Mars more often to see this artwork."

He winked, then with one hand, pulled at the fabric of his pressure suit. "I'm just an old fashioned Filipino. On Mars I'd have to wear this outside. Besides, there are no coconut trees."

"Home is where the heart is." Her smile evaporated. "Sonny, you ready to show me that message? I will not report anything you don't agree to."

He looked down at his computer case, drawing the eyes of Terra and Ness there. Looking back up at them, he said, "This message explains what happened to Apollo, to the rest of the Filipino miners. My sister's husband died on Mars. My father died from the virus. I have to take it first to the quarantine center. Can you get away from here for a few hours?"

She turned to Ness for guidance Ness then said, "You're scheduled for a dinner with the Martian delegation," he glanced at the time reading on his sleeve. "Later today... That's six hours away. The Venus landing is rescheduled for tomorrow morning."

"This message arrived on July eighth," Sonny responded, "It includes Apollo's prediction about the Venus landing."

"We have time," Terra said. "I have thirty hours of filler ready to air, if need be."

"Let's go," Ness said.

Rochelle was excited to have Journalist Terra Newton visit her facility a second time, but was reluctant to allow Terra freedom to intermingle with the patients. Deferring to safety protocols, Terra and Ness remained separated from the quarantine sections, and accompanied Rochelle for a twenty-minute VIP tour. They wanted to give Sonny time with Jenny before revealing the message.

"Jenny, I feel so bad," Sonny spoke through the window separating him from his wife. "If I had talked to Lydia about the message, you wouldn't be here."

Jenny suddenly felt a surging roller-coaster of pent-up emotions; anger at Sonny for not being there, anger at Apollo for bringing the disease home, anger at Celia for not listening to advice. She felt regret for the deaths, the sickness, the quarantine. She knew nothing could be gained by making matters more difficult. The devastating events had overwhelmed everyone. She let those emotions pass, kissed her fingers, and then pressed them to the glass. "This will pass," she smiled, "Maybe its time to think about making a baby sister for Teddy."

Sonny twitched his eyebrows. "After the Lloyds commission for the art recovery, I think we can schedule that. Want to start now?"

"I'd like to," she grinned. "But, we need for you to find out who is after Apollo. If you come in, Director Bond won't let you back out."

Sonny snapped his finger with an exaggerated comical motion. "Pang it!" He then asked seriously, ""How is Apollo?"

"He's eating. His temperature is normal. The virus is disappearing."

"What about the pituitary?"

"He has the strange dreams, a lot of them about Sonia. Nina gets upset about that. They were planning a future together before he went to Mars."

Sonny chuckled. "Are they talking?"

"They're talking. Apollo's sister is in a coma. We are not getting the dreams from her that we got from him. A few of those infected have the dreams, most do not. Teddy no longer has the dreams."

"Good. Terra Newton is with me. I'm going to replay the message in a few minutes on the observation deck. Can you bring everyone up there?"

"Of course. Shall I get them now?"

He nodded agreement. "Jenny, the transmission includes a security camera view of Roberto and Emilio and the rest being killed. Do you think Celia and Nina can deal with it?"

"They know what happened. Apollo explained everything. I'll warn them, if they don't want to watch."

Beyond the pressurized dome of the observation deck, dark shadows stretched across the floor of the Tycho crater, nearly reaching the crater-center metropolitan area. The large, bright globe of Earth created a bluish tint to the dark shadows. The lights of various businesses added sparkles of bright color. Sonny stared out at the empty landscape beyond the man-made bubbles. It had a beauty of its own, but it was not where he would want to stay for long. Sonny had only been at Tycho a few hours, and already he was homesick for tropical Earth. In the visitor's isolation section Sonny seated himself at a table adjacent to the dividing window. A bottle of San Miguel Beer offered him by the galley cart was a welcome treat. He sipped while monitoring his computer console, as Jenny prepared the barrio people on the other side of the partition.

Rochelle and Ness appeared behind Sonny, coming up from the stairwell, followed by Terra and her robot assistant.

Seeing the barrio people, Sonny waved and smiled at the friends he had known all his life. His wife and sister smiled back. Both were tired. Both made efforts to look their best. Jenny did not have to try hard with her natural sensual allure. The twelve coma patients were not in the crowd, but ten alert patients did come with wheelchairs. Twenty walked to the seats. Teddy stood beside Jenny.

Struggling free of his mother's grip, Teddy yelled, "its daddy. I want to see daddy." He rushed to the partition, and banged on the ceramic glass with small, rash-covered hands.

Sonny squatted, put his hand to the glass, and muttered, "I love you, Teddy. I can't be with you, yet." Sonny winked at Teddy. He then stood when Apollo walked in with Nina Perez. They stared at him. He smiled and waved. Sonny turned to Ness and Terra. "I'm going to play the message transmitted to me from Mars. All I ask is that you do not air this until we agree."

Terra immediately agreed. Ness waited, and then concurred.

"Apollo," Sonny asked as he prepared to begin. "Does the barrio know what is on this?"

"Everyone asked. I did not want to say. I asked them to wait for you. I told them everyone was killed, but they should wait for what Sonia sent from Mars. Tita Jenny told me that is what you wanted."

Sonny gave a knowing smile, then spoke to the crowd. "I'm sorry I was not in Manila when this message first arrived. If I had, then only Apollo would be sick. Because I was not there, my father is dead, my priest is dead, my son is infected, and I am unable to hold my wife. My hometown is gone, and all of you are in there. I feel badly."

Everyone looked back at him in sympathy. The barrio people expected Celia to respond. Sonny held up a hand. "Wait to talk. First, you should know what happened on Mars. See for yourself what happened to Roberto, to Emilio and Jun and Doug and Celso." He instructed the computer to begin the replay.

Monitor screens displayed infected, sickly Apollo asking the identifications of the Christmas Rose, Baby, and Cocoanut. Sonny responded with the names and birthdates of Jenny, Madeline, and Carlos. The message continued with a commentary by Sonia. Slowly, the story unfolded on screen about the contaminated fish, the murder of the prospecting crew, and the details of the expedition. The attached security camera recordings showed the graphic killings in the Princess Dejah Canyon mine.

At first there were absolutely no sounds from the quarantined barrio as they watched. Miner Jon Estrella had been a close friend of Sonny's dad back in the old days. Sitting beside Celia, Jon put an arm across her shoulders. With the touch, she could no longer control her emotions. Tears rolled down her cheeks. She turned to bury her face in his arm. Nina and her mother began crying on each other's shoulders. The barrio had been a tight-knit community for as far back as anyone could remember. Suddenly, they were presented with images of five of their most loved men being murdered with poison gas. Terra and Ness sat in stunned silence watching the crowd. Teddy, not clear on what had happened, knew it was something bad; he hugged his mother closely.

Finally, Sonny stood to speak. "I'm sorry to bring this to you. I wish it could be different. You had to know."

Young Lili Morada stared at Sonny. "Celso was on Mars to get enough money to send me to college. Are you going to be able to do something about what happened?"

After scanning the crowd, Sonny focused on Apollo, Jenny, and his son. He glanced at Terra and Ness. He spoke to Lili. "When I saw this message, I promised myself I would find justice. This is why I asked Terra Newton to come for this showing. I need her help," He turned to look at Terra.

Terra stared back. "You have it. Twenty-three years ago, during the war, I watched my best friend die in an effort to save my life. I found the body of my murdered mother in my own house. I know what you feel. I'll help." She hugged Sonny. They both wanted to join the quarantined barrio, but could not.

Chapter Twenty-Eight

Venus Landing

Tycho Convention Center

Earth Date	August 8, 2216
Mars Date	D-Mmon 01, 1174

MARTIAN VIRUS, DAY 39

"Will you be all right by yourself?" Terra questioned. She was at the door, ready to leave with Ness. They were heading for the Tycho Media Center.

"Go!" Sonny watched the automated mobile galley approaching him. "I have to wait for the answer from your husband. The galley unit stopped in front of him. A breakfast tray was lifted up to him.

Terra glanced at the wall, filled with multiple video displays. "Damn. I wish I could be here." She opened the door, pausing to study the images.

"I know, I know," Sonny responded, "Go! Cover the landing."

Sonny was suddenly alone to enjoy his breakfast, and to be a detective. Multiple images displayed on the wall screen included several computer file information panels plus a commercial feed from Tycho media center. In that prerecorded show, Terra Newton interviewed Xuan Zee, the Newton Industries scientist who developed the anti-grav propulsion system. Zee was used to explain how a repulsive gravitational field resulted from passing electrical currents through asteric crystals chilled to near absolute zero temperatures. He elaborated with the development history that included using the anti-grav system to send the first human expedition to an earth-like planet orbiting a distant star. Research into anti-gravity and super-cold technologies had expanded in both fields in the years since that Tau Ceti launch, to where it was possible to operate a cryogenic anti-grav system on the surface of Venus.

Sonny muted the volume on the Mars Broadcasting commercial show he had watched the night before when Terra prepared the prerecorded videos. He continued eating breakfast while reading the other case work displays. He briefly focused on a set of multiple inset views from his mini bumblebee security cameras. Bumblebee cameras could be remotely flown, much like a bee, to attach itself to any surface. From there they transmitted surveillance images. Sonny had them placed in the corridor outside Terra's suite, outside his own room, in his room, and in the hotel lobby. Three agents from Interplanetary Metals, Carl Reston, Scranton Quinn, and Yugo Danford, were in the lobby setting up their own surveillance equipment. Sonny had already checked their credentials. The Martian Global Police listed them, just as they told Director Bond. However, DNA traces, that Rochelle Bond obtained from medical scanners, identified them for who they really were. All three were accounts representatives for Interplanetary Metals, working out of Manila. They were not professional investigators.

Other displays showed the responses of his inquiries into Redrock Mining, Interplanetary Metals, and individual background reports on Redrock Vice President Ghant Travis, Martian Police Chief Ken Sylvester, Geochemist Dave Crane, Fisk Banzar, and Sonia Androff. The Martian Bureau of Mines files concerning mining claims in the Princess Dejah Canyon had been updated during the first week of July. Earlier records on Sonia, Fisk, and Dave had also been modified at the same time. Deeper records on all parties were classified by order of Police Chief Ken Sylvester to protect a homicide investigation.

Other displays showed details related to the virus plus files on patients and staff in the quarantine center. Director Bond had provided these files along with epidemic records from Corrigedor and Baguio. The disease appeared to be lethal for those over fifty-five, or with heart conditions. Children under ten peaked within a day or two, and then the virus slowly disappeared, similar to common flu epidemics. Patients from teenagers to middle aged, when they were susceptible, lapsed into comas. Thousands of lab animals were being tested in search of a serum, but that would take time. Director Bond felt that the malaria cover for the disease would not last long. Any biologist looking at the data would know immediately that this was new.

The dreamscapes of the sick patients created a fascinating mystery, separate from the epidemic. All victims of the virus had the strange dreams at first. However, the Feldermite hormone rapidly subsided within a few days, and dreamscapes became normal dreams. The staff was listing most dreams as normal nightmares, or sexual fantasies. Many of the normal dreams included floating in air, chases, meeting celebrities. Sonny was particularly interested in his son's prophecy dreams about the art exchange in Italy, and a second one that he would be on Mars in August with Brass Newton at the farm of Terra Newton's father.

A C.N.A. recording of Madeline Panahon's dreams appeared to be a vision about one of the Philippine beaches. A nipa hut near the beach was surrounded by tropical plants. Waves splashed against the shoreline of a sandy cove. A short distance down the sunny beach was a rocky outcrop with a lavender amethyst formation that looked like a horse's head. The recording focused on the approach of two people wearing wrap-around dresses; a young female child holding the hand of a woman who looked like a thirty year old Nina Perez. Sonny quietly smiled. If accurate, Nina Perez would return to the Philippines to raise a family. Sonny had seen that beach before, but he could not remember exactly where.

A new small image appeared in the margin of one screen, coupled with a beeping tone and flashing red icon signaling an incoming interplanetary message. Sonny swallowed a mouthful of rice and eggs, and then said, "Replace screen 'A' with incoming mail."

The blond, Nordic face of Brass Newton filled the screen. He looked like a gymnastics poster, but Brass was one of the most gentle, intelligent people Sonny knew. A top Martian biogenetic engineer, Brass had personally modified at least fifty arctic, high desert Earth animals into new species that could survive the harsh climatic condition of the Martian atmosphere. "Sonny, I am amused at your choice of access codes. Now, it's your turn. Remember the full name and birth date of Mosquito."

The picture froze. The message would not advance until Sonny gave the code. Mosquito? Who is Mosquito? Has to be someone they both know, but the rest of the world would not. Damn. Sonny was in trouble. He switched to the comm connection with the Quarantine Center and paged Jenny. After he explained the situation, she smiled and laughed. "Sonny, think back to the case you were investigating when we first got together."

"The Cryogen incident. Sixteen years ago. I don't remember anyone named Mosquito."

"Remember who was with your pilot friend? Why she was going to Mars?"

"Zenia Olsen. She went with Blue Heidelburn to Mars to... recover the body of her sister... a Space Force fighter pilot killed during the war." Sonny's mind began to click. "It was the sister. Blue dated her before she was killed. Blue's nickname for her... Mosquito." Sonny smiled, turned to his computer to ask for the name and birth date of Zenia Olsen's sister. In saying goodbye to his wife, he asked, "How come you remember these things, and I don't?"

"Because you're a man!" She grinned, blew a kiss to the camera.

With the code typed in, the message continued. "Those reports were a surprise to say the least. The virus... I could not match it. However, since you were adamant that this bug originated on Mars, I expanded mt search to every genetic lab computer on the planet. Several weeks ago Doctor Wayne Follett in Sagan City sent a low level inquiry to our laboratory with a diagnosis of the virus. We are unable to locate him. I also found a match in a microbio-paleontology computer. There were fossilized versions of the virus found in fishes that died out on Mars a hundred million years ago. If your barrio is infected with this virus, it is one we have absolutely no understanding of. I'm sending what we have to Director Rochelle Bond. If this bug is as dangerous as you imply, and it's loose on Mars, we have to take immediate action to isolate it."

"Concerning the missing Filipino miners, there is no police information. As you said, the case of Fisk Banzer and Sonia Androff is sealed. I need to get around the security. Terra told me that you intend to come to Mars to do your own detective work. She asked me to arrange for a local detective to work with you. I contacted Jeck Ekakaidis. He agreed to help."

"To help the investigation, you may want to bring Apollo Panahon to Mars with you. Our quarantine facilities are as good as anywhere. If this bug is from here, we need to know what we can, and we need live specimens. Since Apollo's statements are the only evidence we have about those missing miners, and that contradicts official police reports. I am contacting Rochelle Bond with this same request." Brass Newton then concluded his message with a few pleasantries.

Sonny sipped his beer as he sat thinking. He then called back to his wife. "Jenny. It seems everyone around you is quiet at the moment. Is there a soccer game in progress?"

"The Venus landing," she responded, "With the prediction form Apollo's dreams, everyone wants to watch."

"I almost forgot." Sonny adjusted the wall screen settings to highlight three of the commercial broadcast images of Terra, of the crew in the descending Lander, and the view from the ground at the base of Mount Rhea.

"Sonny!" Jenny sounded exasperated. "What did Brass have to say?"

"Sorry." He muted the commercial audio. "Brass hired Detective Ekakaidis. I will work with him. You remember him?"

"Uh huh, we met a few times at the Club Fir Tree, when we were on Mars. I like him."

"Brass also wants me to bring Apollo. The samples of the virus, and Apollo is the only witness to what happened in the Canyon."

A small dot appeared in the sky on the image from the surface of Venus. On the commentary screen, Terra Newton was talking, but seemed calm. The crew of the Lander was hurriedly manipulating control knobs on their instrument panel. Sonny assumed this was related to normal landing procedures.

"If Apollo goes to Mars with you, does that mean he stays in an isolation trailer the whole trip?"

"I doubt there is any way around that. The virus is spreading in the Philippines. We don't want to make matters worse."

"Poor Apollo. Teddy and I will come, too."

"What?"

The dot in the sky above Mount Rhea had grown. It was still descending normally.

"Apollo should not be in total isolation for the rest of the time he's in quarantine. Teddy and I will be in mandatory quarantine as long as Apollo. I'd rather be with you than separated indefinitely... isolated with..." She paused. "I want to come along. If Apollo goes, I go."

Sonny understood what Jenny wanted to say. She needed to get away from the barrio people. Celia had never fully accepted Jenny as one of them, and other barrio women deferred to her on matters of social protocol. He thought about objecting to her plea. He knew better. "I'll see what I can do. I'll talk to Director Bond."

The spacecraft began tilting at a slight angle, although the descent through the air was slow enough. Sonny assumed this was normal. The spacecraft was two-thousand foot above the surface.

"Thank you, Sonny." Jenny forced a smile. "When do we leave?"

"Teka, teka." Sonny answered. "Let's watch the landing. I'll call you back in a few minutes."

"Shall I tell Apollo?" Jenny asked.

"Certainly, he should know. I'll be by this afternoon to talk to everyone. Jenny, I'm going to end the call, now."

"Bye," she responded. "Love you." With that, her image went blank.

Sonny ended the mute of the commercial broadcast.

"...the sulfuric acid clouds," Terra was talking with a clear, steady voice, "coupled with a lighting strike, has eaten into the metal of one of the cooling vanes during descent. Although the entire spacecraft was reinspected yesterday, the information coming in now suggests that there were hairline cracks found in the insulation of those vanes."

The surface camera showed the spacecraft, slightly askew, drifting down through the dense, hot atmosphere, much like a stone falling through water.

"According to diagnostic data, the lightning strike caused globular particles to break loose within the coolant. Those particles are clogging internal filters. Robotic mechanics are trying to bypass the clogged tubes, as the ship is now in free-fall. The coolant is too warm for the anti-grav to work... asteric crystal temperatures have to be within a few degrees of absolute zero..."

The spacecraft drifted to within a four hundred feet of the surface. Dropping slowly because of the dense air, a white cloud of steam puffed from the underside of the vehicle. Seconds later there was a bright flash of white light. The image of the crew within the spacecraft went blank.

The camera tracking the landing from the flank of Mount Rhea followed the final descent of the spacecraft. The clogged coolant line created a temperature rise in the refrigerants, and that accelerated the mechanical cooling pumps. Circuit breakers began cutting power to pumps and fans. Crew attempts to bring the chillers back on line increased coolant pressure in the circulation tubes. The nine-hundred degree temperatures of the crushing atmosphere reversed the cooling, circulating heated liquid with a pressure build-up. Finally, a coolant line burst. Seconds later, the pumps began locking up, then blowing apart. A hole was blown in the bottom of the spacecraft, blasting metal shards up through the cabin.

The surface camera captured the touchdown as the new, experimental Venus Lander hit the surface, then fell over on its side. Clouds of coolant, turned to gasses, were steaming from underneath. There was no sign of life coming from the six crew members inside.

Sonny put his beer down. He gulped. He looked to the image of Terra Newton, waiting for her reaction. She was stunned. She was not ready for this disaster.

Finally, she spoke. "To the peoples of Earth and Mars, I know that two days ago, during my broadcast, this accident was forecast, reported as a reliable prophesy made a month ago. Even though we felt we had reason to believe the forecast, I was not prepared to accept the consequences. Six brave, professional explorers appear to have died before our eyes. I knew them. I dined with them. I interviewed each of them for broadcast. I will miss them, one and all."

"Venus, the goddess of love and beauty, has beaten us once more. We will come back. More Landers are ready to try. It may not be this year, or next year, but we will try again. We will win… we will do it for those who sacrificed everything to put mankind on the surface of that planet. They will not have died in vain."

"With further reaction, we will be going live to United Nations President Charles Petrivich. Wessen, do you have the President with you?"

CHAPTER TWENTY-NINE

TIMESCAPE

Tycho Medical Center

Earth Date	August 9, 2216
Mars Date	D-Mmon 02, 1174

"Celia," Sonny stared at his sister. During her week at Tycho, Celia's hair had grayed a little, and the wrinkles in her faced etched a little deeper. "I understand your feelings. The Panahon kids are all you have left. Papa Raul is dead. Roberto is dead. Father Roxas is dead. Your whole barrio is sick and isolated on an alien world. I want this to be over as much as you do. I promise that the killers will pay; that's why I am going to Mars with Terra. But, we need Apollo. He is the only witness. To convince the Martian authorities, we need him."

Celia began to cry. "Sonny, I know you are right. You are always right. You are also never here when the barrio... when the family... when I need you. You are going to Mars to get even for Roberto. The men you are after will kill you when they know what you want to do.

They will kill Apollo. The only family left is Baby Madeline, and she is in a coma. She may die, just like Papa and Father Roxas. "

"Do you believe the dreams?"

Celia nodded agreement.

"Madeline had a dream that she and Nina were on a tropical beach. They were adults. You see the replay?"

"I saw it." Celia reached for a tissue to wipe her eyes.

"Father Roxas dreamed that this will end soon. Apollo dreamed that he was on Mars a few weeks from now, at the Club Fir Tree in Crater City. If he doesn't go to Mars with me, that dream won't come true."

"Apollo has to go. You have to solve the murders. Your friend Brass Newton has to solve the virus." She blew her nose. "My heart is terrified. My whole world is upside down. What will I do while you are gone?"

"Celia, I wish I could hug you," Sonny was trying to think how to make her understand something that he knew she already understood. "Stay with the barrio. Since Nani (mother) died, you have been the matron of Ulap. You were there when our neighbors got sick. You organized when their children got married or had babies. They talk to you when they have problems. You are right, I was not there. I was away. You have held the barrio together. Right now, right here, they need you more than ever."

Behind Celia, at the entrance to her side of the visitor's booth, the door opened. Nina Perez was suddenly in the room.

"Nina! This is a private conversation." Celia scolded, "You are supposed to knock."

Nina's straight, black hair was uncombed. She looked exasperated. "Apollo told me he is leaving with Sonny… leaving me again to go to Mars."

Celia reached to take Nina's hand to pull her to the bench where she was sitting. "Did he tell you he had to help catch the bad people who killed your father? Tito Sonny and I were talking about this. I don't want Apollo to go. He has to go."

Nina remained standing. She stared at the two of them, stiffening her arms to her side, and yelled, "Before he went to Mars with papa and Tito Roberto we talked about getting married. We talked about having a family. Now, my papa is dead. Apollo is dreaming about sex with a robot and sex with a woman old enough to be his mother. Apollo is supposed to be… my fiancée. You want me to send him back to Mars where everyone else got killed, where I will lose him forever?" Nina started crying. "Apollo is sick and needs my help. I need his help. If Apollo goes back to Mars, I will go with him."

Celia stood, putting an arm around the young girl.

Sonny thought about saying something profound, but held his tongue. After a period of silence, he said, "Someone is tracking Apollo. They followed me from Earth. They came here disguised as doctors. They have a surveillance rover parked outside the entrance to the Medical Center watching right now. You would be at risk."

"I could die here when the virus finally gets to me," Nina responded. "This is the first time I've been out of the Luzon in my life, and it is a forced trip into quarantine on the Moon… to watch my friends and family get sick and die. Tatai is dead. Nanai is in coma. My fiancée is…" She faced the window to plead her case to Sonny. "Tito Sonny, I love Apollo. If he is in trouble, I want to be with him. I want to marry him. I think he loves me."

"Have you talked to your brother and sister? What about taking care of your mother? Have you talked to Apollo?"

Nina nodded. "They know how I feel. Nori and Bing promised to take care of Nanai (mother). Like you, they warned me it may be dangerous, but they did not say no." She paused, and then said, "In fact, they said that if I am going to Mars to be with Apollo, to find Tatai (father), they all want to come. We all have to be in isolation anyway, and our barrio is gone."

Sonny understood. When it came to affairs of the heart, Nina was convinced that Apollo was her future. She was not going to let anyone break it up. Nina's brother and sister wanted to make certain she did not do something with Apollo that would embarrass the family. Sonny was tempted to reject her request out of hand, but Emilio Perez was his friend. Everyone in the barrio was a friend. He had watched Nina grow up.

"Besides," she said, "You reviewed the C.N.A. replay of Baby Madeline's dream. I can't die on Mars. I'll be with her on some beach when we are older."

Other than being nervous about having to accept responsibility for more people while he was investigating the killings, he could not think of arguments against bringing one more. He was bringing Jenny and Teddy, and they were not needed. "Let me talk to Apollo, to your family."

For the first time since Nina walked into the room, she smiled. "Apollo is sleeping. I'll go get Nori and Bing." Nina turned and disappeared through the doorway.

Once she was gone, Sonny spoke to Celia. "After this, no more. I need to move independently when I get to Mars. I don't want barrio people there as a target."

"I understand," Celia forced a smile. "When you leave, tell Jenny that I'm sorry I gave her such a hard time... that the women treated her badly... it's just that... her not being from the barrio... when all these disasters..."

Sonny smiled in return. "Celia, if this was the other way around, and you were the stranger in her world, would my telling you she's sorry make you feel better?"

Celia stared. "I see what you mean. I'll talk to her. I'll organize a bon voyage."

Sonny manipulated the controls on his sleeve. Apollo was asleep. He was still fitted with the C.N.A. helmet, and according to the stats, his hypothalamus and dream centers were active. "Celia, I think that would make a big difference for Jenny. At the moment she is on the observation deck with Teddy and her brother. Go talk to her."

Celia bid Sonny goodbye, and walked away.

"Director Bond," Sonny spoke to his sleeve. "This is Sonny. Are you monitoring Apollo's dreams?"

"Affirmative. This is an interesting sequence. You may want to see it."

"Do you recognize anything?" Sonny started walking down the hallway.

"He's dreaming about a fishing boat in a storm. I don't recognize the people or the location."

"Is it nineteenth century Japan again?"

"Not with floodlights and modern naval satellite traffic locators."

"I'm on my way." Sonny hurried to the surveillance laboratory. Seating himself beside Rochelle Bond on the visitor's side, he glanced through the window at the empty quarantine side observation booth. "No one wanted to come?"

Rochelle responded, "After the Perez girl's reaction the other day, I thought we should be careful. With Apollo reviving, dream privacy is an ethical issue." She pointed to the monitor display of the dream sequence. The screen showed dark blue-gray coloring beyond a boat railing in a storm. That color was uniform for the heavy clouds, the wind driven downpour, and the choppy waves. The view was through an open window of a wooden fishing boat cabin, looking at the deck leading to the bow. Two men on the deck fought the wind and rain to tie down fishing poles and diving gear. A black silhouetted coastline beyond was briefly brightened to the greens and browns of tropical vegetation as a flash of sheet lightning illuminated the area. The screen briefly showed a view of the instrument panel satellite locator monitor below the boat's window. The navigation map pinpointed the boat's location near the entrance of a crescent shaped harbor with one extended pier inside the cove.

The image panned out a window, looking at a deck where one of the drenched men was walking back toward the cabin. Floodlights illuminated his face. He was medium height with a thin face and receding hairline. Sonny recognized him; Blue Heidelburn, looking wet and haggard. Another flash of lightning illuminated a rock outcrop looming near the boat. The boat appeared to be bobbing roughly with the waves.

"Do we have audio?" Rochelle asked the control technicians.

Sonny thought about Blue, who had been the senior partner in E.M. Blue Space Transport. The business he turned over to Bibi Sanchez when he accepted the opportunity to pilot the first manned mission to another star system. Leaving the solar system in the year 2200, that interstellar flight was still five years from Tau Ceti; five years from when they would land at their new home.

Suddenly, the sounds of a coastal storm filled the room; the splashing downpour, the howling wind, the creaking planks being stressed by wave action. A muffled, hoarse, female voice was audible over the storm noise. "Pull to port. There is a rock jetty to starboard.

More power." This was followed by the discomforting sounds of splintering wood. The storm had forced the boat into the rocks.

Jenny and Kai entered the quarantine side of the laboratory observation booth, just in time to see the image tilting. The breaking boat was being heavily deluged with inrushing seawater.

Abruptly, the image and sounds faded into a peaceful blue, then to reddish pink. After several seconds, a view of the laboratory ceiling filled the screen. Apollo was awake, staring at the ceiling. The dream was over.

Staff robots immediately approached the laboratory bunk. As they helped Apollo remove his helmet, he looked to the windows. "Tita Jenny. Tito Sonny. Did you see my dream?"

Sonny adjusted his sleeve controls. "I was a little late, Apollo. You were dreaming about a boat in a storm. Do you know where or when it was.?"

"I think it was your friend, Tito Sonny. Yesterday, Tita Jenny showed me video reports of Blue Heidelburn and Zenia Olsen, and the crew that went with them to Tau Ceti. I think my dream was about them, about Tau Ceti."

"Apollo, at this moment Blue and Zenia are in hibernation, five years from their destination? Do you remember when the dream was supposed to be?"

Rochelle tried to remain professional, but looked astonished. She double checked the surveillance camera to make certain all the discussions were being recorded.

"I am not certain. The details are fading. I do remember Blue cursing the primitive nature of the boat's power plant and rudder control."

Sonny laughed lightly. "Blue was a careful space pilot. He went to great lengths to make certain there were no mechanical problems when he was off the ground. From the looks of your dream, someone broke his boat."

Rochelle spoke to the computers. "Playback just recorded dream sequence. Freeze frame at clear view of navigation locator display on the boat's instrument console."

On the monitor below the window, the image of the traffic locator display appeared and zoomed in. The unit was a standard Startech

Corporation model that used satellite links to establish a precise location. The symbol for the boat showed that it was moving into a harbor, past a rock jetty. Among the informational statistics shown in the borders of the map were three clock readings with time and date for New Manila on Tau Ceti, Crater City on Mars, and New York City on Earth. The eyes of the Earth natives focused on the New York clock; April 14, 2227; eleven years in the future; six years after the pioneers were to arrive at Tau Ceti.

No one was prepared to talk. All were hoping that someone else would offer an explanation of why this was happening. Like Sonny, after the catastrophic failure of the Venus Lander's cooling system, none was willing to doubt the reality Apollo's dreams.

Rochelle finally said, "Terra Newton told me she wants a paranormal professor to look at what we have. Did she forward any of this?" She waved toward the monitor, toward Apollo.

"I'll meet with her in a few hours. I'll ask." Sonny directed the galley cart to bring coffee.

Rochelle accepted a cup of English Gray tea from the robot. "The message you got from Mars… why not give it to the police?"

"That message is not proof. According to the official police reports of what happened in Princess Dejah Canyon, there is no record our Filipino miners ever came to Mars. Apollo is not mentioned. Fisk Banzer is listed as a Redrock mining engineer. Sonia Androff and some unidentified male accomplice are identified as the killers. If we expose Apollo's story now, they will refute the claims, and charge Apollo as the accomplice. Once he is arrested, in official custody… with this strange sickness, he will have a relapse. He will mysteriously die from the virus. No one will be able to prove anything." Sonny turned to see the horrified expression on Jenny's face. "I found that every computer public record concerning the discovery of gold in that canyon was updated within the past month."

"If what you say is true, that means the Martian government is participating in a criminal cover-up."

"The C.E.O. for Redrock is in Tycho for the treaty signing. At this moment, he is having lunch with Martian President Bollen Knotts. I checked both. They were roommates in college. They were officers in the same unit during the war. Redrock has been a major contributor to all of President Knotts' political campaigns."

Rochelle was visibly uncomfortable. She sipped her tea as she looked through the window at Apollo. He sat staring back. She asked, "Have you told this to Terra Newton?"

"No. She saw the transmission from Mars. I figure she will find out on her own. She's good at research. I want to find out what she uncovers on her own."

Rochelle put down her teacup. "My job is to control infectious diseases. Your Filipinos are here because of the virus. We are close to isolating the bug, to finding a vaccine to control it. Still, there are thousands more victims coming." She put a hand on Sonny's forearm. "These dreams... I don't know what to do about them." She tilted her head toward Apollo. "The Redrock issue is not my expertise. However, common sense suggests that you are playing a dangerous game. I hope you don't get yourself and your family killed looking for justice."

"What choice do I have? Until the truth comes out, anyone who knows about the canyon is a threat to the killers. That includes Apollo, me, and you... everyone in quarantine. I'm a detective. I'll find a solution." He sat up. "In the meantime, I need for you to tighten security. Don't let anyone know where Apollo is."

"It's a little late for that!"

"Because of those three phony Martian inspectors?"

"Terra Newton's coverage of the warning about the Venus crash. Other news organizations have pieced together that the warning came from the Filipinos in quarantine. Public officials everywhere are swamped with demands for more information on the prophet. I've been trying to control it, but your barrio friends are communicating with the relatives on Earth. News accounts name Apollo directly." She stood. "I assume you need to talk to Apollo about tomorrow?"

Sonny shook hands with her, thanked her, and asked her not to leave yet. He turned to his nephew. "Apollo, go with Jenny to the observation deck. I'll meet you there. We need to discuss what we do next."

"Yes, Uncle Sonny."

"What is the situation between you and Nina?"

Apollo slowly dropped his feet to the floor. Staring at Sonny, he said, "Nina has been my closest friend… since I was a baby. A year ago we promised to marry when we are old enough."

"I understand. What I want to know… has that changed… in your heart? In your mind?"

A robot medic helped brace Apollo as he stood up. "Nina is the most special person in my life. I love her. I will probably marry her."

"Probably?" Sonny questioned.

"I have this feeling… a sense that maybe it won't work the way Nina and I had hoped."

Sonny again glanced at Jenny and Kai, then returned his attention to Apollo. "Is this related to the dreams?"

"I tried to tell Nina, but she got mad. I think she will not be with me, but with some man named Exxis. I have a feeling that Miss Sonia is trying to talk to me, that we will be special to each other. I know she is too old for me. I am very confused."

Sonny smiled. He addressed the computer, asking for an identification photo of Exxis Potowski from Mars. On screen appeared the image of a husky blue-eyed blond. His facial features looked familiar to Apollo.

"Who is that?"

"That is Terra Newton's nephew. His parents have a farm on Mars, at the base of Mount Olympus. Maybe Nina is supposed to go with us."

Apollo studied the picture. He recognized the face from his dreams. He felt a tinge of jealousy.

"Apollo," Sonny said. "Nina is insisting that she go with us to Mars. She is determined that you are her future. We need to talk to her now, to make a decision."

"I told her that she is still my future, despite what I dreamed."

"We do not have time to argue. Do you want her to come to Mars?"

"She should come. I told here she should. Her future is there."

"Okay, I'll meet you on the deck." Sonny motioned with a thumb to Jenny to go with Apollo. Jenny, remaining quiet, moved toward the door to meet the boy. Apollo disappeared through his own doorway, followed by the medic robot. Sonny glanced at Rochelle, then through the window at Jenny and Kai. "Director Bond, I need your help to leave with Apollo."

"I've already agreed to release him to the Mars Life Sciences Center. What more do you need?"

"I need you to convince the public that he is actually going to Hong Kong University Hospital. Can you do that for me?"

Rochelle eyed him and snickered. "Cloak and dagger. Certainly. Give me the particulars. I'll be part of your game."

Sonny again faced Jenny, and smiled. She already knew what he had in mind. She left to join Apollo.

CHAPTER THIRTY

NOSTRADAMUS SYNDROME

Tycho Conference Center

| Earth Date | August 10, 2216 |
| Mars Date | D-Mmon 03, 1174 |

Tycho Crater was almost completely in shadow, the setting sun no longer visible from the crater floor entrances to the medical center, although a golden light reflected from the far side illuminated crater rim. Under the black, star-studded sky, the ground was visable with a defuse bluish tint from the overhead Earth. Roadway lighting and the glow from illuminated metropolitan buildings created sharp lighting contrasts. Dressed in an off-white sealed full pressure suit, Sonny exited the personnel airlock at the crater base. He walked across the lighted crater floor medical center parking lot toward a lunar rover parked at the fringe of the pavement. Not totally adjusting to the light lunar gravity, he bounced rather than walked. Looking up at a blue-white Earth, he wished he were there. Reaching the vehicle, he plugged a comm cord into the jack adjacent to the airlock. "Good afternoon, men. I am Sonny Ortigas. May I come in?"

"Detective Ortigas!" Carl Reston was surprised by the visit. "Please come in."

The indicator light for the door airlock switched from red to green. The outer door opened, providing Sonny access. Inside the rover, Sonny opened the faceplate to his helmet, and then he shook hands with the three men inside.

Reston said, "Have a seat, Sonny. I must say, I'm surprised. Is there some way we can help you?" Reston motioned toward some seats. Quinn remained at a surveillance console, watching the multiple images from hidden cameras inside the quarantine facility. Danford brought an unopened can of San Miguel beer.

Thanking Danford for the beer, Sonny placed the gloved index finger of his left hand over the beer's opening for the glove's computerized sensors to analyze the contents. The computer confirmed the presence of SWK truth serum. Sonny pretended to sip, then put the drink down. "Just a friendly visit. Yugo, Jenny knows you. She is nervous that you followed her to the Moon. I would ask why."

Carl Reston motioned for Danford not to respond. Leaning against a desk top, Reston said, "I assume Jenny told you that we want to talk to Apollo Panahon. The quarantine prevents that interview. Could you help us with that?"

"You told Director Bond that you are with the Martian Global Police."

All three looked astonished that Sonny would question their credentials. Reston reached for a wallet sized computer clipboard, and handed it to Sonny. "We are Martian Police. Quinn and Danford have been undercover Earth-based agents for years. Here is the official investigation warrant granted us. I'm sorry if our actions made your wife nervous."

Sonny gave a cursory glance to the clipboard. He handed it back, then pretended to take another sip from the beer. "This matches the documents on file with the U.N. Patrol, and the files supplied by the Martian Justice Department in Crater City."

"That's what I said. This is an official investigation."

"I ran your DNA scan through Martian government files. There is no record that any of you were agents for their police. U.N. computers list you as employees of Interplanetary Metals, based in Manila." He pretended to sip once more, and then put the beer down. "Care to explain?"

"Undercover," Danford responded. "Our backgrounds are kept secret to protect our cover."

"Yugo," Sonny smiled, "You make this old Filipino laugh." His smile disappeared. "I don't care what game you want to play, but stop following my family. Apollo is my nephew. Leave him alone." Sonny faked the intoxication he knew was brought on by the truth drug. He reached in his pocket, pulled out a computer plug, and said, "Here is what I know about you at this moment." He handed the plug to Reston. "The news media will have this if you make any further attempts to follow Apollo." Sonny seemed to sip the beer one more time.

"Mister Ortigas," Reston asked, "where is Apollo now? We haven't seen him in the facility since yesterday morning. Did you move him?"

"Oh-oh (yes)!" Sonny knew that the SWK drug was fast-acting, that people using it would blurt out honest answers despite efforts to remain secretive. "Hong Kong."

"Why Hong Kong?"

"To hide from you," Sonny began grimacing, as if he did not want to reveal what he was saying. He stood to leave.

"Where are you going?" Danford grabbed his wrist, "We have a lot of questions."

Sonny burped, "I don't think so." He adjusted a dial on his belt, and then reached with his free hand to Danford's cheek. The resulting electrical shock dropped Danford to the floor. "I've said too much. I have to be at the media center in two hours for Terra Newton to interview Apollo on the air." Sonny turned to the other two in anticipation of an aggressive reaction. Instead, both stood motionless watching Danford fall."

"Interview? What interview?" Reston held up his hands to avoid a taser shock.

"About Apollo's forecast of the Venus crash." Sonny was backing toward the airlock. "He'll be interviewed by long distance comm connection." He reached to his faceplate. "You gave me SWK, didn't you?"

"We wouldn't do that, Sonny," Reston responded. "Stay and talk."

"Leave my family alone." Sonny sealed the faceplate shut, and exited the rover. The three amateur agents made no effort to stop him.

Once outside, Sonny approached the rover's left front wheel. He sprayed adhesive liquid rope from the wheel's axle up the side of the rover, across, then back down to the wheel. A few moments in the vacuum of space would dry that adhesive epoxy rope to the strength of a steel rod welded to the wheel. The rover would go nowhere until a mechanic cut the rod loose. Sonny strolled across the parking lot.

Celia, along with the rest of the Filipinos from Maliit na Ulap, were seated at the edge of the observation deck, looking down at the crater floor, watching for Sonny's vehicular shell game to unfold. Three separate lunar trucks, pulling overland personnel trailers, left the medical center garage airlocks, each heading in different directions. The first turned left, toward the spaceport. The second headed straight for the Tycho resort area, and the third went right towards the agricultural domes. The trailer towed to the spaceport was being launched within the hour to Hong Kong. Across the parking lot, Reston and Danford stood outside their lunar rover checking the damaged left front wheel, agitated that their vehicle was incapacitated while all the traffic activity progressed. The three trucks disappeared from sight. The barrio patients finally drifted from the edge of the observation deck, returning to their slow-paced lives in quarantine of mahjong games, video sports, and taking care of sick friends.

Fifteen minutes later a garbage truck, towing a new passenger trailer was headed for the spaceport. The trailer was loaded in the cargo hold of a Mars-bound space freighter. Waiting quietly in the trailer were quarantined patients Apollo, Nina, Kai, Jenny and Teddy. The launch waited for Sonny and Terra to get onboard.

Meanwhile, Terra attended a luncheon with the signatories to the Venus Resources Treaty. Terra's guest, Sonny, watched from the visitor's booth. Gregg Kim, Director of the manned Venus landing expedition, concluded his podium remarks, "...and I apologize for errors in the manufacturing of the cooling system, in the scan of that system, for our failure to heed the warning we were given." He glanced up at the Martian Broadcast balcony booth. "There will be a complete manufacturing review of the equipment. This brings us to the matter... the source of that incredibly forecast. Ness Trenton agreed to let broadcast journalist Terra Newton explain it. Terra, would you care to come up here?"

Ness joined the applause from his front table, and signaled Terra to go to the podium. Terra allowed the applause to fade before she attempted to speak. She told a few jokes about adjusting to the peculiarities of working on the Moon. After introductory levity, she spoke to the point. "I assume everyone in this audience has heard of dark ages French prophet Michael de Nostradamus." On the wall behind her a portrait of Nostradamus appeared, followed by a collage of historic artworks matching her words. Her personal journalistic perspective continued with details about the ancient prophet. Born in Remes, France in 1503, Nostradamus became noted early during his adult life for work he did with victims of the Black Plague, an epidemic that decimated the population of Europe. However, he is remembered much more for his ability to see the future. According to the historical records, he was able to predict the fate of the French Royal Family, who employed him. He was able to foresee the rise and fall of Napoleon and Hitler hundreds of years before these men were born.

"Based on the way we understand the laws of nature and time, what Nostradamus did does not make sense. If human acts are random free will, then it should be impossible for anyone to predict future actions of people not yet born. Time is supposed to flow like a river." The images on the wall behind her shifted from views of clocks to a picture of a cool, mountain creek trickling through the snow. "A stick in a mountain stream flows with that water into a river, and down to the ocean. Flowing with that river down several waterfalls, that stick can not go back to the headwaters to advise other sticks what to expect. Time flows like water. We can't go back in time to warn friends to avoid accidents or to invest in stocks. Time does not work that way. If we found a way to stop Adolph Hitler when he was a child, at the same time we would alter all of history as we know it." The wall screen images the evolution of history since World War Two. "We would be able to alter the foundation of our own existence.

"The benefits of being able to communicate through time… to prevent disasters, to invest, to know what to expect… are tempting. But, just knowing the future would mean we may try to change that future if we can. If we change it, then it is no longer the future. We can't know the future. The laws of the Universe prohibit it.

"Nostradamus knew the future. He predicted what would happen to his family, his country, his world. How? If the flow of time is only one way, like the stream, and individual actions are random, there should be no way to foresee individual futures. But, Nostradamus was able to see the future, and that means, despite the contradictions, there are natural laws that we do not yet comprehend that allow some individuals to communicate through time, the way that Nostradamus did. There has to be a physical mechanism for it to happen.

"A few days ago the Martian Broadcast Agency reported a prophecy, offered a month ago, that the manned Venus Lander would crash because of a malfunction in the vehicle's cooling system. We were convinced that this source had extraordinary abilities to see the future. Warned of the impending disaster, Martian Broadcasting decided to share this warning in hopes that tragedy could be avoided. Acting on that warning, the Space Agency delayed the Venus landing long enough to check the cooling system. The tragedy still happened just as forecast. Six explorers died before they could step out on the surface of Venus. Today, instead of celebrating victory, we mourn a tragedy.

"That prophecy created a firestorm of attention. People everywhere are asking who is this new prophet? Was it real or was it sabotage? Martian Broadcast is flooded with requests for information. We wanted to protect our source from the public scrutiny for obvious reasons. However, it will be impossible to protect that source indefinitely. For this reason, we decided to tell the world who he is."

An image of Apollo appeared on screen. "This is Apollo Panahon, an eighteen-year-old Filipino I first met ten years ago. Until very recently, he was a happy, shy, normal orphan boy from a remote Philippine barrio." Terra then told an abbreviated story of Apollo, how he came home from Mars as an unidentified coma patient. She told of the subsequent spread of the on-going epidemic. The screen behind her highlighted the quarantine story with images of the isolation wards at John Hay Park and Corrigedor. She left out any mention of the gold strike in Princess Dejah Canyon, the missing Filipino miners, or Sonia Androff. Following a summary of her ten-year-old interview with Apollo as a child, she showed an edited outtake from his message from the El Dorado badlands showing only Apollo's dream of what would happen to the Venus Lander.

Terra then detailed the strange side effects of the virus, with images showing the medical scans of a rare Feldermite hormone from Apollo's pituitary sparking intense, unfamiliar activity in the hypothalamus. Video monitor clips showed the medical staff working with Apollo. Using the C.N.A. images of Apollo's dreams, she showed the 1883 Japanese world of Percival Lowell as Apollo dreamed it. She emphasized that according to his relatives, Apollo had never mentioned any knowledge of Lowell that they could remember, and the images of Lowell before he built his Arizona observatory did not match any video reconstruction available.

When the Lowell dream recording finished, Terra mentioned the dream sequence of a boat entering a harbor in a storm. At various points the playback was stopped for Terra to emphasize what they were looking at. The screen split into four freeze frame images: Apollo's dream vision of Blue Heidelburn on the deck of a boat in a storm; file video of Blue Heidelburn fifteen years earlier, before he boarded the starship bound for Tau Ceti; the boat instrument panel locator display dream image showing a coastline map; and the dream of a time display of April 14, 2227 Seattle time.

"These images came from the Tycho Quarantine Center C.N.A. recordings of a patient in a coma. What you see are dreams of people and places and times that the coma patient did not know prior to this sickness. Apollo dreamed of communicating with Percival Lowell with details that match precisely Lowell's activities of the 1880s. Apollo dreamed of the malfunction on the Venus Lander cooling system a month before it happened. Apollo dreamed about the pilot of our manned mission to Tau Ceti with a boat in a storm eleven years from now. As we speak, that mission to Tau Ceti is five years from landing. The pioneers on that starship are still in hibernation."

The images switched back to a picture of Apollo. "This young man is the source of our prediction of the Venus disaster. His talent to see through time was apparently triggered by an unknown viral infection that put him in a coma. It killed his grandfather and his priest. It spread to thousands of confirmed victims in the Philippines. The Tycho Medical Center has done what it can to save his life, to isolate the infection, to find a cure before the epidemic spreads further. Because of intense public interest in the 'source' of our prediction, the director of the Medical Center today sent Apollo from Tycho to an undisclosed facility elsewhere. We do not know if Nostradamus's visions of the future were caused by an infection altering what happened in his brain, because in the sixteenth century mankind had no idea what a virus was. However, Nostradamus gained his powers of prophecy during a deadly epidemic that killed a third of the population of Europe. This suggests that what happened to Nostradamus may be happening again with Apollo. At this moment, the Tycho Medical Center's Infectious Disease Department is doing everything it can to understand this virus, to attempt to find ways to control and stop its spread. It is researching the Feldermite hormone that seems to trigger Apollo's ability to communicate through time and space." Terra looked from the crowded dining room briefly to the overhanging media booths to one side, catching Sonny's eye. He was ready with the comm control unit.

"A healthy Apollo went to Mars three months ago on a tourist visa. Apollo was returned from Mars in a coma. Sealed in a medic chamber, he was shipped to his uncle, Sonny Ortigas of Manila, a private detective. Sonny wants to find out what happened on Mars. Mars Broadcasting has hired Sonny to investigate this story." She looked over at the Martian delegation to the right of the podium, focusing on President Knotts. "Mister President, I ask your help. I ask that you to grant Sonny Ortigas an official authorization to investigate the circumstances of what happened to his nephew."

President Knotts was caught by surprise. After a few moments, he regained his wits, and spoke. "Terra Newton, I am sympathetic, fascinated with these unusual events you have outlined. However, I am unfamiliar with the virus and with Apollo Panahon's circumstances. Please allow me a few days to look into the situation before I respond."

"I understand, Mister President. Mr. Ortigas is with us at this moment, in the media balcony. He will meet with your staff after this broadcasts. However, as a free lance employee of Martian Broadcasting, with an approved work visa, he will be leaving for Mars in a few hours. We are anxious for him to find what he can."

"We are anxious to know more," the President responded, "What you showed us today changes the meaning of life as we know it. Your documentation demonstrated the ability of this boy to communicate with the past, the future, and with distant worlds. I would very much like to meet Apollo when he is well enough to talk."

"Mr. President," Terra said, "Apollo is sick, and at a secret location, but we do have him connected. Are there any questions you would like to ask?"

Astonished, President Knotts invited Terra to make the connection. Sonny, then did his computer slight of hand.. Apollo's rash covered face appeared on the monitor screen. With a shy, soft voice he said, "Hello, Miss Terra. Hello, Mr. President."

"Apollo, is there anything you would like to say to Martian President Bollen Knotts?"

There was a three-second delay before Apollo answered. "Mr. President, I am sorry about the Venus Lander crash. I hope my dream did not cause the problem."

"Good evening, Apollo. I hope you are feeling better," the President spoke cautiously. "I don't think anyone blames you for the accident. However, we are amazed at your ability to forecast the catastrophe so accurately a month in advance. Are you able to give us more insight into where you developed this talent for prophecy?"

There was another three second delay. "It started while I was on Mars. I found a frozen fish deep in a cave. When I thawed and tasted the fish, I got sick and began having these dreams."

President Knotts responded, "This virus came from Mars? Mars is a desert world with no surface liquid water. How could you have found a fish?"

Terra added her comments. "I have details concerning the fish, Mr. President. I have a copy of the discovery for your use." She pulled two small color-coded cylinders from her pocket, and walked it over to him. "This is an analysis of the fish. The second cylinder is from the Tycho Medical Center research into the nature of the virus and the effect it has on the human body. I have already sent these to the Martian Life Sciences Institute in Crater City."

The President accepted the cylinders, and again stared at the monitor. "Apollo, tell me about your prediction of a disaster on Venus. How did it come to you?"

Apollo answered, "A few days after I tasted that fish I was sick. It was July eighth. It was hard to breath, my stomach hurt, my head hurt… I slept a lot. I woke from a dream that I was with the men on the Venus Lander, watching the camera views of the ground getting closer. I remember a huge mountain below. I remember the instrument panel showing that the cooling system was not circulating… everyone was excited that something was wrong. There was an explosion in the tubing… then a second explosion. Hot Venus air came rushing in… then I woke up. I told the security camera what I remembered. A little later, I tried to eat some rice. That made me sick. The next I remember was that I woke a few days ago at Tycho on the Moon." Apollo's face began perspiring. He was getting woozy. "I remember many dreams. Some seemed real, others seemed disconnected."

"Do you remember seeing the world through the eyes of Percival Lowell?" The President asked, "I mean, other than the C.N.A. recordings that the Medical Center replayed for you?"

"I remember. I did not know it was Percival Lowell when I dreamed it. I remember it like seeing a movie, like talking so someone when they are doing something…"

"Mister President," Terra interrupted, "the medical staff with Apollo just told us that Apollo should stop. He is showing signs of relapse."

"Thank you, Apollo." President Knotts politely ended his conversation with the new media star.

The comm link was ended.

Everyone watching the show was convinced that Apollo was talking to Terra and President Knotts from somewhere in China. Apollo was sealed inside a new, pristine trailer manifested to the Startech Corporation that was loaded on a space freighter for delivery to Crater City. The flight crew was patiently waiting for Sonny to finish his deception.

CHAPTER THIRTY-ONE

CARGO LAUNCH

Tycho Conference Center

| Earth Date | August 11, 2216 |
| Mars Date | D-Mmon 04, 1174 |

MARTIAN VIRUS, DAY 43

The squat-shaped 'Blue E.M. Company' spacecraft energized its anti-gravity field, effortlessly lifting off the tarmac of the Tycho Spaceport. Below, the building and roadway lights of the Lunar metropolitan area sparkled against the dark, shadowed crater floor. The golden sunlit mountain-like rim crest quickly came into view; it then receded, shrinking with distance. More and more of the rugged shadows across the golden landscape filled the rear view screen. Ahead, in the star-studded sky, was the blue and white orb of Earth. Combining the anti-gravity drive with the fusion rocket thrusters would get the ship to Earth in only a few hours, where it would swing around the planet, and in slingshot fashion, gather speed and trajectory for the three-day flight to Mars.

Terra used this time to closet herself in her compartment with Chet, her robot. She wanted to finish her Venus Landing report. Sonny sat with pilot Octan Palmer to talk with her for the first time since the situation began. She detailed what happened at the Wells Spaceport when Flex brought Apollo for her to take home to the Philippines.

The five quarantined passengers sealed in the new Startech trailer in the cargo hold had little to do but watch the screen views of the flight. They were not to speak to anyone outside their trailer until Sonny advised them otherwise. They did not know how long they would continue in quarantine. Nobody knew.

"Tita Jenny," Nina looked around to make certain Apollo was not nearby. "I need to ask you something," The stare of her eyes was focused, "just between the two of us."

Jenny smiled, and then nodded. She briefly turned to the comm console to shut off the audio communicator. "You want to ask about Apollo?"

Nina dipped her head, looking down at the floor. She then looked up again at Jenny's face, "Would it… should we…" She stammered for the right words. She looked around once again. Imaged on one of the communication monitors, Apollo sat with Teddy at the far end of the trailer, watching a large screen display of the spacecraft's outside camera view of Earth. "I want to sleep with Apollo."

"Nina," Jenny sighed, and then continued, "I know you were hurt about those C.N.A. dream recordings of his… situation with Sonia Androff… with the robot playmate. How do you feel about this?"

"How do I feel?" Nina eyes signaled momentary alarm. "Apollo and I have been together since we were children. Now, he doesn't dream of me… he dreams of sleeping with a lady old enough to be his mother."

"How do you… how does he feel?"

"Father Roxas told us to wait. It is a sin. I used to believe that I should wait until we get married. Before, Apollo told me the same. But, on Mars my own father arranged for him to have sex with a robot. He had sex with the blond lady. If I don't sleep with him, what we had will evaporate like a mirage."

"Did you want to do this during this flight? There is me and Doctor Kai and Teddy and Sonny and Miss Terra... and all the monitoring of Apollo because of the virus?

"I thought you would understand. When you were my age you..." Nina stopped herself before she might say something insulting.

"When I was your age I was selling sex for money," Jenny did not raise her voice or change the tone, "Is that what you wanted to say?"

Nina once more bowed her head to avoid direct eye contact. She began to blush.

Jenny placed an index finger under Nina's chin to raise her face. She could see embarrassment in the young girl's eyes. "Nina, I know what I was. I was a prostitute. I was an orphan on my own on the streets of Manila. I had a choice. I could live in an institution with no warmth, or I could live on my own. To survive on my own, the only thing I could do to earn money was sell sex. I haven't been that way for a long time. The women in the barrio think of me as a whore. Do you want this to be your future?"

"That's not true. Tita Celia says that. But, I don't think that. You are the prettiest woman I ever met. All the men like to be helping you. The women in the barrio are jealous because the men all like you."

Jenny was briefly silent in reaction to Nina's words. She had always thought the women of the barrio did not like her because she was not Filipino, because she had more money, because of her childhood history. Jealous? It had not occurred to her before. She thought back to the women being so cold to her, and of their husbands being so friendly. The men of the barrio had always been friendly to her. Jenny previously thought they were offering innocent friendship to the wife of Sonny Ortigas. Suddenly, it dawned on her. Her willingness to share jokes, to play cards with the men, was a direct threat to the barrio wives. She regained her composure, and focused once more on her young friend. "Nina, you are sixteen years old. I don't think you should rush to have sex to hold a boyfriend. If you and Apollo want privacy together, I'll make certain you are not monitored, but I think you should wait."

"Apollo's dreams... what your brother was recording... can you tell me more about them?"

"You know about Percival Lowell… about Tau Ceti… about the Venus landing. What more do you want to know about?"

"Were there any dreams about me? About Apollo and me?"

"What did Apollo tell you about them?"

"Nothing. He doesn't talk to me about the dreams."

Jenny was surprised. Then she remembered Apollo's revelation that he saw Nina's future with Exxis Potowski; saw his own future with Sonia. He had to be as confused with his own dreams as anyone. Obviously, he avoided talking to Nina about visions he knew would upset her. "Nina, Apollo is sick. He just came out of a coma, isolated on the Moon. He feels guilty that he made everyone else sick."

Nina stared, waiting for Jenny to say more.

"I'll make certain that you have privacy with Apollo." Jenny patted her arm. "But, don't rush him. Don't rush yourself. If it doesn't work the way you want, you will feel terrible. I know."

Jenny smiled. She pushed a button on her sleeve. "Sonny!"

An image of the cockpit on one of the monitors pictured Sonny still talking with Octan. He stopped his conversation, and said, "Jenny. Good to hear from you. Are you watching the Earth?"

"Love you."

"I love you, too. How's Teddy?" Sonny turned to his console. He adjusted the multiple monitors. "You're with Nina.."

"Nina wants to be alone with Apollo with no cameras, no microphones, no monitoring."

Sonny paused, and then said, "If it's okay with the doc, I won't complain. I would go crazy if I were watched all the time, too."

"I'll talk to Kai." Jenny winked at Nina. "We'll give you time to be with him."

Nina smiled, stood, and then said, "I think I'll go talk to him now. Watch the space view with him. Can you turn off the recorders for awhile now?"

Jenny leaned to the computer. "Monitor Apollo's vital statistics only until further notice. No audio-visual at this time."

"Acknowledged," the computer responded.

With that, Nina left the cubicle.

"Sonny," Jenny asked, "can we talk about Mars? What are you going to do?"

"In another hour." Sonny rubbed the back of his neck. "Once I've finished the diagnostics of the ship's electronics."

"Diagnostics?" Jenny was puzzled.

"Looking for hidden programs, listening devices, transmitters… I need to be certain."

"They couldn't do that. You were too careful getting us away from Tycho."

"They could have attached something to my equipment… or Terra's. I did it to them."

"Did what?"

"We'll talk after I finish. Go talk to your brother. Have lunch. I'll talk to you in an hour."

Jenny rarely understood the technology Sonny used. She rose, walked to the far end of the trailer to join the others watching the Earth getting closer. A large screen gave a window-like image from the camera outside the cockpit. Jenny seated herself next to her brother. Teddy moved from Kai's lap to his mother. He was still lethargic. Jenny accepted Kai's diagnosis that she was seeing residual effects of the virus, that Teddy would be fully recovered within a few days. On an adjacent sofa, Nina was seated close to Apollo, listening intently as her sweetheart pointed to features on the blue and white Earth; the white peaks of the Himalayan, the green of the Ganges River delta, the blue, cloud-spotted ocean between India and Burma. He tried to get her to find the Philippines. She tried, not because she was interested in spaceflight geography, but because she wanted to impress Apollo with her dedication to his concerns.

Octan piloted the anti-grav space freighter around Earth in a sling-shot maneuver. She then accelerated the ship for the high-speed passage to Mars. Once the spacecraft was in deep space cruise mode, Octan kept the anti-grav field energized to maintain an artificial gravitational field to protect her passengers from the zero-gravity health problems. It took two hours to complete the sling-shot acceleration maneuver around Earth. By that time Teddy had fallen asleep. Apollo remained excited about the images on screen, as Nina snuggled next to him, drowsily listening to him talk.

Jenny and Kai retreated to the dining cubicle for a bite to eat and to discuss how they would deal with the trip. As they discussed Nina's intention to seduce Apollo, Sonny signaled via the intercom.

"Hi, Sonny," Jenny smiled for the camera. "Can we talk?" Five of the screens on the console displayed images of each of the adults.

"We're clean now," Sonny responded. "Terra had two bugs attached to her outfits. They've been deactivated."

"However," Terra added, "whoever planted those devices now knows what ship I'm on." She sounded angry. "Sonny, they know you're with me."

"Relax," Sonny smiled at her. "I expect them to know. I doubt they will try anything rash."

"Sonny, I understand that you and Terra have avoided saying much to us in isolation... to me... about what is going on... the need to keep secrets. If you took care of the bugs, Kai and I would like to know."

Octan, quietly watching her cockpit instruments, nodded agreement. "I'm with Jenny. What are we up against?"

Sonny answered, "You're right. Terra? You're part, or mine?"

"If that recording we have from Sonia Androff is correct," Terra said, "then Redrock vice president Ghant Travis ambushed the prospecting team to steal a major gold discovery for Redrock. However, the Redrock CEO is presently on the Moon with President Knotts for the Venus Treaty is to be granted a special franchise for the Venus minerals. Redrock is also a major contributor to the President."

Octan said, "Do you think the President is involved with these killings?"

"Wait," Sonny held up a hand. "Don't be hasty. Terra, you're a journalist. We should not suggest that scenario yet. There is no evidence that the conspiracy goes higher than Travis."

"There is no evidence that it doesn't. Why don't you explain what you've found."

Jenny, Kai, and Octan focused their curiosity on the detective.

"Years ago, after the Cryogen affair, after I uncovered the United Nations military intelligence infiltration of the Martian security computer system, then-President John Farber asked me to look at the

Martian military computer network. He trusted me… because Terra recommended me… I recommended a way to avoid manipulation of records from outside."

"Farber had you do that?" Octan asked. "You didn't tell him you were creating you own tap in?"

"No, I did not tap the Martian security system." Sonny smiled slightly. "I studied the system, found the weaknesses in their computers. I left it to their specialists to figure out a new coding. However, that did give me direct access to the telecommunications system. Figuring that someday I may need to track suspects on Mars… like I do out of Manila… I inserted a sleeper communications exchange program."

"Sleeper?" Kai asked, "What do you mean?"

Terra said, "He means that if he puts a special code hidden in a message he expects someone to send through Martian computers, that code will activate the program, and track the message where ever it goes. It will identify the receiver, and then track the receiver's subsequent communications, at least until Sonny remotely terminates any tracking."

"It does not break any coded transmissions," Sonny had a sheepish grin, "It only lets me know who gets the message."

"I understand," Kai responded, "What did you find?"

"The message Terra gave Knotts went to his security staff, then to the Justice Ministry… then to the police, and to Sylvester, who routed it to Travis. The two of them caught a flight to Princess Dejah Canyon within an hour."

"That is what I mean," Terra said. "The president sent it to the chief suspect, Travis."

"No," Sonny shook his head. "He sent it to his staff. His staff sent it to Justice. Justice sent it to the police chief involved with the case. That's normal. Now, we know the communications codes for both Travis and Sylvester. We wait and see who they send it to."

"What about your other matters?" Terra asked.

"Redrock has acquired a lot of independent mines under mysterious circumstances."

"Mysterious?" Octan looked at him.

"Independent prospectors who found rich ores. I found eight in the last nineteen months… who had fatal accidents, or got sick… all were listed secretly as Redrock employees."

"Is that unusual?" Kai asked.

"It is if their data records… tax reports, employment records, legal documents… were all modified only weeks before they died… like Banzer and Androff… there are no 'old' official records."

"You mean that Redrock is altering the computer records of prospectors… to kill them and steal their mining claims?"

"He does!" Terra looked stern. "And I am going to expose it as soon as I get to Mars."

"Hold on, Terra," Sonny reacted. "What do you think you are going to expose?"

"Sonia Androff's message from Mars… Apollo's dreams. Redrock is killing people for money, and Redrock is the top contributor to the president. That is what I will expose."

"You move too fast," Sonny put a hand on her arm, "All we have is circumstantial. This could blow up in your face if you air it too soon."

"What more do I need?"

"We know that Travis directed the claim jump with the help of Sylvester. We do not know if the CEO is involved… or the president. They may be innocent. If they are innocent, you would not want to air these charges. If they are guilty, you would not want to do anything until you have more proof."

"Proof?" Terra questioned. "What proof is available?"

"Wait until we get to Mars. Find out what records are available from before the recent updates. Find out all we can about the actual conspirators and their connection to the value of the claims."

"What about Apollo?" Jenny asked. "If he has the ability to see things, maybe he can tell us what we need to know."

There was a moment of silence.

Terra finally spoke, "Sonny and I reviewed all the dream sequence recordings from the Quarantine Center for Apollo. The dream connections seem to be random selections, with no reason for a specific sequence."

Kai said, "So far, we have not attempted to test our ability to control his visions. On Corrigedor they tried the power of suggestion of the visions of those with the virus. There have been mixed results."

"Mixed?" Sonny asked.

"They asked patients experiencing the dreams to think about specific historic personalities. With a few, the suggestion created a connection. With most, it did not."

There was silence, and then Terra proposed the obvious. "Let ask Apollo to think about Ghant Travis."

"If these people have killed for profit," Octan said nervously, "They will consider all of us a threat. They know you're on my spacecraft returning to Mars. What's to keep them from creating an accident for us?"

Terra paused, then said, "I have the Militia commander working with me. We are working on a way to avoid that problem."

CHAPTER THIRTY-TWO

PANAHON DREAMS

Deep Space Between Earth and Mars

Earth Date	August 14, 2216
Mars Date	D-Mmon 07, 1174

MARTIAN VIRUS, DAY 45

The view from the rocky Benget hillside was magnificent. Green pine needles on nearby trees contrasted a pastel blue cloudless sky. The bright sun created sparkles in the flowing stream at the foot of a gorge. It was peaceful, too peaceful. All the Japanese soldiers bivouacking in town were gone. Below, in the distance, the city of Baguio seemed deserted, although hundreds of people were bunched along the rocky hillside, anxiously waiting final liberation. Three women inside the nearest cave quietly attended a pot of rice cooking on a small campfire. A sheet of scrap iron supported by rocks provided a heating surface above the fire. An old man still held one of the paper flyers that had been dropped in the wind by a flight of American planes days earlier. The paper displayed General MacArthur's picture and quoted his rallying message, "I shall return." The flyer warned the people of Baguio to leave, because the American Air Corps would soon drop bombs on the Japanese Army stationed there. The thousands of flyers worked. Town people evacuated the city to the countryside to dig caves, to build lean-to tents, to find some way to avoid the anticipated bombardment. General Yamashita's retreating army also heeded the warning. They were gone from Baguio.

"I see them," a small child yelled out. "Here come the Americans!"

Filipinos all along the hillside began scrambling. Many went for cover in the caves, in the crevices of the rocks. Others found places to sit where they could watch the city below. Several squadrons of silhouetted American B-24 bombers were stark black against the blue sky. There was an occasional glint from their windshields. They came in low, about eight-hundred feet above the ground. As they got closer the planes grew to enormous gray-green American four-engine bombers with painted numbers. Their bomb-bay doors seemed to open in unison. A rain of small bombs then fell in gentle arcs toward the center of Baguio. Bursts of flame and smoke from the carpet-bombing erupted throughout the city. The sounds and shock waves of the explosions followed several seconds after the fire bursts had turned into dark clouds of smoke and debris.

For some of the children, this was exciting. For others, it was terrifying. The desperate resignation to fate was apparent in the faces of many adults who knew their homes and businesses were being destroyed in the bombing. They all realized their sacrifice was part of the cost of liberation from the long horrible nightmare.

The images faded from his mind. Apollo could hear a voice. Was it part of the dream? Nina's voice. He was waking. With his eyes closed, as the dream faded, he sensed someone else's thoughts. He was hearing two voices.

"You're having another nightmare, Apollo." Nina was whispering. "Wake up."

There was an unfamiliar older male voice. "Exxis, are you all right?" The image of a pudgy, balding man wearing a pressure suit appeared. "Exxis, please wake up."

Apollo moaned audibly, then opened his eyes. He was in bed, still in the isolation trailer. He sensed the anti-grav field. Nina looked concerned. Seated on the bed beside him, she stared back into his face. She was so beautiful, so innocent. He eyed her breasts and small dark nipples exposed through her unbuttoned blouse. He smiled, not wanting to talk yet. Had they really slept together? The fog of waking from an intense, unexpected dream seemed to dissipate. Images of an unfamiliar older man calling him "Exxis" disappeared. Yes, they had slept together. It was not one of his multiple dreams.

Hours earlier Nina had asked him not to talk, then closed the cubicle door and crawled on the bed with him. Blushing as she proceeded, she clumsily removed her own clothes. The sudden realization of his long time lust for Nina rushed his arousal, as he silently reciprocated by taking off the sensor-loaded sleepwear he had on. He was stark naked before she was halfway undressed. Remembering Sonia's advice, he then proceeded slowly. Once they faced each other naked, he was able to relax her nervousness by using his fingers to caress her face. He kissed her cheeks lightly, moving his hands to her shoulders. Amidst her hushed breaths that followed were barely audible sounds of excitement. He turned to the side shelf, picked a chocolate from a bowl, and popped it into her mouth. "This is for the sweetest girl I know."

Nina's tension eased. She dropped her gaze to his protruding arousal, blushed again, and then returned her focus to his eyes. Apollo took her hand, pulling her to snuggle, reaching one arm around her waist. In reaction, she hugged him, her face to his neck. She held her breath when his free hand moved to her knee, and then progressed up the thigh. She smiled and slowly inhaled when his finger made light pubic contact. Putting her hand over his, she continued looking at his face, a grin on her lips, as he continued the erotic probe.

Eventually, they stretched out on the bed beside each other. Apollo rolled to his back, inviting her to get on top. He encouraged her to take her time to get through the novelty of her first sexual encounter. Starting slowly with uncertainty, the escalating sexual pleasures soon convinced her to progress vigorously. After they had exhausted themselves they continued to snuggle. Apollo sang a slow ballad for her benefit. They fell asleep in each other's arms.

"You've been asleep for a long time," She offered him a glass of pineapple juice. "What was your dream?"

He reached to rub sleep from his eyes, and then slowly sat up to face her. The blanket rolled down to his mid section. He put his hand to the side of his head. The C.N.A. helmet was there. It had not been in place before he slept. "Did you put this on me?"

"I did," Nina responded. "You fell asleep… rather quickly. I was too… I wasn't ready to sleep yet, so I got up. Tita Jenny asked me to put the helmet on you. They wanted to record your dreams."

"Does Tita Jenny know… about…" He was embarrassed to ask.

Nina's eyes dropped to the blanket. Her cheeks reddened. "I told her I wanted to be with you. She agreed to leave us alone."

Apollo thought of his own discussions with Jenny. He smiled, reached over and brushed his fingers through her hair. He accepted the juice. "Thanks, Nina."

She was about to say something, but stopped herself. She then asked, "What was your dream? You were rolling your head, moaning. Was it bad?"

He sipped the juice. "It was another historic vision, I think. You remember in school … learning about World War Two?"

"Three hundred years ago? You were dreaming about that?"

"It was more than a dream. It was another vision. It was near the end of the war, when the Americans chased the Japanese from Baguio. I was in someone's mind standing on a hillside with a hundred Filipinos to avoid the bombing of the city. I felt the rocks and dirt. I smelled pine trees and boiling rice. I felt the blast of exploding bombs."

Nina stared at Apollo. She held her hand to his lips to stop his talking. She quickly buttoned her blouse. She spoke to the communication unit, as she handed a shirt to Apollo. "Tita Jenny, did Apollo's dream get recorded?"

There was no image on the screen. Jenny's voice said, "We recorded several dreams. Are you descent?"

"In a few moments," Nina slipped from the bed to the floor. "We'll be out there. Did you record a dream about World War Two?"

"Yes, a few minutes ago. You want to see it?"

Apollo slipped into his shirt. "We're coming."

Sitting at the trailer dining table beside Nina, Apollo yawned once more. He accepted a galley-generated breakfast platter from Jenny. "What time is it … in Baguio?" He looked at the console's fifteen screens. Everyone onboard was imaged on a separate monitor. Octan was focused on the cockpit controls. Teddy was sleeping. Sonny and Terra, sitting next to each other in the ship's comm center, were looking at their own panel of multiple monitors. Nina, Jenny, and Kai were at the table with Apollo.

Jenny smiled. "You had a nice sleep, Apollo?"

He nodded.

"You recorded his dreams?" Nina asked. "He woke from one about being in old Baguio."

"We got it." Terra said. "We recorded three dreams. Is that what you remember?"

"I had four dreams during the night."

"Damn," Kai turned from the console. "He should have had the helmet on before he went to sleep."

"That last dream," Sonny said, "matches historic records from March 1945. The American Air Corps carpet-bombed Baguio to drive out the Japanese army. The bombing took place several days after dropping leaflets warning residents to clear out. The Japanese left before the bombing began. Most of the town's people had gone to the hills."

Apollo watched in amazement. Once again his dreams replayed on screen as if it were a recorded movie.

"Freeze frame!" Sonny blurted. On screen was a petite, young Ilocono woman squatting in front of a campfire cooking rice. Dressed in a soiled, colorful wrap-around cloth, she was looking up. On an adjacent screen was a reproduction of a black and white photo of the same woman. She appeared to be about thirty, dressed in a white blouse with lacy collar. Her black hair was neatly styled. It was the same face. "This photograph is from Celia's collection, a picture taken ten years after the war. The woman is related to you, Apollo. She is an ancestral grandmother, on your mother's side of the family. Her name is Lenora Cruz."

Apollo was biting into a roll. He stopped and stared, but said nothing.

"If this woman is an ancestor," Jenny asked, "who is the image coming from?"

"There is no way to know for certain," Sonny said. "Her husband, her brother, her father were with her in Baguio in March 1945. Maybe the view was someone not related. Do you remember anything about the dream that was not visual or verbal?"

"I dreamed I felt happy that the Americans were coming. I sensed fear that a bomb may hit the cave we were in and kill all of us so close to liberation. I was frightened for the woman. She was pregnant. I remember thinking I did not want my child born in a Japanese hospital."

"The viewpoint is her husband, Jon Cruz," Terra said. "If those were the unspoken feelings, it couldn't be anyone else."

"Continue sequence," Sonny told the computer. The image continued for a few minutes, showing Jon Cruz's view of the bombing, of the flame and smoke from downtown Baguio. Abruptly, the image shifted to blue, and then to a view of the older man Apollo didn't know.

"Freeze frame," Terra said. "That is Professor Haff Chester, from the University of Mars West. He is in charge of paranormal studies on campus. He was addressing you when you were waking… calling the name 'Exxis'."

Apollo yawned, and then said, "I understand that Exxis is your nephew, Miss Terra. Is that true?"

"My sister's oldest son is named Exxis. This is too short a segment to be sure it was him." Terra continued. "Is this the only dream sequence you have through his eyes?"

Apollo didn't want to respond with Nina beside him. He looked down at the table.

"I'll tell you later," Sonny said. "Continue the sequence."

The image of the professor disappeared. The screen went to red, then to a view from the pillow of Apollo's bed. Nina was sitting on the bed beside him, her bare breasts exposed. She was offering a glass of pineapple juice. The monitor sequence went blank. Sonny stopped the run.

Nina blushed. She looked down at the table. She asked, "Do you have to keep that part?"

There were several seconds of silence. Sonny said to the computer, "With just completed sequence, delete portion following Apollo's awakening.

Anxious to avoid discussions of the deleted elements, Jenny asked, "What about the other dreams? Are they significant? If they are not personally embarrassing to anyone…"

"No," Terra said, "there is nothing too private to discuss in what we recorded. Sonny?"

Kai reached for a pastry. "These dreams are odd."

"Of course they're odd," Terra retorted. "They appear to be accurate telepathic communications through time."

"Other than that," Kai responded. "Most people recall only dreams in progress when they wake. You recorded three. Apollo remembers four." He stared at the Filipino boy with the dark dots where the rash had been earlier. "Apollo's brainwave patterns do not match normal activity of either sleep or coma. What I see is high neural activity between the hypothalamus and the sensory centers. This duplicates reports from Corrigedor."

"Corrigedor?" Jenny asked.

"Quarantine center. Medical teams are documenting all aspects of this epidemic."

"What were the dreams?" Nina asked. There was a nervousness to her question. After sleeping with him, she wanted to know if Apollo was dreaming of Sonia.

"Nina," Sonny spoke cautiously, "We did not record Apollo dreaming about other women. Besides, this piece on World War Two, we recorded another section about Tau Ceti in the future, from the viewpoint of Zenia Olsen."

"Who is Zenia Olsen?"

"She's the wife of Blue Heidelburn, the starship pilot on the mission to Tau Ceti," Sonny responded. "Blue is a friend of mine."

"A friend?"

"I'll explain later. Let's look at the dreams first."

The other dream sequences were queued on two other screens Sonny first ran a replay of the sequence with identified images of the Tau Ceti pioneers from Zenia's viewpoint. The playback showed Zenia's perspective as she followed Blue and two others from thick, brushy undergrowth out into a sunny meadow. The field, surrounded by tree-sized ferns, was filled with colorful blue and yellow flowers accenting the green grasses. Within a minute of emergence into the sunshine, the hikers were attacked by five large dragonfly-like insects. One landed on the back of a woman. Zenia's voice yelled, "Remi, watch out!" Blue swung a laser rifle around to cut the remaining insects in half, one by one. A man near her used a machete to take out the insect on Remi's back. It was over, the five huge insects dead. Remi bled from the shoulder where the insect bit her. There was a glazed stare in her eyes. Zenia spoke of getting Remi to the infirmary before infection set in. The dream faded.

Sonny stopped the sequence. He said, "We can't verify this dream. However, this last dream sequence is familiar. I was there." The third dream began with a look at wrinkled hands dealing cards to four positions at a table, a view that panned up to Sonny, who was seated across the table. Two barrio Filipinos were seated on either side of the table, each picking up cards. In the image Sonny told a joke as he watched the deal. He sipped a San Miguel beer. He waited for all of his cards to be dealt before picking them up. "Freeze frame."

Beyond the card game was the open wall to the observation deck of Sonny's Baguio house. In the pastel blue western sky the bright sun glared from among a few puffy white clouds. An artificial fir tree was decorated with colored lights and strings of silver beads. Visitors were crowded on the deck. Jenny was there leaning against the railing, talking to Nina and her mom. Lydia was chatting with Bibi and Sonia. Apollo stood with them. The canyon beyond the deck railing was not visible from the perspective of the card table.

"Jenny," Sonny commented. "This look familiar?"

Jenny smiled. "Last Christmas... Our party in Baguio... I don't see Lee Chang. Wasn't he there?"

"He's in the dream. I remember this card game. I was telling a colorful joke during this deal. Roberto was dealing."

Jenny, Kai, and Nina studied the still image. All turned with curiosity to Apollo. Nina asked, "You dreamed you were seeing yourself through Tito Roberto's eyes?"

"I don't know why I dreamed that. It just happened."

"Apollo," Terra said, "Sonny and I reviewed these dream sequences… and replayed the discussions we had before you went to sleep. We want to understand what triggered this series of dreams."

"Yes, Tita Terra."

"Remember, we asked you to think about the men who killed your Uncle Roberto. Dave Crane, Ghant Travis, and Ken Sylvester," she continued. "It seems we made you think instead of your Uncle Roberto. Your dreams put you inside his mind at the Christmas party. The dreams connected you to his direct ancestor from the twentieth century. I don't know why you were connected once again to the Tau Ceti explorers, but you were seeing that planet through the eyes of Zenia Olsen."

"I tried to think about the killers when I went to sleep," Apollo spoke with a hushed, muffled voice. "When I was drowsy I felt I heard Dave Crane talking to someone about us. I didn't hear it clearly … I just felt it. He was thinking about us, trying to plan a way to force an accident on us. It wasn't like the dreams, more like a feeling."

"The C.N.A. did not record that," Sonny said, "Are you positive?"

"Maybe I was only thinking it, because I am afraid," Apollo responded. "Thinking about Mr. Crane scares me. I started remembering Tito Roberto. He was a father to me … I watched him die … I'll try to do better next time."

Jenny reached over to run her fingers through his hair. "You did great, Apollo. I miss Roberto, too. We all miss him."

"I cry," Nina snuggled to Apollo's arm, "when I think of my tatai … and of Tito Roberto… being killed that way. I think about tatai a lot. I cry. I don't know what nanai will do."

Kai added, "We did not necessarily get Apollo focused the way we tried to direct him. His thoughts are with Roberto, not Dave Crane. The first dream sequence was a connection to Roberto from last Christmas. What triggered the other connections?"

"I think I know," Terra said. "Let's run the rest of the Christmas connection. There may be a clue there."

The dream of the Christmas party again began unfolding. As Sonny picked up his cards, he began telling another joke about a priest, an aqua farmer, and a politician stranded in an undersea habitat with a robot playmate wired with the program of a cargo handler. He stopped in the middle of the story to toss coins to the center of the table, calling the bet. Bato started the betting. Andy bet. Roberto called and raised. Bato called. Sonny raised again. While Roberto dealt each their additional cards, Bato asked for the rest of Sonny's story. Sonny smiled, looked at his cards, and then held up a finger to signal he would give the punchline after the hand. Following another round of bets, Sonny won the hand with a straight flush. Before Sonny could finish the joke, Roberto excused himself, asking Emilio to sit in for him. Roberto, in the dream recorded viewpoint, walked to the deck to join Lydia, Bibi, and Sonia at one corner of the railing. Apollo was leaning against the railing, looking out on the canyon. From the new perspective, the rugged pine tree studded canyon was visible.

Jenny took Roberto by the arm, and said, "Bibi told us that Blue Heidelburn's stock option shares of Newton Industries has earned him a fortune he'll never benefit from."

"I know," Roberto commented. "He's three quarters of the way to another star system. He'll never return. What happens to the investments?"

"Blue gave me his share of the Space Freight business," Bibi responded, "and oversight of his investments. I was his office manager since the end of the war… he was leaving."

"Oversight?" Roberto asked, "Why? If he never comes back, why not give you everything?"

"This is an exploratory mission," Jenny responded, "to a planet no human has been to. He felt that if they were forced to abandon Tau Ceti for unknown reasons, it would be nice to have some money when he got back. The starship will reach Tau Ceti in five more years. The first message after landing will take twelve years to get back to us. Then, give a few years to determine if they make Tau Ceti their permanent home."

"I understand," Roberto said. "If Blue stays out there, Bibi has a nice retirement."

Bibi swatted his arm, "I don't need Blue's money. I have enough from my share of the business. The last time I saw Brass Newton, he suggested we use some of Blue's money to send supplies he may need."

"Supplies?" Roberto asked., "We won't know what he will need until he gets there."

"They are going to an ocean world," Lydia added. "The touchdown target is a tropical cove. They brought a small fishing boat. However, Zenia told me before they left that she wished they could bring equipment necessary to explore under water. Maybe we could use the money to send a bigger boat with some small submarines."

"Can we do that?"

"Brass said the anti-grav spacecraft has improved since Blue's launch. He feels we can accelerate to ninety-seven percent the speed of light. It could reach Tau Ceti in fourteen years. He said that Newton Industries and the Martian Government are going to send a test craft with resupply to Tau Ceti. He suggested we include special equipment that Blue might need."

"You are serious?" Roberto asked. "You're going to send supplies before they even get there?"

Bibi smiled. "I think it's a good idea."

"This is too abstract for me," Roberto said. "I'm a simple miner. I wanted to talk to you about something else. He looked at Sonia. "I wanted to talk about what she is here about." The view shifted to Apollo leaning against the rail, listening to the conversation while staring across the canyon.

The recording image faded to a pattern of swirling colors.

"That's the end of it," Terra said, "an interesting sequence. If the focus of Apollo's dreams are targeted by what he was made aware of, this would explain why the next dream was about Blue and Zenia at Tau Ceti."

"What triggered the World War Two episode?" Sonny asked. "We did not discuss that. I don't think Roberto mentioned it in the Christmas party dream."

Nina sighed. "A few days before we left Tycho, Tita Celia was crying about Tito Roberto being gone. Apollo and I sat with her and went through the computer records of the family. She showed us that picture you found of Lenora Cruz. Celia told us the story of the bombing of Baguio."

"Apollo?" Sonny asked, "Last night, were you thinking about Lenora Cruz?"

He looked down at his plate of food to avoid making eye contact. "I don't know. I was trying to think about what you asked. I don't remember."

Octan turned from her cockpit controls to speak. "You have time to sort out his dreams later. I'd like to hear more about the feeling that Dave Crane wants to destroy this ship."

Apollo looked up at the screens again. "I didn't dream it... or hear it. I felt it. I was thinking about how he killed Tito Roberto. I was angry. Then, I felt as if he were thinking about trying to make this ship blow up."

Following a brief pause, Sonny asked, "Your earlier dreams... that we will be at the Club Fir Tree next week. Do you feel that has changed?"

Apollo closed his eyes to quietly concentrate. After a moment, he opened his eyes once more. "I remember that dream. I'll have dinner with you and Sonia at the Club Fir tree. I don't know if it is real."

"This ability to see through time and space is a tremendous event," Terra said. "Apollo, you're giving us fantastic images. However, I'd like to know if you can do it in a controlled fashion."

"My son communicated with me," Sonny briefly rubbed his eyes with his fingers, "when I was in Naples during the art exchange, I could sense Teddy calling me. It was... distracting."

"I know," Kai answered. "We monitored Teddy's brainwaves at the time. He communicated with you mentally with a two-day time differential."

"How do we test it?" Jenny queried. "His dreams seem to be random."

"Not so random," Kai responded. "But..."

Nina, sitting close to Apollo, said, "How about Tita Celia?"

"Celia?" Jenny turned to the two teenagers.

"Apollo told me last night he was thinking about Celia. He felt bad because she was so unhappy on the Moon with us going away."

"Apollo?" Sonny blurted.

Apollo nodded. "Yes, I can feel her. She has been my mother since my own parents died when I was little. I could always feel her with me."

"Think about her. Do you feel her now?"

He nodded agreement again.

"What time is it for her?"

"I don't know."

"With your thoughts, ask her to look at a time display."

Apollo paused, closed his eyes, and concentrated. In a moment he said, "August 6, 2216. 10:44 a.m. New York Time. Tycho Medical Quarantine Center."

"Two minutes in the future." Jenny checked the time reading on the sleeve of her pressure suit.

"Apollo," Terra said, "I'd like you to ask her to send us a message that includes an unusual statement. Have her say the toast was burned at breakfast. Tell her to send the message to the Mars Broadcast Company number six-six-zero-five, extension thirty-two."

Apollo stared at the monitor display of Terra. "That was six-six-zero-five, extension thirty-two?"

"That's it. That's a link to a comm panel that I use for back-up."

A few minutes later a message from Celia at the Tycho Medical Center came through the comm console. "Apollo, this is strange. I think I sensed a request from you for me to call that I burned the toast at breakfast. I did not even cook this morning. Did you really want me to say this?"

With confirmation of the telepathic message the discussions between the isolation trailer and the cockpit were ended. In the cockpit, Sonny, Terra, and Octan needed to discuss the visions.

"Those are interesting recordings." Octan pursed her lips, then blew. "The one that interests me is the one we did not record."

"The feeling about Dave Crane?" Terra asked.

Octan nodded. "If these visions are accurate, what does he mean about an 'accident'? There was no cross reference to when and where."

"If I were in Crane's shoes," Sonny said, "Or part of the caper, I would want to make certain nothing arrived to threaten their house of cards. They'll probably try to hit us when we reach orbit, before we land."

Terra asked, "Has your special computer identified who the threats are, yet?"

Sonny grinned, "It's not that easy. Most of it has to wait until we get on the ground,"

"That's what I'm afraid of," Octan said. "We may not get to the ground."

"Terra," Sonny said, "We need to call General Burch … on a secure channel." .

"He's already has intelligence specialists ferreting details you asked for. What more do you want?"

"This ship. I'd like to temporarily transfer this spacecraft to military ownership."

Octan's eyebrows bushed out. "What?"

"Temporarily," Sonny responded. "As military transport with a classified cargo, the Militia could block customs inspections and prevent police boarding. I have no idea who all works for Chief Sylvester or Ghant Travis. However, I do have confidence that their influence does not reach to Militia Intelligence."

"Good idea," Terra said, "I'll contact the General."

"I have some other suggestions," Sonny said, "I'll discuss them with Burch when you get connected. I think we also need a diversion."

Part E

Mars Return

Chapter Thirty-Three

Redrock Operations

Princess Dejah Canyon
Syrtis Major Region, Mars

Earth Date	August 16, 2216
Mars Date	D-Mmon 09, 1174

The thin, cold air in the huge excavated cavern finally began to clear as the rock dust settled. Dave Crane stood, staring from the safety of the parked, pressurized Redrock laboratory trailer, watching for a minute as the dust continued falling like snow to the mine floor. He returned his attention to the bank of video screens on the control console. The seismic data from the new series of planned explosions created an updated image of the ores deeper into the canyon wall. The gold vein, thinning, continued into the stratified rock. This had to be one of the biggest gold strikes ever. Looking over his shoulder at the Redrock operations superintendent, Crane said, "Ollie, that's it… put them back to work!"

Mine supervisor Oliver Chandler spoke to his sleeve, instructing his crew to bring the boring machine back into the cave. On the screens, the vehicle reappeared at the cave entrance from the exterior work platform, and moved into the cavern. Within moments the boring machine was again cutting into the gold ore, ejecting the broken rocks via conveyor tubes out to the platform, where it was spewing down in an arc to the growing pile of glittering gravel five-hundred feet below.

Crane instructed the computer to transfer the data to the operations trailer parked on the canyon floor. Giving Chandler a thumbs up, he winked, donned his pressure suit helmet, and headed out of the trailer airlock. Out on the steel grating access platform, he stepped into one of the passenger elevators for a descent to the canyon floor. The noon sun cast a bright light on the rest of the colored canyon rocks. The aesthetic beauty of the scene did not interest Crane. A dragonfly plane gliding to the canyon floor from the direction of the valley had his attention. "What now? Did Travis finally resolve the problem?"

By the time the elevator stopped at the flat dusty canyon floor, the plane had landed. Two pressure suited passengers disembarked from the plane to approach the mining facilities trailers.

Crane stepped into the operation's trailer. "Is that Travis?" Dave asked receptionist Gina Lomar. He removed his helmet and then prepared to make himself comfortable.

"Travis and Sylvester." Gina looked over her shoulder at Crane. "They called half an hour ago... asked me to tell you they will be here. Mr. Travis wants a private conference."

"What for? We're ahead of schedule extracting the gold." Crane motioned toward the surveillance monitors. The multiple screens displayed various aspects of the mobile smelting operation. A series of trailer mounted furnaces, connected by conveyors, separated pure gold from the raw ore cascading down the cliff. "The results of the seismic scan I just finished confirms the vein is even deeper."

"Mr. Travis said something about problems with a Filipino detective. Does that mean anything?"

Crane sighed, exhaled audibly, and glanced at the trailer. He was ready to debrief the visitors on his findings in the cavern. This was one of the biggest gold strikes ever. If Travis mentioned a Filipino detective that meant someone was looking for Roberto DeNila, or it was about the Filipino boy who got away with Sonia. "I'll be in my office. Download the seismic results to the main office in Crater City." He put his helmet back on his head, pivoted, and returned to the airlock.

Crane was already seated behind his desk, with his helmet off, when Travis and Sylvester came through the airlock. An open bottle of Champaign was on Crane's desk. Empty glasses were waiting beside the bottle.

Dave began pouring the Champaign. "Before we hear your news, whatever it is, let's celebrate the results of today's seismic scan." He handed each a glass. "The gold vein continues. We have at least another twenty-thousand tons."

The serious expression on Travis' face temporarily softened. He accepted the drink, quietly eyed his partner in this gold strike, and then smiled, "For that, I'll drink your toast." He lifted the glass to his lips.

Sylvester followed Travis' lead. "To the frosting on our cake." He drank the Champaign, and then placed the glass on the desk.

"That's my news. I just finished the tests. Haven't had time to do the complete breakout, but I was surprised you arrived before I called it in," Crane said, then continued tersely, "You told Gina this is about a Filipino detective. Did your agents in Manila finally locate Apollo?"

Travis looked astonished. "Did you watch the Terra Newton show two days ago?"

Crane motioned toward the monitors. Images and data from surveillance, smelting, underground mapping, and chemical tests were on display. "I have time to watch television? No, I did not watch her show. I saw her report on the Venus crash. There was another story about some epidemic in the Philippines." He refilled his glass. "Tell me what your detectives found in Manila. Were they quarantined by the medical issue? I hope your efforts in Manila are better than your search for Sonia. Or, do you have leads on her yet?"

"No leads on her," Sylvester responded. "I have a warrant out for her. It's as if she never existed. None of her acquaintances know where she is. Epsen's employees have no idea, either."

Crane stood, shaking his head in disbelief. "If you hadn't rushed to force that Sagan City doctor, we might have been able to contain it."

Sylvester became edgy at the suggestion of his incompetence. "How was I to know the old man was allergic to SWK? What's done is done."

"You're supposed to be a chief of police," Crane grimaced. "Why can't you get your detectives to track her down?"

Travis responded. "We blew it. Ken has the network looking for her. If she's on Mars, she'll turn up." He put his glass on the table. "The Filipino detective is a brother-in-law to Roberto DeNila..."

"Is he one of those in quarantine on the Moon?"

Sylvester answered, "No. He was on the Moon two days ago with Terra Newton and President Knotts. The detective left the Moon with Terra Newton. They are on their way here. You need to see the show."

An hour later Crane finished watching Terra Newton's shows about Apollo's ability to predict the disaster on Venus. The various segments included Ness Trenton's exposure of Apollo's predictions, the coverage of the crash, and finally, Terra's detailed account of Apollo's ability to see through time. Travis also ran copies of the video Terra had given President Knotts about the nature of the virus infecting Apollo, along with a record of Sonny's credentials. The show ended with a copy of the security camera images of Sonny's confrontation with Carl Reston in the Tycho parking lot, along with a documented report of Sonny's investigation of Interplanetary Metals agents. At the conclusion, Travis said, "The virus that made Apollo sick has made him famous. This Filipino detective is coming to Mars with Terra Newton to look for Roberto."

Crane pondered what he had seen briefly. He turned to the cabinet for a bottle of scotch. "Now, I need something stronger than Champaign." He filled his glass. "Why did you use those business agents in Manila?"

Travis took the bottle of scotch to pour a drink for himself. "They freelance for us through Interplanetary Metals if we need a dirty job done. I did not expect this thing with Apollo, nor did I anticipate that his uncle was a real detective. You saw what he said after drinking the SWK laced beer. At the moment, I have them in China looking for Apollo."

"I saw." Crane seated himself, leaning toward his computer. "Something doesn't look right. Why would a detective with his credentials walk into the trailer of three hostile agents and drink a drugged beer they handed him. He was sharp enough to sabotage their vehicle as he left. He set them up... for a reason. Computer, check the files we just watched for any feedback loops."

"No feedback loops."

"Are there any phone company tracking instructions?" "Normal bill tracking with a Code RXS6 routing."

"RXS6? Not KPT2?" Crane paused, "Check instructions for RXS6."

"RXS6 is classified. No information available."

"What are you talking about?" Travis was perplexed by the conversation.

"I used to work for the phone company... as a computer specialist. The transmissions you got from Tycho should have been routed via a KPT2 switching computer. There is no RXS6 address, unless someone installed one that has not been used in the past." He paused, spoke to the computer again, "The RXS6 switchboard address. How is it configured?"

The computer responded, "The files carry military-classified routing override commands."

"That's it," Crane said. "We can not prove anything without access codes. Ortigas now has a record of everyone who got a copy of these messages, along with their personal access codes. Who got copies?"

"Reston sent it to Van McDermott at Interplanetary Metals in Manila." Travis said, "McDermott sent it directly to me. I sent a copy to Ken."

Sylvester added, "That report Terra Newton gave the President was sent to his staff in Crater City. The President gave instructions to determine what happened to the missing Filipinos and to evaluate Newton's request to grant Ortigas a guest police detective permit. Remy Meyers forwarded to me. I sent it to Ghant."

Crane drank his scotch. "So, our Filipino detective has confirmation that you two are involved. Is he going to get his permit?"

"Terra Newton asked for it on interplanetary television," Sylvester responded. "There is no good reason to object. We could complain that this is interference in an active case, but he will still be here as a private investigator for Martian Broadcasting."

"So, we invite him," Travis said. "We give him leads. We need to find out what he knows, what Martian Broadcasting has. Ken, do you have a friend who can work with him?"

"A friend?"

"Someone you can put with Ortigas, someone who can't be linked to us. We'll have him guide Ortigas into a trap."

Crane shook his head. "The kid, Apollo Panahon… he was a witness to what happened here. Those revelations of his, the ability to talk to the past… talk to the future… predict the crash of the Venus Lander. If he told all that to Ortigas, and the detective shared it with Martian Broadcasting, you know they have his testimony about what happened in the canyon."

"If they have that, why didn't they expose us?" Sylvester asked.

"Ken," Travis said, "You're supposed to be the police. If they know who we are, they want to know who else is involved. That's why they gave the President a coded file."

"That means they suspect President Knotts is involved." Sylvester responded. "Maybe we can use that to our advantage."

"Advantage?" Crane asked.

"Ghant," Sylvester continued. "Send messages that the President's staff is working with us. Also, suggest that the Filipino miners are alive, and being held… think of some place where a mining cave could accidentally collapse on a detective team. Dave, you're good with communications computers. See what you can do to find where the Panahon files are stored."

"You're not asking much," Crane said. "This is getting more complicated each step of the way."

"Damn it," Travis snapped. "You were supposed to make certain we had everyone when we took the mine. You let Sonia and Apollo escape."

"You should have had a team on the canyon floor." Crane focused on the monitors of the mining operations. "I had to be with Fisk," He pointed to the image of the gold mine entrance five-hundred feet up the cliff. "You could have had your men there, rather than waiting in Burroughs Valley."

"Could, should," Travis sat down. "They got away. Now, we have a problem. If we solve it, we are rich. If we don't… we'll be in prison for a very long time. Let's try to work out a solution."

Crane took another slug of scotch. "This virus the boy has, it started an epidemic in the Philippines. Sonia has it, too, doesn't she?"

"According to Dr. Follett's records in Sagan City," Sylvester said, "they were both infected, and in isolation. It's a virus no one ever saw before."

"Terra Newton is covering the story about the boy. Sonia is not with them, or she would have been part of the show. She never left Mars. She stayed with Epsen after Panahon was sent to Earth."

"We can't find Epsen. He disappeared, and nobody in his trucking company is willing to talk without a court order first."

"I know that," Crane shook his head, "For a police chief, Ken, sometimes you can be so dumb. Terra Newton's husband is chief genetic engineer at the Life Sciences Institute. She would have contacted him with the technical details on the virus. Even if she instructed him to be cautious about the authorities, he would have had to send out inquiries related to the virus. Find out who he has been talking to. Whoever is reacting will know something. Go from there."

"How should I proceed… with her husband… with anyone who knows this?"

Travis responded, "We created a computer façade that gives us this gold mine. I don't have to tell you what happens if Sonia Androff shows up at Martian Broadcasting."

Crane finished his drink. "The spacecraft with Terra Newton and the detective… what are the ramifications if it has an accident before it can land?"

Chapter Thirty-Four

Exxis Potowski

Crater City, Mars

Earth Date   August 18, 2216
Mars Date   D-Mmon 11, 1174

"Professor Bernstein!" Tia O'Malley spoke loudly. She concentrated on the classroom monitor at her workstation. The young, beautiful red-haired General Studies sophomore raised her fair-skinned face to look towards the podium, over the heads of other students. "You marked me down for problem sixteen. What was the correct answer?"

At the front of the classroom, Agricultural Sciences Professor Pen Bernstein was occupied with a bank of monitor screens on the desk in front of him. A wall screen behind him displayed an image of the Zepper worm, the topic of today's lecture. Tia's question about the test from the week before distracted him. Following a momentary glance at the attractive student, he focused once again on the monitors, calling up problem sixteen from that test. The wall image behind him shifted from a picture of the worm to the written question sixteen. He verbalized the question aloud. "What is the role of Fechter chromosomes in Martian wheat?"

Professor Bernstein looked up, scanning the thirty students in his classroom. He focused on Tia. "You answered that Fechter chromosomes gave wheat cells a thick membrane, that the thickness permitted necessary internal pressures needed by the cell, and protected the cells from ultra violet radiation. I'm afraid you gave the correct definition of the KX additive to the wheat's DNA." He looked around the classroom. "Exxis Potowski. Give us the definition of the Fechter chromosome."

Exxis Potowski stood from his workstation. Glancing across two rows of students at the stunning Tia, he hoped she would view him favorably, although he was too shy to approach her. "The Fechter chromosome, engineered by Canadian bio-engineers on Earth, year 2032, concentrates in the root cells of Martian grain crops. It protects the roots from extreme cold soil, and produces root secretions that, when combined with permafrost ice, down to 130 degrees below freezing melts the ice, and permits the root to draw the water solution back into the plant as a liquid."

"Very good, Exxis. Thank you. The image on the wall behind the professor returned to the picture of the worm. He readied to continue his lecture.

"Professor!" The activity beacon light at student Roger Lyman's workstation was flashing. "I have an unrelated question."

Bernstein sighed with exasperation. "Mr. Lyman … What?"

"You are a life sciences specialist. The media reports from Tycho… based on what you know about life… the sick Filipino boy, Apollo Panahon… do you believe those cerebral video images are real?"

Exxis had wondered the same thing.

Berstein focused on Roger. "As a life sciences specialist, the news struck me as incredible. Based on my own understanding of the rules of nature, the boy's C.N.A. images are doubtful. I suspect they were staged. However, that does not explain that he predicted, on the news broadcast, in advance, that the Venus Lander would crash because of cooling system failure. In addition, newscaster Terra Newton, to the best of my knowledge, has never aired a phony story. All I can say… I have to accept his paranormal images at face value… I can venture no guesses on how it happened. Does that answer your question?" He wanted to return to his lecture about the Martian Zepper worms.

"Professor," Hanna Grappner raised her hand. "The broadcast compared the boy to the French prophet Nostradamus. Media reports show that millions of people on Earth are convinced that Apollo Panahon is a messenger from God. Even here, in this University, most of the students are talking about those images." Hanna stood up to ask, "Professor is there a scientific explanation?"

Bernstein exhaled in exasperation. He looked over his shoulder at the image of the worm. The students were not focused on his lecture. He turned back to the class. "Show of hands. Discussion of Apollo Panahon? Or, the planned lecture that you will be tested on? How many want to discuss the Panahon issue? Remember, you will still have to take the test on the worm at the end of the week."

Twenty-seven students raised their hands.

Professor Bernstein smiled, laughed lightly, then told his computer to rest. The image of the worm disappeared from the wall, replaced by a lattice pattern matching the other walls. "If you want to talk about the theological or philosophical aspects of this… situation, I am no better prepared than any of you. I am also puzzled. Did Panahon communicate with Percival Lowell… in Japan, 1883? The C.N.A. imaging was convincing. Panahon dreamed about telling Lowell that water from the polar ice, disassociated into hydrogen and oxygen, was piped to equatorial regions. Lowell, at that time, was convinced that there were engineered canals on Mars built to channel water from melting polar snows to the equatorial agricultural regions. Ten years later Lowell used his own inheritance to build an observatory in Arizona dedicated to proving the existence of a civilization on Mars. The C.N.A. imaging suggests that Panahon communicated with Lowell, convincing him that there were engineered canals on Mars."

"The failure of the cooling system on the Venus Lander speaks for itself. The forecast was made on interplanetary television two days before the event happened. The other C.N.A. image shown on the broadcast was about a pilot with the starship mission to Tau Ceti having a boating accident eleven years from now. Adding the twelve light-year travel time for a radio report of this incident, we will not be able to confirm for twenty three more years. Is the dream a forecast of an event yet to come? I do not know."

Tia O'Malley asked, "Is there a physically real basis for a person to be able to see through time and space the way that Apollo does? The way that Nostradamus did?"

Bernstein smiled. He enjoyed talking to pretty Tia. "These are documented observations. That is what science is about... observing the forces of nature, and then trying to understand how and why it happened. You may want to talk to Professor Haff Chester in Paranormal Studies. This is his area of expertise."

Tia responded, "I have his class. He is not in this week. A substitute is handling his classes, and the substitute does not discuss this issue."

"Not in?" Bernstein was surprised. "This would be his... is he sick?"

Tia shrugged. "He got called away. His substitute said it was a family matter." Tia continued her discussion. "The broadcast mentioned that Apollo got sick from a Martian a virus that caused his pituitary gland to secrete a rare hormone that enabled his brain to act in unusual ways. What do you know about that hormone?"

Bernstein moved to the front of his desk, leaning back against it. "Feldermite hormone? I know nothing. It is not in the medical computers. It may be the key." Bernstein looked at Exxis. "Mr. Potowski, you work with the Life Sciences Institute... in fact, you are related to newscaster Terra Newton. Could you give us some insight?"

Exxis blushed. He usually avoided commenting about his relationship to Aunt Terra and Uncle Brass. He wanted to avoid being judged by his famous relations. "I haven't seen her in a month. I never heard of Apollo Panahon before the Tycho broadcasts."

Hanna commented, "Exxis, I didn't know you're related to Terra Newton."

Jack Meyers lifted his hand. "If this new virus gave Apollo Panahon the ability to see through time, what about the rest of the epidemic victims? The reports I saw said an entire town was quarantined to the Moon, that there are thousands of cases in the Philippines. Do other patients communicate through time?"

Susan Kim spoke up. "Supposedly, this virus came from Mars. How much of a threat is it to us?"

Bernstein realized the entire class was emotionally wrought over the Panahon story. Giving up any attempt to return to the assignment materials, he began asking each student how they felt, what questions they wanted to ask. As life sciences students, many asked how this Feldermite hormone could trigger the phenomena. Taking a queue from media reports of mass religious rallies calling Apollo a new messiah, half of the class admitted to being convinced that Apollo had been granted a special talent by God. Exxis was confused about the matter. Quietly observing, the class comments convinced him that everyone was equally confused, equally convinced that this was potentially a great moment.

Multiple aromas of foods wafted through the air at the University cafeteria. After class Exxis got himself a coffee before joining a table with Tia, Hanna, and Roger. Everyone sipped their own coffee as they listened to Roger Lyman elaborate his earlier line of questioning, "If an entire village was quarantined to the Moon… and all the barrio buildings sterilized, then the Health Department considers the virus a serious threat. There are several thousand additional people quarantined on Luzon. The news is, how shall I say it, incomplete. How many are dead? This prophet, Apollo Panahon, was in a coma. How many others are in comas? If that virus came from Mars, are others on Mars infected? Is that virus loose on this campus?"

"If the threat were that immediate," Tia responded, "the authorities would have announced it before this. Why is this such a mystery now? I think they were sick when they came here. I doubt that it came from Mars."

"That's a good point," Exxis stirred his coffee with a spoon. "When I see Aunt Terra… I mean, I'll look into it."

The others stared at him. He had wanted the disclosure to impress Tia, but got embarrassed at using family fame to attract attention.

Hanna asked, "You're really Terra Newton's nephew? Amazing. Why didn't you mention this before?"

Exxis blushed, and nearly spilled his coffee, but caught it in time. He cleared his throat. "I want to be accepted as Exxis Potowski, a student studying life sciences, not the relative of someone famous." A red light flashed on his sleeve. He looked down, pushed a button. Uncle Brass was calling.

Tia commented. "That makes no difference to me." Changing the subject, she continued, "This ability to talk to other people across time and space… if that is real, what does that do to the meaning of existence?"

"I wish I knew," Exxis said. "From what I've seen on campus… on the news… everyone is asking the same questions." He pointed to his sleeve. "Let me answer this call, and then we'll talk."

With no objections, he opened the communications link. "Uncle Brass," Exxis said, "I know I'm supposed to work in the lab tomorrow afternoon. You didn't have to call."

"Can you get away from school for a few days?" Brass' voice was audible across the table. "I need for you to take a Startech trailer to the farm."

"Startech trailer? Why not have one of your regular drivers take it?" Exxis was puzzled.

"A special shipment for your dad. You haven't been home for six weeks, so I figured…"

Exxis did not understand. He thought to himself that it was not like Uncle Brass to arrange this type of home leave. "I have a calculus class this afternoon. Tomorrow morning is genetic engineering. I could arrange a satellite link-up. How soon do you need me?"

"I need you to receive the trailer at the Crater City spaceport this afternoon. This is a special shipment. I'll contact your instructors."

"Are you coming along?"

"I would, but Terra arrives tomorrow. I assume you've been watching her Venus Treaty broadcasts. I need to be here when she arrives."

"The entire school is talking about those broadcasts… especially about that boy with the visions. What do you know about those?"

"Not much more than what's been broadcast."

Exxis had been an intern apprentice genetic engineer with his Uncle for two years (three and half Earth years) since he started college. Brass had never interceded with the instructions before. His appeal that it was "special" meant there was good reason not to mention the true nature of the request. Whenever Brass bought a surprise gift for Terra, or was working on a classified project, he referred to it as special. "Uncle Brass, I'll be there." After getting the information about what terminal, what arriving space flight, and the specific order to pick up, the call was ended.

"I take it that was Terra Newton's husband?" Tia asked. "Heir to the Newton Industries fortune? Life sciences specialists, who Terra Newton uses for commentary on newly engineered life forms?"

"That's my Uncle Brass," Exxis continued to blush. "He is also my boss at the Life Sciences Institute."

"Amazing," Roger asked, "Maybe you can put in a word for us? Get us a job?"

"Roger," Hanna swatted his arm, "that's probably why Exxis hasn't mentioned this before."

Exxis smiled. "I understand. We're all life science majors. I'll put in a word."

"Ask your uncle about the hormone," Tia said. "I'm serious. I want someone to explain it to me."

"You heard the call. I won't see him. I'm taking a Startech trailer out to the farm. I'll ask him, though, when I get the chance."

"Such a shame," Roger said. "You're going to miss Nelson's calculus class. That's our favorite nap time."

"I wish that were true. Uncle Brass will arrange for a satellite link to the classroom. I'll still be there... on remote."

Exxis watched from the pedestrian walk, five levels below the surface, as the Crater City tunnel taxi pulled away from the spaceport office entrance to Startech Corporation. It blended into the traffic, disappearing on its way back to city center. He picked up his travel bag, pivoted, and walked through the entrance. He inserted his identification into the automated wall receptionists for clearance. A small data cylinder dropped into a slot below the identification receptionist. He inserted the cylinder into his pressure suit belt. Automated messages from the cylinder directed him through the maze of hallways and doors to the controller's office.

"Good morning, Exxis," Axel Knudson greeted him. "That you could make it, I am pleased. What you are here for was explained?"

"Mr. Knudson?" Exxis would have recognized his odd accent even without seeing him. He was surprised to see the Startech sales rep he knew as Aunt Terra's close friend since the war. He reached to shake hands. "I'm supposed to take a trailer to my dad." He looked around the office. No one else was there. As a Startech agent, Axel was a regular visitor to the farm as far back as he could remember, filling farm machinery orders for Exxis' parents about once a month.

"Necessary that we be discreet. Everything you need is with you?" Axel glanced at the travel bag. "Follow. I will explain shortly. At the moment, you are towing a trailer to the farm. It goes to the Baxter annex." Axel grabbed his own pressure helmet from a magnetic hook, guiding his visitor out the door into the hallway.

The directive seemed normal. The Baxter annex was a second farm that Exxis' dad had bought from the Baxter family when they no longer wanted to be farmers. Brass used the annex to develop experimental crops he engineered at Mars West University Life Sciences Laboratory. Brass often had Exxis transport shipments to the farm when he wanted to avoid official documentation on the 'special' cargo. This was apparently one of those shipments.

The two of them walked out on the import warehouse distribution dock. A row of twenty new, sealed trailers were lined up in parking stalls. Three identical trailers, connected to overland rovers, waited on the garage deck beyond. Peculiar. Why would there be three rovers, rather than just one with three trailers in tow? Boarding the nearest rover as he followed behind Axel, Exxis was anxious for an explanation. His imagination ran wild. Four people inside were seated around the dining table, absorbed in discussions. Exxis did not recognize them.

"Exxis," Axel began, "Flex Epsen is a trucker from Sagan. His sister served with your Aunt Terra during the war. Jake Andrews, seated next to him, operates an independent air freight business from Wells. John Bushnell and Sweeny Belisario are truckers with Startech. They make deliveries for me."

Exxis shook hands with each. All seemed friendly. He was curious about the mystery of this meeting, but said nothing. A bank of monitors at the console behind the driver's seat displayed interior views of the trailer, with special focus on racks of ceramic covered planter boxes. The leaves of the plants in those boxes were unfamiliar to Exxis, who grew up on a farm, and was studying genetic engineers. They must be experiments by Uncle Brass.

Axel nodded to Jake Andrews. "Go ahead, take off. We have you officially scheduled for Wells, then Electra. Keep me posted."

See you tomorrow." Jake grabbed his helmet, exited via the rover's forward airlock, and disappeared through the garage door leading to the spaceport tarmac.

Flex rose, patted Axel on the arm, and said, "I'm on point. I'll call from Spider's Web." He smiled at Exxis as he reached for his helmet. "Take care of the cargo. It's not in the clear yet." Flex left the rover to board the next vehicle. John Bushnell and Sweeny Belisario followed him out, going to the third rover.

Flex's rover and trailer rolled toward the vehicle airlock. As the airlock door closed behind it, Exxis asked, "What's going on? This is not a usual shipment, is it?"

"Seated, please be," Axel pointed to the table, then asked the computer galley to prepare two coffees. "You'll be leaving in ten minutes."

Exxis seated himself, and accepted the coffee.

"As far as you know, this is a special shipment from your uncle to the Baxter annex." Axel sat down, "The trailer is sealed because of the experimental plant samples you are delivering. No one can open the trailer without preauthorization from the Life Sciences Laboratory."

That was an unusual stipulation for experimental agricultural shipments.

Axel handed Exxis a computer plug. "When I contact you, before you get to the farm... you will review this message. It will explain what is happening. Do not view it until I tell you. Do you understand?"

Exxis dropped his eyes to study the small computer plug in his gloved hand. Unusual, but Axel had his reasons. He would wait. "I assume I am to drive this unit?"

"Five minutes after the other two rovers leave. The auto-driver is already programmed."

Exxis stood, put his bag in a closet cubicle, and then approached the computer console. Pulling a computer plug from his pocket, he plugged it. "Computer, connect me to Mars West University for my scheduled classes. Flag me when I am needed."

"You are connected," a female computer-generated voice responded. "Your calculus class begins in twenty minutes. Do you want the review on screen?"

"Not yet," Exxis looked out the window at the second rover-trailer in motion, heading toward the airlock. "Just let me know when class begins." He turned to Axel. "Are you going with me?"

"No," he continued drinking his coffee. "I'll maintain contact from here. You have a passenger, though." He motioned toward the office entrance at the loading dock where a pressure suited woman walked beside an elderly man. A robot luggage cart followed discreetly. "Haff Chester is coming with you."

"Chester?" Exxis squinted for a better look. "Professor Chester?" I thought he was away from the University on family matters?"

"Flight control put a hold on Jake Andrews lift off," The computer spoke. "The police want to board his plane. They have a warrant charging him with suspicion of smuggling."

Axel ignored Exxis. He spoke to the computer. "How did Jake react?"

"He pulled the plane to a siding to park. He is refusing police access until his attorney arrives."

The Startech woman guided Professor Chester through the airlock into the rover. The sound of the cargo airlock opening outside was followed by the unmistakable sounds of heavy cases being pushed into the cargo hold below the floor.

"Good. That will delay them a good hour." Axel stood to greet the couple. "Professor, I wasn't certain you'd be here on time. Do you know Exxis Potowski?"

"Good afternoon, Professor." Exxis was more puzzled than ever. He decided not to ask questions. Turning to Axel, he asked, "Does this mean we leave now?"

"You leave." With his hand and face, he signaled the Startech woman that they were disembarking. "If you get stopped for any reason, be honest about your manifest... your destination... do not allow anyone in the trailer. Those are experimental agricultural plants. The Life Sciences Institute must supervise any exposure threat. Understood?"

Exxis swallowed, nodded agreement. "I'll see you when I get back in a couple of days." Exxis watched Axel and the woman disappear into the airlock. Seating himself at the driver's position, he offered the passenger seat to the professor. He told the computer to move the rover on the prescribed course. The vehicle began rolling towards the vehicle airlock. Out on the surface, the rover headed west into the afternoon sun, out of Crater City. Directly ahead of them loomed Mount Olympus, a huge, dark shield volcano, bigger than any similar mountain on Earth. The dust in the air gave the sky an orange color, making it look deceptively warm.

"Professor Chester," Exxis said, "I hope you can tell me what's going on.""

Haff Chester smiled, keeping his gaze out the window. "You have a math class in a few minutes. I'll tell you later."

Exxis had not expected that response; not from a Professor he barely knew. Neither Uncle Brass nor Axel Knudson had offered any details. "Why not before class?"

"It's better to wait. Do your math class." The professor pointed to the console behind the driver's seat. "I'll supervise the driving until you're finished."

Exxis shrugged. He asked for coffee, and then shifted to the console station. He connected himself to the math class; and then leaned back to participate.

An hour later he terminated the satellite link to the university. Leaning back, he glanced at the cup on his desk. The coffee was cold. After pouring it into a liquid dispenser beside the console, he stood, looked around, and moved to the passenger seat next to the driver. Through the forward window were the familiar rolling, grass covered Osterman Hills. Without checking, he knew they were forty-five miles west of Crater City, two-hundred miles to go. "Okay, Professor. Class is over. Care to brief me?"

Haff Chester was absorbed with his own academic exercises. On the dashboard, adjacent to the vehicle instruments, a monitor displayed a generic diagram of a human brain. Adjusting neural activity was highlighted in colors. Biological electrical-chemical data tables below the illustration automatically changed with the animation.

"Your uncle did not explain?"

"He called me at school from his lab. We haven't gotten together. He asked me to take this shipment to the farm, as he had to meet Aunt Terra. I think his call was a spur of the moment decision."

Professor Chester smiled, "Aunt Terra?" He turned from his data displays to face Exxis. I'm not used to… her being called Aunt." He reached to the galley cart for a pastry. "Do you remember the first time we met?"

"Vaguely," Exxis said, "I was little."

"Do you remember Zenia Olsen and Blue Heidelburn?"

"Barely. I've reviewed the accounts of their mission to Tau Ceti."

"I assume you are aware of the broadcasts your Aunt Terra made from the Moon… about the Filipino boy's visions of Zenia and Blue having a boat wreck on Tau Ceti."

"Everyone at school is talking about it. They won't arrive at Tau Ceti for another five years. That was a strange broadcast. Is Aunt Terra bringing the boy with the dreams to the farm? She wants you there to evaluate him with your instruments."

"That's part of it. Those dreams were caused by an unknown virus, an infection that is running amok in the Philippines. It has flu-like symptoms that put victims in coma. While they are sick, it creates paranormal dreams. I think your Aunt referred to it as a 'Nostradamus Syndrome'. My specialty is paranormal studies. Terra worked with me before, so she had your uncle contact me."

"Then, you are the special cargo I am transporting?" Exxis smiled. "That doesn't make sense. Oh well, I could use a home break."

"I think you should talk to your Uncle."

Exxis stared. His grin remained, but a hint of uncertainty shown in his eyes. "Computer, connect with Brass Newton at Life Sciences Institute in Crater City."

Moments later Brass' face filled the dashboard computer screen. Following standard greetings, they switched to their personal transmission cipher mode. Exxis then asked the purpose of his mission.

"I'm sorry I didn't have time to meet with you privately," Brass sighed, "but I had to move quickly. I needed a driver I could trust to act without questions."

"Fine, Uncle. I'm transporting your trailer full of experimental plants to the farm. But, I do have questions. What am I really hauling? Why is Professor Chester with me?"

"At the moment, its better that you do not know. Your Aunt Terra is arriving this evening. When she arrives, I'll fly with her to the farm. I'll explain everything then. "

Exxis grinned at the camera. "I'll wait. Looks like I'm about to be delayed. There's a police checkpoint." A quarter mile ahead the road was closed off by police barricades. The police were funneling traffic into four separate inspection lanes. Robot guards were positioned in standard placements, before and after the checkpoint, to deal with potential trouble. "The rover computer registers a police command to pull into one of the check points."

"Don't end this call." Brass' grin disappeared. "Patch in the rover's surveillance system. I'll coordinate from here."

Exxis made the computer adjustments. "What should I tell the police if they ask about the trailer?"

"Show them the manifest. Tell them you are carrying experimental agricultural products for me. The trailer must remain sealed. If there is a problem, have them talk to me."

Strobe lights at roadblock flashed from the barricades. The automatic driver slowed the rover significantly, threading the vehicle's course through the arranged lanes. At a wide gravel highway shoulder it came to a stop. Exxis thought it odd that instead of the highway patrol rovers parked beside the checkpoint, an anti-grav police spacecraft was waiting. Supported by four legs, it was parked in a field of desert grasses sprinkled with small yellow flowers.

Two officers approached the front of the vehicle. One connected a communications cord from his pressure suit belt to a jack adjacent to the front airlock. "Mister Exxis Potowski, driver."

"Yes, sir."

May we come in?"

"Why am I being stopped?"

"A special police investigation. May we talk to you inside?"

Exxis glanced at the monitor image of his uncle. Brass nodded agreement to allow them in, but said, "Ask for confirmation of their identity, first."

Exxis asked. The rover's computer checked the identification data against the camera enhancement of the faces behind the faceplates. Brass checked them against a police roster. Their identities were confirmed as Lieutenant Jon Lee and Sergeant Mack Brian. The computer unlocked the outer airlock door.

The two policemen stepped inside, and lifted their faceplates. "Exxis Potowski," Lieutenant Lee stared at the young driver, and then glanced at the elderly passenger. "Professor Haff Chester. I am placing you both under arrest, and seizing this vehicle."

"Wait a minute," Exxis stiffened. "You can't do that. What are the charges?"

Lieutenant Lee reached to Exxis' exposed cheek with his pressure suit glove. The knockout toxin took effect almost immediately. Exxis's eyes rolled back. He collapsed into Lee's arm. Sergeant Brian used the same tactic to subdue Haff. As they lay the victims on the floor, the Lieutenant glanced at Brass' shocked image staring back from the dashboard monitor. Lee reached to the dash, and one by one, turned off the communications switches.

Brass watched the communications screens go blank. The surveillance views, routing through a duplicate communications link, were still transmitting. The police officers moved Exxis and Professor Chester to rover bunks, strapping them in. They began searching the back of the rover, lifting agricultural trays to look underneath. They stopped when they found a med-chamber with the unconscious Sonia Androff sealed inside. After confirmation, they put the plant shelves back where they had been. Lieutenant Lee took to the driver's seat where he plugged a police computer control peg into the dashboard. Sergeant Brian left the rover to disconnect the trailer. The automatic driver routed the rover away from the checkpoint to a ramp leading into the squat anti-grav spacecraft. Once the rover was secured inside the cargo hold, the spacecraft doors slid shut. Closing of the shielded cargo bay doors disrupted the transmissions reaching Brass. All he could see was static.

Brass breathed deeply, and then exhaled. "Computer, connect me to Terra Newton. Code Y-87. She is still on an E. M. space freighter approaching Mars."

Within thirty seconds Brass was talking to his wife. "We have a problem. The police knew where Sonia was. They grabbed her."

"Knew?" Terra asked, "How could they know?"

"Ask Sonny how he would have done it. They drugged Exxis and Professor Chester, then loaded the rover on a police cargo spacecraft. I lost contact when the cargo bay doors were closed. Sonia Androff is in a med chamber under a shipment of agricultural seedlings. She is still in a coma. They have her now."

CHAPTER THIRTY-FIVE

POLICE ACTION

Burroughs Canyon, Mars

Earth Date	August 18, 2216
Mars Date	D-Mmon 11, 1174

"Boss," Dave Crane's secretary's radio voice interrupted his concentration. "Ken Sylvester is coming in with two shuttles. Meet him at your field office."

Nearly a hundred trailers were parked on the flat dusty floor of Princess Dejah Canyon, giving the facility the look of an industrial complex. Raw ore cascading from the cavern high up the cliffs had created a pile of rocks sparkling with the glitter of imbedded gold. Robot vehicles scooped that ore onto conveyors; feeding the rocks into a series of crushers. More conveyors moved the gravel into the electric smelters to melt the gold out of the rock. Granite, basalts, and other waste rocks were separated to a slag heap. A secondary smelter purified the gold, and then routed the purified precious metal into castings.

Late afternoon shadows from the western cliffs stretched across the canyon floor, hiding a few of the office trailers. The sunset colored sky, the ochre dusty desert, and the almost black shadows made the scene like a picture postcard. Crane and Travis were unconcerned with the natural beauty before them. They had a lot of ore to process, and that task kept them busy. Both watched the loading of pallets of gold ingots into a truck that had just pulled up to the dock. Another loaded truck rolled away through the canyon gorge into the large expanse of the Burroughs Valley.

Crane and Travis, reacting to the receptionist's announcement, glanced at each other. They then looked to the sky. Two anti-grav space shuttles were descending into the canyon. "Why in the hell is he coming here?" Crane mumbled. "He's supposed to be tracking the Sonia."

"She's with him," Travis responded, "in a coma, enclosed in a med chamber, but he has her."

"You knew, and didn't tell me?" Crane lowered his head, focused on the barely discernable face behind the faceplate. "What the hell is going on?"

"She's been in a coma since she left Mooreland. She was being treated secretly at Lowell Canyon by special military doctors. That's why we couldn't track her. They were treating her as a Jane Doe." Travis motioned toward the main office trailer. They walked side by side to the rendezvous. "I didn't tell you because I didn't want to distract you from the gold extraction."

"Terrific. She's alive?"

"Yep. It's complicated. Ken tracked her by tapping Brass Newton's communications."

"Newton?" Crane pushed a button on the side of the trailer to open the airlock. "Oh, yes, Terra Newton's husband. Terra has the boy, so you figure the boy tells her where to find Androff, and she tells her husband. Why are you bringing Androff here? You're asking for trouble."

Minutes later Ken Sylvester joined them in the trailer. Over drinks the police chief updated Travis and Crane on the status of his actions. Sylvester explained that he had learned of Brass Newton's arrangement with Epsen Trucking to bring Sonia to the Startech warehouse in Crater City, that they would help move the patient to his in-law's farm. Epsen had been hiding Sonia from the beginning. They caught her by stopping every shipment leaving Startech that afternoon. She was hidden on an agricultural research shipment Brass Newton sent to the farm, driven by Newton's nephew. A university professor was along for the ride. Sylvester's police at a roadblock arrested and drugged the nephew and professor; and then commandeered the vehicle.

While Sylvester explained events to Dave, Ghant Travis sat himself at the control console to remotely direct the anti-grav shuttle to the cave entrance at the base of the canyon cliff. He extended a ramp from the shuttle cargo bay into the cave entrance, and then had robots off load the rover into the cavern. The shuttle then returned to the dusty aircraft parking area.

"At this moment," Sylvester explained, "Terra Newton, Apollo Panahon, and detective Sonny Ortigas are onboard a space freighter destined for Startech Corporation. The spacecraft docked at moon Phobos this morning awaiting clearance to land. My own agents tried to board with the Custom's inspectors. They were denied access by military intelligence officers. The shipment has a classified military clearance."

"Military?" Travis asked. "When did that happen? Who is responsible?"

"General Joseph Burch, Special Projects."

"Burch," Crane looked at his own computer. He asked for identification, and intercepts with Terra Newton. The computer displayed the answer. During the war Captain Burch commanded intelligence publicity as an aid to General Boch. Terra Newton, Lieutenant Terra Antoni at the time, was a spokesman for the Militia, and worked directly with Burch. Following the war she remained with the Militia reserve, advancing to the rank of colonel. Crane turned from the computer, "She knows enough not to trust your police." He smiled, pointed at Sylvester. "She is using the military to bring the boy back to Mars." He took a swig from his drink. "Smart. Nobody knows she's even on the craft. Military security was not mentioned at all until the freighter docked for clearance."

"Ken," Travis turned his attention from the computer display. "If she knows what we think she knows, this business is over."

"Relax," Sylvester poured himself a fresh glass of scotch. "Customs denied boarding rights to the police, but the Space Safety Board has normal rights to do a diagnostic scan of exterior surfaces. We inserted an 'R-20' on the coolant coils." An R-20 was a miniature six-inch long missile with a signal-activated high explosive.

"R-20?" Crane asked, "You plan to kill Terra Newton?" He carefully studied his two partners. "This is a bit further than I was willing to go. You are crazy. Both of you."

"You've already killed seven. It will look like a mechanical malfunction." Sylvester said, "If she lands with the Panahon kid, and puts his story on the air, we're dead anyway."

Dave paused, looked out the window at the gold smelting operation. "I've been thinking about the time communication story that Terra Newton told about the boy. It sounds like fantasy, but I feel his presence... and Sonia's... as if they are in my head." He downed the rest of the whiskey. "It's probably just nerves on my part. What's the status of the spacecraft?"

Ken addressed the computer, asking for a traffic control check on the space freighter. One of the monitor displays showed that it was still in orbit near Phobos.

"Are you going to finish Sonia Androff?" Crane asked.

"We plan to make her disappear," Travis responded. "Now, it may be a good idea to wait."

"Travis, Travis, Travis... you are supposed to have agents on the President's staff. Why is this happening?"

"Don't Travis me. You were Banzer's confident. You should have checked out these Filipino miners he hired. You should have known that Roberto's brother-in-law was a private detective... and a close friend of Terra Newton."

"Who ever checks an employee's in-laws?" Crane wiped his dry lips with his open hand. He poured himself another drink. "Ken, did you finally get a report on the detective?"

Sylvester had the computer bring up his file on Sonny. "Ortigas does well investigating insurance claims; cases the police have given up on. He's sharp. Not only that, he's a wiz with computers. He's created back door codes for his private access to police and military computers."

"Back doors?" Travis asked.

"Inserted special codes that allow discreet access only for him," Crane responded. "That's how he tracked us. I've done the same on occasion. Did you say the detective is on that space freighter with Terra Newton?"

Sylvester nodded agreement. "And my 'computer specialists' tapped into her computers on Mars."

Crane looked at the traffic locator display. The space freighter was still parked near Phobos. "What about the detective's computers?"

"Don't know what he has. We planted an access code in the Redrock tax records. When he taps the file, transmits a copy back to his computers, and that code goes with it."

"What do we do with your captives?" Sylvester asked. "We have Brass Newton's nephew and a university professor, along with Sonia. Newton was in communication with the rover when we took it."

Crane once more peered out the window at the smelting operation. He panned the area, stopped to focus on the cave entrance where they had moved the rover. "Seal the entrance. Cover it with waste slag. Leave a couple of robot guards inside."

"I like it,' Travis said, "If anything goes wrong, we have something to bargain with. Otherwise, they can disappear... forever."

"We'll disable their communications," Sylvester said. "We can leave them enough food to last... what say... two weeks?"

"Two weeks," Crane agreed. He finished his drink and checked his surveillance computer. "When this next load leaves the smelter, I'll give the crew a couple of days off. Send them to Spider's Web for a few days."

"Terra Newton's freighter is moving," Sylvester pointed to the traffic control monitor. "This should be over in a few minutes."

On the monitor, the traffic symbol for Octan Palmer's anti-grav freighter was moving out of orbit. The traffic locator listed the Crater City spaceport as the destination. Fifteen minutes after beginning the descent, the monitor abruptly began flashing a warning for the shuttle. A malfunction had disrupted the cooling system and shut down all power. The spacecraft began to free fall, tumbling out of control. Moments later, the flashing message verified that secondary explosions were breaking the spacecraft apart as it descended into the Martian atmosphere.

Chapter Thirty-Six

Hostages

Burroughs Canyon, Mars

Earth Date	August 19, 2216
Mars Date	D-Mmon 12, 1174

MARTIAN VIRUS, DAY 50

Nina whispered, "Wake up..."

Exxis closed, and then opened his eyes. He was in bed, in the same rover he had been in. He sensed an anti-grav transport in motion. The police must still be transporting him somewhere. Nina showed concern as she sat on the bed beside him staring into his face. Exxis was mesmerized by the beautiful young Filipina sitting beside him. She was beautiful, and so innocent in appearance. He eyed her breasts poking from her unbuttoned blouse. He sensed his own sexual arousal as he stared at her. His thoughts were almost vocal, "Who is she? Why do I know her name?" The fog of waking from an intense, unexpected dream dissipated. Yes, they had slept together. He remembered it. He remembered asking her not to rush into something she would regret, but she was determined. She asked him not to talk. She removed her clothes before him, and then naked she crawled under the covers with him.

"You've been asleep a long time," She offered him a glass of pineapple juice. "What was your dream?"

A deep male voice interrupted her. "Exxis, are you all right?"

He did not see where the voice was coming from. He only saw Nina. Someone gripped his arm. Something shook him. Nina's pretty Asian face abruptly evaporated into a fog. The image became a solid dark red.

"Exxis, please wake up."

He opened his eyes. He was on a bunk in the rover he had been driving to the farm. Professor Haff Chester's face was in front of him. Nina Perez had been a dream, only a dream. He felt dizzy. His throat was parched. He needed water.

"Good," The professor smiled. "You're conscious."

The dream faded. Exxis began to recall his last memory; specifically the police roadblock on the highway west of Crater City. He had been drugged. It was a strange drug to create such vivid dreams. Was Nina a real girl? "Where are we?" He slowly sat up.

Professor Chester handed him a bottle of water. "Drink! When I came out of the drug I was thirsty. I assume you are, too."

Exxis swung his legs from the bunk to the floor. He accepted the bottle, drank the water. He drained it. His dizziness ebbed away.

Professor Chester had been awake, by himself, for an hour. He explained that they were still in the rover, that they had been moved into a cave somewhere. He concluded that they were near some mining operations. When he woke, loose rock was being poured over the entrance. Two security robots were stationed in the cave, outside their rover. Efforts to use the rover communication were fruitless. The transmitter had been disabled. He did not know if their captors had listening devices in the rover with them.

Exxis got to his feet, moved to the computer station, "What about life support?"

Displays on the console confirmed the professor's words. "Air, water, food, heat… adequate for three weeks. Standard Martian Rover provisions. There is no indication that they had been tampered with. Pressure suits were available, but the helmets were missing.

Exxis studied Professor Chester. One of the most knowledgeable experts on paranormal activities on Mars, the professor was not noted for survival expertise in the Martian outdoors. As a farm boy, Exxis had a lifetime of personal experience getting around the Martian countryside. He did not want to discuss anything significant yet, until he knew if listening devices had been planted in the rover. "Professor," Exxis asked, "What about our passenger?"

"Still in a coma," Professor Chester sat beside Exxis at the console. A push of a button brought an image of Sonia's med chamber to one of the screens, her vital signs to another. Pulse, temperature, breathing, neural activity were all below normal, except for the hypothalamus and the dream centers. They were active.

"Have you tried fitting her with the C.N.A. unit?" Exxis questioned. "Aunt Terra's report from Tycho showed dream sequences from that boy."

"Apollo Panahon," the professor responded. "While Sonia was in the Lowell Canyon facility, the staff recorded several hours of C.N.A. from her dreams. Your Uncle Brass asked for it after he learned about the Panahon boy on the Moon. He showed me some of those recordings to get me involved." He rose from the console to walk to the storage area. "I haven't done anything with her since we left Lowell. We tried to move her surreptitiously." He lifted the shelf of exotic plant cultures from the shelf over her med chamber, putting it aside. "Maybe, we should put the unit on her. It may be the only way to communicate."

Exxis looked down through the transparent cover of the med chamber. The blond, attractive woman in her forties lay sleeping inside the chamber. Her hips were covered with a waste removal skirt. Her life support vest connected transfusion lines and vital signs probes to her arms. Her pale European face was covered with a rash. "I don't think we need the C.N.A. unit."

Professor Chester had pulled a cart sized C.N.A. unit from under another shelf of plant cultures. "What do you mean by that?"

"I know this will sound strange, but I was having the most vivid dreams. It was like I could feel someone else talking to me from within my own mind. I think it was that boy, Apollo Panahon."

The professor stopped efforts to open the C.N.A. console control. He stood to look at Exxis.

"He told me about mixing a serum of Mexerlack VY-6 with Tanchion Selzak. I'm not certain what they are, but the voice told me that combination would revive her."

"Mexerlack and Tanchion Selzak?" Haff Chester scratched his chin. "Are you certain?"

"I'm positive that is what I dreamed. I don't know how much faith to put in it."

"Mexerlack is an antidote for radiation-caused blood poisoning. Selzak is a treatment for swollen glands. You probably have both in the rover's first aid cabinet."

"It was only a crazy dream."

"You saw the broadcasts from Tycho. Apollo Panahon's dreams predicted the crash of the Venus lander," Professor Chester said as he walked to the driver's cubicle. He got the first aid kit from under the seat. "Both of those medications are benign. I'll give it a try."

The professor mixed the serum concoction suggestion by Exxis, and then attached it to the med chamber medication distribution controller. Meanwhile, Exxis checked the rover for cameras and microphones. He understood that, unless their kidnappers were complete incompetents, there could be a dozen devices onboard that he would never find without the proper equipment. Peering through the windows, he saw a huge cave with room for a half dozen rovers. Illumination from the rover's windows highlighted a pressurized, transparent worker's tent near one wall. Sleeping bags, galley facilities, and computers were inside the tent. Geologic work tables outside the tent were covered with tools and sample bins.

"It's working!" Chester's voice interrupted Exxis concentration on what was beyond the windows. "Her vital signs are improving."

Sonia's pulse, body temperature, respiration, and neural activity were returning to normal. Inside the med chamber cover, her lips began moving. She was perspiring. Her closed eyelids twitched. Suddenly, there was a barely audible cough. Moments after that her eyes fluttered open. Her dilated pupils contracted rapidly with exposure to the light. She squinted, moaned, and then coughed again. Her head rolled a little, and then her eyes focused on the two men looking down at her. She tried to sit up, but the med chamber lid kept her restrained.

Speaking with a faint whisper, she asked, "Where am I? When am I?"

The professor glanced to the med chamber computer display. Temperature, normal. The virus seemed to have faded. "We're sorry to keep you in the chamber. You have been suffering from a most unusual virus." He paused, then added, "I can't tell you where on Mars we are, but the date is C-Mmon 54, 1174, or Earth date August 6, 2216, if you prefer."

"2216?" She asked. "Not 2040? ... It was a dream ... All a dream."

"2040?" Exxis asked.

"Who are you?" Her expression flashed anger. "Are you with Redrock?"

"No," the professor responded, "We are not with Redrock. I am Professor Haff Chester, from Mars West University. With me is Exxis Potowski, nephew to Terra Newton."

Her anger faded. "Terra Newton? That means I've been rescued. How is Apollo?"

"Not exactly rescued," the professor answered, "You've been in a coma for a month."

While monitoring Sonia's rapidly improving vital signs, Professor Chester detailed for her what he knew of the situation. As he talked, Exxis offered to get her solid food if she wanted it. He did not want to allow her out of the chamber yet. Professor Chester went on to explain that Brass Newton brought him in on the situation to deal with the C.N.A. recordings of her dream sequences. Brass also had a copy of Sonia's transmission from Sonny Ortigas. He had been able to track Sonia to Lowell Canyon because doctors treating her sent out inquiries for information about the unique characteristics of the virus. Following the Tycho broadcast, Brass convinced the Lowell Canyon doctors he could best protect Sonia elsewhere, which led eventually to the kidnapping. Professor Chester then explained what he knew about the situation for Apollo on the Moon.

Exxis and Sonia listened attentively. This was the most detailed explanation Exxis had heard. The reasons to keep everything circumspect were now clear. "Miss Androff," Exxis asked, "If this virus gave Apollo Panahon a unique ability to communicate through space and time, the way the Professor explains it… do you also have that capability?"

"She looked in their faces with a little uncertainty. "I think so." She stared at the professor, "Did Lowell Canyon record my dreams, too?"

He nodded. "I have not seen the C.N.A. results. Brass was bringing them to the farm. I intended to review what we have when we got to the farm."

"Were they dreams like those Aunt Terra reported from Tycho?" Exxis asked.

Sonia smiled. "I think it would be better if we limited our conversations. We don't know if our abductors are listening." She reached up to touch the transparent dome over the med chamber. "If I can't get out, could you get me a monitor? Get me a camera view of what is outside the rover."

"Rock walls of a cave," Exxis responded. He pushed a button on the side of the chamber, and a monitor panel rose from the side of the chamber. A few feet above the transparent dome, the clipboard-sized screen angled over so that Sonia could look up at it. Exxis connected a coiled comm cable from the med chamber to one of many rover communication jacks. "You're connected. Channel's C-11 thru C-16 have the exterior cameras."

"Thanks." Sonia began surfing those channels, briefly pausing to study the cavern outside. "We're back at Princess Dejah Canyon. The gold deposit is five-hundred feet above us."

"Princess Dejah Canyon?" the professor asked, "How can you be certain?"

"That tent, those work benches, the narrow passage beyond… the Filipino mining crew were surveying this cave. This is where Apollo found the fish, where he infected me."

327

Exxis, Sonia, and Professor Chester each stared at the same monitor displays. Thoughts of being sealed in a cave with the source of the epidemic filled Exxis with terror.

"I sense your thinking," Sonia said. "Exxis, the virus is in a fish, not the air. I got it through intimate contact with Apollo. From what Professor Chester says, the epidemic in the Philippines is related to contaminated food or insects. I don't think it is airborne."

"You can sense my thoughts?" Exxis wondered.

"Yes," Sonia responded. "It seems telepathy is one of the side affects of this virus. From what I see in your thoughts, you've also connected to Apollo. He gave you the serum to get me out of a coma." She paused, "and a view of Nina Perez."

"Nina Perez?" Exxis thought back to the pretty girl he saw in his mind.

"If you can read thoughts," Professor Chester asked, "can you read the thinking of our captors?"

She stared at him, and then stared at the screen. After a moment, she whispered. "Oh, my god!"

"What?" Exxis demanded.

There was a long moment of silence. She closed her eyes, and breathed deeply. Finally she looked at them. "I can't read Ghant Travis or Police Chief Ken Sylvester, but I am able to focus on Dave Crane. Maybe because I know him, I can read his thoughts. I hear what he hears; see what he is looking at."

"What do you get?" the Professor asked.

"They plan to keep us sealed in this cavern indefinitely. They don't want to kill us yet, just in case they need us as hostages."

"Indefinitely?" Exxis asked.

"Chief Sylvester had his men put an explosive on the spacecraft Terra and Apollo were on. It blew up when it was coming out of orbit."

"The Panahon telepathy came through time," Haff said. "Do you have a sense of when this is?"

She asked, "When is now?"

"Exxis glanced at the time display at the console. "D-Mmon 12, 1174 (August 19, 2216). Four dash seventy-seven (11:30 a.m.) Crater City time."

"Same," Sonia said, "I see a clock on Dave Crane's console."

"You are seeing through Dave Crane's eyes?" The professor's curiosity was aroused. "Amazing!"

"His thoughts, his hearing…"

"I should be recording this. Where did I put the C.N.A. unit?"

Exxis interrupted. "Did you say they blew up Aunt Terra?"

Both Sonia and the professor fell silent, turning to stare at the young student.

"This can't be her final chapter," Sonia whispered, "I remember other dreams… dreams of being with Terra Newton later this month. I had visions of being with Apollo in the year 2240."

"2240?" Haff Chester asked, "You mentioned that year when you woke. What happens in 2240?"

"Professor," Exxis was fidgeting. "Let's think about now, first." He looked down at Sonia. "Is this Dave Crane monitoring us?"

Sonia closed her eyes to concentrate. Her breathing slowed. The yellow med suit covering her chest raised and lowered with a steady rhythm. Her dried, chapped lips smirked, and her eyebrows wrinkled.

Exxis looked up at the bank of console monitors. Outside the rover two security robots stood passively at ease. Like normal guards, they appeared peaceful, but intimidating. Exxis recognized the robot line. They had the same face as Chet, Terra's robot cameraman. He wondered if the programming was identical.

Sonia finally spoke. "They are not monitoring the rover cameras. They monitor us through the eyes of the robots." She paused. "They stashed us in here so hurriedly that they did not take time to place listening devices. They do have an explosive rigged to the underside of this rover. If they become convinced they no longer need us, we will disappear."

Exxis again looked at the external camera view. If there were an explosive, he should try to deactivate it. Those security robots would be programmed to keep him from getting anywhere near the bomb.

"Sonia," Chester asked, "This is a most interesting talent. Are you certain of what you are sensing?"

Sonia sighed. "I just woke up. I thought I was on another world, twenty-four years in the future. That was a dream. The last real thing I remember was in Mooreland, being helped by Flex Epsen to escape. I remember a lot since then, but that has all been disconnected dream sequences."

"I did not mean to put you on the spot, Miss Androff. According to Brass, your C.N.A. recorded dream sequences of historical events are accurate, as were those of Apollo. How were you able to focus on the mind of Dave Crane?"

"I don't know. I know him. I wanted to see what he was thinking at the moment. I closed my eyes and suddenly I saw the world through his eyes. I can't explain."

"Do you realize the implications? If this effect of the virus can be controlled, the way you control it, it will revolutionize communications.

"It sure will," Exxis said. "Anyone can get rich knowing what bets to gamble with in advance. Military commanders will know what their opponents plan to do before they know themselves. Thieves will be able to visualize jewelers opening safes."

Both of the older adults stared at him. His words hit like a bucket of ice water.

"Paranormal events have been my life," the professor answered. "This is the most astonishing event I ever witnessed. You make a good argument about the hazards."

"Until Apollo tasted that fish," Sonia responded, "I never gave this sort of thing a thought. At the moment, I have the ability to reach into other people's minds. Now, we need to find a way to survive where we are."

Exxis asked, "Did Dave Crane actually see Aunt Terra blow up?"

"He saw satellite traffic control images of her spacecraft blow up," Sonia answered. "But, if my other dreams are valid, we will see Terra Newton later this month."

"Can you use your 'talents' to figure a way out of this cave?"

"There is a way. Before Apollo got sick, he was like a ferret. He told me that near the location of the frozen fish there is a system of water carved tunnels that leads to the surface above the canyon."

"Can you focus on his mind from when he explored that cave? See where it took him?"

"I can try. But, even so, how do we get past those security robots?"

"We'll think of something."

Once again, Sonia closed here eyes and wrinkled her eyebrows. She took several deep breaths, while her lips contorted. "I get nothing. I can focus in on Dave Crane, but that is all I can sense."

Professor Chester turned to Exxis. "You sensed that Apollo talked to you. He told you to mix the Mexerlack with Tanchion Selzak to revive Sonia. Do you feel he is talking to you?"

Exxis shook his head. "Nothing now. It was when I was knocked out, dreaming. I don't know if it was Apollo. I've never met him. I remember advice about the drugs, and something about heading for Sonia's cave in the El Dorado badlands. Besides that, through his eyes, I was seeing the most beautiful young Filipina girl, Nina Perez."

"My El Dorado cave?" Sonia responded, "Where we hid out for a couple of days when we were trying to get away?"

"I don't sense him now."

Chester rubbed his chin with his fingers. "We are sealed in a cave with two determined robotic guards stationed to make certain we don't leave. Sonia is quarantined in a med chamber with a virus we do not understand. A bomb is attached to this rover that can be detonated at any moment. Sonia, your paranormal dreams convinced you that you will be around in the future. Maybe our best course is to wait to be rescued."

"I don't know if these are paranormal visions," Sonia said, "Or simply ordinary dreams. However, if Apollo communicated to Exxis what was needed to revive me, and suggested we head for that El Dorado cave, maybe we should think of some way to leave this rover behind."

CHAPTER THIRTY-SEVEN

ICE CAVE

Burroughs Canyon, Mars

Earth Date	August 20, 2216
Mars Date	D-Mmon 13, 1174

"We may have a problem," Exxis finished looking through the closets. "Our pressure suits have no helmets." He settled into one of the cushioned seats at the console behind the driver's station. "We won't be going anywhere."

"Amazing," Professor Chester remained at the med chamber diagnostics displays. "The virus is gone from your blood. Nothing is left." He smiled down at Sonia. "If we confirm this, then I would say it is safe to let you out of the quarantine enclosure."

"Professor," Exxis rotated with the chair to face the rear of the rover. "That's nice to know, but, still, we are not going anywhere."

"This means the virus is cured. It means the epidemic in the Philippines is over."

"You think?" Sonia asked. "Can I get up now?"

"Let me run another series of tests." The professor began adjusting the controls to flush and sterilize the sensors. "Test your breath, perspiration, urine, and blood. If it comes up negative again for the virus, we risk opening the chamber."

"Professor Chester," Exxis held out his hands in mock surrender. "Without helmets, it makes no difference. When this Dave Crane decides to blow us up, it is over."

"Such little faith in Sonia's forecasts," Haff Chester responded. "Are you certain there are no helmets?"

"Our pressure suits are in the lockers, but no helmets. There is nothing in the closets, on the bunks, in the storage bins."

He glanced down again at Sonia in the chamber. "You did say you're convinced our captors aren't monitoring the inside of the rover?"

"If you trust my senses. I don't sense anything unusual."

"Exxis, open the 'CR-234' green house container."

Exxis stood. "I opened it. It has eight feet of agricultural seedlings pallets. He walked halfway up the isle of the bus-sized rover. "Are you telling me there are pressure suits under the seedlings?"

"The seedlings were a ruse. Your uncle packed special quarantine pressure suits for those of us who would be working with the patients. You, me, Sonia... four outfits."

"Quarantine pressure suits?" Exxis opened the transparent cover of the container. He lifted out the first two-foot pallet section. Underneath was a second layer of seedlings. He lifted the under layer, where he found a normal wardrobe storage container. Within minutes he had lifted all of the seedling pallets out of agricultural transport box, and opened the wardrobe container. Inside were the four quarantine-rated pressure suits.

"I wonder why Mister Crane did not remove these."

"I think the instructions to the police at the roadblock were to find me," Sonia said. "Once they confirmed they captured me, they brought us to this cave, and sealed us in. There is no internal surveillance, but they have a bomb attached, and they have robot security guards to make certain we go nowhere. What happens if we try to leave the rover?"

"The security robots will probably kill us on sight," the professor responded. He pulled a blanket from a bunk, and placed it on a desk next to the med chamber. He then pushed a button on the med-chamber. The chamber's transparent cover receded into the side walls. He reached for the blanket, and placed it over her. "You can get up, Miss Androff."

Exxis removed three helmets from the container, along with the pressure suits. Each of the green and white outfits had one of their names over the left breast pocket. The fourth outfit had Brass Newton's name. Slowly Exxis placed the agricultural pallets back where they had been, glancing occasionally toward the med-chamber to see if his help was needed.

The professor lowered the side of the chamber nearest him, and then helped Sonia swing her legs around to let her feet drop. He warned her not to stand just yet. After being in a coma so long, she needed time to get her circulation flowing properly.

"That's it!" Exxis muttered, putting the last of the seedlings back in place. "That's it."

"That's what?" Sonia questioned.

Exxis closed the lid, and turned to them. "The security robots; I remember where their weakness is."

"Weakness?" Professor Chester took a pressure suit from Exxis; placed it beside Sonia. He then directed Exxis to turn around. They both took a few steps forward to give Sonia room to get some clothes on. "I did not know these robots had a weakness."

Exxis pointed to a monitor with an exterior view of one of the robots. "These units are the same model Aunt Terra uses for personal security… modified to be her cameraman. As a police security unit, you don't dare attack them. If they consider you a felon, do not try to run. They are programmed to use deadly force if necessary."

"If they are that efficient, how do we get away from them?"

"Don't try."

"I don't understand."

Exxis sighed. "Terra told me that the security units, like the one she has, have a built in override code. In the event that some owner attempts to use the units for illegal activities, using the code will force it to resort to a hard-wired logic and ethics program. If that is activated, and the robot can be convinced that it has been instructed to do anything improper, it will resort to standard, independent police procedures. It's a safeguard to thwart misuse."

"You can turn around," Sonia said. She was dressed in the quarantine-rated pressure suit, lacking the helmet, boots, and gloves. Standing barefoot on the floor, she braced herself with the med-chamber's edge. Professor Chester rushed back to help her to a seat in a nearby chair. "Do you know the code?"

Exxis joined them, taking a seat across from Sonia. "Red, Zero, Nine, Five, Five, Police, 'A', 'Z', Blue!"

"How do you give the code?" Professor Chester pulled a chair out for himself.

"First you have to explain that there is a problem with what the robot is doing. If there is no logic or ethics conflict, the unit will ignore the code."

"That's nice," the professor said. "How do we do that?"

"What is it doing wrong?" Sonia asked. "I think I see what you mean. How should we do this?"

Exxis studied his companions. He knew he was up to taking risks, but the professor was probably not used to exploring caves or trekking through Martian deserts. He would need help. Sonia, an experienced prospector, was probably better than anyone there at navigating under ground, but she looked sickly. She could probably not travel well. They had no choice. He said, "I think we need to get suited up and outside. Bring everything we need."

"Outside?" Professor Chester was puzzled.

"If I convince the security units that a bomb was placed on the rover by their employers, then I can activate the override code."

"Why will we have to be outside?"

"Initially, they will not be able to determine if we are legitimate prisoners or victims. In either case, with a bomb in place, their core program will be to protect us, and try to find a way to get us safely to proper authorities. That means they have to protect us from the bomb."

"Too bad that their employers are the proper authorities... How does that work?"

"I don't know. All I know is what Aunt Terra told me about working with Chet… her security cameraman." He glanced at Sonia. Her eyes were closed.

"Miss Androff?" Professor Chester asked, "Are you all right? Do you need to lie down again?"

Her eyes remained closed, although she gently shook her head. After a few moments, she opened her eyes again. "I'm still reading only Dave Crane. Maybe because he has me so angry but, if the visions are accurate, it could be useful. Apparently Ghant Travis wants to finish us off… detonate the bomb. Ken Sylvester is opposed until they have confirmation that Terra, Sonny, and Apollo were on the craft that blew up. Dave Crane is nervous. He is convinced that I have the same abilities that Apollo has. He agrees with Travis, because he thinks I could communicate with others."

Professor Chester said, "That means we need to move quickly." He studied Sonia, and then turned to Exxis. "I am the oldest, but I am a classroom professor, not an outdoor Martian, not like the two of you. Exxis, you know these robots, so we'll defer to you to get past them. Sonia, you know this cave, and have an idea about which way to go. We'll defer to your judgment if we get beyond security."

They both looked at him, and then at each other. Exxis shrugged his shoulders. Sonia ran a hand through her sticky, blond hair. She sighed. "I'm not certain of my strength, but you are right. Can I take time to shower?"

An hour later they were cleaned, suited up, and ready to leave. Exxis had prepared all the pressure suits, making certain the power generators, carbon-dioxide converters, and nitrate containers were functioning, checking the heat, pressure, and humidity controls. He tested each suit to make certain they could do all their normal functions while outside. He packed enough food, water, and air to last three days. Explaining that normal radio communications would attract their pursuers, he emphasized that conversations between them should be by laser links or steth-o-lines.

Professor Chester wanted to bring his laboratory equipment, including the C.N.A. apparatus. Sonia complained, noting that stuff could be replaced, and there was no way they could carry it all with them if they were going to crawl and climb through several miles of natural tunnels to reach a surface two-thousand feet above the canyon floor. Instead, he downloaded all of the recorded data into computer cylinders, giving a copy to each of his companions.

Finally, Exxis closed his faceplate and stepped through the airlock at the rover's front entrance. Sonia and Haff waited for him to confront the robots. Stepping out on the dusty cave floor, his outfit abruptly bulged in the frigid miniscule air pressure of the Martian surface. The external temperatures of the cave walls were reading steady at one-hundred-and-forty below zero Fahrenheit. He surveyed the dry cavern walls that millions of years earlier had been an underground aquifer. The abandoned transparent mine worker's tent, toward the back of the cavern, was illuminated by window lights from the rover. The tent and mining tools could be useful in the long crawl to safety. He saw motion, like a man moving toward him along the rover's side. Turning to face the security robot, he spread his arms with his open hands. Using a preset laser comm channel normally used by Terra's robot, he said, "Hello, sir. I am Exxis Potowski."

The approaching robot responded immediately. "Sir, you must return to rover confinement. I am authorized to use deadly force if you attempt to resist or escape."

"Officer," Exxis spoke slowly. He glanced at the nameplate on the robot's uniform. "Officer Harris. I do not intend to resist your commands. However, we have a problem that you should be aware of." Exxis looked beyond robot Harris to the second unit positioned at the rear of the rover. The name on the second robot's nameplate read "Ryder".

"A problem?" Dressed in a normal pressure suit, the security robots did not have helmets. Harris' facial expressions were identical to those of Chet, Aunt Terra's cameraman robot.

"The agents who arrested us should have taken us to a police impound. Instead, we were brought thousands of miles from the point of arrest, and sealed in an isolated cave intended for a commercial mining operation. This is not a proper arrest procedure."

"We were advised that this was necessary. The commanding officer is tracking leads for a murder where you are a suspect. You are needed at this location for witness identification."

"It is not proper to seal us inside this cave."

"I will inquire about that."

"Your commander, Police Chief Ken Sylvester, is part of a conspiracy to kidnap and kill us as a means to cover up his involvement in a criminal conspiracy." Exxis swallowed. "They have attached a bomb to the under carriage of this rover, and intend to detonate when they feel the time is right."

"Detonate? A bomb?" There was a sudden head motion on both robots, scanning the rover. "Do you have evidence?"

"I would ask that you investigate. Proceed in accordance with code 'red, zero, nine, five, five, police, A, Z, blue'!"

The expressions of the robots began to change. Harris dropped the aim of his weapon away from Exxis. "You will remain here while my associate searches for the explosive device."

At the far end of the rover, Ryder removed an all-purpose scan packet from his belt. He adjusted it to the wheeled setting, and then placed it on the cavern floor. The unit disappeared under the rover.

Minutes later the robot guarding Exxis spoke. "We confirm the existence of an explosive device attached to the vehicle frame. We also confirmed that our communication links to the global satellites have been deactivated. In accordance with our primary programming, we will now attempt to protect you from harm, as long as you do not attempt to resist or escape."

"Thank you, sir. We will work with you."

"Are the other detainees prepared for excursion?"

Having monitored the discussions, they were already moving through the airlock. In accordance with Exxis' suggestions, Sonia and the professor stepped out on to the cave floor in a slow, non-threatening manner. They allowed Harris to scan them for weapons. Harris led the trio across the cavern to the work benches beside the miner's tent. "We will try to disarm the explosive." He turned one of the work tables on its side, then a second. You three will lay down behind these tables until we signal you that it is safe."

"Officer Harris," Sonia spoke. "If there is an explosion, parts of the rover would be ricocheting all over the cave. Might I suggest the tunnel over there?" She pointed to the small tunnel leading down to the ice deposit where Apollo originally discovered the fish.

Harris studied the tunnel opening. He signaled Ryder to inspect the cave. Five minutes later, Ryder returned. Harris then told the three prisoners to go to the end of the tunnel. "You will have to crawl approximately fifty feet around some jagged outcrops, but there is a large bay at the end. There are ice deposits that have been chipped away by previous explorers. You will wait there until I come for you."

There was no conversation between the three captives. Exxis trailed behind Professor Chester as he followed Sonia and the robot. Using helmet spotlight, they crawled through the rugged rock passageway to a large bay that opened over flat sheet of dust covered ancient ice. To one side were two sets of stalagmites and stalactites, where there had been millions of years of dripping calcite-laden water before the ground froze solid. Officer Harris left to crawl back out to the main cavern. Exxis then pulled two steth-o-lines from his collar, handing one to each of the others. "If I have this figured correctly, those security robots will now protect us from whoever is outside."

"If we can get out of here," the professor said, "Remember the cave is sealed. Sonia, where is that access to the surface you were telling us about?"

"I never saw it directly. Apollo told me about it before he went into a coma. I also had a dream of his following a path to the surface." She looked up with her helmet spotlight illuminating the cave ceiling, "There should be a vertical opening above our heads."

The illumination beams from the three helmet lights began dancing across the bay ceiling. Above the back wall was a triangular space that narrowed into a rough, forty-inch diameter chimney rising.

"How big did you say Apollo was?" The Professor's voice revealed his doubts about the chimney as an escape route.

"Five foot even," Sonia sighed, realizing that the opening would be tight, maybe impossible for the heavy-set professor. "Thin."

Exxis said, "Maybe we can get the robot to use his tools to widen the opening. I mean, if he can't lead us through the front entrance to the cave."

"He would do that?" Sonia was surprised.

"He is a law enforcement robot, and we are his prisoners. He will interpret his duty as protecting the public from us, first. If we do not present a threat, his next duty is to protect us from threats. He will lead us out, if he can."

"I hope you're right. I don't know what…"

A bright reflective light from the tunnel they had crawled through abruptly illuminated the entire bay. The three of them felt a vibration in the rocks they were sitting on. Lasting several seconds, the light slowly faded. As the crawl spaced darkened, a cloud of dust blew into the bay. The three helmet spotlights focused illumination on the access tunnel. The stirred dust quickly settling in the thin Martian air. For the next twenty seconds, the three of them sat quietly, saying nothing.

The professor was the first to state the obvious. "I don't think they were able to defuse the bomb."

Exxis stood. "Wait here. I will look." He disconnected the steth-o-lines, letting it retract into his collar flange. Sonia followed him, while the professor waited. In the main cavern the damage was extensive. The back of the rover had been blown off; pieces of frame and sheet metal scattered everywhere. Broken water lines from what remained of the front of the rover spewed water on the cavern roof. That water froze on contract with rocks. The miner's tent, with multiple holes, lay deflated on the floor. The two work tables had been thrown against a wall. Using their helmet spotlights, Exxis and Sonia looked for the security detail. The chest of one, with the nameplate 'Ryder' was near the rear of the rover. They found "Harris" against a far wall, pieces of steel frame penetrating his body. Neither robot still functioned.

Sonia rummaged through miner's tools, selecting some small picks and hammers. She found no power packs or boring tools. She did take a five-hundred foot reel of communications cable. They explored the rover for anything useful, but the blast had done too much damage to the inside.

When they crawled back to the professor, they formed a circle connected with steth-o-lines. Sonia said, "I don't know if the robots accidentally triggered the bomb, or if it was deliberately detonated when Dave Crane realized the robots were trying to disarm it. The rover and the robots are gone, so we are on our own. I don't know if they realize we are still alive, but if they think we are…" Neither Exxis nor the professor could see her face through the tinted faceplate, but her tone was ominous.

Professor Chester said, "I assume that they will leave us sealed in here to die."

"Do not assume," Sonia responded. "Ken Sylvester knows those robots better than we do. They will understand that if they were attempting to disarm the bomb, then the robots would have tried to protect the prisoners. They will come back in here to make positive we do not remain as witness threats."

"I can scale that chimney vent," Exxis said. "I'm the youngest and strongest of all of us."

"I should go first," Sonia replied. "I remember Apollo's directions, and I am a prospector. I know my way through underground caves."

"Fair enough," Exxis said. "Besides, I think the Professor may need my help to get him up there."

"I'll pull the communications cable with me," she stood, hooking the reel to her belt. "This cable has a tensile strength of twelve-hundred pounds." She handed each a small miner's pick.

Professor Chester finally spoke. "Sonia, are you still able to sense what Dave Crane is up to?"

"Give me a moment." She stood quietly for several seconds. "They know what happened. They were tuned to the robot's communications. They recorded Exxis' discussions with Harris, and our escape into this ice bay. They are coming after us." With that, she walked to the rock wall under the chimney vent. She began stepping up along the rock outcrops. She disappeared into the vent.

With the comm cable connected to the Professor's belt, and a second cable to Exxis, the two listened as Sonia narrated her passage through the vent. After a six-foot vertical chimney, the tunnel angled deeper into the rock at a forty degree angle. One-hundred feet further up it leveled to an ancient, dried underground river channel, about six feet in diameter. That meandered at a more gentle upwards path. She told them to join her, advising care to avoid tearing their pressure suits on the jagged rocks.

Even in Martian gravity, where the professor weighed in at one-third of what he would on Earth, he had difficulty climbing. Exxis helped push him up into the rugged vent. Exxis advised him when he snagged his back pack on the outcrops, when his footing was not solid. It took several minutes for the professor to climb through the six-foot vertical shaft. He kept apologizing for being a hindrance to the other two. When the shaft tilted forty degrees, the next one-hundred foot climb was as easy as climbing a ladder. When they reached Sonia in the larger, more gentle slope of the subterranean channel, Professor Chester stopped to catch his breath.

"Miss Androff," he asked, "How far did you say we have to climb to reach the surface?"

"It's a two-thousand foot climb from the canyon floor to the surrounding terrain."

"Two-thousand feet?" The professor's sounded exasperated. "I will never make it."

"What I remember from Apollo," Sonia said, "is that most of this channel goes up at a gentle climb. He got to the surface and back in an afternoon."

"You are talking about a boy who works in the mines. I'm not up to this. I think I best remain behind."

"Professor," Exxis said, "I'll help you."

"I think it is better for you two to go without me. I will slow you down."

"Professor," Sonia added, "these men killed my partner to claim our gold discovery. They killed Apollo's uncles. They tried to blow us in the rover. You have to try."

"This climb… what is the total distance we have to crawl through these tunnels?"

Sonia paused a moment to think. "Apollo was wearing a hiker's odometer, and he said he checked it when he got to the surface. What was it? Oh, yes… eleven miles, one way."

"You think I can crawl through these tunnels, uphill all the way, stumbling every few feet, for eleven miles? I should take my chance with Dave Crane."

"Professor," Exxis said, "I can't leave you behind. Aunt Terra told me a number of times that your work with the Cryogen mystery helped convince the government to send a manned expedition to Tau Ceti. I can't let you give up. Aunt Terra would kill me, and then be charged with murder."

After a moment of silence, the professor reached over and patted Exxis on the knee. "I doubt that it would be that serious, Exxis. However, I'll humor you for a while."

"We will pace ourselves," Sonia said, "so we don't hit a wall of exhaustion." She stood up and reeled in the comm cable. "We don't want to destroy this cable. We'll use the laser comm. Make certain all of your units are working properly."

Walking, crawling, climbing, squeezing, walking, backtracking, and climbing more; they proceeded, taking turns at telling stories as they went. Sonia told about her childhood interest in prospecting. Her parents were miners. She told about her failed marriage; that her husband left her to run off with Fisk Banzer's wife. She detailed her long partnership with Fisk.

Professor Chester talked about his expertise in paranormal studies. When he was a child his grandfather used to take him on long trips down Mariner Canyon for rock hunting and to explore abandoned early settlements. He remembered a trip his grandfather took alone to the south polar cap. His grandfather had always been bothered by back pains, and could never straighten or move fast. The back pain had started with an accident, before the Professor was born, when his grandfather was a young man. The pain remained the rest of his life. His grandfather died of heart failure during that polar trip. However, the professor's mother woke during the night that he died, saying that she had just sensed talking to her dad. He told her his back was better; that he could walk erect again. His grandmother called the next morning with the news that his grandfather had died. That call convinced Haff to investigate what was involved with his mother hearing from her dead father. He began studying cases of paranormal events, trying desperately to separate the fakes and the wishful dreaming from the real occurrences. He often got frustrated with the discipline, because so many of the reports were impossible to substantiate.

Sonia and Exxis encouraged Professor Chester to keep telling stories as they crawled and climbed and walked up the former aquifer channels. His speech and breathing let them know when he was tired, and needed a rest. Using their helmet lights to illuminate the way, they kept going a good five hours, with several brief half-hour stops to catch their breath. Despite his fear of his own limitations, Professor Chester maintained a fairly descent pace, allowing them to cover approximately a third of the distance in that five hours. Arriving in a large, building sized cavern, Sonia finally suggested that they stop to rest.

"Thank you, Miss Androff." The professor settled down against a rock wall. "I need a break."

"Me, too," Exxis squatted down. He checked his sleeve to evaluate conditions. Since leaving the rover, they had traversed four miles. Oxygen, nitrogen, and water were in good shape. The carbon-dioxide converter was processing air he exhaled, and returning the separated oxygen to the tanks on his back. "Can we lay down a bit?"

Sonia's breathing was rapid and shallow. "I think we all need to. I'm still running a fever." She undid her supply belt, and then seated herself to face them. "I need a rest. I think we are out of range of their ferrets."

"Ferrets?" Professor Chester asked.

Exxis looked around the cavern. Multiple sets of stalagmites and stalactites were around the cavern. The flat surface they rested on was a frozen pond, covered with a thick layer of hardened dust. A dozen tunnels led off in all different directions. The floor was flat and dusty. "A ferret is a bird-sized robotic scanner that can track pressure suit foot prints in the open desert for about twenty miles during daylight. At night, or in tunnels, it will do less than three miles before it runs out of power."

"Then, they will know what direction we went," the professor responded. "Shouldn't we keep moving... keep a little distance. They'll be sending security robots after us."

"I don't think so," Sonia said. "Not after Exxis disabled the other units at the rover. They will be coming after us with live trackers. They have the same limits we do. We need rest, or we will collapse long before we reach the surface."

Exxis asked, "Are you certain you know which tunnel to take?"

"Apollo marked his way when he explored these caves." Sonia said, "Look for green reflectors."

"Green reflectors?" Exxis was surprised. He rotated his head with its spotlight beam. There was a spot of greenish yellow on the rocks adjacent to the tunnel they just came from. Several more were noticeable ahead, spaced at fifteen feet, leading across the flat dusty floor to a tunnel ninety feet further on. "I'll be damned. Why didn't you say something?"

"Sorry. I should have." She paused. "Exxis, you take the first watch. The Professor and I are in the worst shape. We need rest. Wake me in an hour."

CHAPTER THIRTY-EIGHT

EXHAUSTION

Burroughs Canyon, Mars

Earth Date	August 21, 2216
Mars Date	D-Mmon 14, 1174

MARTIAN VIRUS, DAY 52

E xxis barely opened his eyes. Everything was black. His back hurt. Where was he? He was sealed in pressure suit, camping out in a never ending labyrinth of dry aquifer tunnels. He yawned, and stretched. His legs hurt. He had been dreaming again about Nina. Her face, her form, her taunting smile aroused him. He was a little embarrassed. However, this time it was a normal dream, similar to daydreams he had during the semester about Tia O'Malley. All semester he had been infatuated with Tia's Irish beauty, but he was too shy to approach her for more than conversation in the University cafeteria. For months he had fantasized about a non-existent relationship with Tia, an obsession that he knew was misplaced.

These sudden dreams of Nina, like those of Tia, faded quickly when he woke from the fog of sleep.

His body hurt from sleeping uncomfortably sealed in the pressure suit, forced to lie on his side because of the necessary air control backpack. His arm tingled from having slept the night with it under his body. He forced himself to a sit up. According to his sleeve instruments, he had been asleep six hours. The odometer showed they had walked nine miles to this tunnel cavern bay, where they slept for the night. He was thirsty. He needed to brush his teeth to clear his mouth of phlegm. He had to urinate. Turning on the visor's infrared night vision mat, he saw that Sonia and Professor Chester were still asleep. Rising to a squat, he adjusted the front waste removal drain, and quietly relieved himself. Manipulating the helmet attachments, he drank a sip of water, swished it around in his mouth, and then spit it into the receptacle used for oral waste disposal. He poured that bag, and the urination waste, into the water purification unit to preserve as much water as possible. He took another drink of water.

Exxis thought about the threats they faced. Were killers following them up through the tunnels? If Sonia actually read Crane's thoughts, were her personal thoughts being revealed to Crane at the same time? Once they reached the surface, would waiting surveillance devices be ready to detect them when they started coursing through the rugged terrain of the El Dorado badlands. Sitting quietly with his own thoughts, he pondered the reality that he may never see home again.

He was hungry. He whispered to the laser comm low enough not to disturb anyone sleeping. "Anyone awake?"

There were two audible moans.

Professor Chester coughed, wheezed, then muttered, "I feel stiff, but rested. I wish we had salvaged that tent." He rolled to his stomach, pushed himself up, and twisted to a sitting position. "I haven't slept outside in a pressure suit since I was a child." He leaned back against the rock wall. "I wish I had a toilet and a shower."

Exxis laughed, "Don't we all. You do remember how to do it, don't you?"

The professor's breathing sounded labored. "Everyone knows how. I just don't enjoy it."

Sonia was also rising, "That was quite a dream." She leaned back against the tunnel wall. He listened to sounds of her sipping water through a tube inside her helmet. "Oooh, that's not good."

"Not good?" Exxis asked. "Are you all right?"

"A little nausea," She responded. She looked at her med stats display. "Looks like I'm not entirely over the virus."

"How bad?" The professor was in a squatting position. He attached the receptacle to the rump flange of his pressure suit for solid waste relief.

"Temperature is two degrees high," she responded, "I have a headache and feel queasy in the stomach."

"Don't get sick in that outfit!" Exxis stated the obvious. "When I prepped these outfits, I included inhalant flu medication. Take a breath of that before you attempt to put anything in your stomach."

"Thanks," she said, "I'll do that."

The professor coughed. "The dream, Sonia, what was the dream?"

Exxis adjusted the collar to open the feeding tube. He began sucking in pellets of food.

"I don't know if it was a dream, or another of those timescape visions," Sonia spoke slowly after breathing the inhalant. She took a minimal sip of water, and then waited to see what would happen. There was no increased nausea. "It was unlike any dream I ever remember. I was in a house in old Russia... very old. The waterfront, the hills... were the same that I saw outside Odessa at the Black Sea during the family reunion. There was no city, no port... only a small local village. It wasn't even old Russia. The people called themselves Tartars. The houses were made of mud and plaster and wood... with grass roofing. Everyone was dying... an uncle was pulling bodies out of the house I was in... I went alongside the cart with the bodies to put them in a huge fire. Bodies were pulled from almost every house, men, women, children... all covered with pustules and ashen in color. Everything smelled terrible. The uncle talked about the plague as a threat to the whole community... he was convinced that everyone was dying."

"On the Black Sea?" The professor questioned. "Land of the Tartars? The midst of a plague? Wasn't that in the mid fourteenth century?"

"I don't know," Sonia replied. "I don't know why I was dreaming about it. It was strange."

"The C.N.A. dreamscapes we have from Apollo include a sequence from his direct ancestors in the Philippines... from World War II. Maybe you were also connecting to ancestors. How far back does your family line go in that area?"

"I don't know. My grandparents were born in Odessa. I never talked to anyone about family history. If we get out of here, we can research all my dreams."

"Are the two of you ready to move again?" Exxis asked.

"Give me a moment," Professor Chester disconnected and removed the waste canister.

All three stood, strapped on their utility belts and supply backpacks, and started walking, following the glowing green buttons left by Apollo. The passageway abruptly narrowed to a cascading tube that they had to climb on hands and knees for several hundred feet.

"I'm curious," the professor asked, "Sonia, what is your relationship with Apollo?"

"I like him. Other than that, it's a bit personal."

"The casual sexual encounter... he told his uncle that it was a birthday present from you. Is that something you normally give as a gift?"

Sonia was glad nobody could see the embarrassment in her face. "I prefer not to talk about that sort of... but, then, with this epidemic... I won't have much choice, will I?"

Exxis was curious, but decided to let them do the talking.

Sonia said, "I like him. He reminds me of me at that age... innocent, naïve, shy... but adventurous and excited about exploring geology. He isn't like his uncles, who work hard because it is their jobs... he is excited about it. He found this passage we're following on his own. He found the fish and tasted it. Besides..."

"Besides?" The professor asked.

"Since I first met him last Christmas, I had this feeling... that I knew him, that he was someone I was supposed to be with."

"Could this be from these dream connections?" The professor was huffing as he slowly climbed the natural rock steps behind her.

"I don't know. You're the first person I've talked to about this."

"The girl I was seeing in my dreams," Exxis added, "you said her name is Nina Perez... a friend of Apollo..." He was climbing at much slower pace than he was comfortable with. He knew he had to watch out for the professor. "I dreamed of her again. This time it was less distinct. She was just there in my thoughts."

"That's how I felt about Apollo," Sonia said, "with some of the dreams I had before you woke me up."

"You said something about the year 2240," the professor commented. "Did you dream about being with him in that year?"

"Yes," She was eating a food pellet as she climbed. "But, if it is a forecast of things to come, it doesn't add up. In the dream, he was twenty-five and I was forty-nine. We were exploring an island... a cool, conifer covered island, surrounded by a deep blue ocean. The air was like Earth, but there were two moons in the sky."

"Are you all right to be eating? I mean your stomach?" Exxis queried.

The professor said as he panted, "2040 is twenty-four years in the future. If Apollo is twenty-five in the dream, that is eight years from now. The math does not compute."

"I'm famished. The inhalant medication seems to have me under control." Sonia stepped out on a flat, dust covered bay. "Eight years for both of us. Maybe it was just a fantasy dream."

Exxis followed Professor Chester into the new, large bay. Sonia was continuing along the trail of green buttons. Again there was a flat dusty surface covering an ancient ice pool. "Wait, Miss Sonia. The Professor needs a rest."

Professor Chester stopped, bending over to catch his breath, and then stood erect again. "No, let's continue. Just don't hurry."

Sonia felt a sudden rush of nausea, but was able to control it. She stopped to take a sip of water with a tablet of anti-acid medication. "Professor, do you have a health issue we should be aware of?"

They all began walking again, "Just a bit of heart murmur and old age. I'll be thirty-nine (seventy-five Earth years) in a few weeks."

"That plus little exercise and being overweight!" Sonia responded, "Let us know if you need to stop."

Exxis said. "The drug they used to knock us out probably didn't help." He was listening for their breathing sounds. "Professor, do you have a wife?"

Professor Chester began telling about his wife, who had died in an accident at age twenty-one (forty Earth years), and about his now grown children and their spouses. They continued to walk, crawl, climb, and walk some more. Exxis talked about growing up on a farm in the shadow of majestic Mount Olympus, of harvesting bio-engineered wheat from the open fields on the farm. Two hours passed quickly as they talked and walked and paused and moved again. Finally, they saw the bright orange sky filtering down through a jumbled mound of rocks.

"Wait," Sonia said. "We're at the surface." She sat down against a boulder. "Professor, how do you feeling? Are you up to moving quickly?"

Professor Chester was breathing hard. He wheezed, and then coughed. "I'm not certain I'm up to moving at all."

"That medication only goes so far," Sonia's voice was weak. "My muscles ache, and my stomach feels like it will throw out everything if I exert myself." She paused to catch her breath. "Let's wait awhile, take a nap."

"May I see your map again?" Exxis asked. He slid down beside Sonia. "How about I try to make it on my own? If I make it, I'll bring back help. If I get caught, and don't make it back, then you try later."

"We should stay together," Professor Chester pleaded. "We will need your help to get through the desert."

"Exxis is right," Sonia pulled the small computer from her belt, and opened it to clipboard size. "He can move quickly and evade capture better on his own. We will slow him down, get us all killed." She brought up the atlas, zooming to the map of the region.

"You're right," Professor Chester consented. "I just feel the odds are not good either way."

Exxis studied the map, locating Burroughs Valley, Princess Dejah Canyon, the El Dorado Badlands, the John Carter Trail, and the main highway M-24. He asked Sonia to pinpoint where they were.

With her finger, she pointed to unfamiliar areas of interest. "This jumbled rocky outcrop is over the top of the cave where Apollo and I waited for a few days. Inside is a screen that I had used to hide our location. We parked behind it, hidden from even surveillance drones." She moved her finger halfway to the canyon cliffs, pointing to an ancient, distorted, eroded impact crater. The map showed it with a flat, featureless bottom. The crater walls had been cut by dried gully channels from high elevations. "Apollo showed me this on the map, this is where we come out... at the crater rim nearest the canyon cliffs."

Sonia continued to elaborate, "I suspect the underground aquifer channels were cut a hundred million years ago from water flowing down from a lake in that crater. It looks like about a two-mile walk from here to the cave. If my feeling that we should try for the cave is a mistake, then head for the highway bridge." Her finger traced a dry gully from the nearby John Carter trail approximately five miles to the highway bridge over that prehistoric, dried streambed. "Flag down a passing truck, and pray that the truck is not from Redrock."

He carefully studied the map, and then passed it back. He leaned his head back while he sipped some water.

"You should take the map," Sonia offered it to him, "so that you don't get lost."

He waved it away. "I can remember it. If I don't make it back, you and the Professor will have to figure your own way out."

CHAPTER THIRTY-NINE

DESERT TREK

El Dorado Badlands, Mars

Earth Date	August 21, 2216
Mars Date	D-Mmon 14, 1174

Exxis picked his way up the jumble of rocks out of the tunnels and into the open sunlight. Facing east, away from the cave entrance, the mid-morning sun gave him a new sense of awe. He had not seen the sun since being drugged on the way home. He felt he had been granted a special gift to be alive to see the morning sun one more time. In front of him was the dusty floor of the eight-hundred foot wide crater Sonia had shown him on the map. Clumps of wild grasses and flowers were scattered about the crater floor, evidence of permafrost water below ground. The crater's far side looked like little more than a rough curved line of hills. Beyond that rim were the gray and rust colored jutting rock structures that gave the badlands its name.

He reached to his belt to switch on the radio comm unit he had rescued from robot Harris. It was a limited-power, local comm unit.

At first he tried to tune in commercial broadcasts from satellites. There was nothing but static. Exxis figured the receiver may have been damaged in the explosion. He set the receiver to scan local comm traffic, bypassing commercial broadcasts; anticipating limited range radio traffic from Redrock surveillance devices. He got similar static, but there were no signals at all. Although his pressure suit had mandatory comm units for local radio communications, he dared not transmit anything. Such a signal would automatically pinpoint his location for Crane.

He climbed the crater rim behind him, and then walked along it, staying as close as possible to chaotic rock outcrops and boulders. Although the surrounding terrain was only a few feet higher than the crater, there were no grasses or flowers outside the crater floor. That area was too far above the underground permafrost for wild plants to find moisture. In addition, most of the surface was jumbled, dark, hard, basaltic rocks.

Proceeding quickly, walking as close to boulders and jutting rocks as possible, he tried to be obscure. For the first time since they began this escape effort through the aquifer tunnels, Exxis felt dread and truly alone. Determined to escape and find rescue for the professor and Sonia, that sense of purpose checked his feeling of panic. Alone, he felt he was not up to a fight if one was forced on him.

As he moved he searched for the landmarks Sonia had indicated on the map, specific rock piles and distant hills. Two miles into his trek, the comm unit picked up a high-pitched electronic local radio signal. A minute later there was a separate, similar response. Had he been detected by robotic scans, or were these unrelated radio messages from the highway? Fearing the worst, he picked up his pace, dodging under overhangs for brief stops, and then darting across open stretches to another crevice in the rocks.

Exxis's fears that he was heading into a trap intensified, now that there was reason to believe hostile surveillance devices had spotted him. His pursuers would not send another security robot since they knew he had demonstrated the ability to override robot commands. Logic dictated they would follow him with drones, and then have human predators close in. In that event, the cave he was looking for would be a trap, not a hiding place.

It took an hour to follow the remainder of the jagged course he had memorized. Topping a bluff he first saw the graded-gravel John Carter Trail cutting north to south through the desert boulders then closer, almost directly under him, was the obscure cave entrance he was looking for. Listening to the comm unit, he was still picking up sporadic electronic chatter. Maybe it was not surveillance; maybe it was someone Uncle Brass sent to rescue him. Maybe it came from trucks on the main highway. Squatting under the shadow of a rock overhang, he studied the area. There were no vehicles, and no movement. In the distance was the dry, ancient stream bed that could lead him to the highway bridge. He considered taking that path, avoiding the cave. Heading for the highway would keep him out in the open longer, making it easy for drones to track him. However, escape from the cave would be impossible if he was already under surveillance. He had to act quickly.

He descended the hard bedrock basaltic hill to the cave entrance, and then slipped into the shadows along one edge. There were no vehicular tracks in the dust. Was this the right cave? He then remembered Sonia explaining she had used a blower at the back of the trailer when she was escaping with Apollo, just to obscure the vehicle tracks. He slowly stepped another thirty feet further into the cave, scanning for movement. Seeing none, he squatted. He listened to the comm unit. The electronic chatter seemed clearer. He had been spotted. At the mouth of the cave a tiny, dark object floated into view... a bumble bee drone.

Exxis edged deeper into the cave toward what appeared to be the back wall. Touching the surface with his gloved hand, it pushed in like a curtain. It was the mesh shielding screen Sonia had used, still in place, still coated with dust and pebbles. Exxis slipped around the edge next to the cave wall. He then squatted on the other side.

Looking back through the mesh towards the bright light beyond the mouth of the cave, an acidic feeling sank in his stomach. Two uniformed police officers in full pressure suits appeared at the cave. His laser comm unit picked up spoken English commands. "Exxis Potowski, we know you are in there. You are under arrest. Come out at once." He recognized the voice of the Lieutenant Lee from the roadblock. Turning to retreat further into the cave, he stopped abruptly. In front of him stood the silhouette of a government anti-grav spacecraft. He could not see the insignia, but four military pressure-suited figures walked his way.

"Oh, my god." He turned, went back to the other side of the screen. A bright pencil-thin laser beam, from the mouth of the cave, cut a swath toward him. Leaning back to the protection of the jagged rock wall, the laser missed him. It burned a line through the mesh screen.

On the laser comm unit, he heard an unfamiliar male voice yell. "Exxis, get down. We're with the Militia to rescue you."

Before he could react further, he felt a sharp pain in his arm. He looked down. A dart was stuck in his left sleeve. Reaching with his right hand, he pulled it from his arm, and studied it. Then the dart's paralyzer drug took affect. His arm fell limp, and then his entire body. Losing his balance, he fell sideways to the cave floor. Exxis could not move his muscles, could not stop the fall, and could not even wink his eyelids. Landing on his side, he came to rest facing the light at the mouth of the cave. He watched the two police officers cautiously stepping toward him. They stopped abruptly.

"Halt, now!" Through his laser comm Exxis heard the unfamiliar voice of the Militia soldier. He could not see them. "This is Militia Security. You will halt."

One of the police officers coming from the front of the cave raised his laser weapon. He fired another bright, thin beam at whatever was behind Exxis. Before that laser weapon was turned off, a bright flash ignited the police officer's chest, exploding him into multiple pieces. The second officer was knocked sideways by that explosion. Two military outfitted men rushed past Exxis toward the officers, weapons aimed at the survivor as he struggled back to his feet. A new voice yelled, "Stay down! Spread your arms on the ground."

A hand took hold of Exxis's paralyzed arm, and rolled him over on his back. Now looking up, all he could see was a dark, military uniform. Nothing was visible within the darkened faceplate.

"Exxis Potowski, we are Militia. Your Uncle Brass Newton is with us."

A wave of relief went through his mind. He could not speak or move.

"Can you speak? Where are the other two?"

Exxis' mouth would not open.

After a moment, a Militia Sergeant spoke, "This is Callahan. We have Exxis. He was hit with a paralysis dart. He can't react. I'm bringing him in." The soldier reached under Exxis' back and legs, and lifted him. He carried him back to the other side of the screen, and into the open cargo bay door of the waiting anti-grav shuttle craft. Within the cargo hold, he stepped through the airlock of a waiting isolation trailer. Militia Sergeant Callahan placed Exxis on a bunk. He then reached to open his face mask.

Exxis watched the hand of a doctor in a Militia pressure suit stop Callahan.

"He's in an isolation pressure suit." The doctor pushed Callahan back from the bunk. "He may be carrying the Panahon virus. Decontaminate your gear going back through the airlock."

Exxis could not shift his view. He listened as Callahan stepped into the airlock and activated the caustic decontamination spray.

"Exxis, I know you can hear me." The doctor pulled a syringe from a bag. The nametag on his suit read "McDermott". Dr. McDermott said, "This is the antidote for the paralysis dart." He inserted the needle into a sleeve insertion disk designed for giving patient injections. "We can't expose you until you've been tested."

Exxis felt the sharp pain of the needle. He could not move or speak. The only muscles still working were his heart and lungs, and those were slowed.

"Well, I'll be damned." Exxis recognized his uncle's voice. "Terra was right about where to wait. Will he be all right?" Brass moved into Exxis's peripheral field of vision, then directly over him.

"It takes the antidote five to ten minutes." McDermott said. "If he doesn't black out." McDermott inserted a second needle into the sleeve injection disk. "I need to test him for the virus before we do anything else."

With the sharp pain of the second needle, Exxis felt dizzy. He struggled to speak. His mouth would not move. His arms, hands, fingers could not move, either.

Brass said. "Exxis, I'm sorry I got you into this. I hope you aren't hurt badly."

McDermott's voice caught his ear, "No virus. The air in his pressure suit is clean. You can take off the helmet."

Brass opened the faceplate. Exxis smelled the air. After two days enclosed in a pressure suit, normal air smelled so much sweeter. His eyes blinked, and blinked again. He tried to speak. His lips moved slightly, but there was no sound.

"Take your time," Brass said. "It'll be a few minutes." Moisture appeared in his eyes. "I was worried. Are the other two safe?"

Exxis tried to speak. He could manage barely audible unintelligible mutter.

Brass lifted him enough to remove the helmet. He placed a pillow under the head. Brass asked, "If they are safe, blink once. If they are hurt, blink twice."

Exxis moaned, and then blinked once. He tried moving his fingers. They moved a little.

"Your Aunt Terra said you would come to this cave. We've been waiting here since last night."

Exxis raised an arm. It dropped back to his side. He twisted his jaw. "Uncle, is Aunt Terra all right? I thought her spacecraft was destroyed!"

Brass and McDermott slowly opened his pressure suit. "You knew about that? A robot pilot was on the freighter that was blown up. General Burch is working with your aunt; he sent a Militia cargo hauler to rendezvous with the spacecraft in high orbit. Everyone was transferred secretly. Your Aunt Terra and her guests were flown directly to the Baxter Annex. The empty cargo spacecraft was docked at Phobos, and then flown down towards Crater City. The sabotage was recorded."

Exxis tried to sit up. Brass and the Sergeant helped him up. McDermott asked, "Can you move your arms and legs?"

Exxis slowly raised one arm, maneuvering the hand, then the other. He kicked his legs. He had regained muscle control. He had a splitting headache.

"We'll get you home soon," Brass said. "Where are the other two?"

"Water, please," Exxis asked. Brass got him a large tumbler of water, which he chugged.

"During the roadblock," Brass explained, "security cameras on the rover showed you and the Professor being subdued by the police. What happened? Is Sonia still in a coma?"

"When the professor and I woke three days ago, we were still in the rover, but sealed in a cave, down at the bottom of Princess Dejah Canyon. When I was knocked out, somehow I had these thoughts in my head that the antidote was a mixture of Mexerlack and Tanchion Selzak. We gave it to Sonia, and it worked."

"Three days ago?" Brass questioned, "That doesn't make any sense. I'm unaware of any cure for this virus. Where did you say you got it?"

"When I was drugged… I had some vivid dreams… I think I was seeing what this Apollo Panahon was seeing. The antidote came from him. The serum ingredients came from a Rochelle Bond on Earth's Moon."

"Yesterday I was with Apollo at the Baxter Annex. He did not mention anything about this serum then. I was communicating with Director Bond. She made no mention of a cure." Brass stared at Exxis. "This has to be from the future."

"The Professor and Miss Androff," McDermott asked, "Where are they now?"

Exxis turned to the console station, asked for a local map. "They are about two miles from here, at a cave entrance. Both of them are exhausted. We crawled through eleven miles of tunnels from the base of the cliff."

"Eleven miles?" Brass questioned. "The professor was up to it?"

"We had no choice. They were trying to kill us."

All heads turned to the trailer airlock. Two pressure-suited soldiers were escorting a police lieutenant into the trailer. Militia Major Pernell, who had been quietly observing the recovery of Exxis, pointed a laser rifle at the police officer. He signaled the escorts to open his faceplate. It was the Lieutenant from the roadblock.

One of the corporals escorting the policeman said, "Police Sergeant Mack Brian is dead. This is Lieutenant Jon Lee, with the global police. There are no others at the entrance."

The oriental police lieutenant shook himself loose from the grip of his escorts. "What is the meaning of this? You are interfering with an official police pursuit."

"Lieutenant Lee," Major Pernell said, "You are under arrest, charged with kidnapping, murder, and conspiracy to commit fraud."

Lee removed his helmet. "What are you talking about?"

Brass stepped beside Pernell. "Lieutenant, when you boarded my rover and drugged Exxis, he was communicating with me at the time. Two hours earlier, when you stopped Flex Epsen's rover at the Crater City Spaceport, he was also communicating with me at the time."

Lee silently glared at them.

"I gave General Burch evidence of police criminal activities coupled with details of an epidemic originating here. The General ordered a military investigation."

Pernell said, "Chief Ken Sylvester was arrested yesterday in Crater City. Your chain of command is no more. Tell me, what threat do we face on the canyon floor?"

"This situation exceeds military authority. Your actions against me here are illegal."

"Don't bet on it. Do you want to cooperate? Do you have anyone else up here in the badlands?"

Lee signaled with a finger across his lips that he would talk no more. Pernell motioned for the two corporals to escort Lee to a holding cell beyond outside of the trailer. Once they were gone, Pernell pivoted to talk to Exxis. "You said your companions are waiting at a cave entrance. Is there indication that you were being tracked through the tunnels?"

Exxis replied. "Miss Sonia feels that Dave Crane and several others are following. We haven't seen anyone, but she is convinced they are there."

"From what I've seen of those dreamscape replays from her and Apollo Panahon," Pernell responded, "I would not doubt her feelings. Are you strong enough to guide us to the cave?"

Exxis asked, "Uncle Brass, where is Aunt Terra?"

The doctor poured more water into Exxis' glass.

CHAPTER FORTY

STRIKE FORCE

Sagan City, Mars

Earth Date	August 21, 2216
Mars Date	D-Mmon 14, 1174

Sonia quietly listened to Professor Chester narrate how he worked on paranormal stories long ago. She was too tired to think of small talk. She knew she should be in a hospital bed. Her stomach continued to churn. Consequently, she feared she may vomit inside her sealed helmet. She was hungry for better food than the rations they brought from the rover. Her muscles ached with pain that she could not remedy. She needed sleep, but was afraid to close her eyes, thinking she may go back into coma. Leaning against the cave entrance walls, she knew she was vulnerable. Falling asleep would leave her and the professor in mortal danger if Dave Crane caught up through the tunnels, or if Redrock teams on the surface found the cave entrance. Professor Chester liked to talk, and it seemed to relax him.

Sonia saw the sky through the cave entrance if she turned her head to the right. Looking to the left offered a view of the tunnel they had crawled though. She tried to imagine how they would defend themselves if a threat appeared. They had no weapons other than rocks. Those were useless against lasers, unless used by complete surprise. The only choice was to run, either out into the open, or back down through the network of ancient underground aquifer tunnels. She looked at the opposite side of the cave. Her geologist eyes studied the evidence that water had once flowed down through the tunnel systems.

Her attention returned to Professor Chester. He was saying. "… I think that was the first time the C.N.A. units were used to confirm paranormal visions, when the patient had visions from a sister who died in the war…"

"Wait, Professor," Sonia raised her hand. "I saw something."

He noticed her staring at the sky beyond the cave entrance. He looked in the same direction. "I don't see anything."

"I saw movement… like something passing over the cave."

"Do you think it's Exxis?" He whispered through the steth-o-line.

"I don't know. It could be Redrock." Sonia checked her sleeve. The communicator laser link was set for the channel they had agreed to. No signal. Looking again, she saw a shadow cross the sunlit exposed cave entrance. She rose to her feet. "We have to get farther down the tunnel."

Professor Chester rose to join her. They began edging around a rock wall.

Two backlit silhouetted figures appeared at the cave entrance. Abruptly, there was a voice. "Sonia. Professor Chester."

It wasn't Exxis, but the voice was familiar. Sonia thought it might be a friend of Dave Crane.

"Exxis is with us. I am Brass Newton, here to bring you in. Major Pernell with the Militia is with me." The figures stepped cautiously through the jumbled rocks at the entrance.

"Good afternoon," Sonia mustered the strength for a response. "We need help." She walked towards the opening. Professor Chester followed.

Just as she reached to take Brass's hand, Major Pernell raised his laser weapon. Ready to panic, Sonia watched a pencil-thin laser beam illuminate the air in a line past her. She turned. Thirty feet behind was a brilliant flash of light. A robotic ferret exploded.

"Sorry to scare you," the Major said, "It looks like your pursuers aren't far behind. Let's get out of here."

Sonia exhaled. "Yes."

The anti-grav shuttle was waiting short distance past the entrance to the cave. Sonia and Chester were rushed through the airlocks into the isolation trailer where they joined Exxis. Major Pernell sent a platoon into the cave to prepare for threats. The transport then lifted off and head for Sagan City.

At a secluded underground warehouse at the Bradbury Militia Base, Sonia, Professor Chester, and Exxis were transferred to a separate quarantine trailer onboard another anti-grav shuttle. Ready for a trip to join Apollo on the other side of the globe, they delayed to participate via a closed-circuit debriefing with Brass, Terra, Sonny, Jeck Ekakaidis, Major Pernell and his operations staff.

"I thought your spacecraft was destroyed," Sonia said. "That's what I saw through Dave Crane's mind. What happened?"

Terra responded, "Sonny talked General Burch into having the Militia lease the transport. Another Militia ship was sent for high orbit rendezvous to transfer cargo from Octan's transport. What Dave Crane saw was a remotely piloted spacecraft brought to the low orbit Space Base. It then descended for landing. They blew up an empty ship. Apollo and the other passengers are in isolation at an annex to my father's farm. Military quarantine security is guarding the place."

"Sonia," Sonny spoke, "Apollo told me much about you. The message you sent me offered a great deal of detail. Your private and business records don't match what you sent me. However, everything was updated eight weeks ago, just before the murders. Do you have secured copies of you files?"

"Have you checked with Fisk's family, or my sister?"

"Those were updated at the same time."

"Fisk kept a back-up file of everything in his Uncle Bryan's account."

"Uncle Bryan?" Sonny asked.

"Fisk doesn't have an Uncle Bryan. After what happened to Jim Everly, he was afraid something like this might happen. He used a special code to route copies there. He may have copies of my records, too."

"How do I access the file?"

After Sonia explained, Sonny opened the Uncle Bryan files.

"If you are able to get inside Dave Crane's thoughts," Jeck Ekakaidis asked, "Do you know about what's on the ground in the Canyon?"

"I had sporadic images from Dave." Sonia said. "I know the Canyon layout. What do you need to know?"

"How many people are there?" Ekakaidis asked. "What are their security arrangements?"

Sonia stared at him. "With these visions I had momentary glimpses of his thoughts, his conversations. I don't have answers for what you are asking."

"Apollo said the same," Sonny said. "His dreams contained fragments of what others were seeing … usually a few minutes each. Luckily, we have Ken Sylvester's SWK testimony."

Professor Chester questioned that. Sonny responded, "Militia intelligence arrested Sylvester, gave him truth serum, and questioned him. In addition to the mine and smelter crews, Sylvester admitted to a special police contingent of twenty. We are going to question Lieutenant Lee the same way."

"Will these truth serum admissions be useable in court?" Sonia asked.

Jeck Ekakaidis responded, "Normally, this would be a problem. However, the President declared this virus a security threat. General Burch has greater investigation latitude with security threats."

Professor Chester questioned, "The C.E.O. of Redrock is a personal friend and major contributor to President Knotts. Are they suspects in this case?"

"I don't know," Ekakaidis said. "First, we have to secure the canyon to isolate the source of the virus. We are about to do just that. I wish we knew what threats we are facing."

"In the tunnels," Sonia remarked, "I had a sense of Dave Crane's discussions with Ghant Travis. They are searching for me in the tunnels, but otherwise they are closing up in the canyon until things calm down. There is a frustration because the communications satellites are malfunctioning. They can't call anyone outside the canyon."

Major Pernell said, "The Martian communications network has been temporarily programmed to block any signals to or from the canyon. It was made to look like the satellites were knocked off line by solar storms."

Sonia said, "When do you go after Travis and Crane?"

"Tomorrow morning."

CHAPTER FORTY-ONE

CAPTURE

Princess Dejah Canyon
Syrtis Major Region, Mars

Earth Date   August 22, 2216
Mars Date   D-Mmon 15, 1174

"Everything is shut down, Ghant," Mine Supervisor Oliver Chandler's baritone voice was clear on the comm console. It was about the only clear voice Travis was hearing. "We're on our way down."

Travis watched through the window as the elevator descended the steel cables from the mine entrance five-hundred feet above the canyon floor. "Good," Travis answered, "the shuttle. Grab your bags, and go."

"I wish I knew what's going on." Chandler said. "There's a lot of gold in that cave."

Monitor screens showed surveillance views in the mine, including the thin seam of gold that glittered under the floodlights. Travis began pushing buttons. The cave went dark. The screen images went blank.

"A paperwork glitch," Travis replied. "You'll be back soon enough. Enjoy your break."

Travis changed channels again. "Lieutenant Lee, are you reading me?" He got only static. Travis banged his communications desktop with both fists when his attempt to use the Redrock laser-lock satellite system once again gave him the prerecorded message that it was experiencing technical difficulties. He changed channels to systems connecting into the ice cave. Crane and his search team were somewhere in the labyrinth of tunnels following Sonia.

"We're about five hours behind Sonia," Crane responded. "I take it you still can't get through to the outside?"

"Must be a systems failure... possibly a solar storm ionized the satellite. This has happened before." Travis responded. "I can't get Sylvester... or anyone through the satellite. I can't even get Lieutenant Lee, and he's up in the badlands."

"I hope you're right," Crane said. "No radio communication, no laser connection, no commercial leads, nothing. If the satellites are off line, we won't get anyone beyond the canyon. Where in the hell is Sylvester?"

"He should have been back three days ago," Travis responded, "Anything from the tunnel chase?"

"Just footprints," Crane paused on the monitor. "We're eight miles into the passageways. Sonia and the two men aren't far ahead. Lee will get them if they show at the surface."

"Maybe Sonia rigged a cave-in," Travis said, "Let's shut it down and get back to civilization."

Crane said, "Go on, and get out of here. I'll follow the trail for a few more hours. Just leave us an anti-grav. Out for now."

Travis switched to the laser comm to the main office trailer, "Gina, you ready?"

"I've been ready since last night, boss." Receptionist Gina Lomar's image showed on one screen. The rest of the images were blank. "Channel sixty-four is back on?"

"Sixty-four?" Travis reached to his console, "That's Sylvester's police line. It's about time he checked in."

"It's not Chief Sylvester," Gina responded.

Travis switched on channel sixty-four. On screen was a gray-haired, gaunt-built man dressed in a police detective pressure suit. Travis read the name tag on his chest, then said, "May I help you, Captain Ekakaidis?"

"Mr. Travis!" Chief Detective Jeck Ekakaidis looked emotionless, his voice was soft. "Ken Sylvester was unable to leave Crater City. He sent me with a security force. We need to talk… privately."

"Privately?" Travis was suspicious, "Why didn't he contact us?"

"Solar flares disrupted the satellite. He sent me with news about the Filipino boy. Is Dave Crane with you?"

"Wait a minute; I'll be back to you." Travis muted the audio. Switching Crane back on, he then said, "You know Ken's team. Do you know this detective?"

"I've seen him before. He was a chief detective in Crater City. I thought he retired," Crane paused. "I don't know. Sylvester doesn't tell me any more than you do."

"I don't like it," Travis mumbled. He returned to the police channel. "Chief Ekakaidis, where are you calling from?"

"I'm landing at this moment. That's why I can make this direct laser link. Are your officers available?"

"You looking for anyone in particular?"

"Lieutenant Lee and his unit… Captain Steiner and his team. We need to talk to them."

"Lieutenant Lee is out of the canyon. With the satellites down, we can't reach him. Captain Steiner is in the security trailer." One screen image followed the descent of two police anti-grav transport spacecraft. "You want me to send him to you?"

"We'll meet him in security. I'll meet with you in your control trailer." The call ended.

"Hopefully, this is good news," Travis changed channels to talk to Crane. "And Ollie can resume work."

The elevator with Chandler was nearly to the ground. At the main office Gina was packing up. Travis pushed a button. "Gina, did you monitor that?"

"Check. I'm at my desk."

The two police transports quietly settled to the surface. Slowly, access ramps telescoped from their cargo airlocks, whose doors opened. Twenty police officers rushed from each transport. The two teams spread out with multiple groupings heading for various trailers.

"Looks like Sylvester finally has a security team ready for us," Travis said. "Wonder why he didn't come himself."

The police squads entered various trailers. Two military pressure suited men entering through the airlock of the control trailer, then stepped to one side to allow for the next two. Ekakaidis and his aids opened their faceplates.

"Chief Ekakaidis," Travis stepped forward to greet him. "We're a bit anxious. What happened to Ken?"

"Is it just you in this trailer?" Ekakaidis asked.

Travis said, "We can talk privately." He smiled, "What was it Ken wanted to…" He stopped talking mid sentence.

The other three in police pressure suits opened their faceplates. Brass' face froze Travis in his tracks. So did the Filipino face of Sonny.

"Ghant Travis," Officer Ran Fletcher said, "you are under arrest. This compound is being seized by order of General Joseph Burch, Militia special forces commander."

"Militia?" Travis spouted. "What is the military doing here? This is outrageous!"

The three aides to Chief Ekakaidis drew weapons and aimed at Travis. Ekakaidis said, "This compound is a severe health threat. As of this moment this Canyon is closed for quarantine by order of the Disease Control Administration. "

"Health threat?" Travis questioned. "What are you talking about?"

"In addition, you, along with Ken Sylvester and Dave Crane, are charged with grand theft, fraud, corruption of public officials, and seven counts of murder. You have the right to remain silent and to consult with console. Do you understand?"

"This is crazy," Travis yelled. "I'll have your ass for this intrusion. Do you know who I am?" He glanced at the monitors images of the two police transports. Six more transports were descending to the surface.

"Where is Dave Crane?" Sonny asked, "The two of you killed six of my closest friends. You tried to kill me. We have video records of all that. Ken Sylvester and his police conspirators are under arrest."

Travis stared at Sonny.

"Mr. Travis," Brass said, "This evening my wife will broadcast a report detailing the crimes you committed in the name of the Redrock Corporation. We have copies of Redrock manipulations of the Bureau of Mines records. Auditors are at this moment serving warrants to corporate headquarters for Redrock books. Is there anything you would like to say in your own defense?"

Travis said nothing.

Sonny stared back. "Where are the bodies of the seven men you killed? Where is Dave Crane?"

Chapter Forty-Two

Antidote

Corrigedor, Philippines

Earth Date	August 22, 2216
Mars Date	D-Mmon 15, 1174

The cloud cover in the Benget Mountains obscured the view from the Health Service executive aerial limousine. There was nothing for Rochelle to see until the limo dropped down through the clouds, just over the former barrio of Maliit na Ulap. The shadowless illumination and misty rain below the clouds created a depressing eeriness to the desolate image of the hillside village. To the limit of visibility the effects of decontamination spraying were clear. The rice in the terraces, the flowering bushes, the green palms of the trees, and the lawns were all brown, shriveled and dead. The homes of the barrio had all been burned to piles of charcoal. The only remaining structures that could be recognized were charred portions of the cement block walls of the general store and the stone walls of what once had been a church. The limo landed on the gravel surface of a parking lot beside the general store.

Rochelle stepped from the vehicle and slowly surveyed the entire area. Her eye caught the movement of a single vehicle on the winding mountain road below the barrio, moving on a course toward her. She walked the short distance through the barrio, depressed at the sight of the many charred piles that once were bamboo nipa homes. In the side yard of one home there remained an intact picnic table with benches. Nearby, under a denuded palm tree, she found a child's doll. Picking up the doll, she then seated herself at one of the benches. Using a handkerchief, she wiped the moisture of the misty rain from the doll. She sighed sorrowfully.

The United Nations Health Service had vacated the barrio on her orders. They sprayed a defoliant for a half mile in every direction. However, once the epidemic progressed beyond the village, frightened neighbors came through and torched the buildings. The local government expanded the sterilization spraying to an additional mile around the barrio, giving the mountainside the look of a battlefield void of life.

The approaching van pulled in beside the park bench. Carlos Catabunan, the owner of the mine where the men of the barrio had jobs, got out to approach Rochelle. "Director Bond, thank you for coming all this way. This is unexpected."

She stood, glanced back at the rest of the barrio, and then said, "I'm pleased to meet you. I want to discuss the jobs of the men in the barrio, talk about what happens when they are finally out of quarantine."

"I thought I made it clear when you called. The other miners are afraid of this sickness. I will offer some help, but I can't bring the men back. The rest of the miners will refuse to work with them."

"Most of the patients are getting better. They need help to rebuild their barrio," Rochelle said.

Carlos surveyed the damage as he spoke. "Don't bring them back here. There is great fear of this Martian virus." He paused, took a package from his assistant, and handed it to her, "Here is severance payment for all those who were there. I've included bonus checks for each family. That is all I can do."

"What will they do?" Rochelle asked. "It will take at least a year for the vegetation to return here."

"I advise you to relocate them elsewhere. It is sad that their homes were destroyed, but their neighbors are scared."

Rochelle continued to plead on the barrio's behalf, but she realized there would be no compassion as long as the epidemic threat remained.

An hour later Rochelle stepped out from her anti-grav limo on to the helipad tarmac on Corrigedor Island. She wrinkled her nose at the strong odor of disinfectant mixed with insecticide. The warm, humid, hazy air obscured the distant view of Manila across the bay. The island had changed since she was at "The Rock" years ago in her youth. It had been a tourist attraction, not a medical quarantine center. The tourist shops were closed and covered with airtight inflatable domes to protect them from contamination. The tunnel entrances were covered with disinfection airlocks. Illuminated variable message signs at the landing docks read, "Tourist facility closed," "Quarantine Isolation Facility," and "Restricted Access, Medical Emergency." Robotic soldiers, armed with an array of weapons, were positioned every ten feet.

Rochelle was greeted by Aurora Mabini, executive secretary for Health Service Chief Charles Belisario. Dressed in a medical isolation suit, Mabini had Rochelle seal her own isolation suit on their way into the tunnel airlocks. They walked past a series of inflated clear polymer tents over hundreds of individual med chambers. Many of those coma patients were fitted with C.N.A. helmets. Every ten feet were small air purification units using ionization grids to destroy microscopic organics in the air.

At the administration section they stepped into the office lobby for Belisario, who was with his receptionist in the outer lobby, waiting for Rochelle.

"Welcome to the Rock," he reached to shake hands. "Please, step in my office."

Mabini closed the office door behind them. On the walls were multiple large monitor charts showing the status of everyone isolated in the Malinta Tunnels.

"Rochelle, you didn't have to come to Earth. We have secure lines to talk." As he dropped back into his own chair, Belisario motioned for her to be seated. "I'm glad you came."

"Two days ago Maliit na Ulap was burned. My patients are very upset. I needed to see for myself." She settled into the chair. "It doesn't look like my patients can return."

"I have the same problem. Many patients here have improved… even virus free, but the local government wants to keep them in quarantine. They're preparing an island site… it used to be a leper colony."

"Leper?" Rochelle accepted a glass of juice from Mabini. "I guess it's to be expected. However, that's not the reason I came. There is news from Mars… from Brass Newton… the spacecraft his wife was on may have blown up when it got to Mars."

"That wasn't on the news. Are you positive?"

"Apollo Panahon was with her."

"With her? He's supposed to be in China." He paused to stare for a minute. "He was supposed to be in China? Was that a ruse?"

"Yes. Someone is stalking him. The disappearance of that spacecraft may not be an accident."

Belisario stared at his visitor, and then briefly closed his eyes. Opening them again, he said, "If Terra Newton is dead, her fans will be very angry. If Apollo is dead, then we lost our lead to the source of the virus. What can you tell me?"

"Not much at the moment, and there is not much we can do but wait. The other thing I wanted to ask about the Nostradamus syndrome. How much are you getting from here?"

He exhaled audibly. "There are a wide range of dreamscapes. Some historical, some predictions… almost all are short fragments. Many are very personal issues for the patients. It will take time to sort them out."

"On the Moon old people died within a few days. Preteen children overcome the virus within a few days. When they recover they lose the visions. Half of my patients show no symptoms, but the rest are still sick. Some have the dreams. Most do not."

"That's pretty much what we've encountered." He leaned back in his chair, smiled lightly, then said, "However, I may have good news."

"We could use some."

"Two days ago we got positive results with a serum mixture of Mexerlack VY-6 with Tanchion Selzak."

"Mexerlack and Tanchion Selzak?" Rochelle did not change her expression. "We tried those. Both helped with some of the symptoms, but no positive results."

"I know. Mixed in equal portions, we got results."

"Care to elaborate?"

He pointed to one of the data screens on the wall. "That list with twenty green lights next to the names… all twenty were in coma two days ago. All woke after an injection of the serum, and have been improving since. It seems the virus has disappeared from their blood stream rapidly."

Rochelle smiled. "You found a cure?" She stood to look more closely at the chart.

"I wouldn't make that conclusion at this point. It's too early in the game. But, the results so far are promising."

"How many patients do you have here at the Rock?"

"Roughly, three thousand. New cases are coming at about two hundred a day."

"Baguio's John Hay Park is about the same. Have you advised them?"

"I didn't want to advertise it before I was certain," he said.

"Have you had any side affects?"

"Two coma patients were allergic. Both died."

"Can you test for allergies?" Rochelle asked. There was a signal on her comm unit that she was receiving an incoming message. "Excuse me a moment, Chief Belisario." She quietly took her message. She returned her attention to Belisario. "This is a message from Brass Newton, of the Life Sciences Institute on Mars."

"I know him," Belisario said. "I understand his connection to Terra Newton and the Panahon boy. What does he have to contribute?"

"He says he has reason to believe from the dreamscape reports that you may be giving me a serum formula to deal with the virus."

Part F

Panahon Wave

CHAPTER FORTY-THREE

BAXTER ANNEX

East of Mount Olympus
Tharsis Region, Mars

Earth Date	August 23, 2216
Mars Date	D-Mmon 16, 1174

MARTIAN VIRUS, DAY 54

From the air the Antoni Farm Complex was impressive. It was much larger than Sonia had expected, based on books published about Terra after the war. During the war the Militia made her a media star, including pictures of the family farm she grew up on. In those images the farm had three inflated agricultural domes, plus a barnyard dome. North of the domes were five hundred acres of open Martian wheat fields up to the banks of a dried ancient stream bed. In the thirteen years (twenty-three Earth years) since the war, the wheat fields had expanded to thirty-five hundred acres, plus ten potato fields. South of the main road, three pressurized domes covering fields had been added.

Exxis pointed out the window, for the benefit of Sonia and Professor Chester, explaining the crops in each field. Their anti-grav transport glided gently downward toward the isolated farm complex two miles north of the dried gulch. Forty miles to the west of the farm were the cliffs at the base of the huge Mount Olympus, a shield volcano three hundred miles across and eight miles high. The dark basalt of the mound dominated the entire horizon.

"That is the Baxter Annex," Exxis pointed to the unusual array of domes and buildings below, two miles east of the Antoni farm. "Grandpa bought it when the original family decided to give up farming. Uncle Brass uses the Annex to test experimental crops he develops through the Life Sciences Institute … That is unexpected."

"What is unexpected?" Professor Chester asked, and then coughed.

"The annex is surrounded by military trailers," Exxis pointed to the screen. "I guess they need increased security."

Sonia and Haff quietly watched through a window. Their Militia transport settled to a gravel parking area adjacent to a truck entrance airlock. Moments after engine shutdown the cargo doors opened. An automated robotic tug entered the cargo bay, coupled to the isolation trailer, then towed it down the ramp, past four armed robot Militia guards, and into the airlock. Inside the pressurized dome the tug stopped at the side of the barn.

Apollo, standing on the tiled patio leading from a beige colored house, was dressed in shorts and a shirt. He held a small guitar in one hand. Right next to him, Nina held his arm. With her free hand Nina held her artist's electronic comp-pad. Jenny stood beside them with Teddy and Kia. All five looked healthy and normal. Like Apollo, all were dressed casually with loose-fitting short sleeve shirts and slacks.

Sonia looked forward to getting out of the pressure suit. The military doctor back at the El Dorado caves allowed her to change and clean up in the trailer. The three of them had then been directed to stay with the pressure suits until they arrived for quarantine at the "Baxter Annex". Sonia stepped out of her pressure suit. Underneath she was wearing a smug, colorful environ outfit her rescuers had brought her. Exxis also removed his pressure suit, whereas Professor Chester chose to wait until he got to his quarters.

Once on the ground, the three of them surveyed the inside of the pressure dome. Around the perimeter were two-foot-high planters thick with flowering bushes, contrasting the rust colored landscape and the sunset-colored skies.

"Welcome to the Baxter Annex, Professor Chester," Kai reached to shake hands with Professor Chester, "I am Doctor Kai Patterson, with the Tycho Medical Center. Jenny Ortigas is my sister." He motioned toward Jenny. "Terra told me much about you."

"I'm flattered," Professor Chester responded, motioning toward his companions, "This is Exxis Potowski, Terra Newton's nephew, and Sonia Androff."

Jenny and Teddy stepped forward to greet the newcomers. Apollo and Nina followed. Sonia was not certain how to greet him. She read Apollo's thoughts that he was uncertain himself.

After a brief pause, he threw his arms around her. "Sonia, we were worried that something bad might happen. I'm glad you made it."

She hugged him in return, and then stood back. "Your rash is gone." She glanced again at Nina, who looked uncomfortable. She tried to think of what to say to the girl. Sonia had much to talk to Apollo about. She understood he wanted to talk to her. Nina's silent anger made any words seem inappropriate.

"Nina Perez," Exxis reached to take her hand in greeting. "You are as lovely as I imagined."

Nina's expression quietly changed from anger to perplexed softness. She turned to the tall, blond young man she had never seen. "As you imagined?"

Exxis still had his hand extended. "When we were sealed in the cave... drugged unconscious... I had dreams. In those dreams I saw you. I'm glad that you are more than a fantasy vision."

She smiled, looking at him. "Thank you." She reached to shake his hand. "I've been talking to your parents. Your mom is very nice. Your grandpa is funny."

"Talking to them?" He glanced toward the house. "Are they inside?"

"In a visitor's lobby," Kai said. "We're in quarantine for awhile."

Exxis released her hand, looking at the entrance to the house. He turned to Nina. "Could you come with me to see them? I think Apollo and Sonia have a lot they have to talk about."

Nina's eyes flashed, searching everyone. She said, "Miss Sonia, I'm happy you are all right." She followed Exxis into the house.

Kai, standing with his sister, ignored Exxis and Nina. "Professor Chester, I've been reading your papers. You have some interesting perspectives," he glanced at Sonia and Apollo, "on the paranormal. You don't say much about the situation we have here."

"Actually," Professor Chester coughed before continuing. He looked somewhat ghastly. "I say a lot... about prophecies and telepathy. This situation, though, is unique. This is the first time we had a measurable cause and effect, with a means to record the telepathic awareness directly."

"Are you feeling all right?" Jenny asked. "Would you like to sit down?"

Kai suddenly noticed Professor Chester's appearance. "Do you have a condition we should be aware of?"

"Condition?" Professor Chester snickered, "I'm an old man with a bit of a heart condition. Kidnapped, drugged, and forced to flee uphill through twelve miles of tunnels sealed in a pressure suit. That's a good combination."

Sonia took the Professor by the arm to escort him toward the house. "Don't be so melodramatic, Professor. It was only eleven miles."

He stopped to look at Apollo. "Sonia said you went through those tunnels and back in an afternoon. It took us two days one way, and we were following the green buttons you left."

Apollo displayed a quizzical expression and shrugged his shoulders. "I didn't think about it at the time. I was just curious about how far those tunnels would go."

"Amazing." Kai said. "What would you have done if it had gone on underground forever?"

"The same thing I do back in the Benget Mountains. When I get hungry, I give up and go back."

"Oh, to be young again," Haff Chester smiled. "Doctor Patterson, I understand you have C.N.A. recordings for both of them. After I clean up, could we review them?"

Sonia released his arm. Suddenly, she was a little embarrassed. She remembered most of the dreams as if they were real memories. "If those recording have what I think they have," her eyes pleaded to both Professor Chester and Kai, "I hope you can be discreet."

Professor Chester nodded agreement.

Kai said, "I've been reviewing both sets. The two of you need to talk. We'll discuss the recordings later." With that, he directed Jenny and Professor Chester toward the house. "We'll send out beverages."

Once they were alone on the patio deck, Sonia and Apollo turned to face each other. Neither spoke for a few moments. Finally, Sonia motioned toward a patio table surrounded by chairs. There, they sat themselves.

"Brass Newton showed me the broadcasts Terra aired about your predictions of the Venus crash, the dreamscape recordings of Percival Lowell, and of Tau Ceti," She said. "It seems my El Dorado vision of you in a coma on the Moon was accurate. How do you feel now? I mean, with your barrio all but destroyed?"

Apollo, still a little shy, wasn't certain what to say. "Remember my dream about you as a little girl getting a broken leg?" he glanced toward Mount Olympus. "I've been thinking about that these past few days when I look at the mountain. I'd like to go up to the top when I'm better."

"I'd like to take you," Sonia smiled, reaching to hold his hands, "There are some caves up there… actually receded magma vents… with wisps of steam still wafting out. Some of those caverns are lined with asteric crystals." She paused, withdrew her hand. She felt this had to be a mistake.

"Sonia," Apollo said, "When I was in a coma I had dreams about a lot of things…" he paused, then looked down at his hands. "I had dreams about you. It was like I got to know you better than I know my own family." He looked up again. "This is silly, I know."

"I understand," Sonia responded. "We had a little fun… for your birthday… that was all. You are young enough to be my son."

She noticed an automated galley cart coming from the house. "But likewise, the visions... the images of you and your passion for geology. I've never met anyone who loved climbing around the rocks as much I did... not until these dreams showed me you." She chuckled, turned a little red in the face. "Too bad we aren't a little closer in age than we are."

"I'd still like to go up there with you," He took two juice glasses from the galley cart, handed one to Sonia. "Before I go home to Maliit na Ulap... with Nina."

Sipping from her drink, she said, "Tell me about Nina."

"She's been my closest friend since I was small," Apollo admitted, "I care for her very much... but ... She is convinced we should get married and have a family."

"How do you feel about it?" Sonia used a serious tone. "Do you picture her as your wife?"

"I used to," he said, "but, she doesn't care for the rocks. She hates it when I come back from the mine all dirty. She wants to study nursing, wants us to move to Baguio or Manila. I'd rather be where there are no people except for other miners."

Sonia laughed. "Sounds like me." She glanced at the entrance to the house. Kai and Jenny were approaching them. They had their own beverages.

"May we join you?" Jenny pulled out a chair between them. Kai sat across from her. "The Professor is showering. Nina and Teddy are showing Exxis and his mom how to cook chicken adobo. Annie, Exxis's mom is watching from the other side of the isolation glass in the kitchen."

Apollo glanced at the house. "Exxis will love that. Nina is a good cook."

"So," Kai smiled. "Have you two compared your dreams, yet?"

"Kai!" Jenny said. "They haven't been out here that long."

"Sorry, I guess I know more than either of you." He leaned forward, his expression getting serious. "I need to talk to the two of you ... quietly."

"About the dreamscape recordings?" Sonia asked.

"No, I'll let you two work those out." He stared at Sonia. "While you were stuck in those caves in El Dorado, Lowell Canyon sent over your records from when you were in a coma." He stopped. He looked at each one for a moment, and then focused on Sonia. "You are six weeks pregnant!"

Sitting back in her chair, Sonia was holding her glass to one side. It dropped to the tile deck, splashing the remaining liquid under the table. "What?"

Apollo stared, said nothing.

"That can't be!" Sonia said, "I've never been pregnant. The only opportunity in the last twelve weeks was," She stared at Apollo, "... for his birthday."

Jenny said, "That's why we wanted to talk to both of you. Did you have dreams about this, too?"

"No!" Sonia responded. "Not this."

"I know this is a difficult matter to deal with at this moment," Kai said, "but, I thought I should let you know before reporters get it from Lowell Canyon. Once Terra broadcasts her story about the fish and the gold mine in Princess Dejah Canyon, every journalist on Mars will be looking for a piece of this story." He put his drink on the table. "I know this happened as a fluke. On top of that, you conceived when Apollo was sick with the virus, when you caught the virus. You were in a coma for five of these weeks of early gestation. There is no way to know what affect the virus had during conception."

Sonia and Apollo listened silently, neither prepared to say anything.

Jenny said, "If you want to terminate, we could do it quietly. Lowell Canyon doctors are willing to make this information disappear."

"I'm really pregnant?"

Kai nodded agreement

"No!" Apollo said.

The other three looked at him. Sonia reacted. "What do you mean... no?"

He looked at Jenny and Kai, not certain whether to find sympathy. He reached to grip Sonia's hand. "I was raised Catholic. Killing an unborn child is wrong. Lolo Raul and Father Roxas died because of the virus I gave them. I don't want to kill my own son."

"Son?" Sonia asked. "You knew?"

"It was in my dreams."

"Strange, I didn't dream about it." She placed her other hand on top of his. "I'll have to think about this."

Jenny laughed. "Apollo, I don't envy you telling this to Nina."

Apollo gulped, thinking about that uncomfortable situation

"I've reviewed many of the C.N.A. recordings from Lowell Canyon and Tycho," Kai said. "The playbacks of the dreamscape visions both of you had. The historical sequences all seem to check out against the records of the eras you were dreaming about. There are future events in those recordings … well … we will have to see how events unfold. If the Venus crash is an indication, then…" He stopped briefly to take a drink.

Sonia and Apollo stared quietly at him, anxious about what he might say next.

"Both of you had visions about future… relationships… with each other. Some of those recordings were for identical events, only from different perspectives."

Apollo began to blush. Sonia, watching him, looked worried. "Are these recordings going to be made public?"

Jenny said, "Kai and I reviewed them. We know that both of you were suffering from the unusual side effects of the virus, and had no control over what happened in your dreams. It does seem that you two will enjoy each other sexually in times to come, if those dreams are prophecies."

Sonia and Apollo looked at each other. They both smiled, remembering their own dreams about this issue.

"Please don't show anyone," Apollo said. "Especially Nina or Tita Celia."

Jenny laughed. "No, we won't tell anyone. However, Terra is also reviewing all of those recordings for use with her show. I'll ask her to be discreet."

"One of those recordings," Kai said, "for you, Apollo, appears to have you and Sonia together… in the year 2240… at Tau Ceti."

Apollo looked to him, and said, "I know. I remember the dream. It was just a dream, wasn't it?"

"In the cave," Sonia spoke, "When I woke from the coma… just before the Professor administered the serum you gave Exxis… I was dreaming about being with you on a mountainous island overlooking an ocean... the blue sky had two moons. The year was 2240."

Kai responded. "It matches Apollo's dream."

"Let's not worry about that now," Jenny said. "Apollo, how do you plan to deal with Nina?"

"I was hoping to wait, let things happen."

"You need to tell her," Kai said. "Lowell Canyon knows that Sonia is pregnant. Everyone researching this virus will know, and will be curious because of what the virus does. You should tell her before she finds out from someone else."

"Tita Jenny," Apollo pleaded, "could you tell her?"

"No," She responded. "You have to tell her. You owe her that much. I am the only other woman she knows here. Afterwards she will need to be able to talk to me. If I tell her, then she will have no one to cry with. She will be totally alone."

"I'll tell her this evening," he said, "she won't like it, but she'll understand."

After a moment of silence, Sonia asked, "Apollo... the serum to end the coma... Exxis knew about it when we were sealed in the cave five days ago... he claims he felt you telling him about it. When we were rescued yesterday, Brass Newton told us there was no serum that he was aware of. What happened?"

Kai responded. "Rochelle Bond sent me a message last night about it... she just got it from Charles Belisario on Corrigedor. I gave the serum to Apollo and everyone else here," He then asked, "Did you communicate this to Exxis?"

"I'm not certain," Apollo said. "I remember dreams about the serum when I was in a coma. I didn't mention it when I woke up on the Moon, because I thought it wasn't real. That was when I first dreamed about Exxis."

"That is probably how he got it," Sonia said.

CHAPTER FORTY-FOUR

INTERROGATION

Camp Borox
Hellas Basin, Mars

Earth Date   August 24, 2216
Mars Date   D-Mmon 17, 1174

The Hellas Basin, an oval-shaped depression a thousand miles across and two miles deeper than the surrounding southern highlands, was formed from an asteroid impact a billion years ago. Over the eons, the basin filled with water when Mars was a warmer and wetter planet. As the Martian environment changed drastically; the water that did not evaporate, chilled and froze solid. Eventually the ice sublimated from the glacial sea, leaving a desert with a thick layer of sand. Annual dust storms over millions of years added a thicker layer of fine dust to that surface. Although there remained substantial permafrost frozen a few feet below the ground, salt and alkaline contaminations left the Hellas Desert barren, even with the advent of engineered Martian life brought by human pioneers. Most immigrants to Mars opted for the northern lowlands, leaving southern regions like Hellas deserted. This isolation was an aspect the military found appealing; it allowed for remote testing of secret developments. Also, in the middle of the huge Hellas dust bowl, the Militia maintained the high security prison, Camp Borox. Built on a rocky outcrop, with nothing but featureless flat desert to the horizon was in any direction, the camp was well located for isolating high security prisoners. The Militia Security Court opted to secure Ghant Travis, Jon Lee, Ken Sylvester, and all of their conspirators in Camp Borox until the detectives completed an evidence search. Presented with the initial facts of the case, the request was granted in order to prevent the suspects from directing evidence tampering.

"Mr. Travis," Detective Jeck Ekakaidis said. "It looks like your luck ran out." Ekakaidis turned his stare from the relaxed, but silent Ghant Travis to Sonny and Brass seated beside him at the table. The walls of the windowless interrogation room were the featureless off-white. Behind them two Militia guards stood at ease, laser rifle muzzles in hand, butts against the floor.

"It's about time you talked to me," Travis responded with an aristocratic arrogance. "You've detained me for two days on trumped-up charges without access to my lawyer. You will pay a price for this misconduct."

"Oh, we are looking out for your rights, Mr. Travis," Ekakaidis responded. His bushy eyebrows gave him the look of a friendly grandfather. "If this had been a simple murder and theft swindle, you would have a lawyer. You murdered five visitors from Earth, and indirectly caused an epidemic. The health threat makes you a security threat under jurisdiction of the Martian military. A Militia Judge Advocate General reviewed the initial evidence, and granted us authority to hold you incommunicado indefinitely."

"This is ridiculous. I have nothing to do with any health threat. My actions in the Canyon were justifiable protection of a Redrock mining claim. I demand my lawyer."

"I'll let you talk to your lawyer." Sonny smiled lightly. "Where can we find Dave Crane?"

"What are you talking about?"

"We have your recorded communications with him in the tunnels. What was his escape plan?"

Travis smiled, but did not speak.

Ekakaidis said, "You used to be a lawyer. We have security camera recordings of the murder of seven miners in the Canyon. Detective Ortigas, here, has the authority to work with us during this case. He is very talented with computers. He opened and copied all Bureau of Mines records involved with your claims on behalf of Redrock. He also copied Bureau of archive records showing what those claims were before you became involved. There are serious discrepancies between the two. A number of Bureau employees have acknowledged tampering with the records on your behalf."

Beads of sweat had appeared on his forehead. "If you have such an airtight case against me, why bother to talk?"

Brass erupted, "whose idea was it to try to kill my wife?"

Ekakaidis motioned for Brass and Sonny to remain calm.

"You want something from me," Travis suddenly was aware how angry both Sonny and Brass were. "What is it?"

"Mr. Travis. We have enough evidence to have you executed." Ekakaidis said. "Did the President of Redrock conspire with you in the commission of these crimes?"

"I need to talk to my lawyer."

"How much did you take from the mine?"

He said nothing.

Sonny then spoke. "Mister Travis, we have sealed your personal and professional files, scheduling records, electronic communications, and financial transactions. Within a few days we will know more about you that you know yourself. You can keep silent and hope that the evidence we have against you can be suppressed, or you can bargain for you life with a full statement. Keep in mind, Sylvester will be offered the same opportunity."

Travis swallowed audibly. "If you have such a strong case against me, why bother to talk to me?"

"Dave Crane is missing. Where can we find him?"

"Crane?" Ghant smiled, "You had him trapped in the tunnels chasing after Sonia Androff when you arrested me."

"We thought so," Ekakaidis said. "He is not there."

CHAPTER FORTY-FIVE

RELEASE

East of Mount Olympus
Tharsis Region, Mars

Earth Date	August 25, 2216
Mars Date	D-Mmon 18, 1174

"Exxis, it looks like you are caught up," Tia O'Malley's pretty Irish face filled one of the multiple console screens. "When will you be back on campus?"

Roger Lyman's portrait was on another of the screens. "I'm curious... your escape through those tunnels... your Aunt Terra talked about on her show last night... Just how did you get past the robot guards?"

"Give him time to answer the first question," Hanna Grappner appeared on a third screen. "I'm glad you're okay. "When the news broke that you had been kidnapped and your aunt's spacecraft blown up, we didn't know what to think. We feared the worst. Is the boy prophet with you?"

"Apollo Panahon?" Tia said, "And the woman from the mines, Sonia Androff?"

"Slow down," Exxis leaned back from the Baxter Annex communications console, "My uncle told me not to say anything about my experience in El Dorado for a few days, at least until the criminal investigation is wrapped up." He turned to look at Nina. She had been sitting beside him for the two hours session with Professor Bernstein's Agricultural Sciences class.

Nina quietly watched the class, listening to Professor Bernstein's lecture about Martian crops genetically engineering chemistry used to avoid freeze damage. Using her comp-pad artist's computer, during the class she sketched Exxis working with the console. The technical lecture was beyond her comprehension, but she enjoyed watching the classroom interaction of the students. Now, after the class, the friends of Exxis were anxious to talk to him.

"The quarantine will be lifted today," Exxis continued. "The serum they concocted at Corrigedor is effective. Everyone quarantined on the Moon and in the Philippines has been given the serum... they are all free of the virus. So are those here with us."

"Who is with you?" Roger asked, "Apollo Panahon?"

"Yes," Exxis responded. "So are Sonia Androff and Professor Chester."

"Professor Chester?" Hanna queried. "Oh yes, he's the expert on the paranormal. So that's why he's been away from the University. Terra Newton didn't mention his name in her show last night."

"He was with me in the caves," Exxis said. "At this moment he is working with Apollo and Sonia in another room in this compound. All day they've been sorting out the virus-caused visions."

"I hope we can talk to them," Tia said. "I'd like to meet them."

"Well," Exxis remarked, "you remember what the news report said about the Filipino miners murdered in the Canyon? The daughter of one of those victims is with me now. Nina?" He glanced over at his new friend.

Nina waved a hand, whispering "No."

"I was wondering who the girl was," Roger quipped, "She's cute."

Nina turned her head toward the console. "Am I on?"

Exxis displayed a small smile. He pointed to a console camera pointed at her. He then noticed her artwork. "That's pretty good, Nina."

"What's good?" Roger asked.

Nina smiled sheepishly when Exxis motioned for her to turn the sketch toward the camera. Exxis's friends were equally impressed. Following introductions, they asked her about her barrio and the Philippines. Her reluctance to speak waned with time as each of the students talked about their own Martian backgrounds, while asking questions that demonstrated their lack of understanding of Earth and the Philippines. Exxis and his friends then resumed discussions among themselves. Nina returned to quietly sketching.

Exxis' friends asked more about Terra's broadcast from the night before. Terra had reported that Martian military security was heading the investigation of crimes committed by Travis. The second part of her show detailed the escape of Apollo and Sonia from the canyon. As Exxis continued discussions with his classmates, Apollo appeared at the entrance to the communications room. He watched a few moments. He then said, "Nina, can we talk?"

Nina smiled at the console and excused herself. She followed Apollo through the house out to the patio deck, where they took seats at the table. Filling the western horizon, the dark color of Mount Olympus seemed bright in the afternoon sun. Much closer, just beyond the inflated domes were the military security trailers. At the table where they were seated was a platter of pastries and two glasses of mango juice. Apollo's small guitar was there. He picked up the guitar and began playing a slow romance song that he knew to be one of her favorites.

She smiled, sipped the mango juice, and quietly enjoying the music until it was over. "That was nice, Apollo. Did you bring me out here just to make music? I like that."

"Nina, you are special to me. You have always been my best friend."

Nina continued to smile, but her eyes telegraphed that she anticipated something bad.

"You remember the C.N.A. recordings when I was still in a coma on the Moon? The visions that made you angry?"

Her smile disappeared. "I remember." Her brows flared.

"It seems that the... encounter with Sonia means more than we thought."

"More?"

Apollo swallowed and stared down at the table. "Sonia is pregnant. She is expecting my son."

Nina did not speak, did not move a muscle. She simply stared.

"I know this is hard for you." Apollo raised his head to look at her. He breathed in.

Still, Nina just stared.

"I'm sorry."

"You're sorry?" She stood. "I came a hundred million miles with you to... to... here. My father is dead because of you and that stupid fish. My family and my village are on the Moon because of you... and now you tell me that woman is carrying your son?" She began to cry...

"Nina," he rose to his feet. "Let me help you." He approached her, reaching to put an arm over her shoulders.

She pushed his arm away. "Don't touch me. Don't talk to me. I was giving up everything in the world for you... and this is what you offer?" She ran toward the house. "Stay away from me."

Apollo put his guitar back on the table. He stared at the door to the house, where no one was. He felt heaviness in his stomach. He wished he knew what to say to make things better.

As he sat silently thinking, Jenny suddenly appeared from the door and walked across the patio to the table.

"You told Nina?" She asked. She sat in the same seat Nina had vacated moments earlier.

Apollo nodded.

"That's what I thought. She was crying, heading toward her room. She doesn't want to talk to anyone."

"What do I do now?" Apollo asked. "She won't want to talk to me for awhile. We're quarantined together indefinitely."

"Not anymore." Jenny said, "The quarantine was just lifted. Terra's dad invited all of us to dinner at their farm this evening."

"Quarantine lifted?"

"The U.N. Health Service lifted the emergency in the Philippines several hours ago. The patients in Baguio and Corrigedor can now go home. The Martian Medical Emergency Bureau is following suit. The serum seems to be completely effective in eliminating the virus."

"Great!" Apollo was suddenly elated. "Are Tita Celia and the barrio patients going back to Maliit na Ulap?"

"I don't know," She answered. "Sonny said there were some complications. He is coming here in the morning to discuss the situation. He said there were problems going back to Maliit na Ulap."

Apollo thought about it. "If we are going to dinner, what about Nina? I don't think she will want to sit at the same table with me today."

"I thought about that." Jenny picked up one of the pastries from the dish on the table. "I've been waiting for you to tell her since yesterday. I think Teddy and I will stay here with her."

CHAPTER FORTY-SIX

OPTIONS

East of Mount Olympus
Tharsis Region, Mars

Earth Date	August 26, 2216
Mars Date	D-Mmon 19, 1174

Jenny greeted her husband with a warm embrace and a passionate kiss. This was their first opportunity to even touch each other since Apollo arrived at the Manila Spaceport from Mars. She whispered to Sonny, "Honey, I miss this. Want to worry about the briefing later?"

Sonny glanced at all the other people in the room. "Tonight," He patted Jenny's behind, and then withdrew his hand. "Go ahead, take a seat."

Jenny backed away, taking a chair near him at the conference table.

"Where's Nina?" Sonny asked. He sat himself at the end of the table, placing his pocket computer on the table. The unit automatically unfolded to clipboard size. Kia, Apollo, and Sonia were seated with

Jenny on side of the table. Professor Chester was at the end. Brass and Terra stepped out of their pressure suits, seating themselves on the other side. All placed their own computers on the table tuned to Sonny's unit. Terra's robot assistant, Chet, positioned himself to record the meeting. .

Jenny spoke softly, "Exxis and his parents are giving Nina and Teddy a tour of the farm. We can brief her later." She squeezed Sonny's fingers with her hand. "You aren't leaving, are you?"

"Tomorrow," Terra said. "We'll be here for the night. Are you comfortable here, at the Baxter Annex? Dad fixed up the guest house at the main farm. There's enough space for everyone."

"I'd like to spend time alone with my wife and son," Sonny said, "now that the quarantine is lifted."

Following a moment of silence, Jenny responded, "Teddy and I will go where my husband goes." She looked down the table, reading the expressions on the others. "I'm certain Apollo and Sonia would like to see your dad's farm."

Terra changed the subject. "Let's talk about Maliit na Ulap. Then, we'll discuss Redrock and the Canyon."

"Ulap?" Apollo asked. "Did something more happen to the barrio?"

"Celia sent me some messages." Sonny had his computer run a Philippine newscast reporting that vigilantes burned Maliit na Ulap... the homes, the store, the church. The images showed scorched remains of what once had been the barrio; then panned the surrounding hillside showing denuded rice fields and tree stumps. Sonny stopped the newscast. "Maliit na Ulap is no more." He then said, "Director Bond from Tycho tried to arrange for the men to go back to work after the quarantine. Their jobs have been terminated. Other miners fear them, like they are lepers. The bosses don't want them anywhere near the mines."

"Oh, my God," Jenny said, "Where will they go?"

"The national government is arranging to build them a settlement on an isolated island. Nobody wants them back."

"What about the other epidemic patients?" Apollo asked, "Those in quarantine at Park John Hay and on Corrigedor?"

"Same thing… the Philippine government has them isolated. The epidemic is over, but the public is afraid. Many quarantined homes were burned."

Jenny's eyes widened with panic.

Sonny said, "No, they didn't get our place in Baguio. I had Lydia hire a private security force to protect it. Besides, Jenny, there was no public report that you were in quarantine."

Her face relaxed.

"The Philippines needs time to calm down. This epidemic scared everyone." Sonny said, "When they're convinced it is really over, they'll do the right thing." He looked at Apollo and Sonia. "I got another message from Celia. She is worried about Nina. Nina sent her a note about being miserable. Nina is mad at you, Apollo. Is this what I think it is?"

Apollo looked down at his hands on the table. Sonia waited for him to respond.

"I told him," Kai admitted, "that Sonia is pregnant. Apollo told Nina two days ago."

"That's what I thought." Sonny replied, "Nina is upset?"

"Very." Apollo said.

"That will work itself out. We need to discuss it more. However, Terra needs to talk about the investigation."

Terra looked directly at Sonia and Apollo. "If you've been watching my show, you know I'm holding back on your visionary dreams, or details about the Redrock irregularities."

Brass said, "With the arrest of Ghant Travis and Ken Sylvester, military security used a court order to seize Redrock, Bureau of Mines, and Sylvester's records. It looks like we can reclaim the value of everything Redrock took from Princess Dejah Canyon. Sonia, that is a lot. We meet tomorrow with Redrock attorneys at the Club Fir Tree in Crater City. We need to discuss how you want to proceed concerning recovery of what was taken."

Sonny said, "I will step you through the evidence of tampering with Bureau of Mines records, for this case and for Jim Everly's claims. We have the bank and tax filings for Redrock for the past few years. It is an interesting picture."

Sonia accepted a glass of water from a galley cart. "They murdered my partner, Fisk and our mechanic Japa, along with Roberto and the Filipino miners. Are they going to pay for that?"

"Anyone involved with the murders will pay. I am asking what to do about Redrock, the corporation. The C.E.O. claims he had nothing to do with the crimes of Ghant Travis. He is offering full restitution for everything taken from the mine, plus benefits to the families of those they hurt."

"Does that include the victims of the epidemic?" Sonia asked. "If Redrock had not committed these crimes, the virus infection would have been limited to Apollo and me. How do they restore Apollo's barrio?"

Brass shook his head slightly. "The head of Redrock will do what he can to save his company. That's why he contacted me. If you want vengeance for what they did, all of Redrock assets will be tied up in criminal and bankruptcy courts for years. However, if you are willing to deal, you can get a fairly decent restitution."

"And for this deal, what do they expect in return?

"Survival," Brass said. "Ghant Travis and his cohorts will go to prison for the rest of their lives on the murder charges, and you recover what was taken, plus survivor benefits. In return, Redrock itself will be absolved of additional criminal liability. Can you live with that?"

"Let me think about it. I don't have a lawyer. Would Newton Enterprises offer to help?"

"They tried to murder my wife and my nephew. Newton lawyers will represent you gratis. Is that acceptable?"

"Give me time to think," Sonia signaled for the remote galley cart to bring her wine. "Now, I think we should get to the other main issue." She looked to Chester. "The strange side affects of the virus." She handed one glass to Apollo, and then she sipped from a second.

"Are either of you still having the dreams since the serum?" Terra asked.

Apollo smiled and nodded.

Sonia responded, "I'm not so certain. I may be having normal dreams now. I don't particularly remember many the past few days. Those I remember were interrupted when I was waking up. However,

I do read some people's thoughts. When we were in the caves, I was able to visualize Dave Crane's world."

"You explained that when we found you," Terra said. "Dave Crane is still missing. Have you been able to read into him since you came here?"

"No. The only other mind I've been reading is Apollo... and those images are... unusual."

Professor Chester spoke, "Both wear C.N.A. units when they sleep. Since they took the serum, Apollo continues to have vivid dreams about the past, the future, and many things. Sonia's visions have reverted to normal dreams at night... except...."

"Except what?" Terra asked.

"Except when Apollo is dreaming of something to do with Sonia, then Sonia simultaneously has matching dreams from her point of view."

Everyone focused on the boy. Apollo began to blush. Sonia smiled, but did not speak.

"More of those sexual fantasy dreams," Brass smiled. "When I was your age, I had a lot of those kinds of dreams, too." He turned his attention from Apollo to Professor Chester. "Was there anything special about the setting?"

"Do you want me to replay the recording?"

"That won't be necessary," Terra said. "Where was the setting?"

"Apollo looked to be twenty years older, Sonia was as pretty as she is now," Professor Chester smiled at Sonia, then continued. "They were inspecting rock samples on a rocky bluff, beside a waterfall, overlooking a dark green conifer forest below. It looked like the Canadian Rockies... except for the two chalk-colored moons above the horizon. They were having a picnic."

"I remember that dream," Sonia said. She turned to Apollo. "You had the same dream last night?"

Apollo smiled. His face turned redder. He looked down at his hands.

"I reviewed the recordings... we don't need to go further," Terra said. She then asked Professor Chester, "Have you reviewed all of the recordings from Lowell Canyon?"

"I've reviewed them," he said, "I compared recordings from Sonia with those from Apollo. They both had visions of being together on Tau Ceti. Not only that, they both had dreams that many of the people from Apollo's barrio there with them."

Brass added, "Now that they are free of the virus, I'd like to test Apollo at the Life Sciences Laboratory. While he still has the 'gift', I like to evaluate the neural mechanics of what takes place, find out if he can control the communications."

"That would be wonderful," Professor Chester responded, "if Apollo agrees."

Terra said, "We still have no clue of when Apollo communicated the serum to Exxis. Apollo, have you any recollection of that yet?"

"No, nothing I can recall. Are you certain it was me?"

"Exxis feels it was you. He isn't positive, though. I was hoping to finish my report on the escape."

Sonia said, "It wasn't me. I was in a coma with a lot of other dreams... especially those dreams about being on Tau Ceti with Apollo."

Sonny had been expecting that comment. He turned his attention to Terra. "I hope you don't feel the need to broadcast this yet. I don't want these visions forcing actions that would not happen otherwise."

"I agree," Terra replied, "However, those visions are already leading us in directions we would not have taken without them. The Venus crash and the warning of the sabotage of Octan's spacecraft are the most dramatic. He also had visions of Exxis going to the cave in the El Dorado badlands far enough in advance for us to have the Militia there to rescue them."

Sonia smiled, "What can I say? If it weren't for these visions, the connection between Apollo and me would have never gotten more than casual. His life, if we hadn't been sick with the virus, would have been with Nina. Our age difference is too great for it to be otherwise. But now we know more about each other than anyone else knows about either of us. In addition to knowing we will be together for a long time to come, we both had visions that Nina and Exxis will be with each other. What can we say about that?"

There was a brief silence. Finally, Terra asked, "Has anyone told Exxis or Nina?"

No one responded.

Professor Chester finally said, "In the cave in the Canyon, when Exxis and I woke from the drug, he had visions of Nina. He was infatuated with the image of her in his mind."

Brass said, "Let's think about this before we talk to them."

"There is a complication with these matters," Kai said.

"Complication?" Terra asked.

"Last night I tested everyone here for the virus," Kai said. "Everyone is clean of the virus, which we reported." He stopped to look at everyone else, focusing on Apollo.

Jenny said, "What complication?"

"Nina is pregnant."

There was a moment of silence. Everyone focused on Apollo.

Sonny laughed. "Apollo, you are amazing. You made two women pregnant at the same time. Two months ago you were a virgin. "

Sonia stared at Apollo, then at Sonny and Jenny, then again at Apollo. She reached over to put a hand on his shoulder. She smiled. "This would be really funny, if I weren't part of the equation. What can I say?"

"It's a good thing," Sonny quipped, "that robot Tessie can't conceive."

Apollo sheepishly looked at Sonia, at Sonny and Jenny, and at Brass and Terra. He grinned, but did not respond.

"My question," Professor Chester said, "Both of these... these conceptions... occurred with Apollo infected by the virus. What will that do to the fetuses?"

"That is something we will know in time," Sonny replied. "Jenny, Apollo and Sonia will come with us tomorrow to Crater City. Nina will have to know. Can you talk to her while we are away?"

"Again?" Jenny responded. "This time, can I show her the C.N.A. recordings about her future with Exxis? Otherwise, she may go into a deep depression."

CHAPTER FORTY-SEVEN

CLUB FIR TREE

Crater City, Mars

| Earth Date | August 28, 2216 |
| Mars Date | D-Mmon 21, 1174 |

The Newton Industries limousine routed itself through the Crater City maze of pressurized traffic tunnels toward the entertainment district. The eight passengers were as calm as could be expect, given that they were to meet with the C.E.O. of Redrock. Brass and Terra told Sonny and Jenny stories of improvements to the city since the last time they visited. Apollo listened as Sonia pointed to attractions of the underground city; such as the University district, the reservoir and underground swimming pool, and the banking district. John Dorchester, Brass's attorney, continued quietly reviewing his computer files. Terra's robot remained inactive. Stopping at the entrance to the Club Fir Tree, three tunnel levels below the surface, the computer operated limo opened doors to allow everyone out, and then proceeded on to the parking decks.

A receptionist guided them through the main dining hall to the entertainment lounge. On stage the Desert Sunrise Quintet played a medley of popular love songs; music that had the crowded dinner lounge captivated. A few in the crowd were singing along softly. The side walls of the rooms were ceramic glass panels in front of ten-foot deep terrariums; inside each planter were multiple stunted fir trees with ferns and bushes from the American Northwest Mountains. A stream of water cascaded down rocks within the planters, forming little creeks. Holographic electronic murals at the back of the terrariums recreated the dense conifer forests with snow capped volcanic peaks and pastel blue skies. Other walls were covered with cedar panels.

Within minutes club owner Starr Swenson, a friend of Terra's for twenty-five years, joined her guests. "Terra... Brass, it's been awhile" the red-haired beauty greeted them. She recognized the two beside Terra. "Sonny and Jenny?" She smiled warmly. "Welcome back to Mars."

Starr ushered them to a private conference room to meet their adversaries; Wes Chandler, the C.E.O. of Redrock Mining, his attorney Nana Kimberly, and Thomas Manstein, the chief of staff to the President Knotts. As soon as Starr left, Terra signaled Chet to record all activities

"Thank you for agreeing to meet me," Chandler spoke with caution. "After looking at the evidence you compiled against Redrock, I have to say I was shocked. I am deeply disappointed in Ghant Travis."

"You choose words carefully," Terra said, "You reviewed the files?"

"I've reviewed them," he said. "I never realized this was going on."

"Ghant Travis reported directly to you and the board," Sonny stated. "You didn't know what he was doing?"

"I trusted Ghant. He made tremendous profits for the Redrock. He preferred to run his own operations with minimal interference. I had no reason to doubt him."

"Your own auditors filed reports that the accounts for the acquisition of independent mines were incomplete," Sonny replied, "reports forwarded directly to your desk."

"Detective Ortigas," Chandler responded. "You are good at your work. The materials you sent me included minutes of business meetings where Ghant reported to me. Those reports include his defense of criticisms. He was persuasive."

Dorchester interrupted. "Mr. Chandler, as an attorney for the plaintiffs, I recommend that we not go into great detail. You requested this meeting. We would like to hear what you offer."

Chandler cleared his throat. "Mr. Ortigas, the evidence you and Detective Ekakaidis compiled against Redrock is substantial. I assume that what you sent me is only part of it. You are in the position to destroy Redrock if this goes to court."

"If?" Sonny responded. "My sister's husband is dead. Several of my closest friends were murdered by the Redrock Vice President of Operations. They were killed to make a profit for Redrock."

"I'm sorry for the pain he caused," Chandler said, "If I could repair it, I would. Ghant, and those who conspired with him, will face justice. What I ask is for a chance to save Redrock Mining from destruction."

"What do you want?" Dorchester queried. "And what do you offer?"

This time Kimberly spoke, "If you limit prosecution to the conspirators and those directly responsible for the crimes," she looked at Sonia, "Redrock will guarantee fair reimbursement of all wealth taken from Princess Dejah Canyon. The estates of the murder victims will be awarded the equivalent of a corporate executive life insurance benefit. In addition," Kimberly turned her computer console around for all to see, "we will offer a substantial penalty for the trouble caused."

"The murder victims," Terra asked, "do you include those infected with the virus?"

"The virus?" Chandler remarked, "Those were not caused by Redrock."

Sonia spoke this time, "If Ghant Travis had not come to the Canyon, and the epidemic would have been limited to Apollo and me. The epidemic in the Philippines was a direct result of Redrock stalking him, forcing us to ship him to Earth in a coma."

"How many?" Kimberly asked.

"Over ten-thousand were in quarantine. Two-hundred-and-sixty-five died."

"Ten thousand?" Kimberly reacted. "That is out of the…"

Chandler placed a hand on her arm, then said, "We will provide to the estates of those who died. We will do what we can to compensate the rest of the ten-thousand."

"Our investigation," Brass added, "uncovered similar deception against Jim Everly. Ghant swindled him of his titanium discovery. Will this also apply to him?"

"Jim Everly?" Chandler said, "Oh, yes. I agree to repay his widow the full value of that discovery, not just the royalty. Will that suffice?"

"In return," Dorchester said, "I assume you want us to reframe from a civil claims suit?"

"That's what we ask." Kimberly responded. "If you take us to court, Redrock will not survive. Investors and creditors will strip the assets long before you get a judgment. There won't be anything left."

"That's not true." Sonny said, "The Militia court already froze your accounts. No one gets anything until the charges are resolved."

"I understand." Chandler replied, "You can take us apart. All I ask is that you not destroy the entire corporation for the crimes of one man. I sympathize with your anger. I understand a desire for a vendetta. Please think about what I offer." He signaled for Kimberly to hand over the proposal

"Give us a few days to discuss this," Brass responded. "Sonia, do you have a reaction?"

"We'll discuss it." She accepted the computer plug.

Thomas Manstein, the chief of staff to the President Knotts finally spoke., "Terra, the President considers Wes Chandler a friend, and feels that it is important to Mars that Redrock Mining not be destroyed. However, he told me that the crimes warrant severe punishment for all who participated. I am instructed to offer your investigators unlimited access to government files. Any government employee who knowingly participated in this conspiracy will be charged. Will this make it easier?"

Sonny responded, "So far we have not found direct evidence connecting the Executive office with the crimes, but I remain suspicious."

Manstein looked at Sonny without responding, and then turned to Terra, "We can't undo what has been done. The evidence you have will make a dramatic story that will hurt a lot of innocent people. Please consider what we offer."

They wrapped up the discussions. Starr returned to the room, followed by a waiter with drinks. Chandler, Kimberly, and Manstein declined, opting to leave graciously. Starr escorted them to the exit lobby, and then returned to her friends in the lounge.

"What do you think of the offer?" Brass asked when they were alone. He looked first at his wife, and then both turned to Sonny and Apollo.

"It sounds fair," Sonny said, "The money will give Maliit na Ulap survivors a way to rebuild. It will give them more than enough. What they ask of us is reasonable. However, the decision is up to Sonia." He looked at her.

"I'm angry," Sonia said. "I'll be angry for a long time. Fisk was my best friend; my partner for more years than I wish to count. I miss him." She slowly turned to smile at Apollo. She spoke to Sonny and Jenny. "I am tempted to reject the offer, and go for vengeance. But, the visions," She paused, reaching to take Apollo's hand, "laid out a future for Apollo and myself that I want to make a reality, especially now that I am expecting. The settlement would give me the wealth needed to go with Apollo to Tau Ceti."

"The wealth to go to Tau Ceti?" Terra asked.

"Apollo and I have been discussing this. The value of the gold from Princess Dejah Canyon could buy a fleet of fully stocked starship transports. Our dreamscapes suggest that many survivors from Maliit na Ulap will be on Tau Ceti with us. If those visions are accurate…"

Apollo blushed slightly with Sonia's public display of affection. "There were a lot of dreams while I was in a coma that I want to make real." He put his other hand on top of hers. "I want to go with Sonia… and our son."

Jenny smiled, but said nothing. She sipped her drink.

407

Brass commented, "You do realize the age difference will eventually be a problem… In twenty years, Apollo you will be thirty-eight when Sonia is sixty. After menopause her romantic enthusiasm will diminish. Are you two prepared to deal with that?"

Apollo blushed.

Sonia said, "We know. I'll take along a big enough supply of Xanil-Five to keep me sexually active for a long time. In addition, we would bring along playmate robots for when the time comes."

Apollo stared at her, "We will?"

Jenny laughed. "That's a unique solution. We don't need to know more at this moment."

Terra asked, "Have you talked to Nina and Exxis, yet?"

"Not yet," Jenny said. "He took her to the University this evening to see a sporting event. I'll talk to her tomorrow. This is going to be another shock for her."

Sonia released Apollo's hand, and reached for her cocktail. "Has Nina seen the C.N.A. recordings?"

"Yes," Jenny said, "but not all. She saw Apollo's visions of the two of you together for his birthday at the Canyon. She went ballistic over that. Since then, we've kept recordings that involved you, Sonia, from her."

"What about the other Tau Ceti images? The ones with barrio people there? Has she seen any of my C.N.A. recordings from Lowell Canyon?"

"She's a volatile teenager. We didn't show her."

Apollo added, "Nina understands. We talked while we were on the Moon, while we were traveling here. I told her that I saw her with my sister on Tau Ceti when they are both about thirty. She knows my visions have me there. We had no idea how it would ever happen, but after everything else from the dreams, she believes it is destiny."

Sonny smirked, "Amazing. We are determining our lives based on these dreams. This isn't right."

"What would you do?" Sonia asked. "Apollo's dream warning when he first got sick, warned us that Travis was about to kill us. Travis would have gotten rich from the gold strike."

"I don't know. The dreamscapes have been accurate so far. It just doesn't feel right."

"Apollo," Brass asked. "Sonia and Nina are expecting your children. Are you absolutely certain you should be with Sonia rather than Nina?"

Apollo blushed again. "I know Sonia is older than me. Nina has been my closest friend since we were children. She wanted to marry me for a long time. But, Sonia and I share a love for the rocks. We both enjoy exploring caves, looking for ores. Other than being close friends, Nina and I do not like the same things. She gets upset when I come back late and dirty. She is uninterested in exploring mountain trails. She would rather be a nurse, be helping people. The dreams tell me she and Exxis will be happy," He looked to Sonia's eyes, "That Sonia and I will enjoy exploring a distant world."

Starr returned to the conference room. "Would you like to eat in here? We have fresh rainbow trout, if you like it."

Sonny asked. "Are you going to sing tonight?"

She smiled. "I haven't been on stage for a long time."

"The songs you recorded during the war," Sonny said. "I'd like to hear them again."

CHAPTER FORTY-EIGHT

LIFE SCIENCES INSTITUTE

Crater City, Mars

| Earth Date | September 3, 2216 |
| Mars Date | D-Mmon 29, 1174 |

MARTIAN VIRUS, DAY 67

P rofessor Chester finished his adjustments to the Cerebral Neural Analyzer control consoles. "Apollo, I have a clear image of your consciousness at the moment." He looked around him at the multiple console stations. A variety of technicians were monitoring this test. Kai, seated beside Professor Chester, concentrated on medical surveillance.

The image on the screens was of Apollo's view of him at the console. Seated in a comfortable recliner set to the most relaxing position, Apollo's attention shifted to another console where Electronics Scientist Xuan Zee was recording his brain scan signals. He was just another specialist trying to understand the timescape visions. Other technicians were staff employees with the Life Science

410

Institute. Apollo glanced through the window to the observation room. His C.N.A. recording view was of Jenny, Teddy, and Nina, patiently looking back at him.

"I want you to close your eyes." Chester said.

The images on the screen went dark.

"Think about Sonia."

The memory image of the blond woman he cared for appeared on the screen.

"Good. Try to visualize what she is seeing right now."

Apollo opened his eyes. The screen image was of Nina and Jenny as he saw them through the window. "I'm not sure that I want to."

There was a long pause. Both Professor Chester and Zee looked at him, not certain what to say. Jenny smiled, looked to Nina, patting Nina's arm.

"Apollo," Nina smiled, "I've accepted your visions... the futures you see. Don't stop trying now. I want the best for you and Sonia."

Apollo exhaled audibly without speaking.

"Sonny and Brass are with Sonia in the Canyon," Jenny smiled, "What they are up to? Please."

Apollo grinned. He leaned his head back and closed his eyes. He whispered Sonia's name to himself, asking what she was doing.

An image appeared on screen of the underground cavern where he had found the frozen fishes. The exploded rover and the shredded tents were gone. A new "Life Science Institute" Trailer Laboratory was parked in the cave, almost precisely where the other rover had been blown up. The image focused on the multiple tables along rock wall of the cave, just where Roberto's work tables had been. Three men in Life Sciences Institute pressure suits worked with specimen samples at the tables.

"Be careful with those," Sonia was saying, "Don't touch the fish in that ice."

One of the men turned to face her. Brass's voice was clear, "Don't worry. I've been engineering new life forms all my life. I know the protocol. Is Sonny with you?"

"Not at the moment." Sonia responded, "He's in the Redrock trailer studying Dave Crane's records. He'll have dinner with us in an hour."

"Sonia," Brass said. He walked toward the source of the screen image. "Do you sense Apollo at the moment?"

After a pause, she responded. "He's telling me your laboratory in Crater City is testing him. They want to know if he still has telepathy."

Brass responded, "I'm on a satellite link to Han Snyder at the Lab. He is monitoring. He says the C.N.A. is recording our conversation from your point of view as we speak."

Sonia whispered a thought of romance for Apollo, and then said, "It seems his ability is as strong as it was before. I'm not so lucky. I only get him when he tries to reach me. I don't have the dreamscapes anymore." The view panned around the cave to the brightly lit opening leading out to the Canyon floor, then to the trailer airlock. As the airlock approached, she whispered, "Apollo, let's cut it off. I have to go to the bathroom, and would prefer you don't record that. Try to focus in again in two hours. We'll be having dinner with Sonny. Everyone will be out of their pressure suits."

"Do you have any sense of Dave Crane?" Apollo's voice audio was audible from the C.N.A. console, although his lips did not move. "Professor Chester was asking me, since you seemed to be connected to his thoughts when you were hostages."

"No," Sonia's telepathic voice was clear. "I have had no feeling of connection since we were rescued. I know he is unaccounted for, but I feel that he is somewhere in the maze of tunnels out here."

Zee asked, "Is she wearing a C.N.A. helmet? I'd like to track her brainwave patterns simultaneously."

Technician Han Snyder, still on a phone with Brass, shook his head. "No, she's not." He paused. "Brass said he'd have her wear one during dinner, in two hours."

The C.N.A. audio recorded Apollo's voice muttering something to Sonia, and the image went blank. He opened his eyes. The screen image shifted from his perspective of the console, then to his view of the observation window. Jenny and Nina smiled back at him.

"You are supposed to be able to visualize the future." Zee then asked, "Apollo, could you try to connect with Sonia for two hours from now?"

Apollo began to blush. He continued looking at Nina in the observation room.

Professor Chester understood his reaction. He said, "Sonia may be too personal at the moment. Can I get you to focus on someone you don't really know?"

"I'll try. Who?"

Professor Chester looked over his shoulder. "Xuan Zee developed the anti-grav drive twenty years ago. Can you think of him back then?"

"Professor!" Zee was a bit indignant. "This is still too personal. Try someone else. How about the images Apollo had of Percival Lowell? Three hundred years ago takes it out of the realm of personal." Xuan Zee looked at the boy. "Did you study Lowell?"

Apollo shook his head. "I hadn't heard of him before I got sick. Sonia told me a little about him. He believed there were canals on Mars that were actually optical illusions."

"That was Percival Lowell three hundred years ago." Professor Chester said. "One of your recorded dreamscapes was through his eyes. If you try think about him, while you're awake, could you do it again? That's what we want to test."

"I'll try." He leaned his head back. He glanced at Jenny and Nina, smiled, and then looked straight ahead. The images through his eyes were on the monitors. He closed his eyes, and the screens went dark. An out of focus image appeared on screen; slowly it sharpened to the face of Sonia. There were no voices."

"Apollo, you're not thinking about Percival Lowell."

The image faded to a blank red screen. "Sorry." He began whispering to himself. "Lowell... Lowell... Lowell." He yawned. An image appeared. In the foreground was a planter full of marigold flowers under a series of growth lamps. Above the flowers was a transparent dome, and beyond the dome was brightly lit floor of the Tycho Crater, contrasted with the deep morning shadows. The Tycho Metropolitan Center facilities were shimmering in the sunlight. In the black sky above the far rim of the crater was the blue and white crescent Earth. All was silent for a minute, then Celia's voice was audible on the C.N.A. recording, "Madeline, you should be packing. We leave in a few hours."

"I know, Tita Celia. I don't have much to pack."

The image shifted from the view of the crater to the inside of the Tycho Quarantine Center observation deck, focusing on Celia stepping up to take a seat near the image source.

"Are you worried about going back?"

"A little. There is no barrio to go home to."

"But Sonny and Jenny say they made arrangement for us to stay at their place in Manila. You like Manila."

"Tita, the news says the people don't want us to come home because of the virus. I'm scared."

The image showed Celia reaching to take Madeline's hand. "Sonny promised it will be fine. He has Lydia making arrangements where we will be safe."

"I know, Tita. I was just thinking." The image shifted back to the landscape of Tycho Crater. "I was thinking about Apollo. I hope he is better. Nina wrote me that there is a problem, but won't say what it is. I want to see my brother again."

"I think about Apollo, too," Celia replied, "and Nina. I wish I could be there to help them, but I can't."

The image stopped. There was a blank red screen, followed by Apollo's opened eyed view of the equipment in front of him.

"I don't think that was Percival Lowell," Zee smirked.

Apollo again looked to Jenny and Nina through the window, and said, "Madeline is my sister. I think I was sensing what she is doing at this moment."

"Maybe you lost the ability to see through time," Chester said. "or you can't control it."

"I'll try again," Apollo responded. He closed his eyes. He quietly concentrated on what he remembered from the dream he had before of Percival Lowell.

Abruptly an image appeared of a cobblestone street with horse drawn carriages passing by. Remnants of slush and snow spotted the sidewalks. The wintry street was lined with tightly packed Victorian era European city homes built solidly against the adjacent buildings. There were pedestrians, only a few men in wool coats and scarves, with top hats on. The image panned to an opening door, where a butler ushered in the image source along with a second man. Directed through the elaborately wall-papered house into a parlor, the image showed lattice windows, a view of the bare trees in front of the buildings across the street. A kerosene lamp illuminated the room, and a crackling fire burned in a fireplace.

A well dressed late nineteenth-century European appeared. He spoke fluent French. A second man followed him in to the room. Another male voice responded with American accented French. The conversation continued for several minutes, until a technician reaching to Apollo's C.N.A. helmet stumbled, his hand grabbing Apollo's arm. The image abruptly ended. Apollo's view of the technician filled the screen.

"Van, you idiot!" Zee yelled. "We just got started. Look what you did."

Technician Van Wilder backed away from Apollo, grinning sheepishly. He knew better than to respond verbally. He quickly disappeared.

"What were they saying?" Professor Chester was activating the computer access to library files. "I wasn't expecting a French conversation from an American astronomer. Was that Lowell you connected to?"

"I don't know," Apollo replied. "I tried to focus on him, on the man I had the earlier dream about."

"Janna, run a translator on the conversation," Chester spoke to a technician at another console. "I'll track historical records of Lowell going to France."

"Well," Zee said, "There was a difference. The brainwave patterns of the previous two… the connection to Sonia and to Madeline were almost identical. This one exhibited a markedly different frequency pattern. All come from the same portion of the hypothalamus."

Kai said, "The Feldermite Hormones coming from the pituitary to the hypothalamus spiked in all three instances. It tapered off when the connection is broken."

"I have the interpretation." Technician Janna commented.

In response to a hand wave from Chester, she played back the C.N.A. recording with a dubbed English interpretation. The man who met the visitors at the door spoke to the Victorian gentleman in the parlor. "Sir, an American astronomer desires to see you. Indeed, there are two of them. Here are their cards... Percival Lowell... and Alvan Clark."

"Delighted to see you, Mr. Lowell. We Frenchmen are well acquainted with your admirable works on astronomy. You have come for a look at Europe?"

"I'm on my way to the Sahara in search of a place where the atmosphere is perfectly calm. But, I want to first show you the results we obtained from the summits of our mountains in Arizona. It was your book on the planet Mars that set us at work. But, we are no longer in accord with you. You will be surprised, perhaps irritated, at that."

"Quite the contrary, my dear sir. You should know very well that all I desire is progress, and that no one could..." The recording ended abruptly.

"I have it," Chester said, "who this Frenchman was. He was a nineteenth-century astronomer living in Paris... his name was Camille Flammarion. Portions of this very conversation were reported in the New York Times in February 1896. I also have a historical photograph of the two of them together."

"Apollo," Zee asked, "Have you ever heard of Camille Flammarion?" He shifted his attention to the images from three-hundred years earlier, comparing the photograph to the face in Apollo's dreamscape."

"No."

"Amazing." Zee said. "You still have the time-telepathic talent." He glanced at Kai, "And apparently you are totally free of the virus. Isn't that right, Doc?"

"Yes," Kai responded. "He is one of the few. All the patients at Tycho and Corrigedor and Baguio are in recovery. The serum was a Godsend... but only five out of all those thousands still having visions. Six, if you count Sonia."

"But," The Professor said, "Sonia seems to be sporadic, and mostly when Apollo tries to connect with her."

"Could I go to the bathroom?" Apollo's question disrupted the technical dialog. "Please?"

Kai motioned for the technicians to disconnect Apollo. Turning to Zee and Professor Chester, he said, "Let's not push Apollo too hard. Let him go have lunch with Jenny and Nina." He pointed to his own data screens. "I think we have a lot to analyze from what we have already."

With that, Apollo was released for a two-hour break to wander around the Life Sciences Institute with Jenny and Nina. After his bathroom break he joined the women to stroll calmly through the corridors to the surface observation deck gardens. Nina and Apollo spoke cautiously to each other, making small talk observations about the testing, the hospitality, and the scenery. Finally, Jenny said, "I think I will leave you two. I'd like to call Sonny. You both have much to discuss."

"Don't go, Tita Jenny," Nina reached for her arm. "I'd feel better if you were here."

She studied the two of them. "You really need to talk. I've been in the middle for the past two weeks... every since..." She patted Nina's hand. "The two of you have been best friends forever. You should be able to talk to each other, now." Jenny winked, and then departed.

Apollo watched Jenny disappear into a stairway. He breathed out. "Nina, are you hungry?"

"Not really," She showed a slight smile. "A little thirsty, maybe."

He motioned toward a nearby table with chairs. The pressure dome offered a magnificent view of the distant Crater City Metropolis surface structures. Beyond that, on the horizon, was the morning illumination on the dark basaltic rocks of the grand Mount Olympus volcano.

Apollo asked for an automated galley to bring them fruit juices. As they sat, Nina asked, "That image you had of Tita Celia... that was through Madeline's eyes?"

Apollo nodded. "She is leaving for the Philippines in a few hours. She misses us. She misses you."

"I heard. I miss her, too."

Apollo cleared his throat, and then said, "Nina, I'm sorry I hurt you with... with the forecasts. You have always been my friend. I feel bad about it."

Nina smiled, reached to hug his arm, and then said, "Its okay. I've had time to talk to Tita Jenny and Tito Sonny about what is happening. I should have talked to you last week, but I just couldn't.

They showed me recordings… that you had about me and Exxis. They showed both of us."

"You don't feel that these… visions… are sending you to someone you would not have gone with otherwise?"

She looked down at her feet. "I did for awhile. I was mad when you told me Sonia is pregnant. I was angry more when Doctor Kai told me I am pregnant, too. Exxis was there to talk to, and he became my friend right away. When Tito Sonny and Tita Terra told us about your visions of the two of us being together on Tau Ceti, I was upset all over again." She looked up. "But, Exxis is the sweetest, most gentle… We talked for a long time about it. He took me to his University to meet his friends. We figure we will take time to see if we really want to do this…"

Apollo felt a sense of relief. He took her hand in his. "Are you mad at Sonia?"

Nina shook her head. "No. I know she was hurt like the rest of us. She took care of you when you got sick, and sent you back to the Philippines. Her best friend was murdered in the Canyon along with papa and Tito Roberto. She is a good woman, and she will be good for you, Apollo."

The automated galley rolled up to the table. Apollo asked for and retrieved two glasses of mango juice. After sipping, he said, "What about… the baby? What do you want to do? What do we say to Tita Celia?"

"Do you think we should tell her?"

"She will be mad at all of us."

"I talked to Jenny and Sonny and Exxis. They said that if Exxis and I decide to go along with your prediction that I should say it is his baby, not yours. No one in the barrio has to know."

"Exxis agreed to that?"

"He thought about it for about four days. It was his idea. He says he doesn't know why, but he thinks he is in love with me."

"Do you love him?"

"I don't know. All my life I thought I was in love with you. I think I still am. But, right now, with all the problems from this… virus and murders… Exxis is special…. I think I will love him."

"Where is he now? Is he with his Aunt Terra?"

"Exxis is in class. Terra is with that Detective... Jeck Ekakaidis... interviewing people who worked for Ghant Travis. They are supposed to be here this evening. They both felt I needed to talk to you. I've been wanting to... but I was afraid."

He said, "Sonia and I are talking about us. We think we should get married before she starts to show."

"I've been expecting you to say this... that's what Tita Jenny told me. I hope you will invite Tita Celia. She should be there."

"I know. Tito Sonny told us he would have Lydia arrange something in Baguio or at Intermeros in Manila, if we want."

"But, Sonia isn't Catholic. Would she agree?"

"She doesn't have an organized religion. She is willing if they don't force her to be a Catholic."

Nina smiled. "Exxis was raised a Baptist. I think he feels the same way." She reached over and hugged Apollo warmly. "You know, I think everything will work out."

After the long embrace, they separated. Apollo spoke to his sleeve. "Tita Jenny, I think we are hungry now. Would you like to join us for lunch?"

Chapter Forty-Nine

Panahon Wave

Princess Dejah Canyon, Mars

Earth Date   September 12, 2216
Mars Date   D-Mmon 38, 1174

MARTIAN VIRUS, DAY 76

Sonny asked the console in front of him to replay Lydia Sanchez's message from the Philippines. "…and I guess Celia already told you that the barrio thanks Sonia for the new homes airlifted to Maliit na Ulap. They are nicer houses than any of them ever had. They think that when you get back, Sonny, you'll help them get their jobs back at the mine, but they're in no rush. The money Redrock gave them is more than they could make in their lifetimes."

"I made arrangements with Father Alberto DeGuseman at Baguio Cathedral for your double wedding on October twenty-fourth. I assume you still plan to return this month. Celia is organizing the ceremony with the church. You'll have to explain what you told her, because she seems mixed up about this event. I'm confused myself,

420

so I don't blame her. By the way, everyone is asking what the two couples want for wedding gifts. Let me know?"

Her expression became serious. "Jenny… Lee Chang came by this morning. Your job is waiting for whenever you get back, but he is worried. He's gotten word that some underworld organizations have put a price out to kidnap Apollo and bring him in alive. In fact, they have a bounty out for any of the epidemic victims who still have the timescape visions. There are only five or ten here who maintained the visions after the epidemic passed. Two were kidnapped; the rest are in hiding. According to Lee, the people who put out the bounty feel that the visions could make them rich. So, be careful with Apollo when he comes for the wedding."

"I try to keep up with the news, but the broadcasts are, shall we say, limited. I know you avoid sending any details about Apollo's visions, and that Terra Newton is protecting him from scrutiny, but I would love to learn the details. Meanwhile, Lloyds of London has another job for you. I assume you are aware of the Rangoon gold dragon theft. Two months ago a gold dragon loaded with precious stones disappeared from the Burmese palace. The police exhausted their leads, and Lloyds tried another detective agency with no success. They will pay our standard rate to have you look into it, with the usual royalty for recovery. I'm attaching their request, along with copies of the investigations to date. Let me know what to tell them. I know you are busy with the Redrock business." Lydia cleared her throat, "Contact me. Let me know what needs to be done for the wedding, and I'll see to it."

Sonny scanned the files for the golden dragon, reviewing each recorded interview and the accompanying documentation. It took him two hours to get through the records. He could not improve on the files without repeating many of the steps the police had already taken. It looked interesting, but not something he could deal with until the end of the year. He would have Lydia tell Lloyds that if the case were still open after Christmas, he would look into it then. Looking around the trailer, he was alone. His computer located Jenny in the observation trailer with Teddy and Nina.

Another monitor showed Terra and Brass in the conference trailer with Kai and Professor Chester. Along with Life Sciences Institute specialists on viruses, early Martian water life, and neural chemistry, all were captivated by the antics of Zee, who was demonstrating complex formulas to explain the phenomena. Disease specialist Charles Belisario quietly listened, waiting his turn to discuss what he had discovered about the virus from the ice samples.

Sonny caught Apollo and Sonia on a separate screen. Up the cliff inside the gold mine cavern. They were sharing specimens they found while they supervised Newton Enterprises ore extraction. Sonny had been concerned about the romance and eminent marriage of eighteen year old Apollo to forty year old Sonia. It seemed ridiculous. But, after watching them together for a month, it was obvious that the dreamscapes had both convinced that they belonged together. They valued each other's company as much as he and Jenny did theirs.

"Apollo. Sonia." Sonny spoke, "You should be at the conference. They're discussing you."

"Afternoon, Tito Sonny," Apollo spoke to the camera. "Is it all right if I don't go? They've been dissecting us since I came out of coma."

Sonia added, "We'd rather be here in the mine, there are too many curious scientists down there. Let them evaluate what they have, and leave us lab rats to climb around on the rocks."

"I understand," Sonny responded. "I'll cover for you. We will see you for dinner, won't we?"

"Oh, yes," Sonia answered, "especially if Nina is cooking. She's better at that than I've ever been."

"By the way, Lydia sent a message. She's locked in Baguio Cathedral for October twenty-fourth. Celia is working with the church for the arrangements."

"We know," Apollo responded, "Nina got a message this morning from Tita Celia."

"Someone could explain it to me."

Sonia said, "You were busy. We talked to Jenny."

"Okay," Sonny shook his head. "See you at dinner." He adjusted the comm channels. "Jenny?"

"Sonny." Jenny smiled on the screen. "Your son wants to play. You have time?"

"I'm going to join the conference. Lydia says Lee Chang sent a warning that there's a bounty out for Apollo. He said criminals are desperate to get hold of any of the virus victims still able to see the future."

Jenny smiled and blew a kiss. "I contacted Lee when you were busy with Brass. I've warned Apollo."

"Okay. Tell Teddy I'll be by in an hour." He rose and reached for his helmet. He exited through the trailer airlock.

Kicking up little dust clouds as he walked the canyon floor, he glanced at the string of mining operations trailers with "Androff – Banzer" signs mounted over what had previously read "Redrock". Behind the mining facilities were a series of new trailers airlifted in; Newton Enterprises, Life Sciences Institute, Martian Militia, and Health Service. A sealed pressure dome had been installed with inflated tunnels leading to eight private quarters' trailers. Before stepping through the conference trailer airlock, Sonny looked up the sheer rock cliffs to the grated platform five-hundred feet above the canyon floor. Wisps of steam floated from the cavern opening, evidence that a high-temperature boring machine was in use inside the cavern.

At the conference table, Terra was preoccupied with her journalistic responsibilities, "Sonny," Brass welcomed him, "You're in time for Xuan Zee's analysis of the timescape visions."

"Analysis?" Zee smirked. "What analysis? What we have is an observed phenomenon. My analysis compares to a primitive witch doctor explaining a television signal. Neither of us knows what we are looking at."

"We have a lot of information." Neurologist Tate Reins said, "We've determined the chemical reaction between the Feldermite hormone and the hypothalamus. We isolated the nerve cells in the hypothalamus that are electrically active when the Feldermite triggers a chemical response, and we've isolated the brainwave patterns related to these telepathic communications."

"Chemistry and electrical patterns," Zee reacted. "These are secondary indicators. None of this explains what the mental signal is that travels through time and space from one human mind to another.

What is that signal? It's not from the electromagnetic spectrum. I have no idea."

"Nobody has any idea what it is," Reins responded. "It is the newest mystery of the life force mankind has been trying to understand for five-thousand years. In the past three-hundred years we have mapped the molecular structure of life so that we know what DNA elements determine what traits… that's how we've been able to modify Earth-based agriculture to survive on Mars. We modify life forms that nature creates, but we still are unable to create new life from inanimate molecules. Apparently this… this telepathic messaging is a real, but rare natural occurrence within the living brain.

Terra added, "You discovered the anti-gravity phenomena the same way, by observing what happened when electrical currents passed through an asteric crystal at super cold temperatures. Gravity is not electromagnetic, either."

"You are right," Zee looked across at her. "I still don't totally understand any of the forces of nature. All I do as a scientist is observe how they work, and devise mathematical models to explain the forces… for gravity, electromagnetic waves, genetic engineering… and now… this Panahon wave."

"Panahon wave?" Terra responded. "That's the name you gave it?"

"He's the first case study. The word Panahon is Filipino for time, so it's appropriate."

"I like it. I've been calling it the Nostradamus Syndrome, but Pahanon Wave is just as good. I'll use that."

Kai injected, "Working with Apollo, we have come a long way in learning how to control his visions, and in evaluating brainwave activity that takes place with the various telepathic communications. I gather from Charles Belisario, at Corrigedor, that we now know residual telepathic abilities occur only with the type 'Oh-Negative' blood virus victims, and only a few of those. Everyone else lost the telepathic dreamscapes within a few days of taking the antidote. Based on the discussions, the active molecules in the virus that triggers the production of Feldermite in the pituitary are unstable, unwieldy, complicated strings. We think we can reproduce them with a more benign host than the virus, but it will take years of experimentation.

The question is, should we? There is a serious ethics matter related to creating a human telepathic ability to communicate through time. Terra, you identified the issue very clearly in your commentaries."

Before Terra could respond, Brass spoke. "For a long time there were questions about the ethics of engineered modifications to life forms. Will some laboratory bring back the dinosaurs to threaten present day life? Will some military develop a doomsday virus that inadvertently wipes out humans? Will tampering with what nature creates do the same thing? These issues are yet to be totally resolved, but agriculture on Mars would not be possible without it. The Panahon Wave, like genetic engineering, now that we have the knowledge, will remain a threat if it is misused... but it is here, and it offers us the opportunity to maintain real communications with explorers going to the stars... and that is important."

"Which reminds me," Zee looked at Brass, then asked, "Are we sending Sonia and Apollo to Tau Ceti like you suggest?"

Brass said, "Apollo's dreamscapes have all of us convinced that he belongs there with Sonia. Sonia has ordered a fleet of anti-grav starships. The goldmine in this Canyon made her rich enough to afford it. I've decided to have Newton Enterprises finance a resupply fleet for the initial pioneers already on their way."

"When do they leave?"

Sonny answered, ""They were hoping to go next year, right after the babies are born."

"Babies?" Zee was surprised.

"This is exclusive," Terra said. "Do not mention outside this room."

"Who is expecting?"

"Sonia is carrying Apollo's baby." Kai said, "Nina Perez is also expecting. Both babies were conceived with the virus present."

"Interesting," Reins said, "however, if infants are involved, I would not recommend launching to Tau Ceti right away."

"Why not?" Sonny questioned.

"Hibernation is not good for children under the age of three, and for that long flight to Tau Ceti the passengers will be in hibernation for most of the trip. The distance is twelve light years. How long will they be asleep?"

Terra said, "the mission presently under way is traveling at sixty percent the speed of light. Their total travel time is twenty years."

Zee added, "The new starships we have in development can leave the solar system at nearly ninety percent the speed of light. That would get them to Tau Ceti in just under fourteen years."

Sonny, absorbed with listening to the discussions, was distracted by a signal indicator on his pressure suit sleeve. Stepping away from the table, he responded, "Detective Ekakaidis, what is it?"

"My excavation team has finally gotten the waste rock cleared from the pile under the goldmine. We've found the bodies of your Filipino miners."

"I'll be right there." Sonny looked at the rest of the conference participants. "You know," he said. "This is a magnificent discovery, this hormone that causes the Panahon Wave, as you are calling it. However, if you pursue it, it could create serious problems. I am getting reports that criminals are offering a lot of money to capture Apollo. If criminals are able to use it, the threat is enormous." He stood to leave.

Brass said, "Everything related to the phenomena has been classified 'Top Secret'. We are securing the frozen fish. What more would you have us do?"

"You should destroy the fish and any detailed information about the virus." Sonny reached for his helmet. "I don't think this is a technology you want to be available to everyone."

"I hope we can contain it," Terra said.

Sonny shook his head. He donned the helmet, and then exited through the airlock.

PART G

EPILOGUE

Chapter Fifty

Baguio Cathedral

Baguio, Philippines

Earth Date	October 24, 2216
Mars Date	E-Mmon 24, 1174

A pollo lifted his chin, making it easier for Celia to attach the small black silk Filipino triangular tie to the collar of his dress barong (a formal translucent Filipino pineapple fiber shirt worn for special occasions). She adjusted carefully the fit to perfect alignment, and then turned the collar down. "There," Celia patted his arm. "That looks right. Don't touch it."

"I won't, Tita. How do I look?" He smiled at her, and then winked toward his best man, cousin Jon Ortigas from Olongapo.

Celia took one step back. "Turn around, slowly. Let me see."

Apollo did as instructed, then asked "Does my hair look straight?"

"You have a piece in the back sticking up at attention." Angela Reyes stood behind him. When he stopped turning she finished combing his hair.

Sonny walked in the room. "That shouldn't be a problem." Sonny handed Apollo his spit-shined dress shoes. "We better get going. Jenny just called. Sonia and Nina are on their way. Nina doesn't want to arrive at the church before you're all ready." He stepped out of the room to make calls.

Celia guided Apollo to a chair, making certain he did not wrinkle the barong. "Apollo, I know I shouldn't say anything more." She continued looking for any sign of lint on his black trousers. "I really want you to think about going away forever. I know it is a big adventure, but I'm frightened for you."

"Tita, we've talked about this a million times. Sonia and I belong on Tau Ceti."

"I know you think so. But, you've been my little boy for so long. I don't want you to go away."

"But, Tita Celia," Apollo responded. "We don't leave until the baby is bigger. I won't go away right away, you know that. Maybe I can convince you to come with us by then."

Celia, with moisture in her eyes, took his hand, "I know, I am being bad. This is your wedding day. I will be happy for you." She swallowed. "I want you to be happy." She smiled, leaned over, and kissed his cheek.

"Oh, Tita," He stood to hug her. "We will both be embarrassed." He watched Exxis Potowski across the room. Exxis's seventeen year old kid brother Fern, his best man Roger Lyman, and his uncle Brass Newton entered the room, all dressed in Filipino formal translucent dress shirts over black slacks. Celia had all the wedding outfits made in Baguio before any of the wedding couples left Mars. The men were followed by Lulu Alsona and Feli Hernandez, who made certain the other groom's party was properly dressed.

"I kind of like this," Exxis carefully eyed Apollo, and then glanced in a full length mirror to check his own appearance. "This is an odd outfit, but I like it." He was slump shouldered, his breathing somewhat labored.

Noticing the discomfort, Apollo asked, "Exxis, you feeling all right?"

"The gravity... I weigh a ton. The air is so thick and humid."

"It takes time to adjust," Brass responded, "Your heart isn't used to pumping so hard to keep blood flowing. You'll adjust in another day or two."

Celia turned to face him. "Exxis, I wish I had known you longer. I wish you had known Nina longer. Sonny says you are a good boy." She reached to hug the tall Martian. "You make sure you treat Nina right, or I'll be mad."

"Tita Celia," Exxis hugged her back, "I guess I should call you what Apollo calls you. I will treat Nina right… I swear."

"Don't wrinkle the barong," Brass changed the subject. "Exxis, your dad should have brought you back to Earth when you were growing up. You might have learned that Filipinos have been using this for formal wear for four-hundred years. It's too warm in this country to wear traditional suits."

"Traditional suits?" Roger reacted. "No one wears traditional suits. I expected environ-suits. Even with this thin outfit, I am sweating." He walked to the door that opened to the cathedral's main auditorium. The sun filtered through the colorful stained glass widows of the Baguio's Saint Louis Cathedral, adding a sense of festival celebration to the crowd seated in the packed church. "A big crowd. On both sides of the aisle."

Because of the circumstances of a double wedding, the tradition of having the bride's guest on one side of the aisle, and the groom's people on the other, was not workable. For this event, one side of the church included Filipino guests of Apollo and Nina. Across the isle were the family and friends of Exxis and Sonia brought to Earth on a chartered Newton Enterprises corporate spacecraft.

Poking his head through the door, Sonny said, "Brass, the girls are out front. We're on. Let's go." He winked at Apollo and Exxis. "Good luck, boys."

Brass followed Sonny through the door to the entry lobby. There they prepared to escort the brides. Celia led Lulu and Feli to join the congregation just moments before the organ music signaled for the grooms to appear. Apollo gulped nervously, and then looked at Exxis. "Ready?"

"No more than you." Exxis smiled cautiously. "I guess it's too late to do anything about it."

"I have a solution," Roger grinned. "We didn't drink all the scotch last night. Need a little bracer?"

Exxis wrinkled his lips, uncertain how to respond. Exxis said, "We came a hundred million miles for this. I think I'll follow the script." He patted Apollo on the back. "You're first."

The two grooms, along with their best men, slowly filed out of the waiting rooms as Celia had instructed. They followed the hand-woven carpeting to their assigned positions near the altar. Father Alberto Gonzales and two alter boys stepped from behind back panels to take their positions at the altar. The organist played a soft piece from Tchaikovsky's 'Nutcracker' as the prelude to the march. For the first time Apollo surveyed the crowd before him. Not only three-hundred Filipinos with two-hundred Martian guests, but Sonia had invited two dozen distant relatives from Odessa. In addition, Exxis had invited his father's relatives from New Zealand. There were others Apollo did not know.

Suddenly, Apollo sensed a cold chill in his spine. He swallowed, closed his eyes, and focused on the source of foreboding. It was not anything in the church, but he couldn't determine immediately what it was. He silently prayed for nothing to go wrong.

Two men from the barrio slowly opened the doors at the back of the auditorium, exposing the entrance lobby foyer. Beyond the door the brides' party was lined up. The organ music shifted from the Nutcracker melody to the wedding march.

Two pairs of little Filipino girls, dressed in fluffy pink and white dresses, each carrying baskets of flowers, led the parade, dropping handfuls of rose pedals as they sashayed up the aisle. Behind them, dressed in a small white barong over black trousers, marched Teddy, holding a blue velvet pillow displaying the four rings. Next were the bridesmaids, two for each bride, looking like princesses in pink and white formal Filipino silk gowns with flat butterfly sleeves. Young men in barongs escorted each bridesmaid down the aisle to the bride's side of the altar. The escorts then crossed over to line up behind the grooms. The two best men then walked together up the aisle to the entrance to escort the maids of honor. Madeline, Nina's maid of honor, strolled the aisle beside Roger, while Wein Banzer, Fisk's sister and Sonia's maid of honor, followed, holding Jon Ortigas' arm.

The brides waited until the rest of their wedding party were in place. At this point the organ music abruptly became louder, with a slightly faster beat. Nina, wearing a white silk Philippine wedding gown with butterfly sleeves, was almost angelic with her tiara, opaque netted veil, and flowing train. Holding Sonny's arm, she almost floated down the isle. Dressed identically, Sonia followed, holding Brass' arm. Having been married once before, Sonia was more relaxed in her poise. Just before the altar, Sonny handed Nina over to a nervous Exxis, then stepped away to take a seat beside Celia and Jenny. Brass took Sonia to Apollo, and then joined Exxis' parents on the other side of the aisle.

The double wedding ceremony lasted forty minutes. Father Gonzales took time to speak about the special occasion of the dual marriage that binds the two planets together in the wake of the tragedy that cost everyone so dearly. He spoke glowingly in remembrance of the Maliit na Ulap priest, Father Roxas, of Nina's papa, and of Apollo's Uncle Roberto. He gave communion to Nina and Apollo, a Catholic blessing. Their mates watched, but chose not to follow.

He spoke of the responsibility of each to their marriage vows, and solicited from each a vow of lifelong dedication to their spouse, and to their eventual responsibilities for their families yet to come. He guided them through their vows, and then blessed the two couples. He stepped back to make room for Teddy to approach with the velvet pillow. The two best men each picked a ring to hand to the grooms to place on their bride's finger. The maids of honor did the same for the brides. At this point Father Gonzales pronounced them married.

Following their first married kiss, the four kneeled to pray before the priest, and to prepare for the next step. Celia had arranged for each couple to be honored with Filipino customs of having a series of sponsor couples enter the aisle to place white cords connected each bride and groom. Coin sponsors pinned money to each bride's train. The organ again played the wedding march for the wedding party to retreat back up the aisle to the entrance lobby.

The packed church slowly emptied to wait outside in preparation for the two couples's departure. Before that could happen, Celia and Lydia directed the wedding party back to the altar for picture taking.

During the photo sessions, Sonia whispered to Apollo, "Something is wrong. I sense that you feel it."

Continuing to smile for the photographers, he nodded agreement. He focused his thoughts toward her. "I'm not certain… I think something is wrong with the limousine."

Quietly focusing her thoughts, she telepathically replied. "Lydia arranged the limo. What do you think is wrong?"

He paused, and then focused his thoughts toward her again. "The drivers hired by Lydia have been hurt. Someone wants to kidnap the four of us."

"Can you focus on Sonny's mind? We don't want to disrupt this ceremony if we don't have to."

"I'll try." Apollo looked at Sonny, who was talking to Dan Potowski, Exxis' father. Concentrating his thoughts, he imagined telling Sonny that the limo drivers were imposters, a serious threat.

Sonny stopped talking; he raised his hand to stop Dan. He turned to stare at Apollo and approached, "Apollo, were you communicating to me? Don't say it out loud."

"Yes. Did you get my warning?"

"What's wrong?" Celia stepped up to them, sensing the tension.

"Nothing, sis," Sonny patted her back. "Just a minor difficulty Apollo needs me to look into. I'll be back in a few minutes." Sonny walked up the aisle to the entrance. He stopped at a pew where Lydia was seated with her husband, briefly talked to her, and then led her out of the church. Celia decided to follow her brother out to the parking lot.

Nina and Exxis approached Apollo. Nina spoke first. "Apollo, something is wrong, isn't it?" Brass and Terra were right behind them.

Apollo smiled, raised his hand, and said, "Nothing serious. Sonny will take care of it."

Nina grimaced. "Apollo, you've always been a bad liar. What is it?"

"I'm not certain. The limo drivers… the ones outside are phonies… they are bad men here to try to… kidnap us. Tito Sonny is taking care of it."

"He will need help," Exxis said. "Should we go out there?"

Brass started moving toward the door, but Apollo reached out to stop him. "You don't speak the language, Mr. Newton. Sonny knows what to do."

"Do your talents," Brass asked, "Do you see what is going on?"

Apollo nodded. He put his fingers to his temples and closed his eyes. "Sonny recruited six security robots... he's cautiously approaching the limo... Lydia and Tita Celia are with him... the two bad men are in the front, waiting for us to come out." Apollo looked at each of them. "Sonny is telling them he knows they are not with the limo company... he is asking them to leave. The driver is pulling a weapon, aiming it at Sonny... two of the robot security detail fired tranquilizer darts at the two of them. Tita Celia tripped as she was backing away. She is on her rump, but she's not hurt."

"This is terrible," Nina said. "They were going to take us hostage... at our wedding!"

"This is lucky," Exxis put an arm around his bride, "Apollo's telepathic talents saved us." He reached with his free hand to Apollo's shoulder, "Promise me you won't use that special ability at the wrong time with us."

"I'll try."

Sonia smiled. "I'll swat him if he does."

Six hours later the wedding reception, in the packed rooftop ballroom of the Baguio Hilton, was over. The guests headed for home, the dance band packed to leave. In the Potowski bridal suit, located on the top floor adjacent to the Panahon executive suite, the two couples were still sipping Champaign along with their immediate wedding party as they slowly opened their large cache of gifts. Lydia, Sonny's office manager, recorded the details of each gift. Teddy removed the wrapping from any gift he could help with.

During casual conversations that followed, Celia asked, "Sonny, what became of those limo drivers?"

"The police have them locked away safely. I'll interview them tomorrow... Find out who hired them." He put his Champaign glass down. He reached for a candy dish on the coffee table. "They were stupid. Don't worry about it."

"You always tell me not to worry, but this frightens me," Celia said. "Apollo will be in danger as long as he's here on Earth, won't he?"

"We're not worried about Apollo," Sonia said, "Three times his telepathy thwarted imminent danger to him."

"Maybe he can avoid personal disaster," Exxis said, "but the rest of us don't have that early warning system. What happens if the people who want Apollo take people hostage he is close to?"

"I've had that problem," Terra was sitting close to her husband. "I became a target for kidnap threats when I first became a media celebrity. There are still special threats, some against Brass... some against my dad. There are normal security precautions that stop most of these attempts. Exxis, you should be used to that."

Celia said, "I no want you to go to Tau Ceti before because I am afraid for you, for the baby. This afternoon, I become afraid if you stay. I want you to go where no one is trying to hurt you."

Nina finished unwrapping a large gift. "Silverware. This is from Tito Bernie."

"Tita Celia," Sonia looked briefly at her new husband. Apollo was opening a gift. She turned to Celia. "Thank you for this wedding. Other than the problem with the limousines, this was a beautiful wedding. The messages you sent to us on Mars had me confused about what to expect. It was like something out of an ancient fairy tale. Thank you so much for what you did. I will treasure these memories... always."

For one of the few times that Sonny could remember, Celia was left speechless.

Sonia continued, "Our child will be born in March. I would like to ask your help in showing me how to take care of the baby."

"You want my help?"

"Of course. You did a wonderful job raising Apollo into the man I love. It would be foolish not to ask your help with Apollo's son."

"But, if you go away soon to the stars."

"We won't go for several years... Kai warned me that hibernation is bad for infants. Besides, I need time to prepare for Tau Ceti."

"Prepare?" Sonny asked. "Tau Ceti is an unknown Earth-like planet. How can you prepare?"

"I'm a Martian," she answered, "from what I've seen of the transmissions from the unmanned probe... what I've seen in my own dreamscapes, I have to learn how to deal with greater gravity and jungles and oceans and humid air and wet storms. The money from the goldmine gives Apollo and me enough to take time preparing. During that time, Apollo is going to get a degree in geology from the University of the Philippines."

"Tita Celia," Apollo pulled the rest of the decorative wrapping from a three-foot long cylinder container from Nina. "When the baby is born, we want you to be the Nanny, if you don't mind." He opened the end of the packing tube.

Celia's worried smile remained. She was at a loss for words.

Apollo removed the art tube from the cylinder box. He telescoped the large com-pad painting. "Nina! You did this?" He showed it to Sonia. "This is great."

Sonia took it in her hands, smiling as she studied it. She turned it for everyone to see. The computerized painting was like a fine art rendition, with surrealistic coloring of Apollo and Sonia sitting inside a pressurized bubble with the cliffs of Princess Dejah Canyon behind them. Ghost images of Fisk, Japa, Roberto and the rest of miners who died in the canyon were etched along one side of the painting. "Nina, this is beautiful."

Nina grinned. She took hold of Exxis' arm. "I didn't know what else to get you that would be only from me. I'm glad you like it. Exxis picked another for you. It's still in that stack."

"Before we give you your gift," Sonia said. "Nina and Exxis, what are your plans?"

Nina looked to Exxis for him to respond, "Our daughter is due at the end of April. Nanai Ruby, I was hoping, like Apollo asked Tita Celia... that you would help us raise our girl... while Nina gets her degree in nursing. I plan to stay at my Uncle Henry Potowski's farm in New Zealand for awhile to acclimate to living on an Earth-like planet. The thick humid air combined with the heavy gravity makes me uncomfortable. I need to adapt."

Ruby looked at her friend Celia, and then said, "Looks like you and I have a job to do for the next few years."

Nina stood to hug her mother. "We'll discuss it more when Exxis and I get back from Rome."

"There was something I've been waiting to tell you," Kai handed more gifts to each set of newlyweds. "I was going to wait until you got back from your honeymoons."

All eyes in the room focused on him.

"I don't know exactly what this means, but I scanned your fetuses... they both test positive for the Panahon Wave."

"Does that mean," Sonny asked, "what you imply?"

"We don't know, but they will probably be born with Apollo's ability to communicate telepathically through time."

Chapter Fifty-One

Tau Ceti Report

Martian Broadcast Agency
The Weekly Terra Newton Report
Crater City, Mars

Earth Date: Nov 8, 2221
Mars Date: L-Mmon 19, 1176

S onny leaned back behind his desk, telling his computer to turn on Terra's Martian Broadcast with a Tau Ceti update. Ordering a computer-galley delivered San Miguel beer, he was ready to relax.

"Sonny," Lydia's voice interrupted his relaxation. "You have a visitor."

He briefly thought about feigning that he was out. Instead he directed the video display to hold. The image of Terra reverted to freeze-frame on his wall-size video display. "Who is it?"

"Rochelle Bond."

Sonny was puzzled. "Send her in."

The bamboo wall separating Sonny's office from Lydia's slid open. Rochelle walked in. "Good morning, Sonny. I hope I wasn't interrupting anything."

439

"Just a beer," Sonny stood, motioned for her to take a seat. "I just got in from an all-night surveillance." They both sat down.

"If you're tired, I can come back." Rochelle glanced at the screen. "You're watching Terra's report. I'd like to see that, too."

Sonny glanced at the video screen, then again at Rochelle. "Is this a friendly visit?"

"I wish it was. Business. Probably related to Terra's report."

Sonny smiled, and then ordered a rose wine that he knew Rochelle liked. He then signaled for the broadcast show to resume.

Terra was speaking. "Today the pioneers onboard the first manned mission to another star system are landing on the Earth-like second planet of the Tau Ceti star system. If the touchdown goes according to plan, those explorers will be stepping out on the same beach where the unmanned Columbus probe set down twenty-one years ago. This landing is so far away that the television images transmitted from the touchdown will take another twelve years to reach us. It has been over twenty years since that mission began this historic event. Today, we can celebrate its arrival of civilization at the stars."

The printed message across the top of the screen read: 'Terra Newton Chronicles. Starship update.'

On the right were a series of images from the original starship launch, and of the earlier unmanned probe that landed at the same beach on Tau Ceti. These were followed by recently received transmissions from earlier in-flight images of the on-board pioneers in hibernation sleep. The video images then shifted to the launch of a second fleet of new starships.

"Last month a second expedition was launched toward Tau Ceti. These new spacecraft carry a thousand pioneers in an armada, a convoy that includes ten passenger ships with all of the pioneers in hibernation, and twenty unmanned transport spacecraft loaded with supplies. Propelled by advanced anti-grav drives combined with fusion engines, the armada is traveling at ninety-five-percent the speed of light, fast enough to make the trip in fourteen years." The file images showed the construction, loading, and lift-off of the fleet of starships leaving Mars for the long trip through deep space.

"Portions of the armada were built by the Martian Star Flight Administration. The fleet also includes two ships owned privately by Sonia and Apollo Panahon, privately financed. Five years ago a unique viral infection gave Apollo Panahon the ability to communicate through time. Apollo, and two of others with the ability to communicate through time, are now heading for Tau Ceti. When they arrive they will attempt to communicate with friends left behind. Using Cerebral Neural Analysis Units, we will have images immediately about what their landing is like."

"In fact," Terra said, "over the past five years, we recorded a number of Apollo's timescape visions with C.N.A. units, dreamscapes on what he saw through the eyes of Zenia Olsen onboard that first Tau Ceti mission landing now. Here are those dreamscape recordings of the Tau Ceti landing in progress."

The screen view out a spacecraft window during descent showed a wide stretch of golden sandy beach at a tropical cove. Green vegetation beyond the beach was too distant to distinguish. Blue-green seawater in the cove changed to a deep blue beyond the sandbars at the mouth to the cove. Crashing lines of white breakers contrasted the deep blue. Slowly, the cove got closer. The green vegetation became discernable as giant ferns. At one end of the sandy cove was a rocky outcrop with a lavender-colored pile of quartz that looked somewhat like a horse's head. Thirty seconds later the image implied a soft landing on the dried sand near the edge of the vegetation. Out on the sand, with the rest of the pioneers, the images suggested that the one-hundred and forty pioneers were taking time for a religious ceremony before they proceeded further. The images were freeze framed.

"These C.N.A. dreamscapes for the Tau Ceti landing will continue shortly. I have a number of recorded visions from Apollo." She paused, "However, I want to talk about other C.N.A. images I recorded last week."

The images shifted to a portrait of two four-year-old children. Fisk Roberto Panahon, the boy, had blond hair, bright Asiatic eyes, and cherub cheeks. Terra Celia Potowski, the thin little girl, had brown hair and a thin, smooth face with tight, dark eyes. "On board the starship heading for Tau Ceti are two children conceived when their parents suffered from the same virus that gave Apollo his timescape visions.

Both children were born with their pituitary glands producing the rare hormone that scientists identified as the stimulant for the time visions. They have dream visions similar to those of Apollo. At this moment they are settled in for the long hibernation. Before the launch of the starship, we asked Apollo Panahon to use his telepathic ability when he arrived at Tau Ceti to communicate back through time to let us know what they encounter. The normal flow of time and the speed of light will no longer limit human communication."

Several minutes later the show ended. Sonny directed the broadcast to shut off. He sipped his beer, and then spoke to Rochelle. "If I wasn't so familiar with what happened, this would have gotten me confused about what was happening in what sequence."

"That's the problem when time loses its meaning."

"You said you were here because of this?"

"I want to hire you ... as a detective."

"Oh?"

"At the Tycho Medical Research Center ... we had three of the fishes from the cave at Princess Dejah Canyon. We also had had a quantity of manufactured Feldermite Hormone."

"You said you 'had' them?"

"Frozen in liquid Nitrogen. They are missing. So is one of our top researchers, Dr. Max Dolan."

"This is a matter for the police."

"The police have searched. It is as if the samples and Dolan never existed. All of his accounts have been eradicated."

"Do the police have suspicions?"

"Hundreds of individuals have offered big money to get their hands on sources for hormones. They don't know which way to look. I was hoping you could help."

Sonny sipped his beer again.

"You do realize if someone bad has the hormone ... is able to use it ... they will have the power to take control of everything ...."

"Will you take the job?"

Sonny sat for a moment. Then he spoke to the communicator. "Lydia, Rochelle Bond is hiring us."

Breinigsville, PA USA
06 January 2010
230222BV00001B/8/P